ANDROMEDA

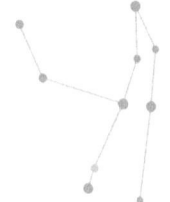

STAR-BLOOD

ANDROMEDA

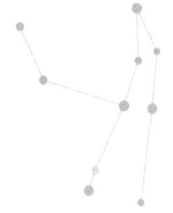

SOFI AGUILERA

*To my mom, who taught me about the stars
and stood outside with me to watch them.*

To my dad, who has pushed me up to reach the stars.

To my sister, who has been at my side through the darkest times.

To abu, who encourages me to aim high at the sky.

To the stars, who always shine so bright.

Chapter I, Verse I

In the beginning there existed only Chaos, the infinite Abyss.
The endless sea of Darkness, untamed and unbroken,
Ruthless in the formless Confusion that brimmed the Void.
It came again, the force that brought no Beginning but neither an End.
Wingless in its flight, weightless in its journey,
Silently from the brink, Time began its reign,
To guide forever all Eras in the Boundless Sphere.
From it arose the Egg, within it the First Born Son,
That held within the gift of all Creation,
But with it also the burden of all Destruction.
He was the first to Love, ardent to conceive what was not yet born.
It sprang forth, the shape of Silence that called for Her,
The bosom of Darkness from which Night emerged,
The first child of Chaos that dwelled in the bottomless ocean.
From the endless sea Death was born, the first one who had a form.
But in confusion she roamed, without a purpose to hold,
For the Soul knew not its dwelling, nor the Spirit its hearth.
A Land there was not, and neither a Sky to behold.
From Darkness and from Death, Light sprang forth,
Ambitious to shine in all the corners that filled the Abyss.
Darkness it suppressed, consuming its power to shine brighter,
Becoming the first enemy that Darkness warred with,
The only force that not even Chaos could control.
And there followed a battle that for ages lasted,
Between the formless shape of Darkness and her blinding Son.

CHAPTER 1

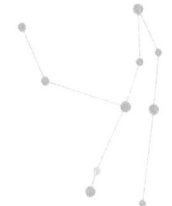

NEVER *let them see your scars.*

I instinctively pulled my sleeves up until they reached my knuckles.

I lay in the darkness, breathing slowly and steadily. The patient in the room next to mine had started to cry loudly, waking me from my sleep. Footsteps drummed outside my room, and a few muffled voices spoke with concern.

I tightened my fists, gripping my sleeves. I had been careful to hide my scars, but it still worried me that the doctors, nurses, psychiatrists or patients would notice. I was fine with them thinking I was crazy—I *wanted* them to think I was absolutely insane, but I couldn't let them find out the truth.

The patient continued to cry, his wailings echoing down the hallway. I exhaled deeply, then sat up on my bed. Faint light came into the room from the window behind me. It illuminated the strange red symbols I had drawn on the wall next to me. The nurses had tried to scrub them away, without much success. They didn't know what the symbols meant, and had asked me about them—but I didn't know what they meant either. I had simply drawn what came to my mind, trying to make the symbols look sinister. After drawing the symbols, I had talked to the wall as if it was my friend. That had earned me a direct trip to the psychiatrist's office downstairs, where I had remained quiet. If I didn't keep pretending I was crazy, they would send me away from the psychiatric hospital and back to my normal life.

I couldn't let that happen.

I pulled back the covers and stood from the bed, then headed over to the window, where my view was partly obstructed by the metal bars. This place felt more like a prison than a psychiatric hospital for troubled teens. I knew it had been a prison once, and that it had been remodeled recently. But it was still poorly maintained. Most of the teens and young adults here were like me—orphans, homeless or teens who had been through the foster care system. People who didn't have money, or anyone who cared enough about them to be able to send them off to a nice place to be treated. Through the metal bars, I was able to see the night. The small flower garden was directly below, surrounded by a tall wall with spikes at the top that looked like jagged teeth. Beyond it was the beach, with sand so dark it was almost black. The ocean behind it rippled with sharp waves that blurred the silver light from the moon into a pool of liquid iron. In the distance, hidden by the fog, was the tiny island with the abandoned lighthouse. The island itself consisted of jutting rocks the same color as the sand. The lighthouse leaned to the side, as if wanting to take a dive into the sea. I wondered how much longer it would remain standing before it toppled over.

By the position of the quarter moon, I calculated that it was a couple of hours after midnight, maybe around two in the morning. I pulled away from the window and went back to the bed, which was still warm. It would have been much easier to note the time with a watch, but they hadn't let me keep the small wristwatch I had stolen a few weeks before being sent to the psychiatric hospital. I also wasn't allowed to have any electronic devices, although I wasn't sure why they were banned. My shoes didn't have laces, and it had taken me a couple of days to realize that any clothing with laces or underwire was also forbidden. I assumed that they were afraid someone would try to commit suicide by hanging themselves.

I lay down on the bed and pulled the blankets to my chin, then turned to face the wall.

"Hello," I said.

I knew the nurses could hear me through the camera at the other end of the room. I didn't expect anyone to be hearing me at night, but I needed to stay in character.

The boy next door was still sobbing.

"It looks like it's going to be a long night."

The wall didn't respond.

I stretched my arm to touch a ragged red line with my finger, but just as I did, my sleeve pulled back just below my hand. A blink of white light illuminated the wall for a second before I buried my arm under the blanket.

My heart broke into a race, thundering inside my ears. I lay unmoving in my bed, expecting someone to burst into my room and drag me away. But no one did. The light had only flashed for a second, and I doubted anyone would notice. Even if they did, they would probably think it had been a glitch in the camera. I took deep breaths, trying to calm my heart as it battered against my chest.

Never let them see the light.

I was glad I didn't have to share a room with anyone. I closed my eyes and continued to take deep breaths. The boy continued to weep.

"A long, long night . . ."

The wall was silent. At least it wouldn't tell anyone my secret.

I munched on the flavor-less eggs with dismay. Like every morning, I craved a hamburger and a milkshake. The patient next to me nudged at my arm. His hair was cut so short that I could see his gleaming scalp in some areas. He smiled as if trying to show off all of his teeth. I calculated he was in his early twenties. No one in the hospital was older than twenty-five or younger than thirteen years old.

"Did you know that these eggs come from humans?" He asked as if he were sharing a government secret. "I saw Nurse Prim poop them out."

I didn't even bother responding, although I did feel my appetite leaving me.

The cafeteria was a wide room, with rows of tables arranged neatly, each with five chairs. It was full at the moment, with laughter and loud voices that I tried to ignore. At one end was the entrance, and at the other was the kitchen, which I could partially see behind the white curtain that covered it. I wondered why they hadn't just built a wall to separate it from the rest of the room. Next to the kitchen was a door that led outside the facility. It was guarded at all times, the guard always standing right in front of the door with a distrustful look in his eyes.

The room always smelled like burnt eggs from the kitchen, sweat and vomit, and none of those smells seemed to ever drift away through the high windows at the back of the room.

On the right, at the top of the wall, was a TV. Most of the times it played videos of animals or the ocean, but I knew that when the patients weren't around the staff would use it to watch the news, and probably movies too. At the moment, the TV displayed what looked like a documentary about giraffes, which I ignored, but some of the patients were watching it.

In front of me was another young patient, probably twenty years old. His milky-white eyes stared straight at me, although I knew he couldn't see me. I was glad that he was quiet today, because most days he would talk about how "ice demons" had taken his eyes away, leaving me wondering what "ice demons" looked like.

The other patients sitting at my table were even weirder. There was a teenage girl who liked to paint her hair and eyebrows blue, and who warned me that in three years America would sink. An angel had told her so. She'd also confided that in fifteen years we would discover another universe, and try to colonize new planets. Since there were no movies I could watch at the psychiatric facility, I found her strange stories entertaining.

On my other side sat the oldest guy at the facility. He was twenty-five and had no legs. He had been in some terrorist attack, or possibly a war in the Middle East. I only knew that he thought metal forks were guns, and that rolled-up socks were grenades. We all ate with plastic forks, and had been instructed not to throw rolled-up socks at him, like I had once done just for the fun of seeing him scream and take cover behind a turned-up table.

"Ohhh!" the blue-eyebrow girl exclaimed as she looked at the TV. I noticed that the noise in the cafeteria had nearly died down as most patients looked at the TV. It had stopped showing the giraffe documentary and had switched to the news channel. I couldn't hear the audio, but I could read the captions at the bottom of the screen. There had been an attack in Paris, where a group of men had decided to start shooting and killing civilians.

According to the news anchor, one of the attackers had been wearing an explosive vest and had detonated it in a public plaza, although I couldn't tell which one.

The news anchor disappeared and an image replaced her. It sent a shiver down my spine. The image showed a symbol drawn in blood on a flaking white wall. It was stranger than the symbols I had drawn in my room, and that one truly seemed demonic. It was a straight line with a curve like a crescent moon on one end, facing outwards. Another, smaller line crossed through the middle like a pair of outstretched arms, and at the other end of the symbol were three more lines. The symbol also had tiny circles at the end of each line.

The image disappeared and a replay video began. It seemed to be a recording from a camera on the street. It showed a busy plaza, where people gathered around a musician playing a guitar. There were at least fifty people on the plaza. Seconds later, people on the right side of the crowd all scattered away. One woman lay on the ground where the crowd had been, lying unmoving. The TV abruptly shut off, and when I turned towards the kitchen, I spotted an old nurse holding a remote control.

"That's the second terrorist attack in France this month, and before that there were a few in England, and there was one in Greece during the summer," said the guy next to me, his near-bald scalp brighter than his eyes.

"Really?" I asked, now mildly interested. "Aren't there always terrorist attacks?"

"Yes, but these are specific attacks," said the blue-eyebrow girl as she turned back to look at us. The TV was now broadcasting the giraffe documentary again. A giraffe munched on some bright-green leaves, lazily swishing its tail.

"These attacks are different," whispered the guy next to me. "That strange symbol always appears somewhere near the attack, drawn with blood." He looked around as if taking care no one else was listening. "They say the symbol belongs to a terrorist group, but they haven't been able to prove that. Different groups of people attack each time, unrelated to one another. It's as if people suddenly went mad." He licked his dry lips, something that I found disturbing. "But priests have said that a demon is causing these attacks. A demon that has escaped from Hell, who has come to punish us for all for our sins!"

I was about to say that I didn't really believe in demons, or in sins, but the blue-eyebrow girl spoke first. "Our end will come soon, and it will all start with the Great Flood."

I nodded politely in acknowledgement to her apocalyptic prediction and continued to eat. The noise in the cafeteria gradually came back, the laughter and voices booming around me.

Once I was done eating the disgusting eggs, a nurse came for me and guided me through the corridors towards the psychiatrist, who was on the same floor as the cafeteria, on the lowest level. The psychiatrist's corridor was darker than the rest. It only had half of its lights on, the rest of the bulbs were missing. At the end of the hallway was the rusty metal door, which the nurse opened for me.

She left me standing inside the psychiatrist's room, which resembled a typical interrogation room in a police station. I had seen several of those in the last two years. There was a metal table in the middle of the room with two chairs facing each other. The psychiatrist was already seated, watching me sternly. Her dark eyes were cold as snow, and her thin lips made her face seem always displeased at something.

On the wall across from the door was a large mirror, but I knew it was just glass, and there were probably people watching me from behind it. I sat down opposite from her at the table, tapping my fingers on the cold surface. I knew the procedure. Didn't she ever get bored of asking me the same questions every week?

She opened the folder and showed me some pictures. She slid the pictures across the table for me to see.

"Do you remember these people?" she asked.

I didn't even look at the pictures. I had seen them so many times that they were clear in my memory. They showed a family of four. The mom had long wavy hair that nearly reached her waist. It looked ridiculous, I had never seen that hair combed, and I always imagined she must have had a hard time washing it. Her face was round and chubby, and she wore a hideous floral dress—her favorite type of dress. The man's hair was dark, streaked with white at the sides. He smiled awkwardly, as if pretending to be happy. I knew that most times his lips were pressed into a thin line, and that he rarely spoke more than two sentences in a conversation. Then there were two boys, standing in between the couple, who were almost the same age. They both wore ugly green shirts, which I assumed their unfashionable mom had bought them. The boys had always been quiet, just like their father.

Of course I remember them, I thought. *They were my foster family for four months.* That was a personal record for me, living with a family for so long.

"Do you remember their names?" the psychiatrist asked.

I didn't know their names. I had never learned them, and just called them Miss, Mister and Kids, like I had always done with every single foster family.

"Do you remember what you did to them?" the psychiatrist asked.

I did remember. I had drawn strange symbols on the wall. Then I had broken windows, vases, glasses, plates and everything

8

else I could get my hands on, yelling that The Voice had ordered me to do it so I could join my brothers and sisters in the sky.

I blinked in response.

She collected the pictures and placed them inside the folder, then slapped it closed. She stared at me for a few seconds, trying to read my expressionless face.

The psychiatrist let out a sigh. "I'll see you tomorrow," she said as she stood up to leave.

For the first time in that day, I smiled.

It was dark outside when I awoke. The scars on my back were itching. That was strange—they never itched once they were healed.

I sat up in my bed and checked that the scars on my wrists were still hidden under my sleeves. They were, and they itched too, although slightly less than the ones on my back. I realized the corridor was silent, without the usual moans or cries of some of the patients. Something felt wrong.

Just as I stood, there was a soft knock on my door. It opened in a silent swing. My heart beat up my throat, but I didn't move. I shouldn't have been surprised that he was here, but felt shocked anyway. I clenched my hands to prevent them from shaking and stood as straight as I could.

He walked inside the room and left the door ajar behind him. He stood motionless as he surveyed me. At the moment Orion's eyes looked dark, but I knew that with light they were amber, almost yellow—like a lion's.

His face looked like it had been sculpted by angels, and even at night I could make out his features—his nose was straight and sharp, his cheeks high, and his jaw chiseled. His full lips scowled as he looked around the room. Unfortunately, his pretty face didn't match his arrogant, stubborn and selfish personality.

Orion was twenty years old, only three years older than me.

"Seriously?" he said, motioning at the room around me. His voice was husky and deep. Orion was over six feet tall, his black clothes tight around his bulky physique. They were the same color as his hair. "Why would you pretend to be mad to be taken here?" His English had an odd accent, a mix of British and German, much like my own. It didn't sound odd to my ears, but people we met normally commented about it.

"You should have seen me talking to the walls. I deserve an Oscar," I said.

His forehead furrowed. "I'm sure the madness came naturally. But why a psychiatric hospital?"

"I had to get more creative after you pulled me out of the police station twice, and stopped me from escaping the country," I said heatedly. "I just wanted to have a taste of freedom."

He looked at me quizzically. "I wouldn't call being locked in a psychiatric hospital *freedom*."

I shrugged.

"Are you really *this* desperate to get away from Zia?" he asked.

"I think my scars can answer that question. Have you forgotten yours?" I asked.

Orion stared silently at me. I knew he wouldn't answer my question. If there was anyone in the world who knew what my definition of freedom meant, it was Orion, but he didn't have enough courage to seek his freedom—or maybe he hadn't felt so much a prisoner as I always had. "You knew I would eventually find you," he said with a smile, his white teeth breaking the darkness around him.

I sighed. "I honestly hoped it would take you longer."

"I found you the day they took you," he said. "But I delayed. Zia knew I was working slowly, but didn't mind. But yesterday she came to my apartment and ordered me to bring you back *now*."

I took a deep breath and leaned against the wall. The corridor outside was completely quiet. Had Orion disabled the cameras? Or killed the doctors, nurses and guards? He was capable of all those things.

"What happened?" I finally asked. "Why would she want me out suddenly?"

He shrugged. "I don't know. I've never seen her this hysterical before." I raised a brow. "She stole some documents. I don't know from whom, or what those documents said, but she went nuts after reading them." He heaved a sigh. "She punished me for not having found you yet."

I shivered at that thought, feeling my own scars tingling on my back and shoulders.

"So now you're supposed to take me back," I said.

Orion nodded slowly, the smile gone from his face. "Sorry, Andromeda. Please don't make this harder. You can escape next month, like you always do, and I'll give you a head start of two weeks."

I didn't want to escape next month; that was too much time, but I knew that with Orion there was not much I could do. I sighed. We walked out of the room together, my shoulders slumping with resignation. I would miss talking to the wall, which never talked back to me the way people did, and never criticized me either . . . Maybe I *was* insane after all.

The hallway was eerily quiet, and seemed to be consumed by an unbreakable darkness. The blinking lights from the cameras were all red. I was distracted, looking at them, when Orion grabbed my arm and forced me to stop.

I turned to him. His gaze was fixed ahead, looking at the unmoving darkness. His hand went instinctively to the knife at his belt.

"Someone else is here," he whispered.

I was about to say that his genius guess was right—the hospital was filled with people. But just in that second, all the patients began to scream.

Chapter VIII, Verse II

Beware of the devil Devil disguised as the savior.
Blood he will spill, death he will spread.
The sky he shall conquer, the earth he shall cleanse.
Fear he will command, Darkness he will consume.
Betrayed by his kin, beloved by his enemy.
One he shall slay, one he shall save.
The blinking demon will ascend.

CHAPTER 2

THE DOORS at my sides rattled. The patients' screams pierced my ears, and for a second, I stood stunned in the hallway.

"Go!" Orion shouted

We raced side by side down the stairs until we arrived at the lowest floor. We ran through the hallway, towards the cafeteria. I knew there was a back door there that we could use.

My heart thundered so loudly that I could barely hear my steps. Orion followed me without hesitation, but I knew he would rather have been the one leading.

I was about to turn left into the corridor that led straight to the cafeteria when I was tackled from the side. I screamed as I fell to the floor, my head bursting with numbing pain. I heard the unmistakable sound of a dagger or knife being drawn from its sheath, then, seconds later, the sound of metal clanking loudly against the floor. Someone grunted, a man, but it wasn't Orion.

The floor swayed left and right under me, and I struggled to my feet. The screams seemed to come from the floor and walls, agonizing cries that made my head spin even faster. I heard Orion's frustrated growl as he fought my attacker, but the darkness seemed to have become denser around me, and I couldn't see anything. I leaned on the wall for support. There was a sharp gasp, and then I heard rapid footsteps echoing away from us.

Orion grabbed my arm. "Are you alright?" he asked.

"I'm fine," I said, pulling away from him. "Who the hell was that?"

"I don't know, but let's get out of here," he said.

There was a loud boom upstairs, like an explosion, and the red emergency lights turned on. The hallway was completely empty, with no signs of the attacker.

Orion's cheeks looked more sunken, and his eyes seemed to have absorbed the crimson color all around us. We remained standing for a couple of seconds, long enough to see the first patient race down the stairs.

It was the teenage girl with blue hair. She held a broken bottle in her hand. Blood covered her white shirt and pants. Her eyes fixed on me.

"Andromeda," she said in a ragged voice. "Now is our time to escape! We have to act before the Wave comes!"

Then her eyes went to Orion, as if noticing him for the first time. She gripped the bottle tighter. The glass cut through her skin and drops of blood splattered on the floor. She lunged at him. Orion was faster, pulling a knife from his belt and throwing it. It sunk into the girl's chest, right through her heart. She fell backwards with a surprised expression, which quickly turned into a creepy smile. The bottle dropped to the floor and shattered next to her.

Footsteps rumbled above us, accompanied by howls of glee.

Orion and I raced away in unison, towards the cafeteria. "Are the patients here always *this* insane?" he asked.

"No," I answered.

And where were the doctors and guards? I hadn't seen any.

I pushed open the metal door of the cafeteria and immediately stopped dead in my tracks. I barely had time to register the carnage. The red emergency light made the scene feel as if the room was flooded in blood. The patients were trapped in some kind of killing frenzy. Shrieks filled the air. To the left the balding patient lay on his chest, his neck twisted at an unusual angle. A patient I hadn't seen before lunged towards us, his shaggy, long hair rippling behind him. Before I could blink, Orion sliced a knife through his neck. Bodies of several patients I didn't recognize lay scattered throughout the room, pools of blood gathering around them.

Orion gripped my arm and dragged me back the way we had come, but the corridor, too, was now filled with blood-thirsty patients. One girl bit a guy's leg. She looked as calm as if she were eating chicken nuggets. Orion dragged me to the end of the corridor and we both pressed our backs against the wall.

One patient stepped forward. He was thin, and so pale he looked like he hadn't seen the sun in years. "Give me my stones!" he yelled at us, but his words were muddled.

I realized why when he smiled. His teeth were gone, and only bloodied gums remained.

Orion pulled a gun from his belt. I wondered why he hadn't used the gun before. Orion aimed forward and shot the man, who fell to the floor without a sound.

The gunshot echoed through the corridor, making all the other patients stop what they were doing and turn to us. There were twelve of them, but Orion didn't seem fazed. His narrowed eyes were set dead ahead. The patients were glaring at us, but their stares were strange, as if they were all sleepwalking—not fully awake but not asleep either.

Simultaneously, all the patients lurched forward. Orion's first shot boomed inside my ears, and the rest resonated across the hallway as one by one the patients fell. It took him less than fifteen seconds to kill them all.

Dark puddles began to spill around the floor, almost covering it entirely.

I had seen dead bodies before, and had stopped being afraid of them by the time I was twelve. But there was something about seeing the patients I had spent some time with, now lifeless and bloodied on the floor, that made me feel very cold. I couldn't feel my hands, only the vague sensation that they were tingling, but it seemed distant, as if it wasn't my own body.

I heard Orion speaking, but his voice was far away. I was barely aware of the strong hand that clasped my shoulder and shook me.

"What?" I said as my vision came back into focus.

The shrieks and screams had turned into a dark silence that seemed to fill the entire building. I wondered why Orion's grip was shaking, then realized that I was the one trembling.

Orion held me steady with his gaze. "We need another exit."

I cleared my head, focusing all my attention in getting out of the facility as fast as possible. Orion held my arm, keeping me upright. I began walking through the hallway again, my legs strangely solid. The dead patients littered the floor, but in my head they were merely obstacles across the corridor, not faces I had once known. I tried not to think as I stepped over the blood, and felt some of it filter through my shoe and lick my foot—it was warm.

At the end of the hallway, I turned right and raced to the glass door. It had been left ajar. It made me hesitate for a moment—that door was never left open. Had someone broken into the facility through that door? There were no signs that the door had been forced open. I pushed those questions out of my head as I walked out.

A cold gust of wind slapped my face as I stepped into the flower garden. The flowers were all dark, and the stone statues stared at me blankly, the maidens frozen mid-dance.

I raced to the other side of the garden, making my way to the metal door built into the concrete wall. I stopped before the narrow door I knew led outside of the facility. It was locked.

"Hurry up," Orion said as he looked back at the building.

The small windows seemed to be bleeding from the emergency light. In the distance, I heard a loud bark, like a mad dog.

"Are there dogs here?" Orion asked.

"No," I said hesitantly.

"Hurry," Orion muttered as he clutched his gun tighter. Unless he had another magazine, I was sure he only had a couple more bullets left.

I turned to the door again, focusing on the keyhole.

I closed my eyes, and imagined the narrow door clicking open and swinging outwards with a moan. I had to *believe* that just by thinking of opening the door it would open. I knew that my mind and imagination were more powerful than that feeble lock.

I imagined it again, the lock slowly turning and clicking open. I summoned all of my strength to make that thought materialize in the physical world. It felt like an electric current flowing through my veins instead of blood. My chest tightened, almost crushing my lungs, and I gritted my teeth.

Open, I commanded inside my head.

I heard a click, and when I opened my eyes the door had already swung outwards. Orion grabbed me by the arm and pulled me outside.

I quickly took in my new surroundings—the dark beach and ocean. We only took one step forward before stopping abruptly.

What in the name of Hell is that?

Standing before us was the biggest wolf I had seen in my life. He was as tall as Orion. The wolf's eyes were molten silver like a liquid moon. His gaze was curious, as if he were analyzing me. His fur was different shades of gray like a thundercloud sizzling with lightning.

Behind the wolf the water from the ocean swayed in ripples and small waves with the wind. It was inky black, darker than the sky above us.

I urged my feet to move, but they were stuck to the sand. Out of the corner of my eye I could see Orion standing frozen like a wax figure. He never froze. My attention went back to the wolf, who seemed to be pinning me with its gaze. The wolf bared its teeth, each of them the size of my thumb and wickedly sharp.

The rest of the world seemed to evaporate from my view, and I could only see those two silver eyes. *Who was here with me?* I wondered. Just seconds before I had been with someone. Was he a friend? A family member? I could only remember he was male. What did he look like?

The silver eyes began to swirl, shining with a sort of intelligence that shouldn't be present in any animal.

What's my name? I wondered. It started with A.

Where am I? Was I back in New York? London? Where had I been living for the past few months?

My chest tightened again, as if I were trying to open another lock. My scars felt as if they were burning with ice. I was suddenly aware of a gnawing hunger. The hunger had a shape, a beast crawling inside my body, waiting to be fed. When was the last time I had eaten? Even as that question crossed my mind, I knew food wouldn't sate that hunger. Then what would? It was as if the hunger had always been inside me, that small hole in my chest, but only now did I notice it.

The pang of hunger blurred the wolf from my vision. My tongue shriveled inside my mouth. I needed to eat.

The wolf smiled, if that was even possible for a wolf, and a low growl escaped from its mouth.

I was hardly aware of the movement behind me. "Alathea was wrong," a woman whispered behind me.

Just then, I was thrown forward with a booming force. A sizzling wave of heat washed over me. I landed at the edge of the beach, on the cold and hard sand. Water soaked through my thin clothes. It was freezing cold, numbing my body.

My vision swirled like I was inside a hurricane. I raised my head from the sand. The entire building was in flames, and the columns of dark smoke became one with the night sky.

The haze of smoke became denser around me with every second that passed. The entire psychiatric hospital seemed to be in flames now, but through the smoke I couldn't see the building clearly. I could only see the fire surrounding the building, like a flaming ghost bursting through the fog.

My thoughts seemed to clear in my head a little, but my mind was still fuzzy. Orion lay beside me, sprawled on his back. He was breathing, and his unfocused eyes met mine. Then my vision blurred again, my eyes watering. I felt a hand on my back, then someone hauled me up, but I couldn't see the person's face. Through my blurring vision the fire melted away, and I could have sworn I could still hear the screams of the patients burning inside.

• — • — •

My mind was engulfed in smoke, my thoughts dissolved. I coughed, my eyes opening slowly. I groaned as I sat up. I had been lying on a hard floor; my muscles felt sore. I looked around. I was in a room that seemed to be under renovation. The wooden walls and floor were covered in plastic.

Behind me was a ceiling-to-floor window, from which I could see the sprawling city, cast in a red glow from the setting sun. The sky was covered in pink and orange clouds.

Unused wood was stacked up on the left side of the room, next to what I assumed was the front door. To the right was an open door that led to a tiny bathroom with only a sink and toilet. Hanging from the ceiling were several bulbs, all turned off at the moment. I could hear the blaring sirens and honking cars outside. How had I gotten back to New York?

Zia crossed the room, her sudden footsteps startling me. I hadn't noticed that she'd been standing in the dark corner behind me. She stood over me, her eyes unforgiving. Her blonde hair was tied in a ponytail. Zia had a beautiful face—it was thin, with rosy cheeks, a straight nose and full lips. I'd never asked her age, but she had always looked the same to me—around thirty years old.

"Did you really think he wouldn't find you?" she asked, her voice honeyed, but her blue eyes were cold as an iceberg. Zia had a thick British accent. I assumed she must have grown up in England, but she had never told us anything about her childhood, or about her past in general.

I didn't answer. I stood up, the haze in my mind clearing. I was still wearing ugly patient clothes.

"What happened?" I asked. "Did you pull us out?"

The image of the dead patients bathed in red light crossed my mind, and I shivered the thought away.

"I was supposed to wait outside the facility until he brought you." She took a deep breath. "But then I saw the building blow up in flames. I found you lying on the beach, unconscious. So I dragged you to the car and drove back here."

Dragging Orion must have been quite a feat, but if there was anyone who could do it, it was Zia. She was a lot stronger than she looked. I quickly scanned the room again, then wondered where Orion had gone. Maybe he had woken up before me and had left.

"So what happened?" she asked, crossing her arms.

"Didn't Orion tell you?"

Her mouth twisted. "I want to hear it from you."

I hesitated for a moment, my lips pressed together. Zia clenched her jaw tight. I sighed in frustration, then reluctantly told her. I found my voice strangely steady, as if my emotions had detached from my body. I knew the patients must all be dead, but I tried not to think about them. I hadn't even known their names, and in a couple of days or weeks their faces would fade away in my memory, just like the faces of all the foster families I had lived with. That thought made my chest feel cold.

Zia paced through the room as I talked, her hands clasped at her back. She muttered something under her breath. Curse algae? I was sure I had misheard that last word. Marine plants were likely not the cause of our troubles.

Once I was done explaining, I asked: "Didn't you see the giant wolf outside? And why would the patients kill each other?"

As weird as my life was, this was something new, and just by thinking of the wolf I could feel my mind numbing.

"I didn't see any wolf," she said skeptically. "And I don't know why the patients killed each other. But it's not your concern anymore. It's over."

I was about to say it was very much my concern because Orion and I had nearly been killed, but I knew it was not worth arguing with Zia. I would have to get my answers somewhere else.

Zia crossed her arms, bringing my attention back to her. The features on her face relaxed as she looked at me. I tensed. She walked closer to me, and she stopped a foot away.

"I like your hair. It's grown," she said. She took one strand of my black hair in between her fingers and twirled it around for a couple of seconds. Then she met my gaze squarely. "How hard is it for you to cooperate? I have tried to give you a life, a home, a family, but you have taken none of it."

Because it's all fake, I thought.

"I want you to be happy, Andromeda." Her voice tightened. "And what do I get in exchange? Convincing the police not to take you to prison, chasing you around the country, and now having to pull you out of a psychiatric hospital."

I didn't answer, because I had nothing to say. Zia walked around me, taking me in. I had lost weight, and probably looked gaunt. I hadn't eaten well inside the psychiatric hospital. The food had been so terrible that most of the time I had only eaten half of what they served me. And after nearly a month and a half, that had taken a toll on my physique.

Zia stopped when she was in front of me again, right where she had started. She heaved a sigh. "I don't know what to do with you anymore."

Leave me alone, was the thought that crossed my mind, but I knew she never would.

Zia smiled warmly. *Here it comes,* I thought in alarm. She unbuckled her belt slowly and my saliva stuck in my throat as I tried to swallow. The belt was white leather and looked pretty much the same as it had ten years ago.

Zia held it in her right hand. Strange, she was left-handed.

Her left fist shot forward before I could blink. I flew a couple of feet backwards. Air was knocked from my lungs, and pain exploded in my gut. My head burst in burning pain as I hit the floor and dark spots danced in my vision. I was seriously concerned Zia had ruptured my lungs, if that was even possible, as I tried to take small gasps of air to keep some oxygen in my body.

Through the blurring pain, I was barely aware of Zia pulling my shirt off and turning me so my back was to her. The cold hit my bare back like a wave of ice.

I was still trying to get oxygen into my lungs when the first lash came. I let out a choked cry as the sound of my flesh meeting the leather belt resonated across the room. My back ached like it had been cut apart by a saw. My nails dug deep into my palms.

Then the second lash came, and the third, and the fourth, and the fifth. I could feel warm blood sliding down my back and onto the floor. My skin felt like it had been set on fire, and the biting pain that it left behind made tears sting my eyes.

It didn't matter how many times she hit me—it always hurt the same.

"How can I make you learn," Zia said from behind me, her voice distant, "that you should always follow my orders?"

I couldn't move from the pain. It expanded to my arms, legs and head like an infection. Some time passed as I stayed on the floor face-down, drifting in and out of consciousness. I knew Zia was still in the room, waiting for me to get up again. I didn't move from the floor. I didn't care if the wounds got infected, or if I bled out right there.

In that moment I would rather have been dead.

It was dark outside when I awoke. I lay face-down, my cheek pressed against the cold floor. There was a dim white light illuminating the room, and it took me a second to realize it came from my back. Instinctively, I felt a pang of fear, but then remembered that I wasn't in the psychiatric hospital anymore. It didn't matter that my scars were uncovered.

I studied the horizontal scars on my wrists. The light that came out of them was purely white, just like the light from all the scars on my back. The light pulsed in tune with my own heart—like a twinkling star.

I stood, groaning, my back completely sore and probably caked with blood. *Great,* I thought. *More scars.* My back would shine with more light now.

Zia sat on a chair a few feet to my left, drinking tea from her metallic-blue mug. The light from my scars made her face look paler. Even though I was nearly half-naked, I didn't feel cold. I was blazing with anger.

Zia regarded me with pity. "I really hope we don't have to do this again. You know I don't enjoy beating you," she said. That was a lie. If she didn't enjoy beating me, she wouldn't have done it so many times. "I have something new for you."

"I'm not going into anyone's house," I spat out, my throat raw. "I'm done with foster homes."

"You're not going to any foster home," she said. The shock must have been evident in my face, because Zia smiled. "You're grown up now, Andromeda, and I can't keep looking after you. I think it's time we part ways."

I blinked in response. Was I dreaming? Was I delirious from the pain? The light from my scars pulsed faster, and it seemed to shine brighter.

"Are you—"

"I'm very serious," she said. "You don't have to see my face ever again if you don't want to."

I was at a loss for words. This had been my dream for years, my only desire—to be free from Zia. But could she really mean it? The lashes on my back had gone numb.

"I only ask one more thing from you," she said in a quiet voice.

Here's the catch, I thought. The pain in my back returned at once like whips of fire.

"What?" I asked hesitantly.

Zia pulled a knife from her belt. It was very beautiful, with a wicked sharp double edge and a white handle, which looked to be carved from someone's bone. Knowing Zia, I supposed it could have been made out of human bone, but I decided not to think about that.

"I need you to kill someone for me," she said.

Time seemed to stop, and I felt the bile in my throat rising. I was a thief and a criminal, but not a killer—that was Orion's job.

"If you do this last thing for me," Zia said before I could protest. "You will never, ever see me again. I promise."

If there was one thing I knew about Zia, it is that she always kept her promises.

Always.

"Never?" I asked.

She shook her head. "Never again. Here's the target." She placed the knife on the floor right next to the chair, on top of a white folder. "There's everything you need to know about him," she said as she motioned at the folder.

"What if I get caught?" I asked. Going to prison for theft was one thing, but getting arrested for murder was something else entirely.

"You never get caught unless you want to," she said with a smile. "And if you do, I'll pull you out of prison like I always do. And then we'll part ways."

"Why don't you send Orion? He's better skilled at this," I said.

Zia's face paled, and the pulsing light made her cheeks look more sunken than they were. For a second, she looked older. I knew there was something she wasn't telling me.

Zia stood from the chair and walked closer to me. She took my cheek into her hand. I began to tremble, but not because of the cold. Zia's eyes seemed to glow as they reflected my light. "You have one week to kill him," she whispered. "And it must be you. Or else I'll never let you go."

The words sank inside my chest, weighting me down.

I nodded, my throat tightening. Zia broke away from me and took a couple of steps back. Her eyes traced me with an expression I couldn't quite place—was that fear? Zia was never afraid of anything. I remembered Orion telling me she had stolen some documents. Was that what was making her scared? What had she read from those documents?

I was missing something, but I knew trying to figure it out wouldn't help me. This was my chance to get away from Zia after years of trying to escape in so many different ways.

Zia smiled. "Once he's dead you can go wherever you want. I won't chase you ever again."

She stared at me for a couple of uncomfortable seconds, her face completely unreadable. Then she turned around and walked to the door. She opened it, hesitated for a second, gripping the knob tightly, then walked out. The door banged shut.

I let out a breath, realizing that I had been holding it.

I looked uneasily at the knife and folder. It seemed as if the knife shone too, but I realized it was just reflecting the light from my scars. Although it was weirdly brighter than it should be.

I took another deep breath, calming my heartbeat, the pulse of light slowing down.

Was I really going to kill someone? Was I willing to do that just to get rid of Zia? In response, the pain in my back returned like a wave of fire consuming my skin. I had seen so many people die yesterday in the psychiatric hospital. What was one more?

The thought of the hospital made the memories of the dead patients rush back to my mind—the girl with blue hair, falling with a smile; the crimson pools of blood gathering around all the bodies.

I began to shiver, suddenly growing very cold. I remained standing, my hands balled into fists. Tears streamed from my eyes, tracing down my cheeks and chin, then splattering on the floor.

I took one more deep breath and unclenched my trembling hands. The patients were dead. There was nothing I could have done to help them. Maybe Zia was right, what had happened shouldn't concern me anymore. I had more important things to think of now.

You can do this, Andromeda, I told myself. *One kill and you walk free for the rest of your life.*

I walked into the bathroom. My own light illuminated the small room perfectly, so I didn't even bother to turn on the light switch. The walls were all made of cement. The room only had a small sink with a bar of soap and a toilet. I would have to make do with that. It wasn't the first time Zia had left me in an abandoned building, although I wasn't sure if the entire building was abandoned or if it was just the apartment I was in. Zia hadn't taken me to her own apartment in two years, ever since I had tried to . . . I batted that memory away. Nothing I needed to think of at the moment.

I looked at myself in the mirror. My eyes were red, which only made the blue iris seem more brilliant, like a lake reflecting the sky. My straight nose was smudged with dirt and my raven-black hair was a web of tangles.

29

ANDROMEDA

I could still feel Zia's fingers looping my hair. I balled my fists, making my knuckles go white. So she liked how my hair looked? I sped out of the bathroom and picked up the knife.

It was light, but the carvings in the handle made it uncomfortable to hold. They depicted strange creatures that seemed to squirm under my hand when I held the knife, as if I had worms under my skin. But when I looked at the carvings, they were all still. I stared intently at them. Was that a centaur fighting Pegasus? There was also a dragon, an eagle, a giant bear protecting a small one, a large snake, a cup, and many other weird things.

I walked back to the bathroom and stared at myself in the mirror one more time. With my free hand I smoothed my hair. It had grown well below my shoulders, nearly reaching my elbows.

I picked up one strand of hair, then cut it with the knife. It was easier than I thought it would be. My dark hair landed on the white floor. I kept cutting my hair, in some sort of mad daze. After some time, I put the knife down and stared at the results.

My hair was now cropped short, reaching just under my ears. It was a shaggy and ugly mess. I smiled.

I put the knife next to the sink and smoothed my hair again. I didn't look *that* bad, but I wouldn't have called myself beautiful with that haircut. I took a deep breath, still feeling the pain in my lungs from Zia's blow. I picked up the knife again, testing its weight in my hand, then looked at myself in the mirror, meeting my own darkened gaze.

I gripped the knife tighter.

CHAPTER 3

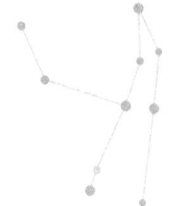

"ANDROMEDA!" Orion shouted.

I had been sitting on the bathroom floor for hours, reading the file Zia had given me, but when I heard Orion's muffled voice through the closed door, I stood bolt upright. I knew that it had been a matter of time before he found me, knowing that Zia had taken him here too. I left the file and the knife under the sink. I didn't feel ready to tell Orion what Zia had offered me, not yet.

I walked out of the bathroom and closed the door behind me. It was already morning outside; bright, warm light filtered through the window. Orion had been hunched over at the center of the room, looking for something in his backpack, but as soon as he heard me he turned around.

His eyes widened in shock as he stared at my hair. His jaw went slack for a couple of seconds. "What did you do to your hair?" he roared. I was sure most of New York had heard him.

"I cut it," I said simply.

He reached me in two big strides, horror spread across his face. "Why would you do that?" he demanded as he tried to take hold of a small strand of my hair.

I slapped his hand away and took a step back.

"It's my hair, not yours, so why do you care?" I asked.

His face flushed red. "I care because I'm the one who has to look at it!"

"It's *my* hair!" I yelled back.

He balled his hands into fists, muttering something about me under his breath. He closed his eyes and took a few deep breaths. I didn't really understand why he was so mad at me. It was my hair and I could do with it as I pleased.

"Why do you always need to have a say in what I do with my body?" I asked angrily. He raised a brow at me, as if he didn't know what I was talking about. "You once dragged me out of a tattoo parlor when I tried to get a tattoo on my arm, and you prohibited me from ever getting a piercing. And now I'm not allowed to cut my hair?" For a moment, I considered going bald just to piss him off more.

He opened his mouth to respond, but then snapped it close again. He shook his head and muttered something else under his breath. Orion walked back to his backpack. "I brought you some clothes," he said.

That's when I realized that I was still only wearing white bloodied pants and a bra. I should have felt embarrassed, but didn't. Orion had seen me in worse states. He placed my new clothes on the floor, next to the backpack, and pulled out an emergency aid kit. He opened it and dipped a cloth in alcohol, then walked to me.

"What do you think you're doing?" I hissed as I took a step back.

"Cleaning the wounds on your back," he said, taking another step towards me.

"I don't need your help," I said as I walked backwards, avoiding him.

He grunted in frustration. "Why do you have to make helping you so hard?"

"Because I didn't ask for your help," I said.

I backed up until I was standing a couple of feet in front of the window. Orion slowly walked closer to me.

He was a few feet away when he lunged forward, pressing my chest against his and wrapping his arms around me. I tried to squirm out, but my wounds roughly brushed against his arms and I screamed out in pain and frustration.

"Let me go, you beast!" I shouted.

"Not until I clean your wounds, you rat!"

"I don't care about my wounds," I protested.

"They could get infected."

"Maybe I want them to get infected so I can just die!"

Orion's grip abruptly loosened, and his hand gripped my shoulder, holding me at arm's length. "Don't. Ever. Say that again," he hissed.

His eyes went involuntarily to the horizontal cuts on my wrists. Those were the only scars Zia wasn't responsible for. I put my hands behind my back so he wouldn't stare at them.

Our gazes locked, his bright-yellow eyes seething with fury. Orion had been the one who found me. If it hadn't been for him, I would be dead.

"Andromeda," he said, shaking me roughly.

"Fine," I growled.

I reluctantly sat on the floor as Orion wiped my back with alcohol. It felt like someone was burning my back with acid, then setting it aflame, but I didn't make a sound. He then carefully bandaged my back.

After ten minutes, he was done. "There," he said. "Was it that hard?"

I only grunted in response. I stood up and walked to the pile of clothes Orion had left next to his backpack. I picked them up.

"Could you turn around while I change?" I asked.

He raised one brow. "Why?"

I let out another frustrated scream as I locked myself in the bathroom. Orion laughed outside.

Putting on my new clothes proved to be a challenge. My back was so sore that every single movement hurt. So I took a while, pausing every few seconds to let the pain subside. When I finally managed to get completely dressed I was breathing hard, willing the pain to go away.

The folder and white knife stared up at me from the floor. I had to tell Orion, but didn't feel ready for it. Zia had given me one week to kill the guy in the file. That was plenty of time. I would tell Orion later today, I decided.

When I came out from the bathroom Orion was staring out the window at the streets below us.

"Let's go for breakfast," he said as he turned to me.

Orion left his backpack behind when we left the room. The building itself didn't seem to be under construction. The floor in the hallway outside was made of volcanic black rock and the other three wooden doors at our sides were closed. As we passed by them, making our way to the elevator, a dog barked inside one of the apartments on our left. We rode the elevator down to the lowest floor and walked out of the apartment building together, immersing ourselves in the cold streets.

Orion had included a warm jacket in the clothes he had brought me, and I pulled it tighter around me. Even though it was still early, there was already light traffic, the familiar yellow cabs racing through the streets. The sidewalks were full of people who were probably making their way to work. Most of them wore formal suits. Tall buildings rose around me, people rushing in and out of them. For some reason, people in this city always seemed to be in a rush, no matter what they were doing, either going to work, eating lunch, going to the supermarket, walking their dogs, going shopping, picking up their dry-clean or getting back home.

The heavy smell of car fumes greeted me as we crossed a street. I had forgotten how much I hated the smell of New York, and rubbed my nose with my sleeve in irritation. There was so much noise—from people talking on phones, honking cars, buildings under construction, street-sellers.

The sky was cloudless, which meant a sunny day awaited us. The windows of the tall skyscrapers around us reflected the blinding shine of the morning sun.

The image of the dying patients pierced my mind like a sudden stab. The bodies all lying motionless on the stainless white floor as blood gathered around them. I tried to push the image out of my brain, but it was replaced with the wolf's silver eyes. Its gray fur moving with the wind.

My foot hit something hard on the street and I nearly fell forward. Orion immediately grabbed my arm and pulled me upright. He looked at my face as we continued walking, as if trying to read my thoughts. He looked away after a couple of seconds.

I didn't want to keep thinking about the dead patients. I didn't care about them, and I was glad that I had no names to remember them by. The patients were dead, and there was nothing I could do about them.

But why had they gone mad and killed each other? And that strange wolf had somehow blurred my thoughts and memories. Where had he come from? I had seen its eyes gleam with human intelligence. Was that even possible? Why had it been there?

Half of my mind wanted answers, and the other half just wanted to forget the whole incident had happened. I cleared my head of those thoughts as I looked around the city. Street-sellers were beginning to line the sidewalks, arranging purses on top of white cloths on the concrete, and others putting their merchandise on plastic tables. Food trucks had begun to open, and the smell of burnt oil filled my nostrils.

I was glad that at least there were some trees planted in the sidewalk; I had always liked to have a bit of nature around me. To me, New York had always been like an enormous cemetery. Every concrete building was like a slab of stone, but instead of marking dead people they represented only the wealthy ones, while the poor withered away like lifeless flowers.

I let Orion guide the way, not noting much of our surroundings. After a few more minutes we arrived at our destination and walked inside the building. The restaurant was small, like most places in the city. On the left was the window with a view to the street, and on the right were metal tables. Red orbs hung from the ceiling as decoration.

A group of four friends sat at one of the tables, eating as they read from some books and notebooks. They looked like high school students, and once they were aware of our presence they turned to look at Orion and me with curiosity. One of the girls stared at Orion wide-eyed, and two of the boys eyed me.

I ignored them and sat a few tables away from the group while Orion went to order our food. He came back to sit at the table, and we were both silent until they brought our food five minutes later.

We ate our hamburgers and milkshakes, not uttering a word. I was thinking how to tell Orion what had happened with Zia, sipping my milkshake, when someone called out Orion's name. He seemed as startled as me. His gaze fixed on someone behind me, then a smile lit his face.

"Hey, Rose," he said as he stood from the table.

A whirl of movement passed by me as the girl I assumed was Rose pulled Orion into a kiss. I wanted to choke on my milkshake at the sight of it.

Rose looked to have stepped out of an eighties movie. Her blonde hair was just above her shoulders, fixed into place with hairspray. Her strong, sweet perfume made me gag. She wore a neon-pink shirt and blue leggings.

Rose pulled back from Orion and turned to me. Her eyes were light brown, and her face had enough makeup to cover a house. She fixed her gaze on me and her cheeks immediately flushed red with jealousy.

"'Sup," I said.

Before Rose could protest, Orion quickly intervened. "This is my sister."

"Oh," Rose said.

Orion shot me a warning glance, and I just smiled. This wasn't the first time I met one of his girlfriends. Rose just looked back and forth between us, trying to find a family resemblance that, aside from our dark hair, didn't exist.

"Well, it's nice to meet you," she said.

She extended a hand to me, but one of my hands was holding my milkshake, and the other was holding my hamburger, so I just smiled instead. Rose seemed offended, retracting her hand at once as if I had bitten it. Maybe I should have.

"How did you find me?" Orion asked hesitantly.

"I saw you through the window," said Rose. She shot me another glare, as if she had thought that Orion had been having breakfast with another girl behind her back. "Why didn't you call me last night, Orion?" she said as she planted another kiss on his lips, making a disgusting sucking sound.

"I had a family emergency," he said.

"Oh, is your grandmother alright?" Rose asked with concern.

"She's getting worse," Orion said with such true distress it almost made me feel sorry for him. Except that Orion didn't have a grandmother. Just like me, he didn't know who his parents were.

"I hope she gets better," the girl said, and added with a smile. "Then you can come over."

Orion smiled. "I will."

He kissed her on the cheek.

"Well, I have to go, I'm in a bit of a rush, but I'll call you. It was nice that at least I could see you for a minute."

She pulled Orion into another kiss, as if trying to make a point to me. My eyes immediately went to my hamburger, which was spilling with ketchup. That was always a welcome sight.

Orion looked after her with a smile as she left. He had a mark of lipstick on his cheek that he absently wiped off with his hand. His smile vanished when Rose was out of the restaurant, and his feline eyes met mine. He smoothed his hair back with his hand.

"Did you have to be so mean to her?" he asked.

"That's what little sisters are for," I said, then added after a couple of seconds, "What happened to your other girlfriend?"

"Which one?" he asked before taking a bite out of his hamburger.

"The one with dark hair," I said, finishing my hamburger in one last bite. I remembered that particular girlfriend well because she looked eerily similar to me, except she had bigger ears, a rounder face and was a few inches shorter.

"Lilly?"

"No, the other one," I said.

"You mean Mary?"

"Yeah, I think it was that one . . . who's Lilly?"

Orion took a sip from his milkshake and shrugged. "Doesn't really matter anymore. Lilly broke up with me nearly three months ago when she realized I was dating her cousin too." He wiped his greasy hands on a napkin. "I'm still dating Maia though."

I shook my head in disapproval. "So you were dating four girls at a time?"

"No," he said, offended. "I dated Lilly and her cousin, then Mary and Rose."

"Why would you date her cousin?" I asked.

"I didn't know they were cousins! They don't even have the same last name."

I laughed, the sound strange in my ears. I hadn't truly laughed in months. The hysterical laughs in the psychiatric hospital didn't count as real laughs. We remained silent for a couple of minutes. I shifted uncomfortably in my chair, as if it had suddenly turned harder.

I still felt hungry, I realized. That was weird. I was always full after eating big hamburgers, and the milkshake had been a large one. The hunger was similar to the one I had briefly felt before the building blew up, as if food wouldn't make me feel sated. But that didn't make any sense. Maybe it was the stress of everything that had happened in the psychiatric hospital. I had heard, somewhere, that people under a lot of stress normally felt hungrier.

"What actually happened yesterday?" I finally asked.

Orion tapped his fingers on the table. "It was on the news this morning. The whole building burned down, so they don't really know much," he paused, bending the green straw from his milkshake. "They say it was because of a 'gas leak' and that the patients and staff didn't have enough time to escape." His gaze met mine again. "Aside from that, I learned nothing new."

"That wolf, it wasn't normal," I said in a hushed tone.

Orion leaned in closer. "No kidding."

"And the patients, they were, like, hypnotized," I said.

I remembered the whisper I had heard: *Alathea was wrong.* I hadn't told that to Zia, but decided to share it with Orion. He didn't say anything for a good two minutes, and instead stared at the table as if he would find the answer scribbled there.

"I'll look into it," he finally said.

"Orion—"

"I'll find that wolf too."

"Just try not to get killed," I said with a sigh.

There was no way to stop him once his mind was set. I knew he would probably find something—he always did. But part of me didn't want him to. I wanted to forget about what had happened, erase those memories from my head.

"Andromeda," Orion said softly. He was looking at my hands on the table, which I didn't realize had been trembling. I clenched my hands to stop them from shaking. Orion traced my face with his eyes. "Do you want to go for a walk?"

Maybe some fresh air would clear my mind and calm my nerves. I nodded. We stood up from the table and walked out of the restaurant. I followed Orion through the streets. The sidewalks were more crowded than before, forcing Orion and me to walk close together.

"If I did get killed," he said as we stood waiting to cross the street. "Would you miss me?"

"Mmmm," I said. "Maybe I would miss your cooking." He laughed out loud, startling the young woman next to him, who, after noticing his presence, swept him up and down with her gaze. I hadn't seen Orion cook for a long time, not since we had lived together with Zia. "You'd have to leave me your recipe book."

"You don't even know how to cook," Orion said, still laughing.

"I know how to make scrambled eggs with toast," I said.

"That hardly counts as cooking."

We crossed the street in silence.

The cool autumn air filled my lungs, but it didn't smell very clean. It smelled like oil from fast-food restaurants and gasoline. I tried to ignore the smell as I kept walking. At least my mind seemed clearer, even though I was still a bit shaken and felt my muscles ache. But I ignored that, focusing on every step I took. I was happy to be walking again. I hadn't been able to move a lot inside the psychiatric hospital.

"How do you do it?" I asked after a couple of minutes of silence.

"How do I do what?"

"How do you hide your scars in the dark from your girlfriends?"

"Oh," he said, his eyes avoiding mine as he looked down at the ground. "I'm usually not around with them at night."

"I'm sure you have a good excuse for that," I said with a snort.

"Yeah. My grandma Zia is dying and I have to take care of her," he said with a mocking smile.

I imagined old Zia lying in a bed, dying, her blonde hair a tangle of white, and wrinkles cutting through her smooth face like cracks. I laughed.

"So you just plan to use that as an excuse forever?" I asked.

Orion grimaced. "It's not like I plan on marrying them. I just want . . . " He paused for a second. "Some fun."

We stopped at another red light, standing among a dense crowd. The tall guy in front of me had a large backpack that seemed to weigh as much as I did. The cars slowly came to a stop and we quickly crossed the street.

"You should try it," Orion said as we passed by a homeless guy sitting atop a cardboard box.

"What?" I asked.

"Flirting with guys, having some fun. Well," he said as he looked at my hair. "Maybe it will be harder now that your hair looks like— Ouch!" he yelled as I drove my elbow hard against his ribs. He rubbed his chest, giving me a glare.

"I'm good," I said.

Orion shook his head. "I really don't understand you. Don't you ever get lonely?"

I didn't answer him. I didn't get lonely because lonely was all I had ever known. The only things I cared about was finding food when I got hungry, seeking out somewhere to sleep, and trying my best to escape from Zia and all the stupid foster families she sent me to.

"And how would you hide your scars if, like . . . " I said after a few minutes, " . . . your girlfriend just wanted to close the curtains to—"

Orion clasped a hand over my mouth. "Stop talking."

I pushed his hand away. "I'm serious. What would you do?"

Orion was pensive for a couple of seconds. "I'll tell her I'm afraid of the dark." I snickered at that thought. "Or I could just keep my shirt on," he added with a grin.

We continued walking, and I let my mind drift away. Cars, buildings and people blurred past me. After some time, Orion grabbed my arm gently, motioning for me to stop. I looked at him, and he motioned towards a bench that was placed against a building made of gray stone.

"Want to sit for a while?" he asked.

I nodded. We sat side by side, watching people walk past us. There was a man in an unbuttoned suit holding a dozen roses while he screamed at someone on the phone. A little girl in a bright-pink sweater held her mother's hand as she looked down at the sidewalk, jumping every crack she saw as if it were an abyss.

Letting my body rest for only a couple of minutes made me feel more tired than before, and the pain on my back returned with a surge of strength. Walking for a while, letting my feet roam free, had made me forget the pain. But now it seemed to protest at me for not staying still in bed. But I didn't want to lie in bed, or on a couch, as I had done many times before when I had lived with Zia. Somehow, being outside, seeing other people walk by with their lives, and letting the sun shine on my face—it made me feel a bit of freedom.

Orion hummed next to me, although I didn't recognize the tune. His left foot tapped on the cement as if it were a slow drum. He looked ahead of us, his gaze distant.

"Hey, Orion," I said.

He must have noticed something in my tone because he turned to face me, the humming and tapping gone in a second. I took a deep breath. There was no reason to keep it to myself anymore.

"Zia asked me to kill someone," I said. He opened his mouth, but I kept speaking. "And in exchange I'll never have to see her again."

Orion clasped his mouth shut, narrowing his predator eyes at me. A few seconds passed in silence. A guy with two German shepherds walked by. One of the dogs tried to smell our shoes while his owner pulled him ahead.

"Why would Zia ask you and not me?" he asked heatedly.

"She said it had to be me."

Orion shook his head slowly, looking at his calloused hands.

"Zia always comes to me when she wants someone dead . . . " His eyes narrowed at me. "I can't let you do this."

I balled my fists. "I wasn't asking for your permission," I said evenly.

He shook his head. "Something's not right here. She would have never asked this of you."

"I don't care," I said, standing up. My butt felt suddenly very sore.

He stood and held my arm harshly. I tried pulling away, but he pulled me closer. I felt his angry breaths on my cheek. "And what happens after? Where will you go?"

"I'll figure it out later," I said.

"You're not a killer, Andromeda," he said. His grip tightened painfully on my arm.

Our eyes locked on each other. I could see the yellow, golden and brown specks in his eyes, simmering with anger.

"You don't know that," I whispered. I pulled free from his grip, my arm aching where his fingers had dug into my skin. "Don't follow me, Orion. I mean it."

Orion's eyes were boiling with fury. "I don't think it's a coincidence—Zia reading those strange documents, everything that happened in the psychiatric hospital, and now this. Something is very wrong here."

"You're just angry that Zia offered me a way out and not you!"

A couple holding hands looked at us dubiously as they made their way around us. A woman holding a phone to her ear pointedly ignored us, speeding past.

"It's not that! I don't care about Zia. She's given me a life. I don't mind my scars," he said hotly.

"Then why won't you let me do this?" I demanded.

Orion opened his mouth to speak, but clamped it shut once again. I hated when he just bit back whatever he was planning on saying. I had forgotten how irritating that was.

I huffed and turned around, leaving him standing next to the bench. Orion was right in one thing—something was strange about Zia's request, but I didn't care.

"You will kill him," I muttered to myself.

My mind was set.

Blood ran freely from my wrists, spilling down my arms and onto the white-tiled floor, which was the only thing I could see clearly. The dark walls around me were a blur, and so was everything else in the bathroom. The pain had first felt like pressure accumulating in my arms and hands, and then the sting had started, as if it weren't blood spilling from my veins but venom instead.

I was tired, my eyes were closing, and I just wanted to sleep—to sleep and never wake up again. I wondered what the other side would look like. Would it be a land of eternal dreaming? Or would I vanish into the nothingness?

"Andromeda!" His shout seemed to come from the other side of the universe, echoing inside my ears.

I couldn't see him. He was just a blurry flash of movements before me, cursing me while he held my wrists, which only made the pain intensify—like a hundred needles piercing my wrists. I never got to hear all he said to me, because at some point everything went dark.

Then I was walking alone through a meadow with lush green grass. Silence dominated my surroundings, as if the universe was sleeping. It was dark, with the full moon shining above me. There were no stars in the sky. In the distance, I could see the outline of mountains, but they were just blurred shadows.

I walked, not knowing where I was going. But no one would come chasing after me. No one would harm me. I was free.

Then the pain started, a dull pounding in my wrists. I looked at them. They were spilling light, and inside that light I could see all the stars that were missing from the sky. I tried to contain it, using both of my hands to cover my wrists, but it was useless. The stars spilled in between my fingers like a river of light.

I gasped, my heart beating wildly. I was not in the meadow anymore. A wave of heat embraced me, and I realized I was lying on a bed, covered with a warm blanket. My eyes were open, staring at the wooden ceiling above me. It shone red with the light from the fireplace.

The pain in my wrists was unbearable. I tried moving my right arm, but that slight movement sent a hot jolt up my arm. I let out a yelp, and spots danced in my vision.

"Andromeda." Orion was next to me then, sitting at the edge of the bed. I hadn't seen him move to my side. His hair was disheveled, and I noticed that there were dark stains under his eyes from exhaustion. He was wearing a long-sleeved black shirt, covering up all of his scars.

"Why would you do that?" he demanded. I turned away from him, facing the fire instead, watching how the flames danced as they blackened the logs. I could hear the logs crackling, and for some reason that sound made the pain fade a little. Orion placed a hand on my shoulder, squeezing it hard. A sharp pain like fire needles stabbing my arm made me whimper, but Orion didn't loosen his grip. "Answer me."

I didn't turn to look at him. "I told you I would find a way to escape."

46

Orion grabbed my chin with his hand and forced me to face him. His amber eyes looked orange with the reflection from the fire. "This is by far the stupidest thing you've ever tried to do," he growled.

"I nearly died and that's all you have to say?" I asked, feeling hurt. Would he have cared if I'd died? Tears burned in my eyes, and my vision blurred.

His face contorted into a mask of anger, his grip painful on my chin. "You're the one who did that to yourself. So stop playing the victim. If you just wanted some attention, you could have called me."

I jerked my head away.

"I didn't want attention, I just wanted to escape," I said, holding his gaze.

His eyes narrowed at me. "I'm not letting you leave. And if you ever do that to yourself again, I'll tie you up in my closet."

"It won't be hard to escape that," I muttered, having been tied up by Zia many times before and managing to break free.

Orion shook his head again, biting his lower lip hard. "I mean it. Stop playing the victim, like you've suffered so much."

"I have *suffered*," I hissed. The tears now fell from my eyes, cutting through my cheeks like cracks.

Orion laughed, the sound of it booming across the room. "Everyone in life has suffered, and if we all decided to take our lives because of it there wouldn't be anyone left in the planet. You think you're the only person with a harsh life?" I looked away from him, not wanting to hear his words anymore. I considered standing up and leaving, but I felt weak, as if all my bones were made out of liquid.

"I don't want to live anymore," I whispered.

"Stop that!" Orion shouted. His hand rested on my shoulder, gently. "If you want to see suffering I can take you on a trip to the police department and show you how all those kidnapped and murder victims suffered, and then you can compare it to your life." His hand

47

tightened on my shoulder, tracing circles on my neck. "Or, you know, we could just watch a documentary on poverty in Africa. Seriously, Andromeda, just because you have scars on your back doesn't mean that your life is a complete misery."

The pillow was now wet with my tears. I didn't want to hear about African poverty and murder victims. I didn't need to compare them to myself.

Orion leaned closer to me, his breath on my neck. "You're staying, like it or not."

I didn't turn to look back at him, and instead focused on the flames. Orion was silent, but I could feel him sitting still next to me, his gaze not leaving my face.

A wave of cold swept over me. I had tried to liberate us both from Zia before, but she had made it clear that we would never win against her. Ever. There was no escape from her. And now, Orion had shown me that there was no escape even from death. He would always make sure of that. I closed my eyes, but that didn't prevent hot tears streaming down my cheeks.

For the first time, I really hated him.

Chapter XXXIX, Verse I

The ears that hear are many, but few the ones that listen.
Sweetened words will all believe, but truth he never speaks.
When the liar speaks the cheater with words deceives,
And observing is the one whose words fool everyone.
Secrets hide in the silence, those that carve his wounded soul.
To no end will his voice harm those who have a trusting heart.
Even the wisest ones to fool for his own cravings to soothe.

CHAPTER 4

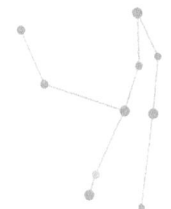

THE WHITE carved knife hung from my belt, hidden under my thick jacket.

I sat on a bench in Washington Square Park. It was Thursday afternoon, and the park was filled with people. Nearly ninety yards in front of me was the huge circular fountain. People sat on the narrow stone benches around it. A light-gray arch that seemed like a giant's door to the park stood behind the fountain.

Most of the people around me were NYU students, walking in groups, getting projects done, or just lying on the grass underneath the shade of a tree to take a nap. I noticed a couple of tourists, taking pictures and admiring the park. For some reason, there were also a lot of elderly ladies walking their dogs, so I got barked at a couple of times, first by a sassy poodle and then by a small brown terrier.

The sun was hidden behind puffy white clouds, and a cold breeze blew through the park, ruffling the leaves from the trees. If I closed my eyes, it sounded like waves washing on a beach. Long shadows trailed behind the trees around me as the sun sank lower.

I sat straighter, my back burning. Even though Zia had beaten me three days ago, the pain was still fresh. I took in a deep breath and fixed my gaze ahead.

ANDROMEDA

My target was eighty yards in front of me, selling ice cream next to the fountain. He was just a boy, probably my age. The file hadn't included much about him, not even his name, which I found a relief. I figured it would be easier, if he was just an anonymous face. The file, however, had information about the guy's school. He attended a private high school whose overly complicated, fancy name I had forgotten. The file also said that he came every day to sell ice cream to Washington Square Park, so I had come to see him for the past two days.

Even though it was supposed to be easier to kill someone I didn't know, it bothered me that Zia wanted him dead—he was just a teenager. I figured that maybe he was some sort of drug dealer hiding cocaine inside his ice cream cart, but he never gave any hints of doing anything of the sort. So why would Zia want me to kill him?

He came to the park every afternoon, probably after finishing school, and set up his small ice cream cart decorated with colorful animals. He spent the next three hours at the park, selling at least ten cones of ice cream. When I first saw him sell ice cream I didn't think anyone would buy it, considering that it was late fall. But apparently ice cream was still not out of season.

I hadn't bought any ice cream myself. Instead, I'd go around the corner to buy a burger with meat and a chocolate milkshake to calm my hunger. I had felt hungrier since I had left the psychiatric hospital. It seemed to be an always-present foe, making me feel as if I had eaten but wasn't quite full. I shrugged the feeling off and focused on the task at hand.

You have to do it today, I told myself, just as I had told myself yesterday. For the last two days, I had waited for him to leave the park then followed him as he pushed the cart through the streets, probably making his way back home. I had never followed him for

52

long, but knew that after he left the park was the perfect chance to kill him. Doing it in front of so many witnesses wouldn't be wise. So today I would wait until he walked through the more deserted streets so I could attack.

Zia had given me seven days to kill him, and I only had four more days left. If I didn't kill him, I would never be free from her. But was I really willing to kill a teenager just to be free from Zia and never have to see her face again?

The boy seemed innocent enough.

From a distance I could scarcely make out his features. He wasn't as tall as Orion, but maybe he reached six feet. He had the build of an athlete, maybe a football player. His hair was like polished copper wires, gleaming crimson and golden with the sun.

At the moment, the boy was selling ice cream to a couple. My attention was pulled away from him when I felt the bench shift weight underneath me.

I turned to my left. There was a guy sitting next to me, smiling. His skin was coffee brown, and his eyes a few tones darker. He had midnight-black hair, the same color as his bushy eyebrows and the stubble that covered the lower part of his face. Hadn't he ever heard of a razor? He looked around my age, but the stubble made him look a few years older.

"Hey," he said with a smile. "You seem lonely sitting all by yourself."

For a moment I thought that maybe Orion had sent him, just to test my flirting skills.

"I prefer it that way," I responded, maintaining a rigid posture.

"You have a strange accent. Where are you from?" he asked. His brown eyes were alight with interest. "I'm Corvus." I stood from the bench, and immediately felt his hand on my arm. "Wait, I didn't get your name."

I narrowed my eyes at him, feeling the smooth surface of the knife against my skin. Two murders in one day seemed inviting at the moment. I tried to pull my arm away, but his grip tightened.

"Come on," he said, narrowing his eyes. "I just want to know your name."

"Let go," I hissed.

"Hey," a voice came from behind us, startling us both.

I turned, nearly choking on my own saliva. It was the Ice Cream Boy. His fists were clenched, and his eyes were narrowed at Corvus—they were so dark they seemed black. His face was lean, and his cheeks rosy.

"Why don't you just leave?" Ice Cream Boy said.

Corvus's mouth twitched into a mocking smile. "Why do you care? Is she your girlfriend?"

"She is," Ice Cream Boy said with a matching smile.

Corvus's hand fell limply to his side, and he paled a few shades. He turned to me. "I'll see you some other time then."

"You better not," said Ice Cream Boy, his low tone menacing.

Corvus walked away with a grimace, towards a cluster of trees thirty yards to my left, where his other teenage friends were waiting. One was a brunette girl, so thin that she looked like a twig. Maybe she had some sort of sickness? Sitting at her feet was a small dog with curly black fur. I also spotted a blond guy with a biker's jacket and dark glasses; I was almost sure he was staring in our direction.

"Are you alright?" Ice Cream Boy said, his words forcing me to face him.

No! My mind screamed. *Ice Cream Boy wasn't supposed to know who I was.*

"I'm fine," I said quickly.

The Ice Cream Boy smiled. "Good," then shrugged. "Guys can be stupid sometimes."

"I've come to realize that," I answered flatly.

He brushed his red hair back. "Do you want me to stay with you?" He turned to look at the cluster of trees, where Corvus and his gang of friends were talking. They stood very close to one another, as if afraid someone would hear them.

"No. It's fine. It was probably just a joke," I said.

The Ice Cream Boy didn't seem so sure about that, his eyes still trained on the strange group of friends.

"Alright then. I'll be over there if you need anything. I'm leaving in around an hour. You should go back home too." He seemed genuinely concerned.

I nodded and sat back down on the bench. The Ice Cream Boy smiled once more, then raced back to his ice cream cart, where two girls were waiting.

I cursed Corvus inside my head. That idiotic boy had ruined my plan. The Ice Cream Boy wasn't supposed to know of my existence. And now I knew Corvus's name. I hated to know the names of insignificantly stupid people.

A new idea began building inside my head. The Ice Cream Boy knew me now, so what if I used that to my advantage? I could say that I didn't feel safe walking home alone and ask if he would accompany me, or at least ask if I could tag along with him for a while. That would allow me to get closer to him and make it easier to stab him quickly.

My scars itched with anticipation. No more scars, I told myself. No more Zia. Maybe I would still visit Orion, from time to time.

The knife felt heavier as it hung from my belt.

I once asked Orion how he endured killing people. He had shrugged and said, "When I kill, I don't think about killing. I just do it. It's easy, pulling a trigger, slicing a knife. There are billions of people on this planet, so how does one less affect it?"

I cleared my head of any emotion, and instead only felt the burn of the scars on my back. That pain was the only thing I needed to feel, the only motivation that would lead me.

I stood. My hands were sweaty, and I wiped them on my jeans. My heart beat furiously, straining against my ribs.

This is the only way, I thought. *You'll forget about him soon. Zia will never touch you again.*

I straightened my back. It stung from the lashes, and I could feel the bandages like a rope tied around me.

I forced myself to take a step forward, then another and another. He was so close to me, but at the same time our distance stretched for miles. The people around me didn't matter anymore; they were only background noise.

My eyes fixed on my target—he was serving ice cream to a small boy. He smiled as he scooped the ice cream into the cone. The smile made my steps waver, and my heart beat even more frantically.

I would make his death quick, then erase his face from my memories, just like I had erased all those dead patients from the psychiatric hospital. He would never see it coming. I just had to trick him into thinking I felt unsafe and wanted to walk with him. Then I just had to stab him. It wouldn't take that long, just a stab in the chest.

I abruptly stopped ten yards away from him. The hairs on my neck prickled, and the wind rustled the leaves around me. The air got heavier inside my lungs. The knife seemed to pull me down with its weight.

Something was wrong.

I looked around me, and my eyes fixed on the cluster of trees at my back. Corvus and his friends were gone. I turned back to the Ice Cream Boy and felt my breath come short. Twig Girl was buying an ice cream, and the boy handed it to her reluctantly. She began to talk to him, but I could see that his replies were short.

Then my gaze switched to the fountain. The blond biker-jacket dude was sitting there, at the edge, and I was sure he was watching me. There was a gleam inside his jacket, right on his left hip. The gleam was gone after a second, and even from a distance I was able to make out the object—a knife. It was double-edged, and the handle was white, like a carved bone.

It must be you, Zia's voice resonated inside my head.

Had she sent someone else to kill the boy, just to test me? The blond guy put a hand on top of the knife and gripped the handle.

The next few seconds seemed to happen in slow motion. I sprinted forward, towards Ice Cream Boy. He kicked Twig Girl away. A carved white knife flew from her hand, and her ice cream splattered on the ground.

Behind ice cream guy, I saw a flash of movement—Corvus.

I reached Ice Cream Boy and pushed him to the ground, then felt the unmistakable cut of a knife on my shoulder. The knife cut through one of my fresh scars, and I bit back a scream. I fell on top of Ice Cream Boy, rolled away, then nimbly jumped to my feet.

Corvus stood a couple of feet in front of me, baring his teeth at me like an animal, his knife dripping blood at the edge. He lunged forward at me, but I stepped to the side to avoid the thrust of his knife, then hooked my right leg with his, and drove my fist into his stomach.

Corvus gripped my jacket and pulled me down with him. We fell in a tangle, me next to Corvus. His grip loosened and I quickly pulled away, scrambling back to my feet. Corvus remained on the ground, coughing raggedly, his face red and purple. Next to me, twig girl was starting to stand, and I kicked her on the jaw. She cried out and shrank away. I looked up. Somehow, Ice Cream Boy and the blond guy had fallen into the large fountain. The blond guy didn't have his knife anymore.

Until that moment, I hadn't focused too much on my surroundings, but when I turned to look around me I realized that a crowd had gathered at my sides, watching the fight with fascination.

Ice Cream Boy shouted, pulling my attention back to him. He had fallen backwards, lying face-up in the water. The biker guy was standing over him, still wearing his sunglasses.

I leaped forward into the fountain, barely feeling the cold water halfway up to my knees. The scars on my back began to burn, as if I needed a reminder of their existence. I waded through the water and threw myself against the blond guy before he could kick Ice Cream Boy in the chest.

We both splashed down. I grabbed his neck and pushed his head underwater, but he was stronger than me. After a couple of seconds, Biker Guy grabbed my arms and shoved me away, making me stumble back and nearly fall. I regained my balance quickly. His head shot out of the water and he took a ragged breath. He pushed me backwards again with unnatural force. I landed on my back, the cold water like sharp knives against my scars. I pushed myself up and stood on wobbly legs at the same time biker guy jumped to his feet.

The sunglasses had finally fallen away, and I couldn't control the gasp that escaped my mouth. The guy's eyes were bright orange, and they had narrow vertical slits like a reptile's.

Out of the corner of my eye I noticed an object whizzing past me. A rock hit Reptile Guy on the chest and he fell back into the water. Someone grabbed my arm and yanked me out of the fountain—it was Ice Cream Boy.

We quickly stepped out of the fountain, water dripping onto the ground. The crowd of onlookers was still staring at us with a mix of curiosity and fear. They parted as Ice Cream Boy and I ran away from the park, passing below the stone arch and onto the sidewalk. Ice Cream Boy waved his arms at the passing cars, and a taxi immediately pulled over next to us. Considering the traffic in the city, that was a terrific stroke of luck.

Ice Cream Boy opened the door for me and pushed me inside, then went in after me. He closed the door. "Take us to Central Park!" he shouted at the driver, who hadn't even turned around to see us. His bald head nodded and the taxi sped off.

I looked out the back window, seeing Corvus and the other two staring after us as they stood on the sidewalk. Reptile Guy had found his sunglasses, and I could see the girl holding her jaw where I had kicked her. Corvus frantically waved his arms at the passing cars, but the few taxis that were on the street didn't bother to pull over.

I lost sight of our attackers as the taxi swerved left on the road, speeding past the buildings around us.

"Thanks," Ice Cream Boy said. "You saved my life."

I stared at him. His hair was plastered on his face, turning it a darker shade of red. His eyes were wide. He was pale, and dripping wet, but aside from that he seemed fine.

"You're welcome," I said.

CHAPTER 5

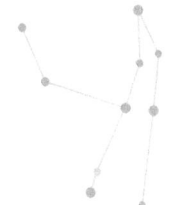

AFTER FIVE MINUTES in the taxi, Ice Cream Boy began to shiver, and I knew it wasn't because of the cold. He held his head in his hands as if it would fall off his neck. His eyes were cast downwards at the black carpet littered with bread crumbs.

I didn't mind being soaking wet, and in fact was starting to dry off from the heat coming from the vent. Even the windows had begun to cloud with steam. The driver didn't seem to notice, or at least he didn't mind. Buildings blurred past us as the taxi drove forward, and I rested my head against the window, closing my eyes. Adrenaline still coursed in my veins, and I could feel my heart thundering inside my chest.

I found my thoughts drifting away. I would still have to find a way to kill Ice Cream Boy, but I wasn't the only one who wanted him dead. The attackers had the same knife Zia had given me. Had she sent them?

You have to be the one that kills him.

So she had known someone else would kill him, or try to. Why hadn't she told me that?

Or had Orion sent them to stop me from killing the guy? That didn't seem likely at all. Orion would never send anyone to do something he could have done himself. But why had Corvus and his friends tried to kill Ice Cream Boy, then? And why would the blond guy have reptile eyes? Had I imagined that?

I closed the plastic window separating us from the driver so he couldn't hear us. "Why would they want to kill you?" I finally asked.

"Huh?" Ice Cream Boy said, meeting my gaze.

"Why would those three want to kill you?" I asked.

"I . . . I have no idea. I've ne-never done anything. I was just selling ice cream," he said, hugging his own arms. The guy was clearly in shock, but there was little I could do about that. "Thanks for helping me."

"Why Central Park?" I asked.

"Huh?" he said again. I was beginning to lose my patience.

"Why did you tell the driver to go to Central Park?"

"Oh, ah. It was the first place I could think of," he said. Then added, "But maybe we should hide somewhere else."

I slid the plastic window open. "Change of plans. Take us to 138th Street in the Bronx, please."

The bald head nodded and took a sharp turn right on the street.

I slid the window closed again.

"I hope you at least have some money," I said.

Ice Cream Boy blinked at me a couple of times, then reached into his back pocket to retrieve his wallet. It was made of dark leather and dripping wet.

We're doomed, was my first thought. But just then he pulled out a credit card.

"This should work," he said with a steadier voice. He clutched the credit card tight. "You never told me your name," he said. I bit my tongue. The boy seemed to notice my hesitation. "I'm Perseus."

"Andromeda," I blurted out, immediately cursing myself for not having invented a fake name.

He cocked his head to one side. "That's a strange name."

"So is Perseus," I snapped back.

Half a smile curled on his lip. "True." The taxi stopped at a red light. Perseus looked out the window. "Where are we going?"

"Somewhere safe," I answered.

"We could go to my house," he suggested as he turned to look at me. His face reddened again. "I-If you want, of course."

"If there are people trying to kill you then most likely they'll know where you live. We'll go somewhere they can't find us."

The sky had already started to turn a darker shade of blue, and with no streetlights our surroundings seemed gloomier.

The building right in front of us was small, squashed in between two old brick buildings. The wall was made completely of gray cement looking dull as always. There were a few cars parked on the street right next to the sidewalk, a layer of dust over most of them. I had wondered several times if people had chosen this desolated street to abandon their cars.

Silence filled the neighborhood, as if it dreaded my return. The construction behind me was still closed. I assumed it had once been a project that at some point had been abandoned.

Perseus stood close enough that I could feel his body heat. He eyed the rusty door of the cement building warily as I walked towards it. The brick buildings at its side seemed empty, even though I knew they weren't.

"Do you have the key?" he asked.

I didn't need a key. I looked at the small keyhole on the right side of the door and closed my eyes. I imagined the door clicking open and swinging inside with a creak. My body was already sagging with fatigue and hunger, even though I had eaten only a few hours before. I had not slept well since I had left the psychiatric hospital, but I gathered all the energy I had left into opening the door.

My chest tightened as I imagined the door opening. The lashes on my back felt as if they were bleeding all over again.

Open, I commanded inside my head, feeling something click inside me.

I opened my eyes and quickly stepped forward to pretend to push the door open just as it gave a loud moan that echoed inside. I walked through the door, feeling Perseus close behind me. He closed the door after he walked in. I let out a breath I didn't realize I had been holding. Hopefully Perseus didn't notice anything weird with the door. My stomach growled loudly, and I knew Perseus must have heard it. Why was I so hungry? Did I have *that* much stress?

I walked forward through the hallway. Perseus's footsteps echoed behind me. I stopped after a couple of seconds, standing in front of the closed door at the end of the hallway. Perseus must have had terrible night vision, because he bumped into me.

"Sorry," he muttered.

I could almost feel his face flushing red behind me as he took a step back. I opened the door and walked through it. Perseus came in behind me, his eyes wide. I closed the door behind him, and locked it with the dead bolt.

The room was huge, rising two stories high. I assumed it had once been a warehouse. The windows at the very top of the left wall barely let any light through, so I clicked the switch that was next to the door, illuminating our surroundings.

Now I could see Perseus in full light. His red hair had dried now, and resembled a coppery mane around his head. He scratched it as he looked around with interest. I had never invited anyone here, not even Orion. Having Perseus in my place made me feel as exposed as being naked.

He looked at the mattress in the left corner. It had a couple of blankets folded on top of it. Next to it was a closed door, which led to a bathroom. Then his gaze traveled to the opposite side of the room, where there was an old computer on top of a desk. Next to it were cardboard boxes grouped together, eleven in total. On the right side of the room was a large couch, placed against the wall, and in front of it a tiny television.

Perseus walked to the computer and clicked one of the keyboard keys.

"Don't touch anything." I didn't mean to sound so menacing, but the echo in the room didn't help.

Perseus jumped back. "Sorry." He faced me, placing his hands behind his back as he warily eyed the ancient computer, which seemed as big as any of my boxes. "So now what?"

"I suggest we stay here for the night, then we'll figure out something tomorrow," I said with a wave of my hand.

Perseus nodded. "Sounds like a plan."

God, he was so gullible. Hadn't his parents ever told him not to trust strangers? But I had saved his life, so he believed he could trust me.

"Do you think your parents will worry if you don't come back?" I asked.

He shrugged. "They're not even in New York."

In that case I assumed that his parents would take a while to notice that he hadn't returned home at all after going to the park, giving me enough time to flee the city.

"Is this where you live?" Perseus asked as he dubiously looked at the mattress again.

I shrugged. "Sometimes."

"Oh," he said. It was true. I came here whenever I wanted to have a couple of hours or days without seeing my foster families, or when I was skipping school or trying to hide from Zia.

I sat on the floor in the center of the room and motioned him to do the same. He sat crossed-legged in front of me like a little kid waiting to play some card game.

"In the meantime, I think we should try to figure out why anyone would want you dead," I said.

He gulped, and I noticed his Adam's apple protruding from his throat. "Well," he said, pulling down the collar of his shirt as if it were choking him. "Now that I think of it, those people could have wanted to kidnap me because of my dad, maybe to get some money out of him."

"Who's your dad?" I asked.

For a moment I was afraid his father would be part of some sort of mafia or drug cartel. During my time in New York I had come across several of those—mostly Orion's fault.

Perseus eyed me warily, and hesitated. "Andrew Wood," he finally said.

"Andrew Wood?!" I repeated as I stood bolt upright.

I paced around the room. No wonder Zia hadn't told me who the guy was. His father wasn't in the mafia, or in any drug cartel, but worse than that—Andrew Wood was known to be the richest man in New York.

He was a real estate investor, and had built some of the most fancy and costly apartment, office and hotel buildings around the city, amassing a fortune. His new home, valued at nearly a hundred million dollars, had been featured on the news—that's how I knew about him.

I turned back to Perseus, who now sat hugging his legs, looking nervously at me as he rested his head on his knees. Andrew had dark hair and light-brown eyes, I knew that about him, and his chubby, round face was nothing like his son's. Perseus had a pointed chin and strong jaw. His eyes were a lot bigger too, and his ears very small. I wondered if he had gotten the red hair from his mother.

"I'm adopted," he said, as if noting my skepticism.

"That still doesn't tell me why someone wants you dead or kidnapped," I said, but still found it interesting that he had been adopted. I didn't know much about the Wood family, so I had never heard they had adopted a child. Then again, rich people were very private when it came to their families.

"If they had wanted to kidnap you, they wouldn't do it in a public park where someone could help you," I said. "And I'm sure guns would be more effective than knives for that."

He nodded absently.

Why would Zia want the son of the richest man in New York dead? And why would other people want him dead too? Had Andrew messed with the wrong people in one of his deals? I found that idea more likely. I couldn't imagine what Perseus could have personally done to anger others to the point where they wanted him dead. And why would they attack him in a public park? Maybe they wanted an audience to make a spectacle of his death. In a way, that would have been a public attack on Andrew too, one that would certainly make its way to every headline in the news. That was the only logical reason I could find.

Too many questions raced through my head. Zia was obviously hiding something from me.

"Maybe your father did business with someone he shouldn't have?" I prompted.

Perseus shook his head. "I honestly don't know."

I began pacing again, looking at the bare cement floor. After a few seconds, a question popped into my head. I abruptly turned to look at Perseus, and he seemed to shrink away from my gaze.

"If your father has so much money, then what were you doing selling ice cream in a park?" I asked.

He shrugged. "My father wanted to teach me humility. He said that I better work hard if I wanted to go on vacation to Greece this winter."

I wanted to protest that selling ice cream in a park was not hard work. I would have loved to see him in a fast-food restaurant, where one out of three customers would call him stupid for not giving them the right sauce, and would yell at him until his face turned the color of ketchup.

I'd never had a job, but had worked with Zia long enough to know what *hard work* meant. I let out a sigh. Outside, the sky was already dark, and at once I could feel the temperature dropping inside. "Well, it looks like we're not going to figure out anything today. So we might as well get some sleep," I said.

Perseus ran a hand through his hair. "Do you have a bathroom where I could shower?"

I pointed to the closed door at the other side of the room. Perseus thanked me and walked to the door. He opened it and hesitated before going in. I bit my lip as he slowly closed the door behind him.

I had to admit, my bathroom was horrible. The showerhead was just above the toilet, and next to it was the sink, making the room big enough for a single person, or two if they were pressed together. For me it was perfect; I could pee, wash my teeth and take a shower all at once. But for someone like Perseus, who was used to marble tubs the size of a Jacuzzi and showers big enough to fit an entire family, my bathroom looked like a joke.

Perseus took his time, and in the meantime I paced around the room, trying to clear my head. Perseus clearly didn't know why Zia or others would want him dead. I could try to find answers later, or maybe I would never know the truth. Asking questions wouldn't earn me my freedom. I looked at the closed door and heaved a sigh. I would murder him tonight. This was the perfect place. No one would ever find his body.

The knife still hung at my side, concealed by my heavy jacket, but it didn't seem so heavy as it had been earlier.

Perseus came out of the bathroom around half an hour later, his hair wet again. He walked over to me slowly. My hand was inches away from the knife, and I could already feel the anticipation building inside my chest. It would be quick; it wouldn't take me more than five seconds to pull out the knife and bury it in his chest.

"I just wanted to thank you again, for everything," he said with a smile that made my stomach flip over. His gentle, dark eyes gazed at me.

He was just a boy, my age, with absolutely no idea of what was about to happen. I swallowed the lump in my throat and smiled. Perseus patted my shoulder awkwardly. His eyes widened and he withdrew his hand as if I had electrocuted him.

"What?" I asked.

He spread his palm before me, and I realized that it had blood on it. I placed a hand on my own shoulder and felt the warm blood there. Corvus had slashed me with his knife. With the adrenaline from the attack, and the already-present pain of Zia's lashes, I hadn't noticed that my shoulder was bleeding.

Perseus's face went pale. "Oh my god. He hurt you. Why didn't you tell me? What do I do?" His voice was loud with alarm.

"Relax, it's only a cut," I said.

He stepped closer to me, and, before I could move away, he pulled down my jacket and shirt. I clutched the jacket tighter, preventing it from sliding down my shoulder and showing the knife.

"It looks deep," he said with wide eyes.

I pushed his hand away. "It's not fatal," I said.

I walked over to my cardboard boxes. The one I needed was next to the computer desk. I quickly opened it. The box had bandages, a bottle of alcohol, and several other things I had stolen from the pharmacy nearby. A shadow loomed over me as Perseus looked down at the box with interest.

I pulled out the bottle of alcohol and a few new bandages.

"Do you need help?" Perseus asked.

"No," I quickly said.

I grabbed my supplies and locked myself in the bathroom, leaving Perseus alone. For a moment I feared he might run away, but at the moment I was the only person who could provide him a safe place to hide in. And even if he wanted to run, he wouldn't be able to open the main door.

I took off my clothes and knife and lay them carefully next to the door. The rest of the floor was soaked after Perseus's shower. I took off the bandages that covered Zia's lashes, then turned around to look at my back in the mirror. The tangle of white lines was topped with the new, bright-red scars that cut through me like red rivers.

Like I'd suspected, Corvus's knife had only left a cut behind. It was three inches long, but not deep enough to require any sort of medical attention.

Since I was already in the bathroom, I took a quick shower. The hot water on my back felt like lava, but I didn't mind. I used my bar of soap to disinfect the wounds again.

I carefully dried myself and bandaged my back with ease. When I put my clothes on again, I made sure to hide the knife well under my jacket.

I opened the door and closed it behind me. Perseus was sitting in the middle of the room staring at the floor, but he looked up when he saw me.

I walked to my boxes again, retrieving the one on the right end, and pulled out two cans of tuna, a can opener, a couple of plastic forks, and some bags of chips and cookies. I took our dinner back to Perseus, who eyed it skeptically, but didn't complain.

We ate in silence for a couple of minutes. I had almost finished eating my can of tuna when Perseus spoke.

"Who did that to you?" he asked.

"Mmmm?" I said through a mouthful of tuna.

Perseus's face reddened again, this time the same color of his hair. "The scars on your back. Who did that to you?"

I hadn't even realized that he had seen them, but assumed he must have when he saw Corvus's cut.

I didn't answer for a long time, instead eating my cookies. "Does it matter?" I finally said.

Perseus looked up. "It does to me."

"Why?" I asked abruptly. "We just met."

He stared at me for three long seconds. "So? You saved my life and we had only known each other for a minute. You didn't even know my name." I wanted to protest that I had wanted to kill him. "You cared for me so now I care for you."

I nearly choked on the cookie I had been eating. That's not how things worked in real life. But I knew he wouldn't let it go.

"Zia," I said.

"Who's Zia?"

"She adopted me, you could say," I began, then decided that didn't quite explain my current relationship with Zia. "Well, actually, she's more like my social service agent now. She finds me foster homes where I can live, and every now and then she comes to . . . visit."

Perseus had stopped eating. "But that's illegal. She can't hurt you. Have you tried going to the police? Or telling your foster parents what happened?"

I ate another cookie. I had tried to tell the police, twice, and my first foster family too, when I had moved in with them more than a year ago. But Zia always had an explanation for everything. She had told them that she had met me only weeks before, when she had "rescued" me off the streets. The scars on my back were old, and I had no evidence that I had lived with Zia during most of my life. We had never even taken pictures. Others had easily believed that I was emotionally and mentally unstable. They thought that I was delusional and had tried to blame Zia for the abuse. I knew Orion had never said anything about his scars, never daring to speak against Zia.

"Andromeda," Perseus said softly, bringing me out of my thoughts. His big brown eyes looked at me worriedly.

"I'm fine. I don't really care," I said.

He crumpled the cookie wrapping in his hand. "My father has connections everywhere. I could help if you need—"

"I'm fine," I said a little louder.

Perseus was silent for a couple of seconds. "Alright, but if you ever need anything now, you know you have a friend who can help you."

I wanted to tell him that he was not my friend, but he stood up and wiped the crumbs from his jeans.

"I'll sleep on the couch, I guess," he said.

"No. Sleep on the mattress, it's better," I said as I stood up too. I preferred to get the mattress bloodied because it would be easier to dispose of than the couch.

"But you're hurt. You should take the mattress."

My irritation was staring to rise. "I normally sleep on the couch anyways."

"Oh, alright then." He hesitated for a second before walking over to the mattress and arranging the blankets.

I walked over to the light switch and turned it off, then made my way to the couch. Even though I could barely see in the dark, I knew my way well enough. I had just settled on the couch when I heard him speak again.

"Good night," Perseus called out.

I didn't answer. I couldn't tell him to have a good night because it wouldn't be one.

Chapter XXVI, Verse I

Silver eyes the beast has in every shape he takes.
Even though the Wolf he prefers other forms he will accept.
For the monster knows no boundaries, not even those of death.
Fear his greatest ally, to weaken those he beholds.
No one to cross his path, except the King with golden eyes.
The war he will fight with Darkness inside his heart.
The Prince to protect so the throne he may seize.

CHAPTER 6

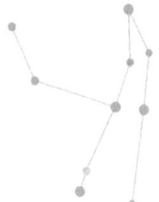

I STOOD over Perseus, holding the knife tightly in my hand. My feet were planted on the floor with shock as I stared down at his torso. His shirt had come up, revealing the bright light coming out of the scar that ran from his belly button to one side.

It seemed as if his bones were made out of pure-white light, and that light was bleeding through the scar in a pulsing river. It was brighter than any of my scars had ever been, almost like a lantern, bright enough to illuminate his legs, and even cast a ghastly light on his face.

He slept soundly, his breaths steady. Long lashes covered his closed eyes, and his copper hair seemed crimson when illuminated by the light from his scars. He had used his jacket as a pillow, and at some point he had pushed the quilts away, so now they were wrapped around his legs.

I looked back at his scar and gripped the knife tighter. To me, the light that came out of my scars had always resembled a twinkling star, every twinkle a beat of my heart. His heart seemed to be in tune with his pulsing light too.

I kneeled down, the knife reflecting the light as if it were a mirror.

If Perseus had known that he had shining scars, then why had he been so careless taking off his jacket, knowing his shirt could come up? Hadn't he grown up hiding his scars? Did his adoptive family know?

I stood up again, taking a couple of quiet steps away from Perseus.

Had Zia known Perseus wasn't human? It seemed likely that she had known. Maybe his murder had nothing to do with his father after all. But one question still remained. Why did Zia and the others want him dead?

By the time Perseus stirred from sleep, I had already been awake for nearly two hours. After staring at his scar for a long time, I had gone back to the couch. I kept waking up with nightmares from the psychiatric hospital, seeing the bodies of the patients lying on the white floor.

I stared at Perseus as he yawned. He shielded his eyes from the morning sun and blinked a couple of times. Surely he was aware that light coming out of a scar wasn't normal, but did he know what he was? I didn't know the answer to that question myself, and maybe he could give me answers.

Had Zia known Perseus wasn't human? I wondered again. If Perseus was like me, then it meant he could manipulate energy too, materializing intangible thoughts in the physical world. Did he even know what he could do?

Orion and I had spent countless hours searching for clues and answers about our origins when we were younger. The only stories that had spoken about shining scars came from conspiracy theories about aliens, angels, time-traveling beings or other stupid things like that. What Zia had told us didn't do much to douse our curiosity: "You came from another world. That's all you need to know."

After dead ends for many years, I had finally stopped wanting to know where I really came from, and the curiosity of not
being human had been overcome more and more with the need
to get away from Zia. As we got older she had beaten us more
frequently, scarring us over and over again. Just like any human
on the planet, I could bleed and feel pain, which made me think
I wasn't so different from them.

But now that curiosity was back again. Not only because of
the tingling I felt in my stomach as I realized there were more like
us, but also because Perseus could know the answers to the questions I'd had for a long time.

Perseus sat up straight, rubbing his hair. His eyes immediately went to me as I sat on the couch.

"Good morning," he said.

I nodded in response. I stood up from the couch and walked
over to the boxes, pulling out a can of sardines and more cookies.
That's as gourmet as my food ever got, so I hoped Perseus liked it.
I walked over to the mattress and put our food down. His expression was groggy, and his eyes were red.

"I feel like I didn't sleep at all," he said in a hoarse voice.

"You get used to it," I answered.

We both ate in silence, but I could feel the tension rising
inside me. He looked human enough. I watched the rise and fall
of his broad chest, how his dark eyes looked distractedly at the
floor, how every few seconds he would unconsciously push his
hair back with his hand or lick his lips. He even had a zit on his
chin.

After we finished eating, Perseus glanced at me sheepishly.
"I . . ." He cleared his throat. "Thank you for saving me yesterday
and letting me hide here. But I think I should get going. I have
a football game tonight and my teammates will kill me if I don't

go." I stopped halfway through retrieving my last cookie from the small box. "You can come if you want," he added.

"Are you crazy?" I blurted out. He flushed red again. "Someone is trying to kill you, but you still want to expose yourself at a football game."

I knew that he would eventually want to go back home, but the notion that he had a football game he couldn't miss tonight hadn't even crossed my mind.

"I'll be safe," he tried to reassure me. "If those weird people come back I'll be ready this time. I can tell my dad what happened and we can hire some bodyguards."

The fact that they didn't already have bodyguards seemed a little bit absurd, but dumber yet was the fact that this idiot was willing to risk his life for a football game.

"What if you just call in sick?" I suggested.

He stood bolt upright. "I can't. I'm the quarterback. I can't let my team down." I blinked in response. "Look, it's nice that you worry about me and everything, but you can't protect me forever. I can take care of myself."

I was silent for a couple of seconds. "Fine. I'll go with you to the game."

His face lit up with a smile. "Great. I'll introduce you to my friends, and you can come to the after party if you want."

I smiled. "Sounds like a plan. Let me just get some things."

I walked over to my stash of boxes. I kneeled next to one at the center, where I had stored away some things that Orion and I had stolen from a zoo, just for fun. I opened it and retrieved the small dart gun. We had stolen that from the elephant cage, and I wasn't sure what the tranquilizer dart would do to Perseus, but I was curious to know. I looked over my shoulder to see him standing in front of the door, fumbling with the knob.

"How do I open the door?" he asked.

"I'll be right there," I responded.

I aimed the gun at him, and pulled the trigger. The small dart hit him in the lower back.

"Ouch!" he yelled as he jumped back. His hand went instinctively to the dart and pulled it out, then let it drop to the floor. He turned to me, his expression a mix of betrayal, hurt, and surprise. I let the gun drop in the box and walked over to him.

"Sorry," I said as he began to slide down the wall, muttering incomprehensible words. He sat down, still muttering nonsense. Then his eyes closed, and his head hit the wall. Well, at least the tranquilizer dart had worked, and I wondered how long it would take Perseus to wake up again.

I walked back to my box and retrieved the rope. Now that Perseus probably wouldn't trust me to keep him safe, I would have to ensure he didn't escape. I walked back to him and tied his hands behind his back as best as I could, then tied his legs.

I wanted him to be in a dark place where I could confront him about his scar. The room was illuminated with light from the morning sun, so the scars wouldn't be visible in the room. I picked him up by his torso and began dragging him towards the bathroom. Immediately I wished that I had lured him into the bathroom and shot him there. Perseus seemed to weight as much a whale, and my arms began to strain with the effort of pulling him. His feet and legs scraped against the floor as I slowly made my way across the room. My back began to ache, and I started sweating, but, after a few long minutes, I finally made it.

I set him next to the toilet with his back against the wall. The floor was still wet, and I knew he probably wouldn't be happy to find his jeans soaked through, but I couldn't do anything about that.

I tried to catch my breath as I leaned against the wall opposite him. Perseus looked so peaceful asleep, and so innocent. I noticed he had a bump in his nose, as if he had broken it when he was little. Without his jacket, I could see his strong arms. His hair was ruffled around him, but I realized he still looked good. I suddenly wondered if he had a girlfriend, then batted that thought away. Why would I need to know that?

After some time, there was a noise outside.

I flushed the toilet and darted out of the room, closing the door behind me.

He was there, of course, eating the last cookie I had left as he looked into my boxes.

"What are you doing here?" I hissed. "How did you even get in?"

He motioned at one of the top windows. One of them had slid open a few inches. I hadn't even known they could slide.

Orion turned to face me, swallowing the cookie. His face was a tone paler than normal, his hair disheveled.

"Did you do it?" he asked in a flat tone. "Did you kill him?"

"Yes," I answered, trying to keep my face expressionless. "He's dead."

Orion didn't speak in a long time, only stared at me. With the morning light coming in from the high windows his eyes looked yellow from a distance, but there was something odd about them today. They looked like a crazed cat's.

"I wish I could have seen you kill him," he finally said after a minute.

"Why didn't you?" I asked. "Sleepover with Rose?" He didn't answer, and that's when I realized that his left hand was twitching slightly. "What happened?"

His face didn't reveal anything as he walked over to me. He looked dead into my eyes.

"Someone kidnapped Zia," he said slowly. "And maybe they'll want to take us too."

"What?" I asked as I felt my hands go numb. "How could someone kidnap Zia?"

I didn't mean why. She had killed, robbed, blackmailed and kidnapped people too. But during our time with her, over ten years, no one had ever been able to hurt Zia.

"I found out this morning so I don't know," Orion said. His expression hadn't changed, but his features were hard as a marble statue. "There was blood in her apartment." The veins in his forehead seemed about to burst. "I know it was her blood, I could feel it. It was already dry, so it could have happened anytime yesterday or maybe even the day before that."

"Good," I said as I felt a smile creeping up my face. "About time she bled."

Orion gripped my arms with so much strength that, for a moment, I feared he would break them.

"Someone took Zia!" he yelled, as if I hadn't understood the first time.

A new thought formed inside my head. If Zia was gone then I didn't have to kill Perseus to get away from her. I was already free.

Orion loosened his grip on me. "Someone might come after us too. After all, we've done much of her dirty work."

I shrugged. "So? We both know how to hide. No one will find us."

Orion pushed away from me and began pacing again. There was something else bothering him, and I sensed that he was about to tell me what it was, so I remained silent. Orion balled his fists then spread his palms, looking at them. "I can't track her," he burst out. "I can't."

It took me a couple of seconds to process those words. "You don't want to find her?"

"I can't find her. As if she didn't exist," Orion replied, not turning to look at me.

I had never heard Orion say that. He could track down everything and everyone he had ever seen.

"How is that possible?" I asked.

"I don't know!" Orion roared. "I was trying to track that stupid wolf and felt the same thing."

He walked back to me, meeting my gaze. "If someone came for Zia then they'll be coming for us. We have to leave."

I didn't know what to say to him. I still had to deal with Perseus. I felt like a weight had been lifted from my heart. I could let Perseus go and continue with his life. If Corvus and his friends wanted to kill him, then that was not my problem anymore. But at least I wanted to ask Perseus if he knew anything about the scars, then untie the poor guy so he could get to his football game on time—assuming he survived that long.

"Andromeda," Orion said as he held my arms. "We have to leave."

"Fine," I said. "On one condition."

"What?" he asked with a scowl.

"You don't try finding Zia," I said slowly. His eyes narrowed even further. "And after we leave the country, you let me go wherever I want."

He stared at me for a very long time. I knew I was asking him something nearly impossible, and that he wouldn't resist for long. But maybe he could hold back long enough to let whoever had taken Zia kill her.

Orion pressed his lips tight together. "Fine."

"Good," I said with a smile. "Give me three hours to fix some things and I'll meet you back in front of Zia's old apartment, the one she sold a year ago."

"No. You stay here." He looked around the room as if assessing how safe it was. "We might be in danger too."

"Fine."

Orion nodded. He pulled something out of his pocket and handed it to me. It was a phone, but it looked as ancient as Orion's fake grandmother. "Keep that with you in case there's an emergency. I have a couple of things to take care of too," he paused. "I'll be back here in three hours. Don't go anywhere."

I nodded. Orion walked away from me and exited the building through the door without sparing me another glance. Even though the front door couldn't be opened without a key, I was sure he would find a way to leave. I just hoped he didn't break my door.

I let out a breath I didn't realize I'd been holding. Zia was gone, kidnapped and probably dead. I hoped she was dead. I had wanted Zia to be dead for so long that the fact that she might be still felt unreal.

I could finally leave the country. I didn't know where I'd go, but didn't care. I could go wherever I wanted to. I would see Orion from time to time to know what he was doing with his life, but now I would truly be able to be alone. That thought sent a thrill of emotions through me.

But first, I had to deal with Perseus.

The night was dark as I walked on the sidewalk, illuminated only by the moon. The streetlights weren't on, and neither were any of the windows from the houses at my sides. I assumed there must have been some power outage, which was perfect for me at the moment.

My heart quickened when I spotted the house I had been looking for. It was two stories tall, made of red brick with rectangular windows on each floor. The path leading to the main door was decorated with small white flowers on each side.

I walked to the edge of the house and made my way around it, towards the backyard. I remembered Orion telling me that through his window he could see the maple tree that stood in one corner of the backyard.

I was no more than a shadow among the grass as I looked up at the house, trying to determine which window might be his. It would be very embarrassing if I accidentally burst into the wrong room.

The two large windows were dark, and I spotted no movement. I guessed I would have to take a look inside. My eyes traveled down, to the large porch with a roof on top to shield it from the rain. It had two columns, and the roof was made of black tiles. I quickly walked forward and began to climb the right column. My shoulders burned with the weight of my backpack, reminding me of its presence. My arms, too, were straining as I hauled myself up to the roof above the porch.

Once there I remained crouched for a couple of minutes, breathing deeply. The windows to the second floor were a few feet above me. I walked to the right one and jumped up, taking hold of the edge. My feet found hold on the uneven bricks, and I quickly peeked inside the window. Right in front of the window there was a king-sized bed with a couple sleeping inside it. That was the only thing I noticed before I jumped down again.

"What are you doing?!" Orion hissed.

I jumped in surprise and turned to the left. Orion was shirtless, leaning out his window to look at me with a furious glare. I walked over to him, his face hovering inches above mine.

"Can I come in?" I said, gesturing at the window.

Orion shook his head in disapproval. Then his hands were below my arms and pulling me inside his room. He let me drop to the floor and closed the window.

"You better not make any noise," he hissed at me. "I don't want my foster parents thinking I sneak in girls at night."

"So I'm the first girl here?" I asked teasingly.

Orion rubbed his head. "I didn't say that."

Orion's back gleamed with the shine of his scars. It was enough to illuminate the room in a dim blinking light that made the shadows look alive with motion.

"Why aren't you wearing a long-sleeved shirt?" I scolded him, remembering all the times Zia had told us to do so. "Someone could come in and see you."

He shrugged. "The door is locked."

I scoffed. Orion was taller than when I had last seen him, already reaching a head above me. And I noticed he had more hair on his broad chest too. I looked at the rest of his room. It was neatly organized. His single bed was to the right, pressed against the wall. To the left was a desk stacked with at least a dozen books and a sketching notebook. I was curious about what he had sketched. I was about to walk over to his desk when he blocked my way and crossed his arms.

"Seriously," he whispered. "What are you doing here?"

"Zia traveled to Europe," I said. "She'll be gone for a few weeks. It's the perfect time!"

He raised a quizzical brow. "The perfect time for what?"

87

I let out a frustrated grunt. "To run away from her, you idiot. We'll have a head start of two weeks." I swung my backpack down. "I already bought two tickets to Brazil."

Orion grasped both of my wrists, which I had left uncovered because they had no scars. I looked into his eyes, but couldn't see what he was thinking. "Are you crazy? We can't just run away."

I pulled my arms free. "It's about time we try," I said. "This is the first time she'll be gone for a long time, not spying on us."

Orion's lips formed a taut line. "Do I need to remind you of what happened last time we tried to escape?" He shook his head. "Have you forgotten what she did to me . . . what she did to you? You couldn't walk for two months."

The hairs on my neck prickled with unwelcome fear. Before those memories could even peek into my mind, I pushed them away.

"She can't hurt us this time," I said with a shaky voice. "We're in foster care now, she won't risk beating us in case we have to move in with a new family."

Orion raised a brow, as if he knew she was quite capable of beating us again without caring about what foster families would say. He was probably right. If she hurt us she could make up a story that she had found us wounded on the street and had saved us. That thought made me sick.

"We have to try."

Orion shook his head slowly. "And then what?"

"I have some money I stole from my foster parents," I said. "And we both know how to steal more, we could rent an apartment, and then—"

Orion grasped my wrists again, with more strength than he'd had before. "We can't run away from Zia." His tone was low. "Didn't you learn that last time?"

"We can try." I placed a hand on his shoulder, where he had the first scar Zia had given him—the brightest scar he had. As soon as

my skin touched his, he jumped back as if I had electrocuted him. "Is that what you want?" I asked as I pointed at his scar. "To live the rest of your life afraid of Zia and just waiting for the next time she beats us until we bleed?"

Orion shook his head again. "It's not that, Andromeda."

"Then what is it?" I asked desperately.

Zia was good at finding people, but never better than Orion. If he knew where she was then we could always avoid her.

"We don't have money, or a house, or a family," he said. "We don't have anything. So how do you expect us to make a life out of that?" I felt my cheeks burning. Orion pulled me closer to him. "Zia may not be the best caretaker in the world, but she's given us everything we need."

"But at what price?" I asked. Orion let go of me as if my question had slapped him across the face. "At what price?" I asked louder. Orion gave me his back. The light was shining more rapidly now, in tune with his heart. I could almost hear it beating with every blink. "At what price?"

He turned to face me again. His face looked thinner now, with the dim light.

"I don't care what the price is. I'd rather live in a house with scars than as a beggar on the street," he said in a deep voice. "I don't mind doing favors for Zia, you know that."

"So you don't mind being beaten? You don't mind broken bones and blood?" I asked.

Orion faced the blank wall above the desk, his eyes unfocused. He shrugged. "We were being disobedient."

Blood boiled in my veins, hotter than the flush that spread across my face. "Those are Zia's words, not yours. Do you seriously believe that?" I asked. "That she can do whatever she wants with us as long as she takes us to foster families, or feeds us and gives us somewhere to live?"

"It's your fault that she started making us live with foster families!" He hissed, every word venomous. I took a step back, and Orion started, as if he hadn't meant to say that out loud. I thought he had forgiven me for that, but apparently he hadn't. He stared at the wall again. "We don't have anything, Andromeda. And if we run away . . ." He looked at his bare feet. "We'll have less than we do now. We need Zia."

I clenched my fists, feeling my hands go numb. Zia had broken him, crushed him well beyond repair. He really couldn't see the monster she was. I bit my tongue to prevent myself from crying. Orion was broken, and there was nothing I could do to fix him.

"Why can't you see her as she really is?" I asked him.

Orion's hands clenched so tightly that I could see his nails digging into his palms. The muscles on his arms knotted, veins sticking out of them. He turned to me then, his eyes drowning in a mix of sorrow, frustration and anger.

He opened his mouth, as if to confess something. Then he closed it again and shut his eyes tightly.

"You don't understand," he whispered.

"No. I don't," I said.

I turned and walked toward the window. My flight left tomorrow morning, and I wasn't planning to let it leave without me. I looked at the big maple tree, which for some reason seemed to comfort me. I opened the window.

"You know she'll send me to find you," Orion said, so quietly that I barely heard him.

"I know," I whispered back.

"Then you know you can't escape," he said. I could feel his eyes on my back. My body turned cold, and it wasn't because of the wind outside. I had seen Orion hunting down people for Zia.

SOFI AGUILERA

I was his new prey.
"I'll find a way," I said before I jumped out the window.

CHAPTER 7

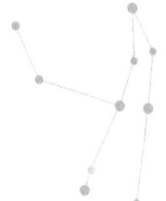

I STOOD leaning against the wall, looking down at Perseus. He had been unconscious for at least twenty minutes since Orion had left, but now he was stirring back to life. He moaned as he opened his eyes. I noticed he was trying to move his arms and legs without much luck. He blinked a couple of times, as if the light bulb hanging from the ceiling was too bright for him. He groaned again, then looked up to meet my gaze.

"I just want to ask you a few more questions before we leave," I said as I crouched down.

The room was so small that our faces were inches apart.

"You could have asked that instead of shooting me with a dart gun!" he yelled.

"I suppose I could have, but didn't know if you would stay," I said.

He blinked at me a couple of times, trying to let his eyes adjust to the light.

"What did you want to ask?" he said hesitantly.

My eyes went to his stomach, and I lifted his shirt up. Perseus jumped at my touch and pressed himself harder against the wall, but didn't protest.

"Nice scar," I said as I looked up to meet his frightened eyes. He had paled a few shades, making his eyes seem darker. I stood up to flip the switch. The bulb turned off, but light didn't fade from the room. I kneeled down again to look at his scar, which was bright enough to illuminate the room.

Perseus's face turned even whiter, like a sheet of paper, the shadows making his eyes seem hollow. Our gazes met for a couple of seconds, but he didn't speak.

I pulled my sleeve up, and my horizontal scars began to shimmer too. They were dimmer than Perseus's. Our light pulsed at the same time, as if our hearts were in tune with each other. Perseus's eyes drilled into my wrists, but he remained silent.

We both stayed like that, letting our scars speak for several minutes.

"You're not human either," Perseus finally whispered.

"No," I said.

"When you saved me, did you know I wasn't human?" he asked.

I shook my head. "I saw your scar last night."

He heaved a sigh.

"Does anyone else know you're not human?"

I knew I was missing a link. Zia asking me to kill Perseus, then going missing days later, and Perseus being not human like me—it all seemed to be connected somehow.

Perseus shook his head. "No one knows, not even my adoptive family."

"Really?" I asked. "It took me one night to discover your scars. Your shirt came up."

Perseus sighed. "With everything that happened yesterday I wasn't really worried about hiding my scars, but I'm usually careful. I never share a room with anyone at night."

I raised an eyebrow. Considering his family was rich, it was possible that he had always slept in a room of his own, and probably had a bathroom for himself too. But for some reason I still wasn't convinced of his explanation. Even though yesterday had been a terrible day for him, he should have been careful hiding his scars if he knew he was going to sleep in the same room as me. It seemed too reckless that he had just forgotten to make sure his scars were hidden all night long, but I let it drop. I had more important things to ask him.

His eyes met mine. They looked black with the white light. "I wasn't completely honest with you yesterday."

"I assumed you weren't," I said. The blinking light made shadows move across his face like ghosts as he squirmed against his bonds.

"Could you please untie me?" he asked.

"Not until I hear the whole truth."

He let his head rest against the hard wall. "What do you want to know?"

"Is there anything strange you can do? Asides from having scars that shine in the dark?" I asked.

He looked at me confusedly. "Like what?"

"I don't know, anything out of the ordinary?"

He shook his fuzzy head. "Not that I know of."

"Do you know what we are?" I leaned forward.

Perseus shook his head. "I'd never found any answers aside from alien conspiracy theories and myths about angels."

I let out a small chuckle. "Same here."

He smiled. "Until a year ago. My dad took us on a trip to Greece and I found something there. It was a strange myth, one that I haven't found in any Greek mythology book, or even on the Internet."

"Greece?" I asked. I had known that my name and Orion's came from ancient Greek myths, but I'd never paid much attention to that. I didn't really find mythology interesting. They were just stories that people told to explain what they couldn't understand.

Perseus nodded. "At first, I just started looking at myths with my name. I knew Perseus was a very famous Greek hero."

"Hmmm," I said.

I had heard of Perseus a couple of times.

Perseus flushed. "Yeah. He's the hero who used Medusa's head to save the Princess Andromeda from the sea monster Cetus."

I stared at him for a couple of seconds. Our names were both part of the same myth, and I didn't think that was a coincidence, but at the moment it didn't matter.

"What else did you find?" I asked.

His eyes were wider now, more alert. "Like I said, it was a myth that doesn't appear on Greek mythology books. It was about Star Children."

"Star Children?" I asked. That sounded more ridiculous than angels or aliens.

He nodded. "The story says that the Stars, or, in this case, Constellations, each created a child of its own and sent it here to Earth. What made these children physically different from humans was that they bled light instead of blood."

I let my head hang back until it hit the wall.

"And where exactly did you find this myth?" I asked.

"In a small museum in Athens," Perseus said. "The myth came from some ancient sheets of paper. They must have once been part of a book that is now lost. I only know that whomever wrote that text was named Alathea."

An electric chill raced down my spine. "Alathea?" I asked.

Alathea was wrong. Those words echoed inside my ears. I didn't imagine many Alatheas living in the world. The book must have been related to the whisper I had heard in the psychiatric facility. So maybe Perseus's story did have some truth behind it, even if I didn't believe in Star Children.

"Who's Alathea?" I asked.

"She was a priestess at the Oracle of Delphi," Perseus said excitedly. "Which means she could see the future. Her book supposedly holds the Prophecies about the Star Children. But I never found the entire book, only those couple sheets of paper that had once belonged to it."

That meant nothing to me except that there was a written text that might explain where I came from. Even though I still wasn't completely sure that the Star Children were real, Alathea was worth investigating.

"But I don't think that some teenagers at the park would want me dead for stealing Alathea's book," Perseus said absently.

"Wait," I said. "You stole the book?"

"No. Like I said, the book wasn't there. The museum only had a couple of sheets," Perseus said. "They were stashed away in the museum's archive. No one noticed I took them, not even my dad."

"Thief," I muttered.

Perseus only gave me a shy smile, his features relaxing as if confessing his crime to me had taken a weight off his back. "The text was really weird though," he added. "A combination of Attic Greek dialect and something else." He squirmed again in discomfort, but I made no move to release him. The light inside his scar twinkled quicker, along with his heart. "A month ago I finally found a Greek book that could help me translate the text into English. But . . ."

"But what?" I asked.

Perseus's shoulders slumped. "Both the original text and the translated copy were stolen about a week ago. They were in a safe in my room, and I'm the only one who knows the password." He clenched his fists behind his back. "There wasn't even evidence that someone had broken into our house. The cameras didn't film anyone sneaking in, and our guards didn't notice anything strange."

I felt my muscles tensing, sending a shock of pain through my scarred back. In the psychiatric hospital, Orion had told me that Zia had stolen some documents from someone and gone nuts. Could it be the same papers Perseus had stolen and translated from Alathea's book? I didn't think it was a coincidence.

My mind tried to tie all the loose ends. Perseus had stolen those papers, and Zia had stolen them from him. She had read something in those Prophecies that had made her go crazy and she had asked me to kill Perseus. Maybe the ancient text had information Zia didn't want anyone else to know, not even Perseus. But why?

"What did the text say?" I asked.

Perseus shrugged. "Ancient prophets tended to make their Prophecies very confusing, and most of the text is too ambiguous or awkward to make any sense. The Prophecies that I stole spoke specifically about a blinking demon named Algol, and how it would spill blood and conquer the sky, or something like that."

"Hmmm," I said. Hadn't Zia mentioned something about Algol? I had mistaken it for algae, but the two words sounded alike. The more Perseus talked, the more I was convinced that Zia had stolen those papers from him and didn't want anyone else to know about them. But why had she sent *me* to kill Perseus? And why would Zia even want those Prophecies? Perseus wanted them because they might offer an explanation of where we came from. But why would they be important to Zia? It didn't make sense, and I knew I was missing something.

"Sorry," Perseus said, his face flushing slightly. "I don't remember what the Prophecy specifically said. My memory isn't that good."

"Don't worry." I leaned forward and began untying him. He tensed as I worked on the ropes, holding his breath.

When I was finished untying the ropes, Perseus immediately leaped to his feet. I stood too. The room was so narrow that we were both pressed together, his chest inches away from mine. He chuckled nervously and slid closer to the door, then opened it and walked out.

The bright light from the sun blinded me for a moment. The scars on my wrists didn't shine anymore, but I covered them with my sleeve anyways. Perseus stretched. His wrists now had red marks, but he didn't seem to mind.

"So can I go to my football game now?" he asked.

I sighed. "Sure."

I walked to the door and unlocked it, even though he could have done it himself, but he seemed too shy to do it. Maybe he was afraid I would shoot him with a tranquilizer dart again. I opened the door and motioned for him to step out. Perseus hesitated, placing his hands behind his back.

"Would you mind walking me home?" he asked sheepishly.

Half an hour had passed since Orion had left. Two and a half hours was enough time to accompany Perseus and come back before Orion noticed I had been gone. And even if he did find out, I didn't really care.

Against my will, I smiled. "Okay."

We stepped out of the building together, and walked through the mostly empty streets of the neighborhood. There were some children playing football in an empty parking lot, their shouts filling the air. I didn't know where Perseus wanted to go, but he seemed to know where he was going, even though I doubted he had been on this area of the city before.

"So now that your pages were stolen, what do you plan to do?" I asked.

Perseus shrugged. "I still have a copy of it in my room, of the original I mean. So I guess I'll have to translate it again."

My heart gave a little leap. If Perseus still had some of those papers then I could read them and know what had made Zia go crazy. But Orion and I were leaving New York in a few hours. I would probably never get the chance to do so. Or could I convince Orion to stay in New York for one more day?

I looked around us. Red-brick houses rose at our sides. The houses looked old—the bricks cracked and their color washed almost into white. There was a man watering the front lawn to our right, even though the grass looked yellow and dead. There were no cars on the one-way street.

Could Orion be right? Could the people that had taken Zia want to take us too? Would they know where to find us? I didn't want to have to worry about that. I patted my side and felt the hard outline of the knife. If someone did try to take me, then I wouldn't make it an easy job.

Perseus turned to look at me. With the sun up high, his hair looked like copper and gold mixed together. "On winter break I'll go again to Greece to try to find more clues." He looked at the cracked pavement, his cheeks red again. "You can come with me if you like. After all, you deserve to know whatever I find."

"Sure," I said to Perseus.

He smiled at the pavement.

At the moment, I didn't want to ruin his invitation by telling him that after I left New York I probably wouldn't see him ever again. Although I did plan to go to Greece someday to try to find Alathea's book, just to see where it led.

The sun was unusually warm as Perseus and I walked side by side talking. I didn't say much about myself, except that I loved hamburgers and milkshakes.

I learned more about him. He had been adopted seven years ago. Andrew and his wife Martha couldn't have any children, so Perseus's other three siblings were adopted too.

"I'm lucky he adopted me," Perseus said.

He didn't elaborate more on that. Andrew loved them as if they were his biological children, and always took them on trips all over the world. I told him that I'd traveled around the world too, and knew that I had been born somewhere in Europe. I had lived in France, Italy, Germany, England and Poland before moving to America.

"So you know how to speak French?" Perseus asked me.

"*Oui*," I responded. "Only a little bit. I also speak some German and understand Italian."

"So *that's* why you have a weird accent," Perseus said, as if he had been thinking about it since I had first spoken, but hadn't wanted to say anything.

I nodded. I had always preferred English, since it was the language Zia always spoke, and hadn't cared much to learn other languages except to say the basic things.

I had to admit that walking with Perseus was quite a pleasant experience.

"If you had the choice, where would you live?" I asked.

"I'm not really sure," he said as we crossed the street. A little girl with a scooter raced past us. "I've lived most of my life in New York, so I don't imagine myself living anywhere else. How about you?"

"I liked living in Europe," I said as I looked at the tall glass buildings around us. "I like small villages more than big cities, everything is just closer. The streets are cleaner too," I said as we passed by some trash littering the sidewalk.

New York was the first big city we had ever moved to.

He nodded. "That's actually what I like about here. Being in a big city where I can just get lost, and not everyone has to know who I am."

We walked for a couple more blocks in silence. I wouldn't miss New York, that was for sure, but I still found myself looking around the city—the yellow cabs racing through the streets, tourists with dozens of shopping bags walking by, the occasional guy in a costume. There was a man dressed only with a loincloth in the middle of the large sidewalk, and even though he seemed ugly to me—with his overgrown beard and shaggy long hair—several girls seemed to find him attractive enough to take a picture with him.

"He looks like Tarzan," Perseus whispered into my ear.

"Yeah, even his face looks like a gorilla's," I whispered back.

Perseus laughed as we continued walking.

"Perseus!" someone shouted behind us.

Before he could turn around, a girl hugged him from behind. For a moment I felt a pang. My hand had instinctively gone to the knife. Once I realized that, I let go of the knife and dropped my hand to my side. The girl pulled away from Perseus and faced me.

I felt my muscles tense, and her jaw dropped.

"This is my new friend, Andromeda," Perseus said as he proudly put a hand on my shoulder. "Andromeda," Perseus said motioning at the other girl. "Meet my sister Rose."

Rose glared at me as she looked me up and down, no doubt noticing I was wearing the same clothes as when we had first met a few days ago. Her hair was still in that ugly and unfashionable eighties style. She was wearing a floral dress, a little too revealing at the top for my taste, and very short at the bottom too. Since she was Perseus's sister, he didn't seem to notice, although every guy that passed by her did.

"'Sup," I said to Rose.

Orion was dating Perseus's sister? It seemed too big of a coincidence, one that made me feel anxious. But Orion and I would leave soon, and hopefully never run into Rose ever again. Seeing her twice in the same week felt like bad luck.

She pressed her lips close together. "Is this why you didn't come home yesterday?"

Perseus flushed redder than he ever had before, and even started going purple. His strangled gaze traveled to me, and I caught its warning. We couldn't tell Rose what had happened at the park yesterday.

"Yes it is," I said with a smile. Rose's light-brown eyes seemed to want to drill into me like knives.

Perseus chuckled, or rather choked, nervously at her.

"We're just friends," he tried to explain.

I nodded.

Rose didn't seem to buy it. Her gaze still bore into me. "Well, now that you're here," a mocking smile pressed on her lips. "Tell your brother that he better answer my next phone call or we're over."

"Sure," I said. "I'll tell him."

Perseus switched his gaze between Rose and me. "Alright then, I'll see you home."

Rose gave me one last glare before she angrily turned on her heel and walked away. I didn't know why she was so angry with me. Was it because I hadn't wanted to shake her hand when we met?

Perseus and I walked away from her, and neither of us turned to look back.

"So your brother is dating my sister?" he asked.

"My foster brother," I quickly said.

"What a crazy coincidence," Perseus said. I nodded. "Well, if that's true then you could invite him to my football game. Rose will be there too." I simply nodded as we continued walking. I didn't think Orion would like that.

By that time we had arrived at Times Square. It was the part of New York that I hated the most. It was always so crowded, and I hated random people bumping into me. There were bright screens in front of every building, featuring ads that varied from new albums, to movies, to food, to new shampoos. Several ads on the screens featured a boxer dog against a flaming background, although I couldn't tell what was burning behind him. I had seen that dog before, I realized. He was part of that superhero movie where he had super speed and a bark that could cause entire buildings to crumble. That movie had been fun. Maybe the ads were about the sequel? There was also one big screen showing a handsome actor in underwear. My eyes lingered there a bit longer than they should have, and when Perseus caught me looking I quickly turned away.

There were so many people around us that Perseus and I were forced to walk side by side, pressed against each other. Perseus didn't seem bothered, and walked lightly next to me.

We were just about to cross the street to get out of Time Square's main plaza when I felt Perseus's hand grip my arm. I glared at him, trying to pull free, but his eyes weren't looking at me, they were looking at the other side of the street.

I followed his gaze—Corvus was there.

He was standing next to the reptilian blond guy, who was wearing dark glasses again. There was no sign of Twig Girl, which only made me more nervous.

Next to me, Perseus was so tense that he might have turned into a statue. I was about to tell Perseus that we better run and get lost in the crowd, but just then the building across the street exploded.

Chapter XIX, Verse I

Beware of the uproar that the golden one shall uphold.
With skin stronger than immortal shields,
And claws sharper than iron swords.
In the silence he will walk, to prey on the victims that he stalks.
To fight the enemy he chose, the one with silver eyes of night.
Until the sun to set and after a blood moon to rise.
The pawn he shall then become, for the Liar to play ahead.

CHAPTER 8

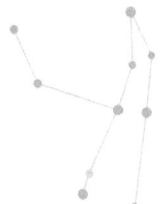

I FELT the scorching heat and saw the bright-red light of the explosion seconds before the impact sent me back against Perseus. My head hit his chest and we both tumbled to the street, me on top of him.

There were screams all around me, and my head felt like it was about to burst. I scrambled to my feet and looked wildly around. Corvus and his friend were both sprawled on the street in front of us. Around us people were scattering in all directions. They passed by me, bumping or brushing against my arms.

I looked down at my feet to see Perseus there, lying on his side. He had no visible injuries, and that sent a wave of relief through me. I hauled Perseus to his feet with all the strength I could muster, not wanting him to get trampled by the crowd. He groaned, fluttering his eyes open. After a few seconds, he stood, leaning against me, his weight pushing me down. I dragged him against the wall of an intact building behind us, away from the one that had exploded, stepping over glass shards that cracked under my feet. I hoped they didn't pierce through my shoes.

Perseus's dark eyes were unfocused, and I worried he might have a concussion. A man pushed past us and Perseus fell down again on his side. I sat him up against the wall and stood next to him, breathing hard as my heart battered inside my chest. Perseus's head rested against one of my legs as he moaned.

I looked at the scene around us, feeling that I was outside of my body, as if I was staring through someone else's eyes.

On the other side of the square, nearly fifty yards from where I stood, one of the buildings had blown up. The upper half of the building had crumbled down onto the street, and I could see some cars trapped underneath. What was left of the building was up in flames, creating a column of smoke that rose into the sky. Most windows of the adjacent buildings had shattered and sprinkles of glass littered the street. The air smelled acidic, as if a chemical lab had spilled all of its liquid flasks.

I realized that most of the screens had gone black. Some of them had cracked and still emitted blurry images that blinked frantically. I pressed myself harder against the wall, and Perseus hugged his legs. People continued to flee out of the buildings and stores around us. Their faces were all pale masks, some with tears, and others painted with dread and horror.

I felt myself trembling, cold. Smoke covered the sky above us, clouding the sun. I knew that there must be people still trapped inside the building that had just blown up, but at that moment I wasn't thinking about them. Instead, I was aware of the sharp pain that beat inside my skull, and that my bones felt like they were crumbling down. I could feel the sidewalk moving beneath me, as if it were still reverberating from the blast.

I slid down the rough wall and sat next to Perseus. He was breathing hard, and his eyes were closed. I was no doctor, but was sure that he had a concussion. His head rested against my shoulder, and he moaned again.

"Andromeda," he whispered.

I couldn't answer back, and only felt my body shivering violently against him. Thin smoke began to gather closer around us, and it smelled like melting iron mixed with something else I couldn't place.

The bodies that lay on the ground were unmoving, and I knew they must be dead. They reminded me of the patients from the psychiatric hospital. They were already dead, and there was nothing I could do for them.

I thought of hauling Perseus up and running away, but my legs weren't answering. They were shaking as badly as the rest of my body and felt weak, as if my bones were made of dough.

Maybe Orion would find me. At least I knew he would be safe. Orion hated Times Square as much as I did, and he would have had no reason to spend his last few hours in New York here. Maybe he had seen the explosion, if not heard it from wherever he was. Or the news channels would be broadcasting it, sending emergency alerts. Either way, he must have known the explosion happened, and was probably now aware that I was here. He always knew where I was.

Police, ambulance and firefighter sirens wailed in the air somewhere distantly, but they were muted by the sounds of the people around us. A woman's scream echoed somewhere close to the fallen building, but I couldn't tell where.

A flash of movement pulled my attention away from the building and towards the other side of the street. Corvus had stood up, but I couldn't see where the other guy had gone. His face was ashen, and his grip tight on the white carved knife as his eyes drilled into Perseus. My trembling hand went instinctively to my belt, but my knife was no longer there, and looking for it wasn't an option.

Corvus lurched towards us. My body seemed to act on its own, moving before my mind could process it. I picked up a shard of glass next to me. Corvus was almost upon us. Just as he raised his knife, I sprang forward, wrapping my arms around his legs and sticking the glass shard into his thigh. I knew the wound wouldn't be deep or fatal, but it still made Corvus howl in pain.

We both fell down to the pavement. With my head spinning, I sat on top of him and pinned his arms to his sides. He squirmed, but couldn't get out of my grip. His dark eyes looked up at me with murdering rage.

"Leave him alone," I hissed.

"Why are you protecting him?" Corvus asked.

"Why do you want to kill him?" I ask.

Corvus smiled widely. "I'll kill anyone it takes to get to that book."

So he *did* want Alathea's book.

"Why do you even want that stupid book?" I asked.

Corvus's eyes widened, and his lips curled up into a smile. He chuckled, but it sounded more like a cough.

"I see," he said slowly as the police sirens got closer.

"I don't see," I said. "So you better tell me."

Corvus opened his mouth to speak, but instead began laughing as he coughed. "You have no idea, do you?"

"About what?" I said as I gripped his wrists tighter.

Corvus winced. "Algol—"

He didn't finish because, just then, another building exploded.

My ears rang, and for a moment I couldn't remember where I was. Images from the psychiatric hospital flashed inside my eyes— crimson light bathed the corpses of the dead patients, the pools of blood that gathered around them were black.

I opened my eyes. The sky was black and red, and I was vaguely aware of the screams around me. I groaned as I sat up. I was surrounded by gray smoke that made me cough wildly into my sleeve. My eyes burned and began to water, so I shut them as I kept coughing.

Two strong hands pulled me up, but I couldn't tell who it was. I tried to stand, but my legs gave away as I opened my eyes and looked ahead. A hundred yards in front of me, another one of the buildings had crumbled down into a pile of glass and dark rock. Fire burned atop it, the flames licking the debris. Firefighters had begun to crowd around it, using their water hoses to put down the fire.

A man carried me into his arms, and I realized he was a cop, but couldn't make out his features very well with the smoke and my burning tears. I could see, however, that we passed several unmoving bodies. One of them was a woman, a bag of groceries still next to her—eggs and milk were spilled around her.

The police officer left me sitting against a building close to where Perseus and I had been moments before. I looked around, but couldn't find Perseus. I dried my tears and looked among the dead bodies littering the ground. None of them had his bright-red hair, but that didn't mean anything.

"Perseus!" I shouted, but my voice sounded hoarse and my throat felt raw.

I coughed into my sleeve.

"Perseus!" I shouted, this time making my throat sting so badly that I clutched it and coughed wildly.

My mind was beginning to slip away, spinning like the toxic gray fog around me. Hot tears streamed down my cheeks, and I licked my dry lips, badly wanting a sip of water for my burning

113

throat. My lungs felt like they had been filled with ashes, and every breath became a scratching pain in my chest.

Someone shouted in the distance, and the voice sounded familiar, but my eyes were beginning to close, and the ringing in my ears was getting louder.

Just then I felt a hand upon my shoulder, and a flame danced in front of me. I was shaken awake, and through my blurry view realized that the flame was Perseus's hair. His wide, dark eyes were filled with concern, and he had blood running down his right temple.

"Andromeda," he said again as he shook me.

My head was pulsing, and every pulse sent a shock of pain through the rest of my body. I wiped the blood from Perseus's face with a shaky hand.

"Looks like you're not going to make it to your game after all," I muttered.

I didn't wait to hear his answer, because my eyes closed, and all the pain washed away.

There was a hum that filled my ears, and I could feel my body reverberating with it. I slowly opened my eyes. My head felt like it weighted a hundred tons. As my vision slowly came into focus, I realized that we were inside a car. I was in the backseat, and could make out the figures of two men in front of me.

I coughed wildly, and felt the seatbelt around me like a lash against my chest.

"Andromeda!" Perseus exclaimed next to me.

I turned to see him sitting next to me. A goofy grin lit up his face, even though it was smeared with ash and dried blood running down one side of his face.

"Hey," I managed. I realized we were on the highway, driving quickly past other cars. "What happened?" I croaked. My throat still felt raw.

"The police think it was a terrorist attack, at least they said so on the radio, but no one knows for sure," Perseus said in a hushed tone, as if the terrorists would hear us. "They still don't know how many people died."

His head hung back in the seat, and I could see tears welling in his eyes. I didn't feel so inclined, knowing those people were already dead, and I couldn't have done anything to prevent the attack.

Corvus and his friend had been there. Even though I hoped a building had crushed them, I somehow knew we would see them again. I wondered how they had found us in Times Square.

Perseus wiped his nose with his sleeve. "Then Bruno found me carrying you through the streets and he took us with him." Perseus jerked his chin to indicate that Bruno was the man driving the car. I could only see the back of his head, which was hidden behind a cap. "Bruno works with my dad," Perseus explained.

"Where are we going?" I asked.

Perseus licked his lips. "Oh, ahhh . . . my dad is in Dubai right now, and he doesn't want me to stay alone in the city. You know, in case there are any other attacks." His eyes didn't meet mine, but I already knew where this conversation was going. "I didn't want to leave you alone in the city, so I decided to take you with me."

I didn't answer, and simply looked out the window again. I wondered what Orion would think about this. Obviously, he would chase after me wherever I went, like the mad hunting dog he was, but I didn't want him meeting Perseus. If he ever found out that he was the guy I was supposed to have killed, but hadn't, he would probably kill Perseus himself.

"I know you're homeless right now—" I turned to look at him and he blushed as he diverted his gaze out his own window. "Sorry, I didn't mean it to sound like that, but—"

"You're right," I said.

That wasn't completely true. I had my secret warehouse, but I had planned to leave that behind anyways. Now Perseus was offering me a free ticket out of the city, and possibly the country.

"Where are we going?" I asked.

Perseus gave me half a smile. "I'll tell you on the plane."

"And your siblings?" I asked warily, not wanting to share an entire plane ride with stupid Rose.

"Oh, they're alright. They left New York already," Perseus said with relief.

I wasn't so relieved myself. Shaken as I was, I tried not to think about the attack and instead thought of Orion. He was very likely already after me, and we would need to get away fast or else he would catch up to us. I would let Perseus take me out of here. Then I'd meet Orion wherever Perseus dropped me off.

I could only hope we were going far away, because now I definitely had no desire to ever be back in New York.

CHAPTER 9

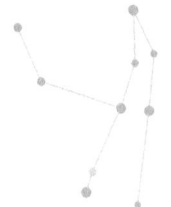

WHEN PERSEUS said we were flying somewhere else I had expected to board a large passenger plane. Instead, we would be flying Perseus's private plane, which, to me, looked as large as any commercial plane.

"My dad has several planes," Perseus explained with a shrug, as if all parents had several private planes.

We had driven for nearly an hour, and arrived at a private hangar that was close to the John F. Kennedy International Airport. The hangar had white metal walls and was empty except for the plane. Judging by the size of it, the plane was big enough to fit at least fifty people comfortably.

Bruno, apparently Perseus's driver, ushered us quickly towards the stairs to climb abroad the plane. Once at the top, I stood awestruck at the entrance. It looked like the inside of a house. The brown carpet was soft under my feet, and lights shone brightly on the walls. On the right were a couple of seats facing each other, with an empty chess table in the middle. On the left were a few couches as if we were in a living room. Behind that was a small bar, where I could see a chef making us what seemed like sushi. Above the bar was a large TV that hung against the wall.

Perseus gently pulled me in and motioned at the seats. As soon as I sat, I felt myself sinking in relief. My head had begun to pound with pain that pulsed behind my eyes and drummed inside my skull. Perseus seemed nervous, glancing at the entrance of the plane.

There was a vibrating noise inside the pocket of my jacket and I pulled out the ancient phone Orion had given me. I had forgotten about it. The screen was cracked and parts of it had gone black, but it seemed to be working.

I answered the call.

"Andromeda!" Orion shouted on the other side of the line.

"Hey," I said.

"Are you alright?" he asked, his tone full of concern.

"Yes," I said.

Perseus was watching me curiously, probably wondering whom I was talking to.

"You disobeyed me." His tone was low with anger. "Where the hell did you go?" I bit my lip. Until I touched down wherever Perseus was taking me, he wouldn't know where I was.

"I left," I said simply.

He was silent on the other end, probably trying to contain an outburst of curses. "I felt Zia again," he said after a few tense seconds. "Only for a second. She's alive."

Every single muscle in my body seemed to knot with tension. I looked at Perseus, who was staring eagerly at the food on the bar behind us.

"Look, Andromeda," Orion said. "I know you don't want me to find her, but—"

I hung up the phone and stood bolt upright, startling Perseus. I walked to the entrance of the plane, next to the cockpit, and threw the cellphone out. It crashed on the cement floor.

I walked back inside the plane and sat down. Perseus must have noticed something in my expression because he remained silent, looking at me with his dark eyes as if he could find the answer written somewhere on my face. The pain in my head throbbed harder, like a sledgehammer trying to break my skull.

Zia was alive, and Orion was going to go look for her. If he found her, then everything would go back to the way it was before. I shuddered to think about it. The best thing I could do was leave with Perseus. But if Zia was alive, and she came back, she would want Perseus dead.

My thoughts were interrupted by footsteps coming from the plane stairs.

Bruno, and another man with thinning white hair, came inside. The stairs curled up behind them and the door closed. I looked at the older man, who had a leathered face with more wrinkles than a crumpled paper. He clutched a briefcase tightly to his chest, and looked curiously at Perseus and me. Then he walked past us and sat alone in the seat behind Perseus's.

Bruno walked to the pilot's cabin and shut it behind him.

"He'll be our pilot," Perseus explained.

How convenient—a chauffeur and a pilot. Could Bruno navigate ships, too?

"Now can you tell me where we're going?" I asked, hoping it would be far away.

Perseus opened his mouth to speak, but just then the plane lurched forward. I gripped the seat and put my seatbelt on.

The plane rode out of the hangar and steered right, into the runway. It raced forward, the engines roaring louder. Seconds later, we were in the air.

I was tempted to look out the window, but I didn't want to risk seeing the column of smoke from the bombed buildings. I knew we were far away from the city, and the devastation probably wouldn't be visible, but still . . .

I didn't want to think about what had just happened. *They were people without names,* I reminded myself. *You didn't know them.* So I banished those dead people from my mind. But even then, I felt myself shaking.

After a few minutes I leaned closer to Perseus, and was about to ask him again where we were going when the older man walked to us with his case.

"Let me have a look at you," he said to Perseus, who in turn looked at me.

"This is Doctor Jahan, he's the family physician," Perseus explained.

Of course they would have their own doctor. I had never gone to a doctor myself. I had never felt sick, now that I thought of it, and was sure that Zia had never vaccinated Orion or me. I assumed that if we weren't human, we probably didn't need them.

Thinking about Orion and Zia again made me feel dizzy, so I looked down at the rug instead. I found myself thinking of the attacks. In less than a week I had almost died twice, first in the psychiatric hospital and then in New York. Something stirred uneasily inside me, trying to connect both attacks, but the rational part of my mind argued that they'd had nothing to do with each other—patients going crazy in a hospital was entirely different than terrorists bombing a major city. I'd just had very bad luck.

I looked back up at Perseus again. Dr. Jahan confirmed that he did indeed have a concussion. Perseus winced when Dr. Jahan detected a bump forming on his head, behind his left ear. He gave him some medication and asked Perseus a few personal questions, checking his memory, then asked him to repeat a few sentences that made no sense to me. He told Perseus that if he started to get a strong headache he should notify him immediately, and that meanwhile he should apply some ice to the bump.

The doctor walked to the bar where the chef gave him a plastic bag full of ice cubes. Then he walked back to us and gave the bag to Perseus, who eyed it for a second, then dutifully held it to his head.

Dr. Jahan then turned to me with eager eyes.

"I'm fine," I said quickly, not wanting the old man to come any closer, but he did so anyways. He smelled like scented lime oil, something I found unnerving.

"I must check you too, dear," he insisted.

"Nope, I'm good," I said as I tried to sink further into the couch.

"It's alright, Andromeda," Perseus said with a smile. "He won't hurt you."

I knew he wouldn't, and if he did I would bite off his fingers. But I didn't want the doctor too close to me, and I definitely didn't want him poking me around like he had done to Perseus to check any broken bones.

The doctor spent a good ten minutes trying to convince me that he only wanted to check if I had a concussion too, or any broken bones, despite my assuring him that nothing hurt. If I had a concussion, it didn't appear to be a fatal one. The headache would probably go away soon. My memories seemed to be intact, as far as I knew, and I was almost sure I had no broken bones.

My eyes went to the doctor's bony hands, and I sank further back into the couch. "I'm fine," I said for the hundredth time.

The doctor's clear eyes regarded me with irritation. I assumed he normally didn't have much trouble checking people, but I didn't like doctors. I had always been afraid of doctors, and was glad Zia had never taken us to one. I felt as if just by checking my pulse they would discover I wasn't human. I had seen enough movies to know what would follow—they would take me to some weird governmental facility and do experiments on me.

Dr. Jahan kept insisting that he wanted to check me for a concussion and fractured bones. I didn't care what I had; my body would heal eventually and I would live on, like I had always done.

Throughout all this, Perseus remained silent, switching glances between the doctor and me with amusement. I wished he could just tell the doctor to leave me alone.

"Arghhh," said the doctor after fifteen minutes. "Fine! But if you pass out on the plane, I won't be responsible for that."

He stomped off towards the bar at the other side of the plane and ordered a drink from the chef.

Perseus rubbed his chin with his hand. "I think you should at least change your clothes," he said as he looked me up and down.

Now that I got a good look at him, I realized that he looked like a homeless person too. Ash smeared his face and his hair, which was a wild mess. His jacket was ripped and had a burnt hole on one side. Perseus's jeans looked like he had dragged them through all of New York before putting them on, and his shoes looked like he had bought them in a dumpster.

"With what?" I asked.

He shrugged. "I think Rose may be the same size as you," he said, pensive. I clutched the seat tighter. Perseus turned around to look at the bar. "If you walk past the bar, you'll find a door on the right. There should be a small closet and bathroom. I'm sure Rose won't mind if you take her clothes."

I knew that she would very much mind, but thinking about pissing off Rose gave me an odd sense of relief. I just hoped that she'd left her eighties-style outfits back in New York. Did she even have normal clothes?

I stood from the seat, feeling my legs straining with the effort as if I had run a marathon. Dr. Jahan directed a hostile glare at me as I passed by him. I smiled in return. As Perseus had said, there was a closed wooden door on the right. I opened it and walked inside, then closed it behind me. A light automatically turned on.

The closet was very small, narrow enough for one person to be standing inside. But being on a plane I hadn't imagined anything bigger. Both sides had drawers, and I opened them all to see what was inside. Each drawer had something different—socks, underwear, sweaters, jeans, sweatpants, pajamas, winter jackets, blouses, and even dresses. The dresses were all ugly, but I was surprised to find that some of the blouses and jackets seemed normal enough. I didn't like sweaters; they were always itchy with my scars, so I closed that drawer.

I opened another drawer on the right that had jewelry inside—necklaces, bracelets and rings. Below them was a picture. I pushed the jewelry aside and pulled the picture out. It showed Perseus, Rose, and a boy with dark skin—the three of them smiling as they stood in front of an oak door. I remembered Perseus telling me that he had three other siblings, so I assumed one of them was missing in the picture, or maybe hadn't been adopted yet. Rose looked a lot younger, with her wavy hair past her elbows. She seemed somehow uncomfortable to be standing in between the two boys.

Perseus looked younger too, his shaggy red hair below his ears. There was something different about him in the picture, something I couldn't quite place. As if the Perseus grinning widely in the picture was different from the one inside this plane. I shrugged it off and put the picture back in the drawer, then closed it.

At the end of the room was another door, and when I opened it, I realized it was a bathroom. It didn't have a shower, but a sink with fresh-smelling soap and toilet was all I needed. When I looked at myself in the mirror my own ash-stained face stared back. I looked like I had come out of a Halloween haunted house. My hair, even though short, seemed to have found a way to be in tangles, my eyes were red, and the left side of my jaw was beginning to swell.

I washed my face first, watching all the dirt drain down the sink, then I used the soap to try to wash my hair. Tiny rocks and even glass shards clattered against the sink. As soon as I was done washing my hair I realized that my hands were shaking, and tears were beginning to well in my eyes.

"Keep it together," I told myself through the mirror, feeling my throat tighten. "You're alive and that's all that matters."

The giant gray wolf materialized in my vision, those intelligent silver eyes staring at me. Then I was looking into the red-orange reptile eyes from that strange boy in the park. I shook my head, trying to shake away my thoughts too. As strange as those creatures were, there was nothing I could do about them. So I picked up those memories and deleted them.

I stripped off my clothes, which looked like dirty kitchen rags. That's when I remembered that my knife was gone. It gave me a sense of relief, that the temptation to kill Perseus wouldn't be hanging from my belt. But if Zia was alive, then she would never let me be free unless I killed him. I had tried everything to escape, everything . . . This was my last chance.

I shook my head in frustration. Was I really considering killing him just for my freedom? Now that I knew Perseus a little better, my heart seemed to stop beating at the thought of killing him. He was an innocent boy, and didn't deserve to be a part of Zia's devious plans. But did I deserve to pay the price for letting him live?

I pulled my wet hair back with my hand. Orion had said that he knew Zia was alive. But maybe she wouldn't be for much longer.

If Orion couldn't trace her then something else was going on—something that neither of us could understand at the moment.

I removed the bandages. Luckily none of my wounds had bled again, but they were all an angry shade of red. Since I had no bandages available at the moment I washed the wounds and let them be. They would heal soon, as always, and sometimes leaving them uncovered after they had stopped bleeding made them heal faster.

Since I hadn't let the doctor check me, I decided to check myself. After finding that none of my bones hurt, or at least didn't hurt too much, I concluded that I had no broken bones but would have several purple bruises and feel very sore the next day.

I washed myself as best as I could with the bar of soap and sink, then dried myself with the little towel and went back to the closet. Perseus had been right, I thought with irritation. Rose and I were indeed the same size. I wondered what Orion might think of me using her clothes. I tried on a soft blouse that wouldn't irritate my scars further, and a thick jacket. I also found a pair of jeans and some hiking boots. The blouse had a strange blue floral pattern, but it was either that or a neon-pink one.

I walked out of the closet and went back to my seat to find Perseus eating sushi from a plate. He looked like he had gone to the bathroom to clean himself up too. So there was a girls' bathroom and closet and a boys' one? I wondered. Perseus looked much better. He had combed his fiery-red hair, and his face was clean now. He wore a new pair of jeans and a navy-blue jacket.

There was another plate on the chess table, which I assumed was for me. Perseus was looking back towards the bar as he ate, and when I followed his gaze I realized why.

He was looking at the TV above the bar. The chef wasn't looking at it, and the doctor was already sleeping in one of the couches. There was no sound, but I could clearly see what was happening. Images from the attack in New York flashed up on the screen. The government had reported that it had been executed by a group of terrorist extremists, although it wasn't clear why. The death count was already over a hundred, and more bodies were being found. There was an image that lingered on the screen for a couple of seconds. It made my hands go numb.

It was that strange symbol, the same one I had seen on the TV at the psychiatric hospital—the straight line, a curving line like a crescent moon on one side, those other smaller lines like arms on a stick-man, and the little circles at the end of each line. It seemed to have been drawn with blood on a cracked window. The image disappeared, but it stayed branded in my head. One of the patients in the hospital had said that there had been several attacks where that symbol appeared.

I tried to shake away the image from my mind. The attack had just been bad luck. Being in the wrong place at the wrong time. I looked away from the TV when pictures of Times Square appeared on the screen.

I focused instead on my food and began ravaging it. A couple of seconds later Perseus turned too, although he seemed to have lost his appetite and left half of the meal on the plate, setting it on the table. I must have been quite a spectacle as I ate, nearly choking on my rolls of sushi as I tried to eat them in one bite, but Perseus smiled shyly at me nonetheless.

I felt calmer after eating, like I always did, and my hands didn't shake anymore. But I still felt hungry, as I'd felt for the last few days. I tried to ignore it. I had already eaten twelve rolls of sushi. I didn't need any more.

"So where are we going?" I asked Perseus.

He leaned forward. "Right now we're heading to London, but we could go somewhere else if we wanted to." His eyes widened with excitement. "I was thinking, I'll be gone from New York for at least a couple of weeks, or until my parents think it's safe to go back, and you'll be gone too, so we should use this time to look."

"Look for what?" I asked.

"What if we went to Greece to look for more clues on Alathea's book?" He asked excitedly. "We have nothing else better to do!"

I fell silent for a couple of seconds.

Greece was far enough from Orion, and I had been planning to go there someday anyways.

"Sounds good," I said.

Perseus smiled. I knew that Orion would eventually come to find me, but Perseus's private plane would probably take us directly to Greece. I imagined Orion would have no such luck. And he would try to find Zia first, so it would be a while before I saw him again. As long as Rose didn't come, I guessed things would be alright.

As I leaned back in the couch, I realized that I hadn't told Perseus what Corvus had said to me, so I quickly told him.

"So he *did* want me dead because he thought I had the book," Perseus said with a frown.

Zia had wanted him dead too, and I was almost sure that it was for the same reason. There must have been something important about those Prophecies if both Zia and Corvus were willing to kill for them. But could the Prophecies be real? I didn't believe in Prophecies, but maybe other people did.

"He also mentioned something about Algol," I said.

Perseus seemed pensive. Zia had also mentioned Algol, and had in fact cursed it. Was Algol an object? I wondered. Or was he a person?

"What if Algol is another Star Child?" Perseus said. "I don't know all the names of the Constellations, so he could be one."

"So you do believe in the Star Children?" I asked him flatly.

His eyes widened. "At the moment it seems like the best explanation we have."

It did seem like a good explanation. Our names were all part of Greek myths, our scars shone in the dark, and very strange things had occurred in the last couple of days. But I didn't completely believe that Constellations had created us.

"Okay then," I said. "Let's assume Algol is another Star Child like us, or something like that. What is so important about him?"

Perseus looked at his shoes. "The Prophecy said Algol would spill blood and conquer the sky, and that it was a blinking demon. That's all I can remember."

I didn't know what to think of Algol. Zia and Corvus had both mentioned him, and he was part of the Prophecy book. From the things that the Prophecy said, he seemed to be a threat. But would he be a threat to us?

"But I think our main concern should be Alathea's book," Perseus said. "It could have more Prophecies that could help us understand Algol, and our very existence."

"Aren't you worried that someone else will try to kill you if we find another one of Alathea's Prophecies, or the entire book?" I asked.

Perseus shrugged. "They already think I have it, and are trying to kill me anyways. So I might as well *have* the book."

That seemed like a fair argument. "Alright then," I said as I stretched my legs in front of me to make myself comfortable. "Greece it is."

"Great," Perseus said with a lopsided grin. "Now I just have to convince Bruno to take us there instead of London."

Perseus unbuckled his seatbelt and walked to the cabin. He knocked, entered the room, and shut the door behind him. He spent a good ten minutes there, and finally came out with a grin. "Greece," he said as he sat down. "Here we come."

"And once we get to Greece, where will we go?" I asked. "Back to the museum in Athens? Maybe they have more of those Prophecies."

Perseus shook his head. "I took all the sheets the museum had. Every Prophecy had Alathea's name at the bottom of the page, and according to the museum archives they had all been found in the same place—at the Temple of Apollo at Delphi. That's where Alathea was from." He clasped his hands together. "It didn't specify where exactly they had found the Prophecies, but I'm sure we'll find something at the ruins of Delphi."

"If Alathea was from Delphi," I said as I twirled my wet strands of hair, "then why haven't people gone to look for her Prophecies there instead of trying to kill you?"

"That's the thing," Perseus said with a smile. "No one except me knows Alathea was from Delphi. There were many different oracle sites throughout Greece—Dodona, Trophonius, and a couple of other minor ones." I nodded as if I knew what those strange words meant. "The point is, she could have been from anywhere in Greece."

"Well, going to Delphi sounds like a good plan then," I said.

Perseus smiled. "It'll be a long ride until we get there, so you might want to catch some rest."

That sounded like an excellent idea. I closed my eyes, but found my mind racing with thoughts. If Zia was alive, then what would I do with Perseus? I opened my eyes again. Perseus was still awake, his gaze lost in his own thoughts as he looked at the carpeted floor. His big eyes were drowsy.

I won't kill him, I decided. I would find another way to escape from Zia, but I couldn't bring myself to even think again about killing Perseus.

With that thought settled, my mind began to drift away, and I felt the welcoming darkness. I had no dreams, and no thoughts while I slept, letting my mind slide into the nothingness.

I awoke sometime later, feeling groggy and, like I had predicted, sore in every muscle in my body. The lashes on my back still itched with pain, but I ignored them. I opened my eyes and realized that someone had placed a quilt on top of me, probably Perseus. He sat across from me on his sofa, his features relaxed as he breathed softly.

His red hair had come undone again, a messy mane that covered his head. His lashes were long and dark as they covered his eyes, and I noticed that they, too, were a very dark shade of red. I hadn't realized before that he had a large freckle next to his left eye, or that his ears stuck out a little.

Perseus stirred and opened his eyes, then smiled when he saw me. "Good morning," he said.

I wasn't even sure it was morning, but felt myself smiling anyways.

"How much time until we arrive?" I asked.

I wanted some fresh air, and to move around, two things that would be complicated to do inside a plane.

Perseus looked around the plane, until his eyes set on the cockpit. I turned too and realized that there was a small clock next to the door that seemed to be counting down the time of our flight.

I curled into a ball on my seat. Three more hours of sleep sounded good. I had the eerie sense that I wouldn't be getting much sleep for the next couple of days.

Chapter XLIII, Verse I

Thunder lights the darkened sky.
The earth trembles when lightning strikes.
The shriek of the eagle the sky controls.
A vantage from above to see the enemies below.
A long way he has traveled, over desert and sea flown.
To the aid of the young who Darkness opposes,
In a journey to end in the fiery abode.

CHAPTER 10

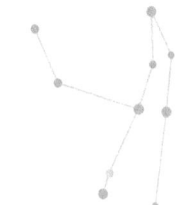

I HAD never been to Greece before, and imagined Athens would be a beautiful city. I had seen pictures of it, and even a couple movies filmed in Athens. The pebbled streets had always been clean, lined with small shops and restaurants, the short buildings colorful and well kept, the ancient ruins of the city visible at the top of the tree-covered mountains.

I was disappointed to discover that I couldn't see the ruins, or even the mountains, because the buildings blocked my view. Most of the streets we traveled by were as dirty as New York. The buildings on our sides were pressed uncomfortably against one another, graffiti lined almost every wall, and we were slowed down by the heavy traffic. It didn't help that the streets were very narrow, barely allowing enough space for two cars side by side. I noticed a lot of trash bags on the sidewalks in front of the buildings. They were about to burst with trash, and seemed to be waiting for a truck to pick them up and take them to the dumpster.

I wondered if the Athens I had seen in pictures actually existed. Or maybe the Athens I had expected was just the tourist section at the center of the city and this was how its inhabitants actually lived.

We had landed just before midday in Athens, and a car had been waiting for us. Bruno had given Perseus another credit card and some cash so we would be able to survive the next few days. Perseus and I had also packed some clothes into a couple of duffle bags. It had been stressful to have to choose from Rose's horrible clothes. The shirts and blouses were mostly of neon colors or with strange patterns, like pink camouflage, which wouldn't actually work as camouflage, or one that looked like a rainbow had exploded. In the end I did find some acceptable shirts, among them a plain white and black one. I also took a couple of tank tops to wear underneath, a hoodie, a pair of sweatpants to sleep in, some underwear, which looked new and I hoped she hadn't used, a pair of jeans, and another pair of boots.

Bruno and the doctor remained on the plane. That was perfectly fine by me. I didn't want to have to spend more time with Dr. Jahan and his glares. I'd asked Perseus if his parents would be okay with him being alone in Greece with a girl they hadn't met, and he said that his family didn't really mind. His mother was apparently too busy in London and his dad was still working in Dubai, and neither paid much attention to Perseus now that he was out of New York.

Once we got inside the car Bruno had rented for us, we programmed the GPS to take us to the ruins of Delphi—Perseus would be driving. Bruno had also reserved a hotel for us near the ruins. I wished Bruno had given us some lunch to take in the car too, but I didn't have time to ask before he climbed back into the plane.

According to the GPS, we would make two hours to Delphi. But the time had started to stretch when we got stuck in the traffic. I calculated it would take us double the time to get to our destination.

After half an hour in the car, I began to shift uncomfortably. Perseus didn't seem bothered by the traffic. A smile lit his face, even though we had barely moved and people kept honking at him. I wondered if he had a license, or if anyone else on the street did; by the way they drove they didn't seem to.

I looked out the window, noting that the only ancient ruins in the city appeared to be the buildings we passed by. Next to me, one of the buildings had a crumbled wall, revealing empty rooms inside. I wondered why no one had repaired the building, or demolished it to build a new one.

"So," Perseus said as I shifted again. "What's your favorite color?"

"What?" That seemed like a very stupid question.

"We're going to be stuck together in this car for hours with nothing to do but talk," he said as he kept his gaze focused on the red car in front of us. "So we might as well get to know each other better."

I grunted. I didn't really want him to know me better.

"Purple," I said as I looked dismally at the red light that hadn't turned to green in the last five minutes.

"Mine's red," he said.

"Like your hair?" I said, pointing at his copper mane.

He shook his head. "More like blood red."

"Sadist," I muttered.

He laughed. "Now it's your turn."

I thought for a couple seconds. "Before you were adopted," I said. "Where did you live?"

I noticed his hands tightening around the wheel. Maybe I should have asked what his favorite animal was.

"I was homeless," he said in a low voice. I wondered where he had lived before. "What's the first thing you remember?"

I had asked myself that many times. I didn't seem to remember anything before a certain age. Orion was my first memory. I had been playing with him in a puddle, both of us jumping up and down on a rainy day to see which one of us could splash more water at the other.

"I remember playing in the rain. I think I was seven years old, or maybe a bit younger," I said.

The light finally turned green and we drove through the intersection. Perseus didn't say anything as we passed by some buildings under construction.

In the distance, past the buildings and standing atop a barren hill that was raised like a platform, I could see the unmistakable ruins of the famous Acropolis. They seemed like a skeleton trying to hold a body that had died long ago. The many columns arranged in a rectangle were nearly intact, I noticed, but the ceiling was missing, as if blown away by very strong winds over time. The columns were made of a stone that could once have been white, but now looked very light brown—like an ancient bone dug up from a tomb. From a distance the ruins were small, but up close I imagined them to be large, as if to house giants inside. The ruins were soon gone, as another building blocked my view.

"My first memory is from when I was eight," Perseus finally said after a minute. "It's like before that I didn't exist."

I found that strange. Orion didn't remember anything either before he was nine or ten; he had told me so. But he had never said what his first memory was. Did he remember us jumping in puddles too?

"So you don't remember your real parents?" I asked.

A shadow seemed to cross his face as he shook his head. "Andrew and Martha are like my real parents."

I nodded. I couldn't really count Zia as a parent.

I didn't remember my real parents either, which I thought was better. If I had no images to attach to my real parents then

I didn't have to miss them, or feel anything towards them. They were faceless and nameless ghosts.

"Have you ever kissed anyone?" Perseus asked abruptly.

"Have you?" I asked.

I could see his face turning bright red. He took a couple of seconds to answer. "Just two," he said shyly.

I was silent for a couple of seconds. "One," I said.

"Ohhh. And who was that lucky guy?" he asked.

"No one you'd know," I replied.

Perseus laughed as we drove on. We continued talking for the rest of the ride. We had left the traffic behind us as soon as we drove out of the city and made our way towards the mountains.

"So how many languages do you speak?" I asked Perseus. He already knew that I spoke a couple of them.

He shrugged. "Just English, and at school they tried to teach me some Spanish. But I'm afraid that if I ever visit Mexico again the only thing I'll know how to do is order tacos."

I laughed at that.

"What do you want to study in college?" he asked.

I bit my tongue. Going to college had never even crossed my mind. The first time I had gone to school had been when my foster families forced me to. Every foster family I'd lived with had sent me to a different public school, but I'd always skip class to go to the park, walk aimlessly on the streets, go to my secret lair, or to eat lunch.

"I'm not sure," I said to Perseus. "You?"

"Archaeology and Ancient History," he said. "But you maybe already guessed that."

"Sounds interesting."

After that particular conversation we both remained quiet, each of us lost in our own thoughts. I rested my head on the seat as I looked out the window, enjoying the view.

The highway we drove on had several cars around us, but no traffic. Every now and then there would be a house or building next to the street, but most of them seemed older than the Acropolis, giving way to plains of grass. Mountains rose in the distance, but they looked more like lazy waves instead of the huge mountains I had seen in Germany and Switzerland. Those seemed to rise until they met the clouds with their sharp peaks as if they were giant stone spears.

Clouds covered the sun above us, but they didn't look heavy enough to bring rain, which was just as well. I wasn't in the mood to tour ruins in the rain.

I still wondered how we would find a book, or at least pages of it, among ancient ruins. I didn't find it likely that we would just find the book lying open on the ground. If Alathea had never been mentioned in history or mythology, it was very likely that the book she had written had been destroyed. When I shared my thoughts with Perseus he didn't seemed fazed by it. He had found part of the book, and he was sure he could find the rest of it.

At first I had thought that maybe he was trying to hide something from me, but then I realized that he was so excited about the stupid book that he had probably never thought it might not exist anymore.

An hour before our arrival in Delphi, I began to get very hungry, so Perseus parked so we could eat at a small restaurant right next to the highway. The food was edible, but not good. It consisted of a meat soup, rice and a dessert that looked like vanilla pudding but didn't taste much like it.

It didn't leave me completely satisfied, but by then I wasn't surprised by the hunger that had been chasing me for the last few days. Once we were done eating, we continued our trip north.

Once we were close, Perseus pointed at the mountain the ruins were in. The mountain was easily the biggest I had seen all day. Even from a distance I could make out the steep slopes. When we were at the base of the mountain, we began to drive up, circling around it.

Trees lined one side of the street. Beyond them the mountain sloped sharply into the large valley below. As we drove forward, I realized there were cars parked on the other side of the street, and even a few tourist buses. After a few minutes, we found an empty parking space between two other cars.

Perseus shut down the engine. As soon as I stepped out of the car I was slapped by a cold gust of air. I shivered inside my jacket, glad that I had decided to bring it along. The hot sun above us didn't seem able to penetrate the force of the wind bellowing around us. Thankfully, my hair was short now, so I didn't have to worry about pushing it out of my eyes or tying it back.

We were almost at the top of the mountain, and I could see the highway we had been on before. The cars looked tiny from a distance.

Perseus walked around the car and stood next to me, his eyes alight like torches as he looked at the ruins before us. From where we stood they were nothing much to look at, just a couple of crumbling rocks that could have once edged a pebbled street.

"Come on," he said excitedly as he began to make his way to the ancient stairs a couple of yards to our right. I didn't find myself in such jovial mood, but smiled anyways. Perseus turned around to look at me, and his smile broadened. "If I get killed for the book, at least I'll die knowing what it actually said."

I looked up the stairs, wondering what we would find above, whatever it was I didn't think it was worth dying for.

CHAPTER 11

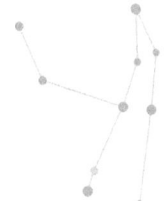

I FOLLOWED close behind Perseus as we climbed the wide stone stairs. There were only a few of them, maybe a dozen, leading further up the mountain. They were modern, the stone polished and with a metal railing on each side. Trees lined the stairs, swishing with the wind. There were already excited tourist groups at the bottom of the stairs, waiting for their tour guide to start leading them up.

"So what was Delphi?" I asked Perseus.

Perseus turned to face me excitedly, but said nothing. The stairs ended abruptly and we were met by a stone ramp that led us to the right. Perseus stopped at the top of the ramp, gazing at the ruins before him. I joined him. I wasn't much a fan of ruins, they were just old rocks, but by the size of the place I imagined that this could have looked impressive once. By the smile on Perseus's face, I didn't think he thought the same as me.

To the right was a rectangular platform, with six remaining columns on one side. The platform was tall, probably reaching up to my shoulders. The columns were made of circular disks stacked atop each other. I wondered how they hadn't crumbled. The platform itself was uneven, with some of the ground caved in with green patches of grass growing inside. Some rectangular rocks remained atop the platform, but they varied in sizes, and I assumed that they could have once been walls. Around it was a small fence to keep tourists out. To the right, the ruins gave way to the valley, which dropped below with a few more ancient rocks that looked like cemetery slabs to me. I could see the mountains in the distance, dark in contrast to the light sky.

To our left was an amphitheater—at least that much I did know about ruins. It had a strong resemblance to a modern theater, but it was made purely out of stone. The stage was just a small circular platform of stone at the bottom. Did ancient people watch plays here? The stone benches had patches of green plants that had somehow broken through the stone. A pair of tourists next to us took a picture of it excitedly, as if having pictures of rocks on your phone was so cool.

"People from all around Greece used to come here. They thought this place was the center of the world," Perseus started.

I at least tried to sound interested. "Why?" I asked, wondering why people would want to walk up that steep mountain.

"It was the most famous Oracle in the ancient world, in honor of the Greek god Apollo. The priestess here would tell you your future. She was called the Pythia," he said as his eyes fixed on the amphitheater.

I guessed there was something about knowing your own future that drove people to walk all that way. Unlike those ancient people, I found the notion dumb. I wasn't interested in my future. I preferred to focus on more present matters—my current concern being finding a bathroom. Did this place even have one? Or would I have to pee behind a bush? I noticed several of them behind the amphitheater.

The sun was already halfway down the horizon, and I wondered how long we would stay here. Perseus began to walk through the twisted path that led up the mountain. I walked beside him. We were passing by a cluster of trees when I stumbled on a rock and nearly fell over. Perseus grabbed my hand to steady me. I muttered a thanks, but he only nodded and didn't let go. His hand had a strong grip, and I was probably not going to get out of it very easily. Soon he seemed to forget he was holding it.

"Every great leader would consult the Oracle before making any important decisions, believing that whatever the Pythia said was knowledge from the gods," Perseus said as we continued up the zigzagging path. Pebbles crunched under my feet as we walked. At least the wind had died down, and my body was beginning to warm up. I realized my cold hand was warm in Perseus's grip now, and somehow I didn't feel so irritated about it anymore.

"So if every great leader consulted the Oracle," I said, "Then whatever priestess was here would actually decide over major political decisions and events."

Perseus nodded. That seemed absurd. Whether the priestess could actually see the future or not, she could move every single leader as a puppet to do whatever she wanted.

I looked at the ruins that now lay below us, and then upwards, as the path led us past more overturned rocks, pillars, and one or two surviving buildings that looked like rock sheds to me.

"Those were treasuries." Perseus pointed at the sheds. "Where the city-states of Greece would make offerings to the gods."

I eyed the sheds cynically, imagining some sacrificed goat, or maybe some looted gold.

"So the priestess would just walk around Prophecies." I waved my free hand at the ruins around us.

"No, I don't think so," Perseus said. He pushed his hair back with his hand. "She was right down there."

He pointed at the structure next to the amphitheater—the stone platform with six columns. I imagined that in ancient times it'd had more columns, and maybe a roof.

"So she would just stand there?" I asked.

Perseus licked his lips. "According to the myths she sat there, right next to the columns. She would inhale fumes that would come out of a chasm, or cave, underneath the ground. Those fumes would connect her to the gods and inspire visions."

I saw no chasm nor cave anywhere, and wondered what kind of fumes she had been inhaling. She could have been drugged and delirious most likely, rambling nonsense, but people would actually take her advice to heart.

Perseus and I continued our way up, walking past more ruined buildings. I didn't ask him anything else. Instead I just looked at our surroundings. It was quite a beautiful place, with all the trees and shrubs giving a sense of life. But the mountain we were on, compared to all the others around us, was barren at the very top, exposing dark brown and gray rock. I found that strange.

There was noise around us—the chatter of all the tourists. Most of them talked in English, but their conversations were jumbled with each other and I couldn't make out a particular conversation. There was a group of French tourists ahead of us, I realized. The tour guide was pointing down at the amphitheater, explaining how it had been constructed.

The air smelled of pine trees and humidity, as if it had rained recently, but I couldn't see any traces of rain, or even clouds in the distance. Even the rocks seemed to have their own smell, which was a strange one, like that of a very old, musty book.

Surviving columns rose up here and there, defiant against the wrecking force of time. But after some time the ruins just blurred around me, as if I were driving top speed past them. Perseus would talk to me every now and then, saying things that I mostly ignored. For me it made no difference why one of the rock sheds was more important than the other, or why one particular lonely column would be interesting.

Perseus's red hair would wave at the wind like a flame, his dark eyes wide as he looked around. I imagined that he would make a good history professor, or maybe even a tour guide. That is, if he found a crowd actually excited to hear what he said, unlike me.

"And there is a huge stadium at the top," Perseus said as he pointed at the top of the mountain. I groaned. My legs were already straining. I knew I had some bruises on my thighs, and the soles of my feet felt like I had been walking barefoot for hours.

As I looked at Perseus I realized that he didn't look much affected by what had happened in New York. Maybe that's why he had decided to come to Greece, and particularly to Delphi. The excitement of exploring ruins and looking for an ancient book would make him focus on something else. I wondered when we would actually start looking for the book instead of just walking around with the rest of the tourists. Maybe Perseus wanted to see all the ruins first?

"You know what," I said. "I think I'll just stay here. But you go up. I'll wait."

Perseus eyed me for a couple of seconds. "Alright. Just don't leave the ruins."

He let go of my hand with a smile and began to walk away, at a more eager pace as the snaking path continued to go upwards. "Tell me if you find the book!" I shouted after him.

He didn't respond.

I took a deep gulp of air, and sat on a rock that was conveniently behind me. The flow of tourists swished past me, going up the same way Perseus had gone. Some of them eyed me suspiciously. I imagined that the rock could have been part of some important building around here, but it was not part of anything now. So I didn't think it would matter much if I sat on it.

I closed my eyes for a moment, feeling a sense of fatigue that my body had been trying to avoid. My muscles burned as if I had run all the way from New York to here, and I knew that I must be covered in bruises underneath my clothes. The sun was hot on my back, and I enjoyed the warmth it gave me.

My thoughts drifted to Orion. He probably already knew I was here, and I could picture him shaking his head in frustration and disbelief, wondering what I was doing in some ruins. Maybe he thought I was hiding here. He would come find me, and I felt a sense of dread spreading like a virus inside my chest. I didn't want him to find me, even if I still had a couple of days before he did. It all depended on how soon he found Zia, or if he found her at all. I wanted her to be dead, so then I wouldn't have to worry about Perseus. If she realized that I hadn't killed him, what would she do to him, and me?

Spending the last hours with Perseus had been a relief, a way to just take a gulp of air before submerging myself into the ocean again. But I didn't want it to end, not this time.

I heaved a sigh, rubbing my temples. I thought of Alathea's book. Now that I had seen the ruins, or at least part of them, I was sure that we wouldn't find it here. There was nothing but rocks and trees and bushes, and to much of my distress—no bathrooms. Where would Alathea have even hidden the book? Under one of those rocks? In a secret treasure chest? The ruins must have already been thoroughly explored by expert archaeologists. So what where we supposed to be looking for?

Then I thought of Zia and Corvus. Clearly the book had some importance to them? But why? Did they really believe in the Prophecies it contained? Maybe the book had some value, being ancient and all, and they wanted it to sell it in a high price to a museum or in the black market. But even Perseus had said that no one in the museum in Athens had noticed the Prophecies had been stolen. They hadn't even been on display.

My mind seemed to go round and round, trying to connect all the dots while I sat. After a few minutes my butt began to hurt and I stood up. I started to walk down the mountain. It wasn't such a big place as to get lost, and Perseus would surely find me when he reached the bottom.

I let my feet guide me down, trying to ignore my weariness. I focused on the nature around me—the grass that grew among the rocks, overpowering the sacred constructions that mankind had once made, the sparse trees around me. Some of them were thin and resembled spears, and others were large and swaying with the wind. The leaves hadn't fallen off them, not yet, gripping the stems with all the force they had.

I imagined my life would be much like this if I ever got my freedom. Walking wherever my feet took me, getting lost without a sense of where I was going. I wasn't scared of it. I liked being alone. I would manage fine by myself, I always had.

By the time I was at the bottom of the ruins the top of the mountain seemed much bigger, rising behind me like a wall. I wondered why they had decided to build the ruins so far up.

I sat on another rock next to the amphitheater, trying to count, without much luck, how many rows of stone benches it had.

After some time, I felt a hand on my shoulder. I jumped and whirled around, then realized it was only Perseus.

"Sorry," he said.

"Find anything interesting?" I asked.

"The stadium was cool," he said.

I assumed the stadium must have been rocks too and was glad I hadn't seen it.

"I have an idea," he said. "I asked a couple of tour guides and they told me a few interesting things that could help us find the book."

"What did they say?"

Perseus smiled. "Let's go get some dinner and I'll tell you all about it."

He quickly walked down the path, his pace faster than normal, as if eager to get away from the place. He seemed anxious too, his hands clenched unconsciously as if waiting for a fight.

I frowned but followed after him, wondering what could have made him so nervous.

Chapter XV, Verse II

A promise to be made to the one who ends in sways,
Then to part on their own ways to meet maybe once again.
Hunted by his past, by all the hurt that she provoked.
For destiny he cannot fool no matter how much he risks.
With an arrow to shoot, aimed at the heart of one he loved.
Over blood and sand he shall decide the one who will be next to die.
For a new era he shall be present if in the storm he survives.

CHAPTER 12

"**IS THAT** even legal?" I asked.

Perseus rubbed his hair. "No, it isn't."

We sat facing each other, each at the edge of our separate beds. After dinner we had driven to the hotel. To my dismay, we would have to share a room, because on such short notice, it had been the only one available.

The hotel was fifteen minutes away from the ruins at Delphi, at the base of another mountain. When I had first seen it, the hotel had resembled a very big, modern cabin. It was made mostly out of wood, and had huge windows on every floor.

Our room was nice. It had two twin beds on one side, with a small glass table in between them. On the other side of the room was a small living room with a couch facing a plasma TV on the wall. Next to it was the bathroom, which was also very nice. It had a large bathtub and a shower.

Opposite from the door was a floor-to-ceiling window. At the moment the view was darkened, but I could make the mountains and hills around us like looming shadows in the distance.

During dinner, Perseus had told me what he had learned from the tour guides. And as soon as we had entered the room, Perseus had shared his new plan.

"So we should sneak into Delphi at night to try to find the book?" I said slowly.

I had already told him that I didn't think we would find anything in the ruins. Archaeologists had probably already found anything there was to find. But Perseus was sure that everyone who had explored the ruins before us had missed *something*.

Perseus nodded. "I already told you." He stood up from the bed, probably too restless to remain sitting, and began pacing in front of the beds. "The tour guides told me that there were myths of a secret chasm under the Temple of Apollo. The book *must* be there."

"Okay, fine," I said. "Let's assume the book is in the chasm. That can't be the same place where the museum in Athens found the Prophecies you stole. Those must have been somewhere else, or the cave wouldn't be a myth. Shouldn't we be looking for *that* location instead?"

Perseus was giving me his back now, his shoulders were slumped. My thoughts traveled to Zia again. If she was alive, what would she do? I couldn't let her kill him. But how could I protect Perseus? Could I tell him the truth?

No. I couldn't. I didn't want him to know that I had been sent to kill him. He would hate me after that.

"I'm sure we can find the chasm," he said. "The book is there."

He said it with such conviction that I wanted to believe him. Instead, I sighed.

He turned back to me. "Most myths of Delphi mention the chasm. Remember I said that in the myths the priestess would supposedly inhale fumes?" he asked. I nodded. How to forget the drugged priestess. "Well, the fumes supposedly came from a chasm underneath the temple, which was a giant cave."

"But no one has found that cave," I said.

"Not yet," Perseus said. He shook his head. "We have to look for the entrance."

"Alright," I conceded with another sigh. "But what if they find us?" He raised a brow. "The people who want to kill you."

"Oh, them," he said, letting his shoulders slump again.

I wondered why he hadn't asked his father for a bodyguard. Maybe he didn't think his killers would follow us all the way to Greece?

Perseus walked over to his duffle bag and opened it. My heart gave a slight start at the sight of the gun. "If they come again, I'll be ready this time."

I felt my stomach tightening. I knew we could probably fight Corvus and his friends again. But if Zia was alive, she would send Orion to get us. And if it came down to a fight between Orion and Perseus, I already knew who would win. Perseus walked closer to me and put a hand on my shoulder.

"Don't worry. I won't let them hurt you." A smile lit his eyes.

"Do you know how to use it?" I said, pointing at the gun on top of his suitcase.

"My dad taught me," Perseus said. "We'll be fine. Don't worry." His tone was soothing. "We'll find that book and get the answers we need."

"Fine," I said.

We remained silent for a few seconds. "I'll go shower," he finally said.

I lay face-up on the bed while Perseus took his shower. The room was peaceful, and the mattress was comfortable enough to start lulling me into sleep, but I was still restless.

We weren't safe. Perseus wasn't safe. I knew a lot more of the danger he was in, and having to carry that with me made me feel uneasy. I didn't want to have to worry about him, and I didn't want him to worry about me.

For the first time, I regretted having met Perseus. He was a weight I had to drag with me. I couldn't worry about myself because I had to worry about him too. That's why I had always preferred being alone.

After Perseus finished showering, it was my turn. I retrieved a pair of sweatpants and a tank top from my duffle bag and entered the bathroom. The hot water felt like it was disentangling the knots in my muscles, and for a couple of minutes, I just let the water soothe me. I then changed into my new clothes. Wearing a tank top felt strange, as if I was naked. I had never slept with a sleeveless shirt. I had also packed a hoodie, I remembered. That would work well enough. Even if Perseus already knew I had scars, I didn't feel comfortable having them exposed at night.

I stepped out of the bathroom. Perseus had placed a towel on one of the beds. He was holding scissors in one hand, and a phone in the other. His back was to me.

"Yeah, Dad," he said into the phone. "Tell Mom not to worry. The hotel looks perfectly safe." He paused for a few seconds. I could hear a deep voice on the other end, but couldn't make out what it was saying. "Yeah." Another pause. "Yes, Dad . . . No, you don't need to call me every night. I'll be fine . . . I'll send you texts . . . Yes . . . Okay, bye." He hung up the cellphone and left it on his bed, then turned around.

"What are those for?" I asked, pointing at the scissors. He smiled and looked at my hair. I shook my head. "Oh no you're not."

He gave me a lopsided grin. "My mom used to work at a salon before she met my father. She taught us how to cut our own hair. I know what I'm doing."

I pressed myself against the wall. "I'm not sure I trust you with those scissors."

"You need a haircut," he said.

"It's fine as it is. I cut it myself," I said.

Perseus tilted his head to one side. "That's what I was afraid of. Now, sit down and let me fix it." I shook my head again. He left the scissors on top of the towel and walked over to me. "Come on, what are you afraid of? Your hair can't look worse than it is now, and I promise I won't hurt you."

I looked him dead in the eye. His own were wide with amusement. He was right about both things, but I didn't want him touching my hair. In fact, I didn't even like him standing too close to me, like he was doing now. It made my stomach flutter and my heart beat faster.

"Please," he said with another smile. "I promise it will look great."

I let out a breath I had been holding and pressed my lips tight together until they hurt. I slowly walked over to the bed and sat down without facing Perseus. He didn't say anything either.

My hair was still wet, and the water dripped softly onto my shoulders and back. Perseus placed a towel there. He softly brushed my hair back with his hand, sending hot jolts through my skin. I closed my eyes. I could hear the scissors cutting, and felt my hair as it fell down.

He took a good fifteen minutes, turning my head, and cutting away whatever he thought needed to go. All that time I felt myself tensing again, and it wasn't because he was holding a deadly weapon, but because he was touching my head.

"There," he finally said. He took away the towel from my shoulders. I stood and walked into the bathroom. As I looked at myself in the mirror I realized he was right. He hadn't cut much of my hair, but had simply evened it out. It was cut just above my ears, shorter than I'd ever had it, but it looked fair now.

"Do you like it?" Perseus asked as he walked inside the bathroom to look at his work. I nodded. "It will grow evenly now. So you probably won't have to cut it again in a while."

I walked out of the bathroom. Perseus had already cleaned away the towels. There were still a couple of strands on the floor though. Perseus turned off the lights, but instead of being plunged into darkness we were lit by the white light from my scars. Only the ones on my wrists, shoulders and upper back were exposed, but they were bright enough. I felt Perseus's warm hand on my shoulder and jumped back. The light blinked faster.

"Sorry," Perseus immediately said. He looked down at the floor, flushing red. "I just wanted to see your scars."

He looked up again, not meeting my eyes but looking at the scars on my arms and shoulders. His eyes seemed darker, big like an owl's. I wished I'd put on the hoodie earlier.

"There's not much to see," I said with a shrug. "They're just scars."

"But you have so many of them," he said softly. He walked closer to me and placed his hand again on the scar on my left shoulder. This time I didn't move away, but rather stood firm like a statue under inspection. "No wonder you ran away," he said after a few seconds. I was aware of his hand still on my shoulder, emitting heat as if it was made of hot coals.

"I try to run away," I corrected him. "But I can't really escape."

"Zia comes looking for you?" He asked.

At the moment I didn't want to mention Orion, so I just nodded. "It's always the same. I run away, but never for too long, and then I'm back where I started with a few new scars."

Perseus shook his head. "That's not right," he whispered. I didn't think it mattered much, what was right or what was wrong. "Have you tried leaving the country before?"

"Three times," I answered. "I've tried everything."

My eyes went instinctively to the horizontal cuts on my wrists. They shone the faintest, but were still noticeable. Perseus followed my gaze and his eyes widened. His other hand traced the scars on my right wrist. I noticed his face had paled.

"What can I do to help?" he asked.

"What?" I asked, not because I hadn't understood his question, but because I didn't know what he meant with it.

"How can I help you escape?" he asked, this time slower.

I shook my head. "You can't help me, they'll always find me. As long as Zia's alive, there is no escape."

Perseus held my gaze with his. One of his hands was still on my shoulders, the other holding my wrist. A dark shadow flickered across his eyes.

"I'll find a way to help you." His tone was deeper, and his eyes set with a dark determination I hadn't seen before.

I didn't ask what he meant by that, maybe because I was afraid of what he would answer. But the truth was that no matter what Perseus tried to do, he couldn't beat Zia, and he would definitely never beat Orion.

Perseus's head leaned down towards mine. His hand let go of my wrist and instead held on to my waist.

"Your eyes look silver with the light from your scars instead of blue," he whispered.

Then his lips were on mine, soft and warm. Heat spread in my chest, and my stomach felt like it had made a somersault. His other hand softly traced the scar on my shoulder.

My own hands went to his red hair, wanting to know how it felt. It was still wet, but soft. His strong arms wrapped around me. My heart was beating fast, and I could feel it pulsing inside each of my scars.

Perseus pulled back. "I promise I'll find a way," he said. "You *will* be free."

I pulled up his shirt, just enough to see his scar. The blinding light seemed to have a life of its own, and was brighter than any of my scars or Orion's. It was almost like a lighthouse. I wondered why his scars would be brighter. I traced my finger through it. The light emanating from the scar had a strange vibration that seemed to reverberate through all my bones. Perseus pressed my hand against his scar, as if trying to make me cover the light, but it simply slipped in between my fingers—just like blood.

He leaned down to kiss me again. I didn't move away or push him back. Instead I pulled him to me, closing the space in between us.

Now I really wished that I had never met Perseus.

He screamed, and it immediately woke me from my sleep. I opened my eyes. Perseus had slept shirtless, and his scar was uncovered, lighting his sweaty face. His light was blinking frantically. He was breathing hard, holding his head in between his hands.

"Are you alright?" I asked.

He gave a startled jump. "Sorry, I didn't mean to wake you."

"It's alright," I muttered. "Nightmare?"

He nodded. His hair was a dark shade of red. "I was thinking about . . ."

"New York?" I guessed.

He nodded again.

"It's just that . . . They're dead. They all died. They—"

"There's nothing you could have done," I said.

Perseus didn't answer. I knew he must have felt some sort of survivor's guilt, wondering why he had lived while everyone else died. I had already buried the memories inside my head, along with the deaths of the patients at the psychiatric hospital, but I didn't think Perseus could do the same.

"Go to sleep," I said, trying to comfort him. "There's nothing we can do to help the dead."

"It's not that," he whispered. He let out a deep breath and lay back on his bed. He pulled the quilts up, cutting off the light. "Andromeda?" he asked in a low tone.

"Mmm?" I asked, my mind already half-asleep.

"It's just that . . ." He let out a sigh. "Never mind. It's just a nightmare. Goodnight."

"Goodnight."

There was a loud knock on the door that woke me from my dreamless sleep. My head felt muddled and heavy. I sat upright, looking warily at the door. We hadn't closed the curtains, so the bright light from outside bathed the room in warmth.

Perseus was immediately out of his bed and on his feet, walking towards the door. His scar didn't shine anymore, and I looked at his muscular back.

Perseus opened the door and was immediately pushed back. My heart leaped into my throat at the sight of Orion. He stood, full height, hands balled into fists. His eyes swept the room before settling, wide-eyed, on me.

"Hey!" Perseus shouted. "Get out of our room!"

"Our room?!" Orion growled. He looked at Perseus's rumpled bed, then at my own. He unclenched his fists, but his eyes narrowed at me. "What do you think you're doing?"

All the drowsiness from sleep vanished as I stood from the bed.

"What do you think *you're* doing?" I asked.

"Do you know this guy?" Perseus asked as he stared at Orion. He was taller than Perseus, and a good deal stronger too. If Perseus noticed this he didn't seem fazed. He stood with his hands curled into fists, looking dangerously at Orion as he stood two feet in front of him.

"Unfortunately, I do," I said as I walked closer to Orion.

"And who is this?" Orion said as he poked Perseus's bare chest.

"Her boyfriend," Perseus said with a smile, the same one he had shown Corvus at the park a couple of days ago. But now I realized that he might have actually meant it.

A ripple of emotions washed through Orion's face—surprise, anger, disbelief, shock. He turned to me, the veins in his neck bulging, then looked at Perseus. Orion's fist shot towards Perseus's face. Perseus deflected the punch with his arm and at the same time kicked Orion in the thigh. Orion staggered back, probably not expecting that. He lurched forward at Perseus at the same time I leaped for him. I crashed against Orion's side and we bumped against the wall, then fell to the floor with me on top of him. Orion squirmed like a worm under me. Perseus hauled me up to my feet and made me stand behind him, facing Orion, who leaped to his feet like an enraged cat.

His eyes focused on the two of us.

"In the hallway, *now*," he said to me through clenched teeth.

He stamped out of the room and I followed after him. Perseus grabbed my arm before I stepped out of the room. "Are you sure it's safe?" he asked.

"He's my foster brother," I explained.

Perseus's grip relaxed, but his gaze didn't. He stepped back. "If you need anything, just scream and I'll shoot him."

I knew he meant that, and it disturbed me a little. I nodded and walked out of the room, closing the door behind me. Orion was leaning against the opposite wall, arms crossed over his chest. At the end of the right side of the hallway was a huge window that let the morning light through. The five doors on each side of the corridor were closed. On the other side of the hallway I could see the stairs curling into the floor below. Orion leaned forward, making the wooden floor creak underneath him.

"Boyfriend?" he asked mockingly.

"You're the one who told me to start flirting."

"I didn't really think you would!"

"Why are you even angry?" I demanded. "I've never tried to attack any of your girlfriends."

He gritted his teeth, letting out a hiss in between them. "That's different," he spat out.

"How is it different?" I asked hotly. He shook his head but didn't answer, and then bumped his head on the wall behind him.

Orion stared hard at me. "There's something I don't like about that guy."

"There's also something I don't like about any of your girlfriends," I said, crossing my arms.

"I mean it," he said. "There is something weird about him."

"Like you're so normal," I said.

"Andromeda, listen to me," he said, his eyes alight like two angry suns. "There really is something wrong about that boy. You'd do good to leave him behind."

I couldn't believe that he was saying that. He had no right to criticize a guy he had met for less than a minute.

"Please, just stay away from him. Date any other guy," he pleaded, but it sounded more like an order. "Something in my chest is warning me against him."

I wanted to tell him that his chest was as stupid as his peanut-sized brain, but didn't want to start an argument in the hallway, where other tourists could hear us. I rubbed my hair. It felt strange, since it was so short. Orion looked at it curiously, and I wondered if he liked my new haircut better than the last one.

"Why are you here?" I asked.

His face turned hard as stone. "I came here for you," He spread his arms. "Why else would I be here, in the middle of nowhere, in Greece?"

"How did you even get out of New York so fast?" I asked.

Orion let his arms dangle at his sides. "I took a boat to Canada and then took a plane here." He eyed me up and down. "Did he see your scars?"

I shook my head. "I followed your advice and wore a hoodie." I had put on the hoodie before going to sleep. I still hadn't felt comfortable sleeping with my scars uncovered.

Orion's eyes narrowed even further, and his nose flared angrily. "Good."

"What about Zia?" I said, trying to distract him from my scars. It seemed to do the trick, because his face went slack.

He shook his head. "I haven't found her yet," he said. "But I will."

I tightened my fists. "Then what are you doing here?"

He eyed me again, looking at my new haircut. "I wanted to see you were alright," he said. He stood upright, his chin raised high. "I'm going to find Zia. If she's alive . . . I'll find you again."

"And if she's dead?" I asked.

Orion didn't answer right away, but I noticed how his entire body tensed. He walked closer to me, making me back into the wall. "If she's dead then I'll also come find you, and I'll have a word with your *boyfriend*." He looked at the door of my room.

As if on cue, Perseus burst out of the room, regarding Orion with hostility. He had put on a shirt. Orion and Perseus seemed to share a bitter conversation as they looked into each other's eyes. After about ten seconds, Orion looked away and stamped down the hallway, his footsteps loud as thunder. He disappeared as he turned right, but not before he shot us one last angry look.

I let out a breath I didn't realize I'd been holding. At least Orion didn't know who Perseus was, or else I was afraid he would have killed Perseus.

I walked back into the room.

"How did he even find us?" Perseus asked after closing the door behind us.

I shrugged. "Don't know."

"Is that the guy who's dating Rose?" Perseus asked, sleepily rubbing his hair back with his hand. I hesitated for a moment as I looked into his big dark eyes, then realized that there was no harm in Perseus knowing a truth. I nodded. "Then maybe she told him we were here." That seemed like a plausible explanation for Perseus. "He didn't seem to like me though." He rubbed his arm where he had deflected the blow from Orion's fist.

"Don't take it personally. He doesn't like anyone," I said.

"Sorry I told him I was your boyfriend," he said sheepishly. "I didn't mean it." He hesitated. "Unless you want me to mean it."

I stared hard at him. His face was red, which mean he was serious enough.

"I . . ." I was at a loss of words. "I'm not sure."

He nodded slowly. "I know. I mean, we just met a couple of days ago." He ran his hand through his hair. "But I really like you."

"I like you too," I said. As soon as those words came out, I realized they were true. I hadn't wanted to admit it, not even to myself. But the truth was that I liked being with Perseus more than I liked being alone.

But there was also the small issue that he had a life in New York, and I would probably spend the rest of my days stealing and traveling throughout Europe, and maybe Asia.

We looked into each other's eyes for a couple of seconds, as if it were a staring context. I finally blinked.

"If you want to find the cave at Delphi, we better start planning something," I said.

Perseus nodded. "I was thinking . . ."

•——————•——————•

The sun was hot above our heads as we sat on the overgrown grass. In front of us was a small lake we had found. The water was bright blue, reflecting the cloudless sky, but there was no way to tell how deep it was. On the other side of it was a small mountain covered in trees. I couldn't see beyond it.

Behind me, I could hear the leaves of the trees rustling with the soft breeze that made my hair flutter around me. The water rippled too. The air around us was heavy with heat, and so humid that with every breath I felt I would drown.

We had been sitting in the sun for around half an hour when Orion gave a grunt and stood up. He pulled his shirt off, revealing his muscular abdomen and back. His scars were a white tangle of lines on his shoulder blades and back, like the map of a city. He had fewer scars than I did. I could easily have counted his if I wanted too, while mine were just too many to tell from one another.

"I'm going in," he said as he took off his pants, leaving only his boxers. He left his clothes bunched up with his shoes right next to me.

Beads of sweat ran down his spine, and I felt my own body yearning to go into the cool water. Orion walked away from me and stood at the edge of the lake, looking into the water for a couple of seconds. Then he jumped. Water splashed in my direction, but I didn't complain—it was refreshing. He disappeared under the water for a couple of seconds, then his head bobbed up as he took a gulp of air. He turned to me with a smile, his head the only thing visible above the water. The lake must have been deep.

"Aren't you coming?" he asked without meeting my gaze.

"Zia said we better be back by nightfall," I said. "She won't be happy we stopped here."

"And since when do you care about what makes Zia happy?" he asked as he swam backwards.

I looked at the sun, which was already starting to make its way down the sky, then fixed my eyes on the car parked a few yards behind me, under the shade of a large oak tree. I couldn't see them from here, but I knew that the new weapons we had acquired were safely stored away in the trunk. We didn't know why Zia wanted those guns and rifles, but Orion and I had guessed that she had made us steal them so she could sell them again.

Stealing them had been easy, all things considered. They had been left practically unguarded in the basement of the house. Our biggest problem had been the guard at the backyard, but Orion had taken care of that easily. Then it had just been a matter of unlocking all the doors in the house and basement.

ANDROMEDA

This was probably the last mission Zia would give us for a while. In a week we would be moving in with different foster families. Bile rose in my throat just to think about it. I had never been away from Zia or Orion, and as much as I hated her, I didn't know how living in a foster family would be like. Would there be other foster children? Would my new foster parents beat me too if I misbehaved? Would they take pity on the poor "homeless" girl they thought I was? Would they send me to school? I had never gone to school before, and didn't like that idea at all.

Zia was a coward to send us away, and part of me was angry that she had done that. But the other part of me was glad that I would be away from her. The broken bones, bruises and lashes from her last beating had finally healed—but I'd had to rest in bed for over a month, unable to move. I hadn't known that Zia was strong enough to break so many bones, or that her lashes could cause me to nearly bleed out.

The only good thing about foster homes is that I would have an actual chance at escaping. But even that thought sent a dizzying wave of pain, as if Zia were beating me all over again. I breathed slowly to calm my drumming heart. I needed to try to escape again, no matter how badly Zia punished me this time. I looked at Orion. He was looking intently at me. He wouldn't try to escape, not again. Not after what she had done to us last time . . . Maybe I should let a few months pass, and then try to convince him again.

"Zia doesn't have to know we're here," Orion said. "We'll tell her we got stuck in traffic."

I didn't answer and simply closed my eyes, letting the faint breeze soothe me as much as it could. I remained like that for a couple of minutes, letting my mind clear of everything.

I wished, again, that I could just sit anywhere in the world, feeling the sun on my back and the heat enveloping me without having to worry about Zia.

I heard movement in the water, but paid no attention to it. Seconds later, a large shadow loomed above me, instantly blocking the heat of the sun. I opened my eyes to see Orion standing over me with a grin. Water dripped from him and onto the grass.

"Oh no, you—" I began to say, trying to push myself away from him. He pulled me to my feet and hauled me over his shoulder, then began walking back to the lake. "Wait!" I squirmed uselessly in his arms as he laughed.

Orion stood at the edge of the lake. "One."

"Don't you dare!"

"Two."

"I'm serious, Orion."

"Three."

"I'm going to—"

My stomach lurched and I felt the wind against my face before a shock of cold washed over me. I swam frantically towards the surface and reached it in only a couple of seconds. I took a gulp of air and coughed out some water. I couldn't feel the bottom of the lake, and wondered how long I could last swimming without tiring.

Orion's head surfaced the water. He laughed hysterically, swimming in circles around me.

"You're the worst," I gasped.

"I know," he said.

The water wasn't cold anymore, and in fact felt warm around me. I pushed my hair out of my face and glared at Orion. He smiled in return, his amber eyes bright as the sun above us.

"What are you going to do, drown me?" he asked.

"I'll try," I said as I began swimming towards him, my blouse floating loosely around me.

Orion was a fast swimmer and began to circle me like a shark, always a few yards away. His head would momentarily disappear underneath the surface and pop out suddenly some-where else.

I went underwater too, opening my eyes. I could barely see, but the blur of movement in front of me was unmistakably him. I did the best dolphin impression I could muster and swam towards him. Either he hadn't expected that I would reach him so fast, or he had wanted me to come, because he didn't move away.

I wrapped my arms around his torso and pulled him down. His own arms went tight around my back and pressed me hard against him. I could feel the heat of his chest against my own, and the strength of his arms around me. We stayed like that for a couple of seconds. Then I kicked my feet and we both went to the surface. I took in a gulp of air.

"I'm not sure that's how you drown people," he said.

His arms were still around me, and his eyes fixed on me like a nail to a wooden plank. I didn't answer, instead searching his face, trying to discern his current emotions without much luck.

"Are you still mad at me?" I asked him.

Orion took a couple of seconds to answer. "I was never mad at you," he said quietly, almost in a whisper, as if he didn't want Zia to hear us even if she was miles away. "I know you were only trying to do what was best for both of us, but . . ."

"But . . . " I prompted.

He heaved a sigh. "But now . . . because of what you did to Zia . . ." His Adam's apple bobbed out of his throat as he swallowed. "She'll never let us live with her again. And she's made it clear she doesn't want us to live together either."

"I'm sorry," I whispered, even though I didn't regret what I had done.

Orion didn't seem to hear me. His gaze was distant as he looked beyond me.

"I don't like this, Andromeda," he admitted. "Even if we live close by, I don't like the idea of being in a foster home. We'll have to be more careful to keep our secrets." I didn't worry about that. All I had to do was wear a long-sleeved shirt at night or lock my door.

Orion looked into my eyes with a gentleness I hadn't seen before—one without fury or the alertness that had always accompanied his gaze.

"I won't be able to make your life miserable so easily now," he whispered.

"Neither will I."

A bird chirped somewhere distantly, and the trees rustled with a gust of wind, making me suddenly feel cold. Then there was a strange stillness around us, as if the air had decided to hold its breath for only a second.

Next thing I knew, Orion's lips were on mine. The cold was gone at once, replaced by heat that radiated from my chest and stomach. Then his hands were on my face, tracing my cheeks and nose, and my own hands were on his strong back, exploring the map of scars.

Whether it was a simple impulse that didn't make me stop him, or the curiosity of kissing someone, I didn't know. At that moment all I could think about was that I liked how the heat inside my chest felt, and how I enjoyed his fingers gently tracing my face and neck.

His hands then moved to my back, gently exploring my scars. No one had ever touched them, only me. Orion knew that, but he did it anyways, as if by tracing my scars he would know me better.

His scars were rough lines that cut through his smooth skin, like cracks in a porcelain vase. I could feel his pain inside them, an ache in his heart that he didn't want to acknowledge. I had never seen him cry when Zia beat him, or in any other situation, but I knew he suffered just as much as I did.

Maybe that's what had driven us to kiss, to know that we shared the same kind of torment that we couldn't escape. And that no matter who we met or where we went, we would always be haunted by the secrets that we shared. Secrets that not another soul would ever be able to know—not even Zia.

The sun began to sink lower in the sky, making the water turn from blue to orange. Our fingers began to look like raisins, and the water got cold around us, but we didn't care, and stayed there even after the sun had sunk under the horizon.

Once the sun had set, our scars began to shine under the water, emitting a strange white glow that rippled to the surface. Our hearts beat as fast as the light did. We stayed in the water a little longer, watching the light, feeling it, knowing that next time we were in the dark, we would be alone again.

CHAPTER 13

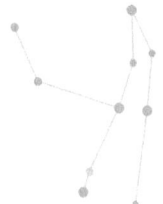

THE NIGHT was cold. The dim light from the moon barely made our surroundings visible, shedding a silvery glow over us. The ruins were silent, only silhouettes against the stark night. The sky was studded with stars. I marveled at the tiny blinking net of lights, which all seemed to twinkle in tune with my heart.

Perseus stirred next to me. Both of us were wearing black clothes, which were warm as much as they were good at camouflaging. There were no artificial lights in the ruins, which worked to our advantage. There were also no cameras, which I found strange. I thought that maybe no one would want to break into Delphi at night, and if someone was going to vandalize ancient ruins, they probably wouldn't want to climb a mountain to do it. So our only problem became the guards. I spotted three of them.

Perseus and I lay on the cold grass, right in front of the temple. To our right was the amphitheater and, further away, the jagged path that led up. We'd had to climb by foot, so no one would hear the noise from a car. It had been a steep and grueling climb. Once at the ruins, we had found a small crevice at the side of the mountain, right next to the remains of the temple where the priestesses had supposedly once resided. There, we could lay flat and remain hidden under the shadows.

I could see the six columns atop the stone platform twenty yards in front of me, but at night they seemed more sinister, like a giant's ribs protruding from the ground. Directly in front of me, one of the guards slowly circled the rectangular platform, which rose up to his shoulders. He had a flashlight, just like all the other guards, but for some reason only kept it trained on the ground— as if looking for spiders.

Another guard was walking along the stone benches of the amphitheater, as if waiting for a music concert that would never start. There was another guard walking up the zigzagging path, and I soon lost him from sight. Perseus guessed he might have gone to check the stadium and other ruins at the top, and I assumed that there could be another guard at the very top of the mountain.

Perseus was looking at the temple wide-eyed, as if this moment would define the rest of his life. He seemed so sure that we would find something here. His body was tense, and his hands clenched. He had spoken very little on our way to the ruins, and hadn't met my gaze. That had made me feel like there was something he was keeping from me, but what could it be?

After nearly two hours of waiting in the shadows and monitoring the movements of the guards, Perseus nudged at my arm. From my back pocket, I pulled out the three small fireworks we had bought in the market earlier today. The market had been in a small village a few miles away from the ruins. We had stayed there all morning, then had gone back to the hotel to change our clothes.

The fireworks were thin sticks, like miniature rockets, and had a pull string on one side. I handed them to Perseus. He didn't look at me when I did, his eyes fixed on the ruins before us.

Perseus had been worried that the fireworks might damage the ruins, but the lady selling the fireworks had assured him that they were harmless.

Very slowly, Perseus stood from the ground and pressed himself against the rocky wall of the mountain behind us. To someone not looking closely, he could have been just another shadow in the dark.

I heard him take a deep breath. He pulled the string and threw the first firework. I couldn't see where it landed. He quickly did the same with the other two, and the fireworks disappeared into the night.

There were a couple of seconds of still silence when neither of us breathed. Then right at the bottom of the snaking path, nearly a hundred yards away from us, light exploded in sparks and shot upwards, blowing up into a cloud of bright smoke nearly twenty feet off the ground.

There was a shout from the guard in the amphitheater, followed by the explosion of another firework in the middle of the path. The third one blew close to one of the stone sheds at the bottom of the path, momentarily illuminating it in bright light. I wondered how Perseus had thrown them so far away, but then remembered that he was a quarterback on his football team.

The guard next to the temple immediately raced away, climbing the crooked path to investigate the mysterious fireworks. The other two guards were already there, looking around and talking among themselves, their flashlights cutting through the night as they waved them along the path.

We both knew that after throwing the fireworks, the guards would be distracted, searching the ruins. It would give us a maximum of ten minutes to find the entrance to the cave where the ancient book was supposedly hidden.

ANDROMEDA

After arguing for hours during the afternoon I had finally given up and decided that if Perseus wanted to look for the cave, I wasn't going to be able to convince him otherwise. But I still felt uneasy, knowing that unless Perseus knew exactly where the entrance was hidden, we wouldn't have enough time.

Perseus pulled me out of my thoughts as he grabbed my arm and yanked me to my feet. I barely had time to register that before he set out running towards the temple. I followed beside him, but his grip didn't loosen, as if he was afraid I would run away. The ground underneath us was so uneven that I had to keep my gaze down. There were rocks, and roots from trees everywhere, and even some plastic bottles.

Before I knew it, the temple was before us. The stone platform rose to my neck, and I could barely see above it. We ducked below the fence that kept tourists out, crawling in the dirt. I got back to my feet and we walked around the platform. On the opposite side was a ramp leading up; we quickly climbed it. Perseus finally let go of my arm and slowly walked forward, staring intently at the rocks under our feet. I looked at the path in front of us and noticed that the guards were quickly making their way up the mountain, waving their flashlights madly around them. They seemed completely unaware of our presence.

I turned back to Perseus, who stood in the middle of the platform where a large patch of grass had grown in between the rocks. There was a large, six-foot-wide rock in the middle of it. Perseus stood in front of it.

I followed after him, trying not to stumble on the uneven ground, wondering what he was looking for. I was at Perseus's side after a few seconds. I didn't even have time to ask what he was trying to do. Perseus planted his feet firmly on the ground and began pushing the six-foot rock out of the way. He grunted with the effort. I imagined it must have weighed a lot, but under Perseus's strength it was beginning to slide to the side, over the smooth grass. He was much stronger than I had guessed. The rock seemed to rumble as Perseus pushed it. I turned to look at the guards, worried that they would hear us. They were almost at the top of the curling path, and none of them turned to look in our direction.

Perseus stopped and took a deep breath, then pushed again, managing to slide the rock a few more inches.

"What are you doing?" I whispered. Shoving a giant rock hadn't been part of the plan.

He kept pushing. That's when I realized there was a hole below the rock. It took Perseus a whole minute, but he managed to push the rock away, revealing the hole completely. It was around three feet in diameter, barely enough space for us to fit.

Perseus wiped the sweat off his forehead with his palm, his breath ragged. He looked down at the hole. For the first time tonight, he looked up at me. His eyes seemed darker than normal, black as the sky.

"After you," he whispered, motioning to the hole.

"Are you serious?" I asked.

"Quite," he said.

There was a shout above the mountain, and the rays of the flashlights waved frantically around. I couldn't see what was going on, but it seemed as if the guards had begun arguing with each other, shouting what sounded like insults.

"Come on," Perseus said.

I barely had time to think as he pulled me closer. How had he known there was a hole there? What was actually happening with the guards? Where did the hole lead?

The last question was the first to be answered. Before I could protest, Perseus pushed me towards the hole and let me fall. I let out a small scream as I felt my stomach fly up to my throat. Then I hit the ground, hard, and a hot jolt traveled up my legs, which gave under me. I fell on my back, grunting. I took in three deep breaths. Then I sat up on the cold, damp rock. I was surrounded by an impenetrable darkness. The smell inside the cave was strong. It was a sweet scent, but at the same time acid—like lemonade with sugar and a rotten lemon. It was slightly dizzying, making my head feel lighter, as if it had been filled with helium and was about to float away like a balloon.

Perseus dropped right next to me, his grunt echoing off the invisible walls. The pain from my feet and legs stopped throbbing a bit. I had broken enough bones in my life to know I hadn't broken anything this time, but had maybe sprained my ankles.

A sudden light blinded my eyes, and it took me a second to realize that it was Perseus's scar. He had lifted up his shirt, improvising a flashlight. I let my eyes adjust for a couple of seconds and then looked around.

We were in a large cavern. Compared to the night outside, I realized it was actually warm. The air around me was moist, making drops slide off the dark walls as if the cavern was sweating. The ceiling above us was low, and I realized that we were standing in some sort of flat and round platform, nearly fifty feet in diameter. Below the platform the ground fell into . . . was that a river I heard?

I crawled to the edge of the platform and looked down into what was unmistakably a river. There wasn't even a staircase that led down into the river, and I really hoped Perseus wasn't thinking about jumping down again. The river was at least thirty feet below us. The water was white with the foam it formed, drawing a stark comparison with the black rock that made up the entire cavern. The foam seemed to evaporate, and hovered a couple of feet above the water like thin mist.

As I looked around the platform, I realized that there were drawings over it, one in fact right where I was kneeling. I made out a snake that seemed to be curled around a tree.

I looked back at Perseus, who was looking down into the river with a blank expression.

"How did you know that was the entrance to a cavern?" I asked, still baffled that he had actually found it.

My voice echoed off the walls, sounding distorted, as if someone else had spoken, someone a lot older than I. Perseus gave a startled jump backwards, his light flashing more rapidly, and he turned to look at me.

"Took a wild guess," he said in a low voice, but still loud enough for an echo.

I didn't believe that, but didn't see what I could do about it. Perseus walked back over to me and gave me his hand. I stood, my feet sore to stand on, but nothing I couldn't handle.

"So now what?" I asked, rubbing my hands together.

"Now we find the book," he said, walking again to the edge of the platform.

I followed behind Perseus and stood next to him, opposite from where I had been kneeling. As I looked down, I realized that there was a ladder. It didn't look old, and in fact resembled one I could have bought in a supermarket. It was made of metal. One end had two hooks that clung to the edge, while the rest of the ladder slid down parallel to the cavern wall. It didn't reach the river, but instead stopped a few feet above it. The mist swirled below the ladder, but it didn't look very inviting.

So we weren't the first people to discover this cavern. I looked at Perseus, whose eyes were narrowed as he looked down. Had he known that the ladder was there?

He tied his shirt in a knot right above his ribcage, so our light wouldn't extinguish, and began climbing down. Immediately darkness surrounded me, the light becoming dimmer as Perseus went down the ladder. I could feel the moist around me like the cavern was alive and breathing, and the acid-sweet smell seemed to get stronger, clinging to me. I looked up at the hole we had dropped through, which was as dark as the walls of the cavern, and wondered how we would be able to climb back up. This didn't seem to concern Perseus, who was already halfway down.

The ladder looked strong enough to hold us both so I went after him. The metal ladder was cold to my touch, and it trembled slightly as I descended, making me cling tighter to it. As I climbed down, the smell got even stronger, and I felt that my head would float away from the rest of my body at any second. My hands tingled.

Perseus stopped at the very bottom of the ladder, and I realized that there was a hole carved into the side of the platform, which resembled a miniature cave. It was wide enough for at least five people, and two times higher than me. There was only one thing there, a chest. Now it was really starting to feel like a treasure hunt.

Perseus swung himself from the ladder and landed inside the hole. He extended his hand and helped me swing away from the ladder and land next to him.

I realized that his hand was very sweaty, and that the light from his scar was beating faster. I shook my head, trying to clear it, but it felt wobbly, like it had turned to jelly. I walked closer to the chest. It was the only thing there, made of oxidized metal. It reached up to my knees and was three feet wide. The rest of the hole was made out of coarse black rock, which seemed to absorb the light from Perseus's scar.

"I assume you don't have the key," I said in almost a whisper. Perseus shook his head. "No, but you can open it."

He was right about that. I kneeled down, seeing the chest. The metal had once been silver, but now it was rusty red. There had also been Greek letters drawn all over it, but most of them were now blotted or gone. I realized that there wasn't even a keyhole to open it, only a lid. I tried to lift it, but it was stuck.

I closed my eyes, imagining the lid opening with a swing. Immediately I felt my scars tingling and burning, and my heart beating faster, but there was something else too—a hunger inside my chest, as if my own power wasn't enough.

I imagined it again, the lid from the box swinging open and revealing what was inside. When I opened my eyes the lid hadn't opened, and my muscles were already sore with trying. I closed my eyes.

Open, I commanded in my head, but the lid didn't budge. Maybe it was stuck? I had opened more sophisticated safes; this couldn't be more difficult than those.

I shook my head and imagined it again. The oxidized silver lid opening, because not even its ancient power could compete with mine. I could open anything I wanted, and this wouldn't be the exception. I took a deep breath—the silver chest opening, yielding to the power of my mind.

There was a creak, and when I opened my eyes, the lid had already cracked open. Perseus was immediately beside it. He pulled the lid back with a loud squeak and looked inside.

I peeked into the chest too. I was expecting to see an actual book, but there were only withered sheets of paper. There were many of them, maybe a hundred or more, and all of them were of different sizes. The paper was thick, and the edges were irregular, as if a two-year-old had cut them. I didn't recognize the script. It was written with dark-red ink, which made me wonder if it could be blood.

I pushed myself away from the chest and rested against the wall while Perseus leafed through the sheets with excitement.

"I told you we would find the book!" he said excitedly, sifting through the papers with a smile on his face.

I couldn't answer because, just in that moment, a cold chill swept through my back. I clenched my fists.

"Perseus, how did you know I could open locks?" I asked. "I never told you I could do that."

He stopped sifting through the papers abruptly. "I-I guessed you could. When I saw you opening the lock of that door in New York." There were a couple seconds of silence.

"You're a terrible liar," I said.

Perseus carefully set down the papers in the box. "I know."

I didn't even see him pull out the dart gun, only felt a small pinch on my shoulder as if he had squeezed my skin hard.

"Hey!" I said as I jumped to my feet, but even as I did, my head began to spin, feeling like it had been filled with rocks. The smell of the cave became sweeter, like cotton candy.

"Now we're even," Perseus said.

The last thing I saw were his eyes—they were dark with regret.

Chapter XX, Verse I

In the shadows he dwelled until by fire awakened.
Long past are his darkened days, those of old he forgets.
His silent breath to spark into the fury of night.
The enemies that cross his path to ashes they will crumble.
The protector he is of all that is sacred.
But the first treasure will be lost from his grasp,
Into the hands of the fiery-red one.

CHAPTER 14

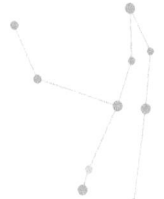

MY EYES slowly fluttered open, heavy, as if they were made of metal. I lay on something hard. The warm sun was high up in the sky, bathing me with light. Tall trees surrounded me on all sides. Birds chirped happily around me, but I couldn't see where they were.

I groggily sat up, resting my back against a tree behind me and wondering what had happened and how I had gotten there. The trees had thick trunks and were tall, creating a canopy above me that nearly covered the entire sky. They were beautiful, a combination of shades of red, orange and yellow. I spotted a few green leaves, but they were scarce among the trees. Underneath me, the soil was dry and cracked, mostly covered in brown leaves.

There was a rustling behind me, and Perseus stepped out from behind the tree I had been resting on, a backpack slung across his left shoulder. His eyes immediately fixed on me, startled.

"Oh, you're awake," he said with relief. I stood up on wobbly legs, fury rising inside me as I began to remember what had happened at Delphi. "Are you hungry?" he asked.

I charged forward, faster than he could move away, and crashed against his chest. He fell on his back with a loud thud, and I landed on top of him. Leaves crunched underneath him, and the backpack fell away, landing a few feet to his right. Perseus's hands immediately grabbed my wrists.

"Stop!" he shouted as I tried to wriggle my hands free.

I leaned forward and bit him hard on his arm. He let out a scream and pushed me backwards. I landed hard on my back, leaves springing up around me. The metallic taste of blood settled on my mouth.

"You shot me with a dart gun!" I said, spitting out his blood.

"So did you!" he spat back. "And I never bit you."

Considering the position of the sun so up in the sky, I realized I had been unconscious for hours. I wondered where Perseus had found the dart gun and tranquilizer darts.

I stood up, every cell in my body sore. I wiped the blood from my mouth, happy to see Perseus holding his forearm in pain. He glowered at me.

"Why would you do that?" I asked.

His eyes went blank for a couple of seconds, and that's when I realized that I had more important questions to ask him.

"You *knew* that cavern was there, and the book hidden inside it. You had been there before," He didn't answer, but I didn't need him to. "You knew I could open locks. Who told you that?"

He opened his mouth to speak, but then closed it again. He let his arms drop to his sides and walked closer to me. I didn't back away, but simply clenched my fists.

"What aren't you telling me?" I asked.

He was a foot in front of me, looking into my eyes. He didn't answer, and instead leaned down and kissed me hard. The taste of blood danced between our lips, but he didn't seem to care, as if he had tasted blood before and liked it. I tried to give a step backwards but he wrapped his arms around me and kissed me again, hard enough to bruise my lips. Then he pulled back. I had a sudden urge to slap him hard across the face, but restrained myself with great effort.

"I was being honest when I said I liked you, and I still do," he said.

"You don't shoot girls you like, you idiot!" I screamed as I pushed him away from me.

My head was spinning, the colored trees blurring around me. I leaned on a tree to my right for support.

Perseus walked back to his fallen backpack a few feet in front of me and opened it. "I'll tell you my truth when you tell me yours."

"What does that even mean?" I asked.

Blood stopped flowing from my heart, and I felt my face go cold. Perseus had pulled a knife from the backpack—my knife. Its white handle was still clean, and the double edge shone with the light from the sun.

"I . . ." My words died on my tongue.

Perseus threw the knife at my feet and looked me straight in the eye. Even though the sun was bright on his face, his eyes were black—I could see the pain inside them.

The sky darkened as a cloud covered the sun, and the forest grew colder. Perseus knew the truth, I realized as I looked into his dark eyes, but he wanted to hear it from me. How had he known? For how long? Had he seen me with the knife the day I took him to my liar?

I let out a deep breath, as if to empty my lungs completely. "I was sent to kill you." The words came out sharp as a stab, but Perseus didn't flinch. He had been expecting that answer. But now that the truth was out, the rest of it was close at its heels. "Zia sent me to kill you," I blurted out. "She said that if I did, I would never have to see her again."

Perseus's eyes were cold as black ice as they narrowed at me. "But you didn't kill me. Why?"

"I-I don't know," I said. "I was planning to, but . . . couldn't. I'm sorry."

An apology didn't seem enough to someone I had been planning to murder, but it was the only thing I could say.

Perseus stared at me for over a minute, and I could feel his gaze like lasers cutting through my skin.

Then his gaze broke away, and he turned away from me. "I *had* been to the cave in Delphi before. I knew the entrance was there because I discovered it a few months ago," he said. He pulled something else out of his backpack. It was another knife, exactly like mine. Perseus didn't look at me, but instead let the knife drop at his feet.

"I knew you would kill me. I was waiting for you to attack me so I could kill you first." He looked up then, our gazes locked. "But then things turned out differently and I thought that taking you to Delphi so you could open the box would be better."

My mind went numb, as if my brain were submerged in ice.

"What?" I asked, rather dumbly.

"I was sent to kill *you*, because I knew you would eventually kill *me*," he said slowly, as if I were a child. That didn't make any sense at all. How could he have known I would kill him? I hadn't even known I had to kill him until a few days ago. And who had sent him?

"Why didn't you kill *me*?" I asked, meeting his gaze with challenge in mine.

Perseus smiled. "You didn't kill me."

"That's not enough," I said.

He shrugged, heat creeping up his cheeks. "I told you, I like you."

That made even less sense. It crossed my mind that Orion had been right. Something had been wrong about Perseus and I hadn't seen it. Before I could regret not having listened to Orion, there was a familiar bark in the woods, one I had heard only once before, in the psychiatric hospital.

The hairs on my neck prickled, and I instinctively clenched my fists. Too many thoughts raced through my head as I looked back at Perseus, trying to find a logical explanation. Before I could think, there was a loud growl behind me, and I didn't need to turn to know that the wolf was standing there, its silver eyes locked on my back.

I had tried so hard to banish that wolf from my memories that hearing it behind me was like stepping into a nightmare.

"Lupus," Perseus said calmly. "Stand down."

I didn't turn to look at the wolf as he passed next to me, his soft fur brushing against my face. My feet were paralyzed like roots planted on the ground. It was indeed the same wolf I had seen at the hospital. No other wolf could have been that tall. It moved to stand next to Perseus. The wolf's hair was several different shades of black and gray, and I tried not to look into his eyes, instead looking into Perseus's.

"You were there," I said, the realization striking me like lightning as I said those words. "You tried to kill us at the psychiatric hospital."

I remembered, before Orion and I had walked into the cafeteria someone had knocked me down and fought Orion. But neither of us was able to see Perseus through the darkness. I shook my head, feeling dizzier than ever and wanting to vomit even though I hadn't eaten anything.

"I knew you would eventually try to kill me," Perseus said. His voice was steady, but I could see his hands trembling slightly.

"How could you know?" I asked. Perseus had tried to kill me before I had been sent to kill him.

Perseus looked back towards his backpack. "It's in the book. The Prophecy says that one of us will kill the other." His eyes met mine, and there was no hint of a joke in them. "*The Princess and Prince to death they shall battle. After three wars one will have triumphed. To ashes and blood one will be slaughtered.*" I felt each of those words like a punch in the gut. Perseus paused, presumably looking at my face for some kind of reaction.

"Zia stole the Prophecies from me," he said. "She read them, and knew you were the only one who could kill me, and that I was the only one who could kill you. So she sent you to do it without telling you the truth."

"WHAT?" I said so loudly that the birds on the trees flew away, rattling the branches. Even the wolf growled in surprise, pulling its lips back into a snarl. "Are you telling me that everything that has happened for the past week is because of some dumb Prophecy?!"

Perseus gave a step back as if I had insulted him, then his eyes narrowed at me. "You still don't believe me, do you?" He took a step closer, eyes wide with anger. "The Star Children, the Prophecies, they're real."

I let that revelation settle in my head. "No," I said.

"What do you mean *no*?" Perseus asked.

"I don't believe in that nonsense," I said, more slowly. I knew that there had to be an explanation to our existence and to all the strange things that had happened. I just didn't believe that stars had created us and that Prophecies were real. That just seemed like a stupid explanation ancient people had made up. But even as I thought of that, I couldn't deny that Perseus might be right.

The wolf gave a low growl, and Perseus just stood blinking at me. Then he shook his head. "Well, it doesn't matter what you believe, we're leaving anyways." He turned around to walk back to his backpack.

"I'm not going anywhere with you," I snarled.

He slowly turned to look at me, his eyes cold again. "I wasn't really asking. We're leaving, and if you're not walking, then Lupus can drag you."

The wolf growled again, baring its huge teeth. I made a determined effort not to look into its eyes. I could feel them. I could have outrun and maybe fought off Perseus, but there was no way I could fight that wolf.

Fury seemed to bleed from every one of my veins as I watched Perseus slinging his backpack on his shoulders.

I gritted my teeth and walked after him.

We had been walking through the forest for hours. I didn't even try to remember the way. After some time, all the trees began to look the same. The wolf walked a few paces behind us, and even though I could barely hear its silent steps I could feel its gaze on me. Perseus always walked close to my side, turning to look at me every now and then. He hadn't tried to talk to me.

My mind seemed to be going a lot faster than my feet, trying to figure out where everything had gone wrong.

Perseus had stolen a couple of pages from Alathea's book, and I wondered if he had actually found them in a museum archive. Then Zia had stolen those pages from him, but even if she had read them, why would she want me to kill Perseus? I didn't think it had much to do with Zia worrying that he would kill me first.

Was it because she believed that I was the only one who could kill him? Was that why she had sent me instead of Orion?

At the same time, Perseus had known that I was the only one who could kill him, so he had tried to kill me at the hospital. But in the end neither of us killed the other. Then Perseus had thought it would be a good idea to take me to Delphi so I could unlock that stupid chest so he could have the rest of his dumb Prophecy book.

And now I was here. Perseus had said someone had sent him to kill me, so that meant there was someone playing him behind the curtains. Someone I assumed I hadn't met yet.

But all of this was considering Zia believed in the Prophecies. I had never heard her speak about them, but clearly she thought they were real. There could be no other explanation. I wondered why she had never said anything about them to Orion and me.

My mind kept going over those thoughts, thinking about how one thing had led to the other. I kept busy with that, because I knew that if I didn't, my emotions would surface. I hadn't let myself feel the hurt and anger from Perseus betraying me. I had trusted him; he had been the only person I had trusted, and it had been a mistake. Zia had been right in one thing—we could never trust anyone else.

For the first time in my life, I wished Orion would find me.

Every now and then I would turn to look at Perseus, who kept his gaze fixed ahead. His red hair was disheveled, and he had made no effort to comb it. I realized that his hair was the same color as the leaves from some of the trees around us. He walked with a light step, but I could see the tension in the muscles of his arms as he tightly gripped the strap of his backpack.

Even if I didn't believe in Prophecies, he did. So that meant that both of us were stuck in a game to see who would fulfill the

Prophecy first. Who would kill the other? I very badly considered making Alathea's words true and hitting him in the forehead with a rock, or stabbing him with a fallen branch, since he had kept my knife. The only problem was the wolf, who would very likely rip me to pieces before I could do it.

After hours of walking, we came into a very small clearing with a narrow stream cutting through the middle of it. The clearing was at least thirty feet wide, but with Perseus and the wolf it felt much smaller than that. I noticed there was almost no grass, only a few patches. The ground was light brown, as if made of rock, and with twigs and small pebbles everywhere.

"We'll wait for her here," he announced.

I didn't know who *her* was and, at the moment, didn't care much.

The wolf went to the other end of the clearing and drank some water from the stream, which was two feet wide at most. I noticed the wolf's tongue was black. Once he was done he jumped to the other side of the stream, crossed the clearing, and walked into the forest. I lost sight of him after a couple of seconds.

I considered escaping again, but knew that the wolf probably wouldn't go so far. And I had nothing to fight Perseus with, not even a rock.

I walked to the stream, kneeling and lowering my hands to cup some water into them. The water was freezing cold, and it numbed my hands as soon as I touched it. I drank it, and felt my body temperature lowering, but I didn't care. I'd rather be cold than dehydrated.

After I was done drinking, I wiped my hands on my jeans and turned to look at Perseus, who pulled two sandwiches from his backpack. He sat down cross-legged a few feet to my left and offered me one.

I shook my head and went to sit to the other side of the clearing, my head still spinning. I sat with my back against a tree, the stream to my right. The ground was hard and uncomfortable, but I didn't care. Perseus came right after me and sat in front of me. He threw a sandwich at my lap.

"I'm not hungry," I said as I threw it back to him. The sandwich landed close to his feet. I was indeed very hungry, and my stomach had been growling for hours. I hadn't eaten anything in a day, but I had survived much longer without food. As long as I had some water I would be alright.

"I had visited the cave several times before. No archaeologist had been able to find it," Perseus said after a couple of silent minutes. I turned away from him, looking at a patch of grass next to me, but he kept talking excitedly. "There is something supernatural about that cave, something that prevents radars and other stuff like that from detecting a cave underneath the ruins." I heard him munching his sandwich. I spotted an ant climbing one of the grass blades. "Although I'm not sure what it is. But I'm sure Alathea must have known there was something different about that cave when she hid the Prophecies there. Maybe only Star Children can find it?" I heard him take another bite. Meanwhile the ant fell from the grass blade and scrambled on the dirt. "The rock I moved yesterday used to be attached to the ground. The first time I went to the cave she moved the rock, somehow ripping it free from the ground. There were also other rocks that—"

"I. Don't. Care," I snapped, looking up at him. "So could you stop talking?"

"Come on," Perseus said, his eyes drooping like a sad owl. "Don't be mad."

"DON'T BE MAD?" I exploded as I stood upright. "You planned to kill me, used me to find a stupid book, shot me with a dart gun, kidnapped me, and you expect me not to be angry?"

Perseus took a bite out of his sandwich. It appeared to be a cheese and ham sandwich. "Just to get things straight," he said calmly with his mouth full. "You were sent to kill me, used me to get out of the country, and shot me with a dart gun."

"I didn't use you to get out of the country," I snapped. "You offered to take me away." Another thought occurred to me. "If you already knew that the book was at Delphi, then why didn't we go get it the first night? Why wait?"

His face flushed the same color as the dying sun. He didn't meet my gaze, looking at his muddy shoes instead. "I wanted to spend more time with you," he said in such a quiet voice that I barely heard him.

Anger swelled inside me. "Because you knew that after finding the book you would have to kidnap me and I would hate you."

Perseus shrugged. "What else do you want me to say? Sorry? You don't even believe the things I tell you."

"Because they make no sense," I said, sitting down again as my eyes seemed to spin inside their sockets. My head had begun to throb again, and I held it in between my hands. The temperature was dropping as the sun lowered, and I hugged myself tight.

"Seriously?" He asked. "You have scars that shine in the dark, you can open any locks with your mind . . ." He turned towards where the wolf had disappeared. "And you met a massive wolf who can paralyze people with its eyes and you still don't believe me?"

I had to admit he had a point. Maybe the problem wasn't that I didn't believe him, but that I didn't *want* to believe him. My beliefs had always been simple—find food, water, shelter, and get away from Zia. That was practically my religion. What Perseus was telling me didn't fit into that.

"Andromeda," Perseus said softly.

"Don't say my name," I hissed.

Perseus swallowed another bite of his sandwich as if it were made of thorns. "Look, yes, I was sent to kill you, but I don't want to."

"Well how nice of you," I said.

He gripped his sandwich harder, as if wanting to crush the life out of it. "You still don't understand, do you?"

"Nope," I admitted, not even wanting to understand.

"The Prophecies that appear in the book tell everything that's going to happen to us. And from leafing through them the future doesn't look very good for any Star Child—especially not for you and me," he said.

I had a few things I wanted to say about those Prophecies, but was interrupted by a sudden movement in the trees. I hadn't noticed that the sun had already fallen below the trees, and that shadows were cast around us. The wolf stepped out of the trees, looking towards Perseus.

Perseus tensed, lowering his sandwich. He stood. "I believe you'll want to have a few words with her."

"With who?" I asked standing up.

She stepped out of the trees behind the wolf, and her eyes immediately settled on me. How had she even gotten here? We were twenty feet apart, at least, but it seemed like she was standing right next to me.

"Hello, Andromeda," Zia said, then gave me a disgusted look as she stared at my head. "What did you do to your hair?"

CHAPTER 15

ZIA SAT in front of me. Her hands and feet were tied together with a length of rope that Perseus had procured from his backpack. He hadn't tied me, knowing that with my abilities I would be able to escape. So I sat with my back against the tree, wrapped tightly in my jacket.

The sky was already dark above us, and some stars had begun twinkling in the sky. The moon was shining bright, almost full.

"How did you get here?" I asked Zia.

She rolled her eyes, as if the answer was obvious. "Perseus kidnapped me a couple of days after I sent you to kill him," she said. I imagined that must have been the day before the incident at the park.

"But how did you get *here*?" I motioned at the forest around us.

She sighed. "I don't know." She pursed her lips. "I fought him in my apartment, that's the last thing I remember. Then, when I woke up, I was here . . . tied to a tree and with that wolf making sure I didn't escape." She looked at me, her eyes bitter. "And now you're here too."

Orion hadn't been able to track Zia, I remembered, as if something had blocked him. Could the wolf be acting as some kind of shield? Orion hadn't been able to track him either. I sighed. Whatever was blocking Orion's ability to track us meant that he would probably not find us anytime soon.

I looked around the clearing. The wolf lay next to the stream, looking at the water rushing by. Perseus had gone inside the forest and hadn't come back for at least ten minutes.

"You should have killed him," Zia hissed at me. "You had one job, to kill that stupid boy. But nooooo. You let him manipulate you!"

Her words felt sharper than any of her lashes, and thinking of lashes I realized that she didn't have her white belt anymore. She looked strangely naked without it. Her black pants and blouse were dirty with mud, which I knew probably bothered her, but muddy clothes were the least of her problems.

"You didn't tell me the truth," I said to her.

Zia's hair was disheveled, and I could see that her arms were covered with bruises. It gave me an odd sense of satisfaction to see she had been hurt.

Zia huffed. "The truth," she muttered. "I'm guessing the boy told you some of it, didn't he?" She bit her upper lip, then added. "What exactly did he tell you?"

I hesitated for only a second, then told Zia everything that I knew. She listened with her eyes closed, and I realized that her left eye was bruised too, and so was her jaw.

When I was done explaining, she simply let out a sigh. "Well," she said as she squirmed in her bonds. "He's right in everything he told you."

"Oh, come on," I said. "You seriously can't believe in all that Prophecy nonsense."

Zia opened her eyes and raised a brow at me. "The Star Children are real, and so are those Prophecies."

"You never told us," I hissed at her. Anger swelled inside me like a fire. "If you believed in all this then why didn't you ever say anything?"

Zia was silent, her eyes closed again, although I knew perfectly well she wasn't sleeping. She looked as if she was trying to meditate. "You should have killed him," she whispered after a few seconds. "That boy will kill us all. He's got the star Algol in his blood."

"The blinking demon?" I asked, bewildered.

The more Zia spoke, the less things made sense. How could he have a demon star in his blood? But something else dawned on me, something Perseus himself had said. That Algol would kill and spill blood. He had been talking about himself the whole time. But what did Algol actually mean?

My head was blazing hot, trying to make sense of everything. It was like trying to make a puzzle without half of the pieces and not knowing what the picture actually was.

"*Beware of the Devil disguised as the savior.*" Zia said. Her eyes were open as she looked at the dark sky above us. "*Blood he will spill, death he will spread. The sky he shall conquer, the earth he shall cleanse. Fear he will command, darkness he will consume. Betrayed by his kin, beloved by his enemy. One he shall slay, one he shall save. The blinking demon will ascend.*"

As soon as she was done speaking, those words settled like a weight in my chest. "That's his Prophecy?" I whispered.

"Only one of them," Zia answered. "Every Star Child has several."

I still refused to believe what she was saying. I didn't want to believe in the Star Children or Prophecies. It made my head spiral like a kite in a storm. I wanted to worry about escaping from Zia, not escaping *with* her. She must have sensed something in me.

"Think, Andromeda," Zia said, looking at me. I realized her features were sagging with fatigue, and she suddenly looked years older, as if she truly were Orion's dying grandmother. "Where do you think the light inside you comes from? Orion and you can materialize intangible thoughts into reality. You're not human, you've always known that, so why is it so hard for you to believe in stars?"

"Because stars are stupid," I blurted out. "They just twinkle in the freaking sky! There's nothing to believe about them!"

Zia's face remained unreadable. "Yes, they are stupid and only twinkle in the sky. But we're not stars, Andromeda, we're their children."

"*We?*" I asked, looking at her.

Zia smiled. "Just because you haven't seen my scars doesn't mean they don't shine."

I only blinked in response. Zia was also a Star Child? Somehow that was harder for me to believe than Star Children in general. I had never seen her do anything out of the ordinary like Orion and I could do. She was strong, fast, and a very good fighter, but asides from that she was pretty normal. But Perseus hadn't been able to materialize anything either, as far as I knew.

Before I could ask Zia anything else, the sky seemed to grow darker, if that was even possible. It was entirely black now, with only the moon shining over us. The stars had vanished, hiding from whatever threat had come upon us. Shadows moved among the trees with a life of their own, and I swore I could hear their whispers.

Perseus stepped out from the line of trees on the other side of the clearing and walked towards Zia and me. She glared at him with fury, but Perseus didn't seem to notice. He was looking at me with that stupid smile on his face.

"She wants to meet you," he said.

"Who does?" I asked.

"Arianna," Zia said in a whisper, as if to not be heard.

"And who is Arianna?" I asked.

"She's darkness," Zia said.

"What?"

"Literally," Perseus explained. "Arianna is darkness."

I couldn't quite imagine what that looked like, but knew I was about to find out. I stood from the ground and followed Perseus to the edge of the clearing.

The wolf was sitting, ears thrown back and his eyes narrowed at the forest beyond us. Perseus stopped a few feet in front of the line of trees, looking uncertainly at them.

"This is Andromeda," he said as he motioned at me, as if I were a pet that he could proudly display.

She came out like a shadow from the dark, a hooded figure of darkness. I felt a sudden pain in my scars, as if they were burning with ice, and my stomach seemed to shrivel, just like my tongue in my mouth. There was a pang in my chest—that strange hunger again. It was like a worm inside me, wriggling its way through my organs.

Her features appeared suddenly as if they had been there all along and there had never been a shadow. The woman's face was so pale it looked almost translucent. Dark lashes rimmed her eyes, which were piercing blue. Her nose was small, and her brows thick. Her lips were thin, set straight as a line as she looked at me. Her hair was black as a raven's and so curly that it spread out of her head like small, twisting snakes.

"Andromeda," she said, her voice sweet and lulling.

She wore a black dress with long sleeves. The woman stepped closer to me and I realized that she was over six feet tall.

"You're Darkness?" I asked skeptically.

Perseus laughed nervously. "She's still trying to process the whole truth. Don't take it personally, Arianna."

Arianna watched me with her light eyes, blinking slowly as if trying to decide how stupid I actually was.

"Hmmm," she said. "So this is the girl who will kill you," she said to Perseus, so matter of fact that it gave me a slight start. "Unless you kill her first."

I turned to look at Perseus. His face was as pale as Arianna's. "I . . ." He trailed off.

Arianna's eyes seemed to shine brighter, like two blue orbs. "But now that we know what the other Prophecies say . . ." Arianna looked at me, and the smile she gave me made my bones shudder. "I think I can find another purpose for her." Her eyes went back to Perseus, who was so stiff that I was sure he had forgotten how to breathe. "Keep her alive."

Then she was gone, just like that, as if she had never been there and I had been staring at a shadow curled on the grass. Perseus let out a breath of what I assumed was relief. He turned to look at me with a shy smile.

"So now what?" I asked.

"Huh?" He asked.

"What happens now, Perseus?" I said, crossing my arms.

He looked up at the dark sky, and I did the same. The stars above us were back, bright and twinkling, but looking at them after everything I had learned that day made me feel dizzy.

"Now we wait," Perseus said. He walked away from me and jumped to the other side of the stream where the wolf was. I didn't know what he was waiting for, but I certainly didn't want to be there when it arrived.

The wolf was staring at me, and it looked ready to lurch in my direction at any time. I gave a sigh of frustration and walked back to Zia. Her eyes were open, staring distractedly at the distance.

"Now you have met Darkness," she said.

"She doesn't look like Darkness," I said to Zia as I sat down. "I mean it, Zia, what's going on?"

She didn't answer, but simply closed her eyes again, resting her head against the trunk of the tree behind her. "Just go to sleep, Andromeda, you're going to need it."

I didn't sleep for a long time, nor even tried to. I wondered if Orion would find us. He wouldn't give up until he did. But if he did find Zia and me, then what would happen? Would he be able to kill the wolf, and what would we do with Perseus? Zia would definitely kill him if she had a chance.

Thinking of Perseus sent shocks of pain through my chest. Why had I been stupid enough to trust him? Because he had seemed so innocent? Or was it because I had thought he was my prey, when all along I had been his. I tried to contain the anger rising inside me, but it seemed impossible.

I was hurt. It was a pain different from the physical one. It was like a bruise inside my heart. It made my throat tighten so much I felt I would choke. The pain made my eyes sting with tears.

I should have just killed him and walked away. I had been better by myself. I always had been. But maybe I had been attracted by the idea of not being alone anymore, of having someone that actually cared about me and wanted nothing in exchange. It had been a trap—having people around me was always a trap. But I did believe that Perseus cared about me, and that drove me mad. Only a monster like him would ever care for me.

There was a sudden rustle next to me that made me open my eyes. I tensed as a blanket was dropped onto me. I hadn't noticed I was cold until I began feeling the warmth of the blanket. Perseus sat beside me. I sat up and clutched it tight around me, glaring at Perseus.

"Sorry," he said. I huffed. "I didn't mean to hurt you."

"No, you only meant to kill me," I said flatly.

His eyes looked straight into my own. "I do care about you, Andromeda."

I couldn't say the same thing to him, so I said nothing instead. He inched closer to me. My muscles were so tired, feeling like they were made of water, that I didn't move away. The heat from his body seemed to flow into my own as he sat next to me. From inside his jacket, he took out the sandwich I had refused to eat earlier and gently placed it next to my feet.

Then he looked up at the stars, his dark eyes wide. My blood froze as a sudden realization struck me.

"Your eyes," I said. I remembered the picture I had seen in Rose's drawer, in her closet in the private plane—the picture that showed young Perseus, Rose and another boy.

"Hmmm?" He asked, looking at me with a brow raised.

"Your eyes were blue," I said, remembering his clear eyes from the picture. They had been bright blue, or maybe gray. I didn't know why I hadn't realized it before.

Perseus didn't seem surprised that I knew his true eye color. "They used to be blue and green."

"What happened?" I asked, now truly curious.

Perseus shifted uncomfortably then rose to his feet after a couple seconds. "I met Arianna." His voice seemed distant, as if he weren't really talking to me. "I took too much from her."

He walked away without another word, crossing the stream again to join the wolf, who seemed wide awake, his nose sniffing the air suspiciously.

I took too much from her. His words seemed to vibrate inside my chest. He had taken too much of what?

My stomach growled in answer and I looked next to my feet at the sandwich, which was covered up with a napkin. I picked it up, unwrapped it, and silently munched it, facing away from Perseus the whole time. I didn't want him to see me eating. The sandwich was made of ham and cheese, which both tasted bland.

After I was done, there was a growing wave of heat inside me. Then I was curling into a ball again, sleep finally overcoming me.

I seemed to come in and out of dreams, but couldn't remember what I had dreamed once I was awake. If it wasn't for the moon moving down across the sky, I wouldn't have been able to tell if I had slept at all.

Then I was suddenly very awake, and I wasn't sure what had awoken me. I lay very still and closed my eyes.

"No," Perseus said quietly. "I can't do that."

"You can," Arianna said in a sweet voice.

There was a moment of tense silence, in which not even the air dared stirred around me.

"There has to be another way," Perseus said. "Please."

Arianna sighed. "I have already explained this, Perseus—fulfilling your Prophecies is the only way to escape them."

"But—" said Perseus.

"Do you want to be free?"

There was a long silence that stretched for a few seconds.

"Yes."

"Then follow your Prophecy," Arianna said. "We have three more nights until the blood moon. So enjoy your time."

Then everything was quiet again. Perseus sniffed hard behind me, and I didn't need to look at him to know he was crying.

Chapter XIII, Verse II

With lashes and threats her leash upon them.
To keep them protected from the force of the ancient.
At midnight the deed done, whispering to the dead.
Vexed by the horned one she will follow,
unable to see his true intentions.
Her buried secrets she will never confess,
not even with the threat of death.
Hidden they will remain until
the Hunter seeks them out of revenge.
Her last dwelling shall provide the truth
for why she abandoned them in youth.

CHAPTER 16

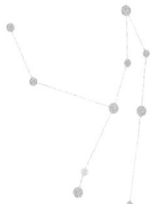

I CRACKED one eye open and looked at the sky. It was covered in clouds, the sun hidden somewhere behind them. I assumed it had to be morning, the birds were chirping happily, contrary to my mood; the air smelled fresh.

After a few minutes lying motionless on the ground, I pushed the quilt away and stood up, my head still heavy with sleep.

"Good morning," said Perseus from across the clearing.

I noticed that his eyes looked red and puffier than normal, and his face was ashen gray. But he was still smiling at me. He started walking closer to me at the same time I took a step back. His smile dropped.

"We're leaving today. I thought you might want to know that tonight you won't be sleeping in the forest," he said.

I didn't answer. Where would he be taking me?

"We'll be leaving in a while longer. I'll go get some breakfast from my backpack so we can eat while we wait," he said. He walked back to the other side of the stream.

I looked around and noticed Zia was awake too, her back against a tree. I still had a few questions I needed to ask her. I walked over and sat cross-legged in front of her. In the daylight, she looked even more beat up, I realized with a smile. Her left cheekbone had a large purple bruise that made her face seem deformed with the swelling. Her eyes were red from lack of sleep, and her wrists bled from having been tied for so long.

"How long have you known?" I asked.

"What?" Zia said, her blue eyes scanning me.

"How long have you known Orion and I were Star Children?" I asked.

"So you *do* believe," she said, amused.

"Answer me," I said in a more menacing tone. Zia's expression hardened. "For once in my life, be honest with me."

She hesitated for a couple of seconds. "I knew since I found you both," she said, shifting in her bonds.

"Is that why you took us?"

Zia eyed me warily, as if not sure of what to say. "Partly, yes. You were both orphans and needed a home. And I knew that having young Star Children around would be useful."

"So that's it?" I spat out. "If we hadn't been Star Children you would have left us on the street?"

"But you *are* Star Children. So it doesn't matter what would have happened if you hadn't been."

"It doesn't matter because either way we ended up being your prisoners and doing all your dirty work!"

Zia sighed. "You helped me, and I helped you. I've always made sure you and Orion have everything you need."

"Except our freedom," I hissed.

"Oh freedom," she said with a laugh. "There is no freedom. We're always prisoners of something—parents, partners, society. But you never truly saw that. What you wanted wasn't freedom, only rebellion, and I wasn't going to stand that."

My blood was hot in my veins, and it surged up to my face.

"You used us!" I growled. Zia couldn't hurt me, not now, and that gave me an overpowering sense of strength. "You never cared about us," I said, raising my voice.

"I did care," she said simply. "Just maybe not in the way you wanted me to."

"No, you didn't care," I said angrily. "You only wanted our abilities." I stood up, fuming with rage as I paced back and forth before her. "You knew Orion would be able to track down any-one, and that I would be able to open locks."

"I didn't know about your ability, that was a surprise. I only knew what the myths spoke of you." She sneered at me. "Andromeda, the princess—beautiful, but useless, chained to a rock until Perseus rescued her." She licked her dry lips. The fury felt hotter in my veins. "Orion however . . . he was the best hunter the world had seen. There was no beast he couldn't track and kill. Some myths say he was a demigod, the most handsome man to live." She smiled mockingly at me. "And he has grown to be just that—the best hunter and handsomest man I've met."

"What does Orion being handsome have to do with anything?"

Zia regarded me with amusement. "I thought you wanted me to be honest with you." I stopped pacing, and felt all my mus-cles stiffen. A mocking smile curled on Zia's lips. "Oh, I'm sorry. Did you really think you were the only girl he had kissed?"

Her words were like a punch in the stomach, knocking all the air out of my lungs. Rage traveled through my veins so hot it chilled my bones. Even if I'd hated Zia with all my guts, she had always been a mother to Orion. I felt I would throw up, turning my stomach inside out. Why hadn't Orion told me anything? Or had he tried to tell me somehow, and I hadn't noticed? Zia had made me bleed many more times than Orion, but somehow this seemed worse. How long ago had it happened? Why had Orion let her? Why hadn't he told me? How had I not noticed? Had she just kissed him or had she gone further than that?

I lunged forward and tackled Zia to the ground. We both fell with a heavy thump next to the tree. Zia struggled underneath me, screaming in rage. She had always been stronger than me, but Zia was no match for the fury inside me.

She had hurt him worse than she had ever hurt me. All my scars were on my back and shoulders, but Orion's scar would always be deep within him—it wouldn't shine, it wouldn't heal. Why would Zia do that? I knew she was a monster, but this was worse than anything I could have imagined her doing.

I couldn't see her fury-red face anymore. I was blind with a black curtain of wrath. She was a distant shape now, and so was I, as if we were both only part of a dream. I couldn't feel her scratches on my arms, nor the pain in my fists.

Two arms wrapped around me and I was pulled backwards. The curtain of rage vanished. I breathed raggedly as I stared at Zia. Blood ran in rivers from her nose. Her face was red from my punches.

"How dare you touch me?" she hissed in fury, spitting out blood.

I tried to lurch forward again, but the arms around me were tight as iron bars.

"HOW COULD YOU?" I roared at Zia.

I was beginning to lose sight again, rage clouding my senses. There was a loud growl next to me that made the anger momentarily fade. The wolf was standing five feet away from us, looking murderously at Zia. It was only then that I became aware that Perseus had been the one holding me back.

I tried to push away from him, but Perseus pulled me around so I could face him. His hands tightened on my waist. Now that I could look clearly into his eyes in broad daylight, I noticed that they were truly black. He was breathing slowly.

He leaned down to kiss me, and I was so surprised that I didn't back away. His lips tasted sour, as if he had drank rotten blood. He broke away.

"I promised," he said in a whisper.

"What?" I asked.

His eyes were set determinately. "I promised I would free you."

He pulled back. I frowned in confusion, unsure of what he meant by that. He stepped away from me and faced Zia, who was glaring at him. That's when I noticed Perseus had a knife in his hand—it was my knife, I instinctively knew it.

The next seconds passed in slow motion. Perseus raised his hand and threw the knife at Zia. It cut silently through the air, then found its mark on Zia's chest, right in her heart. Blood began to spread around the white knife, staining her shirt, dripping. She fell slowly, her eyes fixed on me, as if she had wanted to say something else but knew she never would. Then Zia was on the ground, and her face was slack, her body unmoving.

I wanted to scream, I wanted to run, but I didn't do anything. Zia was dead. Perseus had killed her. My mind didn't seem to accept that fact, and merely let it float around my head as if I would wake up from this terrible dream. I was angry, but with whom? Perseus for having killed Zia? Or Zia for having been with Orion?

Then Perseus was next to me, his hands on my face asking if I was alright. His arms were around my waist holding me. He hadn't even flinched at killing her. How many had he killed?

A loud growl pulled me back to reality. It was cut off abruptly with three loud booms. I turned to look at the wolf. He was lying on his side right next to the stream, twenty feet away from us. The wolf yelped, trying to stand up, and Perseus was immediately at his side.

A hand grabbed my shoulder tightly, and it took me a split second as I turned around to realize it was Orion. He was staring at me with his eyes narrowed, saying something I couldn't understand. He grabbed my arm and pulled me away, and then we were running through the forest. The trees blurred around me. Red, orange, yellow and brown mixed together as if I were running inside a painting. My muscles seemed to act faster than my head, following Orion as we raced away. Perseus shouted somewhere behind us, but I didn't turn.

Orion had surely seen Zia's dead body, and maybe even seen Perseus kill her. How had he found us? I wondered. But there was no time for asking questions. I ran faster than I had run in a very long time, always keeping pace with Orion. I looked at his hand and realized it was empty. I assumed he had shot the wolf with a gun. Had he dropped the weapon? Had he run out of bullets? Would the wolf recover?

The forest blurred faster around me—a small lake to my left with bright-blue water, a wall of dark rock to my right, a steep slope right ahead. We had to slow our pace as we raced down the slope, our feet sliding on the muddy ground. I didn't know where we were going, and I didn't care. My head was beginning to clear, banishing away all thoughts except the one of getting away from the forest, and fast.

My muscles burned like they had begun to melt, and sweat made my shirt cling to my body. Orion didn't seem to be tiring. He would turn to look at me every few seconds, as if to make sure I was still there.

After some time, I heard the beat of wings above us, like a very large bird flying over the trees. The leaves fluttered with a sudden burst of wind. We both looked up, but through the canopy of trees I could see nothing except a blur of white that looked like a very fast-moving cloud.

We kept running, but the beat of wings became louder, almost deafening. There was a horse's snorting, and the sound of branches breaking apart. Orion put a hand on my chest to stop me. At the same time, the canopy of trees broke apart, branches and leaves raining before us. A horse landed ten feet in front of us, thumping loudly and whinnying as he shook away leaves from his shining white mane. Only then did I realize that the horse had wings.

"You've got to be kidding me," I said out loud, making Orion turn to look at me. "Is that a unicorn?"

"It's a Pegasus," Perseus said as he slid from the horse. He had a knife in one of his hands—it was still dripping with Zia's blood.

Orion noticed it too and snarled, his nostrils flaring. I looked again at the horse, not sure if I was delirious or if it was really there. It seemed real enough, looking at us with eyes dark as Perseus's.

"Nice to see you again," Perseus said to Orion, who stood between him and I.

"Leave or I'll kill you," Orion said. I noticed his voice was raspier than normal.

The sun stepped away from the clouds, bathing the forest in light, but I still felt very cold. There was a wall of rocks to our right, marking the base of a mountain, and right ahead of us, through the trees, I could see a distant lake, probably the same one we had passed earlier. Leaves silently fell from the trees, but they seemed to do so in slow motion.

Perseus met Orion's gaze challengingly. "I'll leave if you give her to me," he said, motioning at me.

Orion's amber eyes were bright yellow with the light, looking at Perseus menacingly.

"I can't do that," Orion said.

Perseus held the knife tighter. "Very well then."

With lightning-fast movements, he pulled out a gun from his back and shot thrice. Orion tackled me to the ground a second after I felt a small pinch in my arm. Orion and I rolled over the dead leaves then were back on our feet again.

"Dart gun," I said as I pulled the tranquilizing dart out. I was getting tired of those things, but I guessed it was better than being shot with a real gun.

Orion had been shot too. I could see two small darts on his back. But his eyes were still bright and alert.

"Go!" he shouted at me.

"I'm not leaving without—"

He pushed me away and I nearly stumbled down. "Go, I'll catch up!" He roared.

Then he leaped towards Perseus. The horse gave a startled jump back, flapping its wings like a chicken. Orion and Perseus fell to the ground in a tangle of limbs, and I didn't have time to see anything else because I was already running away.

My mind kept screaming at me to go back and help Orion, but my survival instincts were faster, making me run through the forest with a rush of adrenaline. Maybe that's what kept me awake for a while longer, the adrenaline running through me.

But after a couple minutes, spots began to swirl in my vision, and my legs felt like they had turned to rubber. My hands were already numb, and so were my feet, but they were still moving, stumbling over tree roots and rocks.

The spots in my vision blinded me completely, and then I couldn't tell if I was moving or not.

●———●———●

"Let's take her," a man said above me.

I couldn't open my eyes, or even move a single muscle.

"Are you sure?" a woman asked shyly.

Someone nudged my leg with a foot.

"We're going to need her," said the male voice with a sigh. "Pick her up."

●———●———●

The rage flowing inside my veins was hot as lava. I could feel it traveling through me with every thumping beat of my heart. Every second that I looked at Orion, the anger seemed to swell more, as if my veins were about to burst.

Orion lay face-down on his bed, his breaths ragged. The bandages on his back were wet with dark blood. The bed was already bloodied too, the once-clean sheets now smeared with dry blood as if a canvas with sharp brushes of paint. Orion's sleeping face was turned towards me. I brushed his dark hair off of his sweaty forehead. His mouth twitched, but he didn't wake up.

This is my fault, I thought. Zia had punished Orion because of me. It had been my idea to escape, not his. Zia had known that. She had also known that punishing Orion would hurt me more than anything she could do to me.

A tear slid from my eye. Orion would hate me because of this. He had tried to convince me not to leave. He would hate me. I tried to swallow the knot in my throat, but it felt like trying to swallow a hot coal.

We had no other choice, *I thought. We* needed *to escape. How much longer would we last with Zia until she broke us completely?*

I hate her, *I thought.* I hate her so much. *Zia had changed. She hadn't been like this before. In the last couple of years, she had become more violent, more aggressive, more demanding of us. She didn't see us as people—much less teenagers—only as objects she could use as she pleased. And when we resisted, we got a lash on our back. The hatred inside me gnawed at my heart and chest. Zia didn't care about us. I wondered if she ever had, or if it had all just been an act. I tried to remember the times when we had actually been happy living with Zia, but those memories had faded away from my mind, replaced with the scars she had left behind.*

I leaned back on the wooden chair I had placed next to Orion's bed. The shutters on the left side of the small room were closed, and outside the street was quiet—as it always was. But a fragment of silver light penetrated through the top right of the window, where the shutter was broken. The shard of light rested on the floor next to me as an elongated triangle.

The walls of the room were white and bare, and so was the ceiling, which only had a single circular light. The nightstand on the other side of Orion's bed had a notebook, a knife, and an old book—the cover so withered that I couldn't even make out the title of the novel. Those were Orion's only possessions.

I clenched my fists as I looked back at Orion's sweaty face. He had been unconscious for hours. I had stayed with him, disinfecting and bandaging his wounds as the last rays of the orange sun had sunk under the horizon and the shy light of the moon had begun to creep out.

Another tear fell from my eye, sliding down my cheek.

Zia was out of control, and someday she would end up killing us. We couldn't stay here anymore. That's what had finally convinced Orion to leave. He knew what Zia was—what she had turned into—even though he didn't want to admit it. Why was it so hard for him to see who she really was? His eyes were wide open but he wasn't looking.

We need to escape, I thought for the thousand time. But last night Zia had made it clear that there was no escape from her, and if we tried she would make us bleed for it. She shouldn't have known how to track us down; we had a head start of four hours and had changed cars twice. She didn't have Orion's power, so she couldn't have been able to tell our exact location. But she had. Zia had known exactly where to find us. If we escaped, she would search for us until the ends of the earth and she wouldn't stop until she found us.

There was no escape from her.

I took a deep breath, feeling my beating heart. My pulse throbbed through my whole body, and I could feel it in my fingers and toes.

There was no escape unless . . .

My gaze slid to the knife on top of Orion's nightstand. My fingers tingled as if fire ants were racing through them. She'll end up killing us someday, I told myself, knowing that it was most likely true. She'll break us until we're ground to dust.

I stood from the chair. My steps were silent as I walked around Orion's bed, towards his nightstand. The knife stared up at me. My hand reached down and picked it up—it was cold to the touch, very cold, as if I were holding ice. I gripped it tighter. I gripped it until the cold disappeared, replaced by a heat that seared my hand.

"Don't." I startled and looked down at Orion. His eyes were wide open, his dry lips parted as if he wanted to say more but couldn't bring himself to do it.

"She'll break us, Orion," I whispered. "She'll beat us until we die."

Orion sighed, but it sounded more like a whimper. "She didn't mean to hurt me," he said, then after a pause added, "We should never have tried to leave."

The heat inside me turned to frost, and my hand numbed until I couldn't feel the knife in my grip anymore.

"Look at you," I whispered, my voice strangely even and devoid of emotion. "You can't even stand up. What happens next time she gets angry? Zia said she would hurt us both worse than this. She's sick, Orion. She's become a monster."

He opened his mouth to speak, but no words came out. *Why can't you see it? I asked him inside my mind. Why was he so afraid of her? Orion was taller, faster, stronger and a better fighter—she had trained him for that. He could have beaten her in a fight, he could have defended himself when she beat him. So why didn't he?*

I was missing something. Orion met my eyes, and I saw it starkly. She broke him.

I could see it, pieces scattered everywhere, smashed well beyond repair. What had she done to him? This wasn't just the beatings—It was something else entirely. I could see it so clearly inside his eyes, but at the same time the truth was just beyond my reach. What did she do to you? *I asked him inside of my mind, as if he could hear my thoughts. I wished he could. I wanted Orion to see himself through my eyes, to notice how damaged he was.*

I searched his face for an answer, but he didn't give anything away. I scoured my memories, thinking of anything I could have missed. And it was there—Orion shrinking away from Zia, giving her short responses, not meeting her eyes, trying to avoid being left alone with her and instead sticking to my side.

What did she do to you? *I wondered again. Orion pressed his chapped lips together, as if he knew what I was thinking. We knew each other so well that he probably did.*

"Please don't do this," he whispered. "She does care about us."

Fury took over me.

My memories of walking out of his room are lost. The next thing I knew, I was standing in the living room. The room was blurred around me, my eyes fixed on Zia as she lay face-up on the couch, everything else just shadows in the background.

Her chest heaved slowly every time she breathed. The right side of her face was illuminated with the light of the moon that filtered through the window, but the left side was left in darkness. It made me feel as if I was looking at two Zias. The one illuminated by silver light was the Zia I had known before, her features relaxed, soft, light. The other side was rigid with shadows under her eyes and cheeks, dark just as her gaze was every time she looked at us.

I walked forward silently. Then I was right next to Zia, standing over her with the knife tight in my hand. She didn't stir. Her right sleeve had a red stain—Orion's blood.

I held the knife high.

Zia opened her eyes.

I was flying backwards before I realized that she had kicked me, the air knocked so hard out of my lungs that I couldn't breathe. I crashed on the floor with my back, a spasm of pain running through my bones like an earthquake. The knife was out of my hand, and I couldn't see where it was. I couldn't see anything except the yellow and black spots twitching in my eyes.

Then I felt the sharp pain on my jaw, as if a hammer had hit me. I yelled out, but that made my jaw feel like it had cracked apart. The spots were gone, and I was staring at the dark wooden floor. Zia was screaming at me, but I only heard her words in fragments. ". . . Dare you! . . . to me! . . . should have! . . . harder! . . . bitch!"

I didn't feel the first lash, or the first kick or punch. It all mixed together in a mosaic of pain. Ripples of fire and ice went through me. I could feel my skin tearing, my muscles contracting and my bones cracking. I was being ripped apart, piece by piece. The agonizing pain was so much that at some point my body just stopped feeling, as if my pain receptors had turned off. I wondered if she would kill me, or if I was already dead and that's why I couldn't feel anymore. I didn't hear Zia's screams, nor my own. I could only hear my heart—it galloped as wildly as a horse trying to escape a forest fire. It felt suddenly very heavy in my chest, as if it just wanted to drop all the way to my stomach and lay there.

Eternity stretched around me. Then it abruptly ended.

I still couldn't feel the pain, but I could feel my breaths. They were ragged, my throat so raw I was sure if I spat only blood would come out.

I lay on my back, staring at the bare ceiling that was illuminated by a timid golden light. Was it morning already? How long had Zia been beating me?

The pain struck me like a spear through the chest, so sharp I almost passed out. I was suddenly aware of every inch in my body. I could feel my lungs, shriveled and sore; my intestines, squirming like wounded worms; my brain, pulsing at the same time as my heart, wanting to break free from my skull. My skin felt like it had been flayed completely, and my bones so heavy I couldn't move them. There was a warm liquid that spread around my head, back and legs. Was it blood or pee? I wondered. Or both?

Zia's whispers were suddenly right next to my ear. I hadn't even noticed she had kneeled. "You are mine," she hissed like a snake. "You belong to me until the day you die. You can't escape, and you can't kill me." I couldn't see her face, didn't want to see her face. She pulled a strand of hair that I didn't notice had been across my forehead. "You may hate me, but he loves me. He won't dare escape again, I'll make sure of it. He's mine, and I won't let you take him from me."

Zia stood again, and her footsteps echoed down the hallway. I stayed on the floor for what seemed like hours and seconds at the same time. I fell in and out of a fevered sleep with no dreams. I could taste the blood in my mouth—metallic and salty. I could feel the blood on my back, first warm, then cold as frozen water, then like a crust that hardened on my skin.

At some point, the room began to grow dark again, the golden light replaced by the silver one. I shivered. My bones and muscles were frozen, and I couldn't command them to move.

There were footsteps somewhere behind me. They stopped for a few seconds, then continued. I tried to move, but could only manage to uncurl my clenched hands. My fingers were stiff.

I heard a sigh. Orion kneeled next to me. I could feel the warmth from his body even before he gently touched my arm.

Orion groaned with effort as pulled me into his arms as if I were a baby. I was in so much pain that I couldn't even tell where it was coming from—it seemed to emanate from every single cell in my body. My head was heavy, and I struggled not to let it roll to the side.

I was expecting Orion to scold me for being so stupid, to tell me that I shouldn't have done that. He would say that he hated me, that he had been beaten because of me, that it was all my fault.

He remained quiet, staring into my eyes. His face leaned closer to mine, and I felt his warm lips press softly against my forehead. He pulled away and looked again into my eyes. His gaze was the same one I'd had the night before as I stared at him. He saw me as clear as I had seen him.

I was already broken.

CHAPTER 17

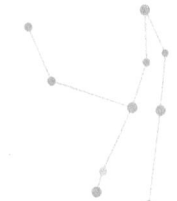

I COULD feel the sun's rays heating my skin. The heartbeat was loud in my ears, rhythmic as the air blew silently around me. It took a couple seconds to realize that the sound was not my beating heart but someone else's. I opened my eyes and noticed that my head was resting against someone's chest—I was being carried away.

I jerked completely awake and heard a startled cry. The grip around me loosened and I fell flat on my face. I grunted, looking at my surroundings. To my right were thin trees stretching as far as I could see, and to my left was a large, lazy river. Its water was bright blue and green, sparkling with the light from the sun. On the other side of the river were mountains covered with more trees.

I stood on wobbly legs, staring at the three people standing before me.

"Not you again," I said with dismay.

"Afraid so," said Corvus.

He still had that ridiculous stubble that couldn't be called a beard, making him look a few years older than me. His bitter dark eyes were staring at me curiously. His cocoa skin seemed more tanned than last time I had seen him, as if he had been standing in the sun for a week.

On his left was the girl I had seen at the park, and now that I was looking at her up close, she truly seemed too thin. I wondered if she was anorexic, or if she had been starved to death. Her skin clung to her bones, and her arms and legs looked like they were about to snap in half like feeble twigs. Her eyes were a warm color of brown, and she had freckles splashed across her cheeks. Her jaw was bruised, and I remembered I had kicked her while we were at the park.

Standing on Corvus's other side was the blond boy with sunglasses. I shivered when I remembered that he had weird reptile eyes. I noticed he was taller than all of us, and looked stronger too, so he had very likely been the one carrying me.

They were all wearing thick coats and carried backpacks, as if they had been camping here. I wondered how they had found me again, but realized that it wasn't the most important question.

"What do you want now?" I demanded.

Corvus huffed. "We find you unconscious on the woods, scraped and bruised, so we decide to help you and now we're supposed to want something?"

"Then why did you help me?" I asked.

The blond boy shrugged. "We help our own."

"Our own what?" I asked.

The three of them looked at each other, a conversation passing in between their eyes. I didn't have time for their games.

"Did you see anyone else in the forest?" I asked.

Corvus seemed surprised at my question. "Well, as a matter of fact we did see your boyfriend with—"

"He's not my boyfriend!!" I bellowed, so loud that the three of them gave a startled jump back. "And if I ever see Perseus again, I'll stick a knife through his ribs."

The girl gulped hard and took a step closer to Corvus as if to avoid the same fate as Perseus.

"Alright then," Corvus said with a smile. "Looks like we're on the same side."

The blond boy looked back over his shoulder. "We should get moving."

Corvus took my arm gently and we started walking at the edge of the river. The trees shaded us from the sun, but the light that reflected on the lake shone on my face. I noticed Corvus was limping a little, and I remembered that I had stabbed him in the leg while we were at the terrorist attack in New York. I felt suddenly very guilty about it.

"Why did you want to kill him?" I asked Corvus.

"So he doesn't kill us first," he answered simply. "And last time I saw you, you were trying to save him. So what changed?"

I wasn't sure I was ready to answer that question. "Why would he kill you first?" I asked.

"Oh," said Corvus. "I forgot you probably don't know about the Prophecies."

"Seriously?!" I asked, forcing them to stop again. "You believe in that too?"

"You don't?" asked the girl, tucking a strand of hair behind her ears.

The water next to us rippled with a sudden gust of wind, and, despite the sun, I shivered inside my jacket, which I was glad I still had.

"Why should I?" I asked.

Corvus pursed his lips as if not to explode with laughter. He turned to look at the other boy and nodded. The blond guy removed his sunglasses, revealing those disturbing red-reptile eyes.

Now that I was able to look at them more closely, I realized they were red and orange instead of just red. The vertical slit in them narrowed into a line.

"I don't believe we introduced ourselves," said Reptile Boy. "I'm Draco."

"I'm Virgo," said the girl.

"What is this?" I asked. "The Terrible Names cult?"

Corvus shrugged. "If you want to call it that, then yes. Welcome to the Star Clan."

I shut my eyes for a moment and took three deep breaths, then opened them again, finding the three staring at me curiously. "You're Star Children?"

"What else would we be?" Corvus asked. "Now let's keep moving before your ex catches up to us."

He took my arm again and we started walking. It seemed like I was living inside a dream. But I knew I wasn't. I had been trying so hard not to accept the truth, but it seemed to be crashing with me like an inevitable wave.

Pebbles crunched under our feet as we continued forward. My legs felt like they were going to dissolve to mist.

"Whoa," said Draco, pulling me to him so I could lean for support. "She doesn't look alright, Corvus."

"Of course she's not," Virgo said. "We need to sit down to rest a little bit."

Corvus looked around suspiciously. "Not until we meet up with Leo. I don't feel safe out here." He waved a dismissive hand at me. "Just carry her."

Without further argument, Draco hauled me up into his arms before I could collapse. I groaned, but didn't complain.

"So it's real," I said after a few seconds. "The Star Children."

"Yup," Corvus said as we continued our trek.

My head was pulsing, throbbing with pain as if my brain were bleeding, which I really hoped it was not. I groaned again and shut my eyes.

Corvus turned right to lead us deeper into the forest, leaving the lake behind us. *What had happened to Orion?* I wondered. He hadn't found me yet. That could mean that . . .

"I have to find him," I blurted out, trying to escape Draco's grasp. His arms wrapped tighter around me, and I tried to wriggle away from him.

"Find who?" Corvus asked. "Perseus?"

"No!" I shouted. The last thing I wanted to do was see Perseus again. "I need to find Orion."

"The tall guy with black hair right, and those creepy yellow eyes?" Corvus said as he scratched his beard.

"Yes!" I said, finally succeeding in standing again. Draco held my upper arm in case I fell.

"That's Orion?" Virgo asked with wide eyes. She turned to Corvus. "I told you someone that handsome had to be Orion!" Corvus grimaced in distaste.

"Did you see him?" I asked. Corvus exchanged a glance with Draco. "Did you see him?!"

"He's alive," Virgo said. "But Perseus got him."

"What?" I asked. How could that happen? Orion never lost a fight.

"The wolf was there," Draco said. "I'm not sure he was able to escape. But Virgo's right. He's alive, and will continue being alive for a while longer, so don't worry about him."

"Why would Perseus keep him alive?" I asked. I also wondered how they had seen Perseus without being spotted, but didn't consider it important enough to ask.

"Orion's the only bait he has," Draco said.

"Bait for what?" I asked.

"Humph!" Corvus said. "You really don't know what's going on."

All the questions and empty answers in my head seemed to vanish at once. "I don't," I said simply.

"What *do* you know?" Draco asked, rubbing his head.

I hadn't even noticed, but we had started moving again, our feet stepping over patches of grass and gray rock.

I took a deep breath. I didn't see the harm in telling them what I knew.

So I told them everything since my escape from the psychiatric hospital, and how things had spiraled on from there. They never interrupted me, although Corvus seemed to want to do so, but always shut his mouth at Virgo's glares. It was only when I told them about the chest we found in Delphi that Corvus exploded.

"You found the book?!" He asked. "And you let Perseus take it?"

I didn't know why he was so mad. They sky was pink above us, sunset approaching. I had been unconscious for a long time. I wondered where Perseus had gotten the tranquilizing darts. Had he stolen them from the zoo too? Or had his rich father bought him a dart gun? Was he even Andrew Wood's adopted son? He hadn't talked to his parents since the night we had spent at Delphi.

The air blew harsher, tearing more colored leaves from the trees.

"It's not her fault," Virgo said.

"It is!" Corvus cried. "She let him take the book!" He muttered something incomprehensible under his breath, then walked away from us, not looking back. "I'm going to find Leo. You stay here and make camp."

He walked up a curving path to our right that led further up the mountain. Then he disappeared after a few seconds behind a cluster of trees.

"I'm guessing that Perseus having the book is bad news?" I asked.

Virgo sighed and unslung her backpack, then sat on a broken log. Draco left his backpack next to her and sat cross-legged on the ground.

"Sit," he said, motioning me down next to them. "It's time you know the truth."

Chapter XVI, Verse I

The weaving one her loops she counts.
From the three Wise Ones her knowledge comes.
Hands tainted with the blood of those she killed.
Consumed by her power, which she has used in excess.
A memory she will grasp, one that will lead to her survival.
The Three Sisters in compassion shall take her from the grave.
Her near death shall announce the arrival of the Prince,
Who will awaken when he hears the wailing of her screams.

CHAPTER 18

"ALRIGHT then, I think we should start explaining from the beginning," Virgo said. I sat on the ground, which was covered with a blanket of fallen leaves. The light in the forest was almost gone, only dark-red rays from the sun illuminating our surroundings. I shifted uncomfortably, not feeling quite ready to know the full truth. "There are three aspects of the Universe that you should know about—Destiny, Fate and Prophecy."

"Okay," I said. That seemed easy enough to remember.

"Destiny is unalterable—the outcome that you will arrive at one way or another." Virgo said slowly, as if explaining to a child. "Fate is a predetermined set of events that take you to your Destiny. That means that different Fates can get you to the same Destiny." She paused, and I nodded. "But Fate cannot alter Destiny—that's important to remember."

"Look at it as if it were a map," Draco said. Looking into his eyes was distracting, as if I were talking to a big serpent. "There are many roads that could take you to, say, Paris. So Paris is your Destiny, and the different roads to get there are your Fates."

"That sounds a bit boring," I said. "I mean, if there's Fate and Destiny then there's no free will, right? And if all of our lives are programmed to turn out a certain way, then what's the point in living them?"

"There is no free will," Draco admitted. "But people don't know that."

"Not having Fate and Destiny would make the Universe erupt in chaos," said Virgo.

"Why?" I asked. "What's wrong with choosing how to live our lives?"

"It would be like traveling the world without a map or any idea of where you're going. Everyone would get lost," Draco said. "Fate and Destiny guide all creatures."

"It still sounds boring," I said.

Virgo rolled her eyes. "Getting lost would be the least of our troubles. If there is no Destiny then the Stars could die, and if they die Darkness would take over, and if that happens, we're all dead. There can only be life if there's light. It's that simple." She took a deep breath. "Let's continue. The Stars are the ones that control the Destiny of every creature in the Universe. Then there are the Weavers . . ." I noticed she tensed, her fists clenching. "The Weavers give Fates to each person so they can arrive at their Destinies. Each person is given a certain number of Fates when they are born."

"Who are the Weavers?" I asked, curious about their strange name.

Virgo paled a shade, and Draco shot me a warning glance.

"They live at the bottom of the Three Wells at the end of Eridanus," Draco said, and before I could ask what all that meant, he continued. "They decree Fates, and they are also the ones that channel the energy of our thoughts into actions."

"What does that even mean?" I asked.

"You said you could open locks just by thinking about them, right?" Draco asked.

I nodded.

"All of us can do that. I mean, not open locks. But we do different things."

"We call it materializing," Virgo said. "Because we materialize intangible thoughts into physical actions."

I knew that was true because I had been doing it most of my life. Orion could do it too. He just thought of someone or something, and then he knew exactly where that person or object was.

"The Weavers are the ones that transform the energy of our intangible thoughts into physical actions." Draco said. "They do the same thing with Stars. Whatever Destiny Stars choose for each person, the Weavers materialize that energy through the Fates they give."

"Okay . . ." I said, trying to keep up with the explanation.

"Then there's Prophecy," Virgo said. She scratched her cheek and looked down at the ground, as if trying to find the easiest way to explain. "We Star Children are different than other creatures." She finally said. "We don't have Destiny or Fate, but something in between."

"How can we have something in between?" I asked.

"We're made out of Star stuff," Draco said. "We believe that the Stars made us just by thinking about it. We don't have any parents, or family. We're literally a thought materialized into life." He stood up, as if too restless to be sitting down. "Stars can't give Destinies to other Stars, and that includes us."

"So we have Fates?" I asked, not wanting to think about the implications of a Star having created me out of its pure thoughts.

"No," Virgo said. "Since the Stars didn't give us a Destiny, that energy, then the Weavers can't give us Fates."

"So we call it Prophecy," Draco said. His eyes were fixed on the sky above us. "Because of Alathea's Prophecies. We have a set of predetermined events that will happen in our lives, like Fate."

He paused, looking at me again. "So I guess it would be like having two or three different Destinies that we can choose from."

They were then silent for a couple of seconds, letting the information sink into my brain. Only one thought crossed through my head.

"Perseus and I," I said. "One of us will kill the other. Perseus said that he had read that from the Prophecies."

Draco and Virgo exchanged an alarmed glance. Even though I had told them earlier that Perseus and I had been sent to kill each other, I might have forgotten to tell them that it was in the Prophecies.

"Are you sure?" Virgo asked.

"Yes," I said. "He read it from the Prophecies he found first. The ones Zia stole from him."

The thought of Zia made my head go numb as I recalled her death. I shook my head, trying to drive away that memory. I had more important things to think about. My hands began to shake, and I clenched them into fists so the others wouldn't notice.

"Are you sure?" Draco asked again. "We stole those Prophecies from Cassiopeia, I mean Zia," he said quietly. "And she didn't have one that mentioned you and Perseus killing each other."

"Cassiopeia could have destroyed that Prophecy," Virgo said. "I think it's true, Draco, even if we didn't read the Prophecy."

Draco's lips pressed into a line for a moment. "So you see, your Prophecy is either you kill Perseus or he kills you, and you can decide which one happens."

"I think I'll choose to kill him," I said.

"Smart choice," Draco said.

"So this leads us to why the book is important," Virgo said. "Perseus now knows about each of our Prophecies. So he can use them to manipulate us all into getting to the outcome that he wants."

"Like killing you," Draco said, not meeting my gaze. "And probably finding a way to kill the rest of us."

I closed my eyes, burying my face in my hands. Now I understood why Corvus had been so hysterical that Perseus had the book. Perseus had the future in his hands, literally, and he could control it in any way he wished. I wondered what kind of Prophecies the others had.

"Is there another way to know of our Prophecies?" I asked. "Does Perseus have the complete book of Alathea? Or are there other sheets of it still lost?"

Maybe we could find other sheets of the book in museums, like Perseus had first done. Had he even found those sheets in a museum? Or had that been a lie too? I looked up at Virgo and Draco.

"Perseus only has one part of the book," Virgo said.

"So there are other parts?" I asked, hopeful.

Virgo shifted uncomfortably on the log. "The book is divided into three parts." She explained. "The first part explains how the universe came to be, how the Stars were formed, the primordial wars that were fought and all of that." I didn't really know what she meant by "primordial wars", but didn't want to interrupt. "The second part has the Prophecies of each Star Child. That's what you and Perseus found at Delphi. The sheets that Cassiopeia stole from Perseus are also of the second part."

"And the last part?" I asked.

"No one knows." Draco said with a shrug. "The first and third part of the book haven't been found yet."

"So Perseus has the most important part of the book," I said. If he really had every single Prophecy of every Star Child then he was more dangerous than he had been before.

Virgo nodded solemnly. Draco began to walk around us, picking up twigs and piling them up a few feet to my right.

My mind raced with thoughts, all of them trying to make sense of what Virgo and Draco had just told me. I felt more confused than I had been before, and new questions arose.

"How do we exist?" I finally asked after a couple minutes. Virgo dangled her legs on the log, and once again I was amazed by how thin she was. I was compelled to buy her a hamburger. "I get it, the Stars made us, and the Weavers materialized us." At the mention of the Weavers, Virgo flinched. "But did different Stars make each of us? How many of us are there?"

Draco carried a large log towards us, the fallen leaves crunching as he stepped on them.

"Oh," Virgo said, as if remembering that she hadn't explained that yet. "The Stars are divided in the sky, much as our planet is divided into countries."

"How are they divided?" I asked.

"Constellations," Draco said as he dropped the log onto the pile. "There are forty-eight of them in total. Or at least forty-eight *real* Constellations, because later on people invented more of them that really don't mean anything. So that means that there are only forty-eight Star Children in the world." He kneeled in front of the pile of wood and began arranging it into a pyramid. "We really don't know much about the Constellations, only that they all control different Destinies."

"Huh," I said, pensive.

"For example, Andromeda," Draco said, bringing my attention back to him. "Your Constellation represents the myth of a princess chained to rocks to be sacrificed to a monster. So the Stars in your Constellation control imprisonment, sacrifice, and escape."

"Really?" I asked. I found that ironic, considering I had been Zia's prisoner my whole life.

Virgo nodded. "So all the people that go to jail or escape from it are controlled by your Constellation."

"So are the myths themselves true?" I asked. I didn't know much about mythology, but was familiar with some of the Greek myths and gods.

Draco shook his head. "No, as far as we know myths were just a way to explain how each of the Constellations worked. A way for people here to understand the star maps they saw in the sky—how Destiny and Fate worked."

Virgo rubbed her hands together. "We don't have the full power that each of our Constellations control, only a small fragment of it. For example, you can't materialize sending people to jail or freeing them, but you can open locks."

"Some Constellations are more powerful than others, and a few of them have what astrologers call the Behenian Stars," Draco said. "They are the most powerful Stars in the sky, and their power can be independent from the Constellation."

"Independent from the Constellation how?" I asked.

"Like Perseus and Algol," Virgo said. I felt my stomach twisting at the mention of Algol. "In mythology, Perseus is just a demigod. He cut off Medusa's head and saved Andromeda." She paused, looking at the growing pyramid of twigs and logs Draco had made. "We honestly don't know what Perseus can materialize, or what he *should* be able to materialize, because we have never seen him do it. But since he has Algol in his Constellation, he can draw power from that star."

"What does Algol do?" I asked, already dreading the answer.

"It's the most unfortunate star in the sky," Corvus said behind me. I startled. I turned to see him standing next to a tree five feet away. He crossed his arms. Corvus's gaze was bitter, I imagined still resentful for having let Perseus steal the book. "Algol controls war, massacres, terrorist attacks, mob violence, death by hanging, beheading, electrocution."

"Algol is part of Perseus, as much as his heart is part of his body, and he can use the power of the Star whenever he wants," Draco said. He brushed away the leaves that crowded around his pyramid of logs. "But Algol has existed long before that, creating the worst attacks in humankind."

"What attacks?" I asked.

"St. Bartholomew's massacre in France, where thousands died," Virgo said. Her gaze was fixed on her muddy boots. "It caused the Holocaust when all the Jews were sent to be exterminated, the French revolution, where all those people were beheaded, the massacres in Rwanda where millions were killed, the attack on Pearl Harbor in the United States . . ."

"And the list goes on," Draco said solemnly.

Knowing that a single Star could do so much harm made my stomach shrivel.

"Algol has been feared by all civilizations since the beginning of times. It was depicted by ancient astrologers as piled-up corpses," Corvus said. "If you trace its movements across the sky, you'll realize that it's linked to all the disasters Virgo has mentioned, and likely more murders than we can count."

I wondered how they traced the star, and thought that maybe it had to do with astronomy or astrology, but at the moment it didn't really matter. I was beginning to finally understand what made Perseus so dangerous.

"So if Perseus has Algol . . ." I prompted.

"He can use it at his will," Draco said, having finished his pyramid. "Like the terrorist attack in New York." His red eyes met mine. "The one we were in."

"But . . . " I said, finding myself at a loss of words. "How is he able to do that?" I thought again of the massive destruction I had seen—the buildings, all the dead. "I thought we could only control a fraction of our Constellation's true power."

"That's what we thought too," Virgo said, crossing her arms. "But Perseus can materialize to a much bigger scale than the rest of us. He shouldn't be able to do that, not even with Algol."

Corvus nodded. "Normally, he should be able to cause one car accident, or maybe one death by electrocution, but not all those attacks, not all those deaths." He shook his head. "He's way more powerful than he should be."

Virgo pulled out a tablet from her backpack and motioned me to sit on the log next to her. I immediately stood and sat at her side. The log shifted underneath us. I wondered how she had Internet in the middle of the forest. Virgo was flipping through a news channel, where the headlines were all of terrorist attacks.

"Algol makes people go into some kind of killing frenzy," Virgo said.

"The word alcohol was named after Algol," Corvus explained, and before I could ask what that had to do with anything, he continued, "That means Algol makes people go drunk with blood, maddened and full of hunger for killing."

I looked back at Virgo's tablet, watching the headlines. There were dozens of them, all from attacks that had happened during the last year. One of the headlines caught my attention—a group of men in France shooting dozens of civilians in a plaza, then setting off their explosive vests in a suicide bombing. I had seen the news while I was in the psychiatric hospital.

The hospital.

Perseus had been there when the patients had begun to kill each other in that mad frenzy. I suddenly felt very dizzy, like the log was spinning in circles underneath me. Perseus had done that. He had killed all the patients. He had killed all those people in New York, and he had been responsible for countless other deaths.

His big dark eyes and smile appeared inside my head, the way his face turned red whenever he felt embarrassed. How he had seemed so passionate about history, and so curious about it. I could hear his laugh in my ears, feel his warm lips on mine. I wanted to puke. How could he have killed all those people? Had he felt any remorse?

I remembered when he had woken up at the hotel, screaming. I'd thought that he had been traumatized by the attack. But I was wrong. Had he caused the attack on purpose, or was Algol out of his control?

As Virgo scrolled through pictures of the attacks, one of them caught my attention—the symbol drawn in blood. Those lines and little circles made me go dizzier.

"That's Algol's symbol," Virgo said, her eyes trained on the screen. "It always appears drawn somewhere in the attacks, but we don't know who draws it, or why."

"Perseus?" I guessed. I hadn't seen the symbol drawn in the psychiatric hospital. But the building had burned down, so that's probably why no one had been able to get an image of the symbol.

Virgo's brows knitted together. "No, it's not him. There's something or someone else doing that . . . We're missing something."

"Two nights from now," Corvus said. I turned to him. The forest was almost fully dark now, only illuminated with the faint light from the moon. "There will be a blood moon—a lunar eclipse—and Algol will rise to its full power."

I had heard Perseus and Arianna talking about the blood moon, so Corvus must have been right.

"So he wasn't at full power before?" I asked, feeling sicker than before.

Virgo shook her head. "It's not that he wasn't at full power, but whatever he does two days from now will be more destructive and will cause more deaths than any of his other attacks."

I stood up abruptly from the log, feeling like I was about to fall back down again. But my legs were so stiff that I stayed upright. "How do we stop him?"

Corvus glared at me and spoke in between gritted teeth. "Since we don't have the Prophecy book, we don't know."

A sense of urgency rose in my chest. I had seen the book. It had been right in front of me.

"So what do we do now?" I asked.

"We fight," Draco said, arranging the logs and branches into an orderly pile. "And we try to kill him however we can." He turned to me. "And by that, I mean you try to kill him before he kills you."

"Why her?" Corvus asked. Virgo quickly explained the Prophecy to him.

Corvus's face betrayed no emotion. "So now it makes more sense," he muttered. I shot him a questioning look. "Why they kept Orion alive, I mean."

"Why?" I asked.

Corvus glowered at Draco and Virgo. "You didn't tell her?"

Virgo shrank away, and Draco remained silent, still piling up the branches.

"What?" I asked.

"Orion is bait to lure you in." Corvus met my gaze. "Your Constellation, Andromeda—it's the chained princess, but also the sacrifice victim."

"So?" I asked.

Corvus clenched his fists. "So he wants to sacrifice you! To spill your blood when the red moon appears to make himself more powerful!" His eyes bore into me. "If he does that, he wouldn't need blood moons to cause more deaths and destruction, your blood would give him that power whenever he wants it—he would become unstoppable, capable of destroying entire countries." I felt like I had been shot in the chest. "He knows you'll try to save Orion, because if he doesn't kill you, he'll kill him just to make you suffer."

There were a couple seconds of tense silence.

"You could have said that in a nicer tone," Virgo said.

"I'm not sure there's any nice way of saying that," Corvus retorted.

They kept on arguing, but I wasn't hearing them anymore. My ears were ringing with the blood that rushed inside them.

I traced the scars on my wrists, which were shining alongside the beats of my heart. I wondered if Orion had known—that he had saved my life so one day I could save his.

CHAPTER 19

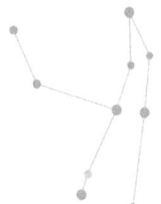

"ANDROMEDA?" Virgo asked, reaching for my arm but unsure whether to actually touch me. Her hand hovered above me.

"I'm fine," I said in a quiet voice.

"I'm pretty sure you're not," Corvus said, leading me back to the log so I could sit on it.

"Of course she's not!" Virgo shouted somewhere to my right. "How would you feel if you were going to be sacrificed?"

"Well thank the Stars I don't have to feel it," Corvus said.

"We have to kill him," I said, a little louder than I intended. The fog was beginning to clear from my thoughts. "We have to find him and kill him!"

"That's the plan," Draco said. "But it's not as easy as it seems."

"Why not?" I demanded, already picturing myself driving the knife through Perseus's chest.

"He has Lupus, for starters," Virgo said.

"The wolf?" I asked.

Draco nodded. "He's a Star Child too."

I blinked, trying to make sense of that.

"Not all Star Children materialized into people," Virgo explained. "Some of them are animals, monsters or objects."

"Great," I muttered.

"Perseus has Lupus and that stupid Pegasus," Corvus cursed.

"And Arianna," I said, remembering that strange woman.

"WHAT?" Corvus demanded. He rushed to my side and gripped my arms tightly. "Darkness?"

"In the flesh," I said.

Corvus looked straight into my eyes, his own wide with terror. Then he let go and took a step back.

The three of them looked at each other.

"Why in Heaven's name would she be here?" Virgo asked. Her gaze traveled to me, questioningly.

"I don't know; she was just there, and she seemed to be friends with Perseus," I said.

"No, no, no, no, no," Corvus said as he paced around. His eyes settled on the pile of wood. "Make a fire."

Virgo grabbed my arm and feebly pulled me away until we were standing ten feet away from the pile of wood Draco had made. I noticed how weak she was, and wondered why it was so.

Corvus stood next to us, eyes set on Draco. Draco stood a few feet in front of the pile. He took in a huge gulp of air, his chest rising. He waited a couple of seconds, then blew out. Fire exploded from his mouth like a hose of hot flames. The trees were suddenly illuminated in red, and the leaves around Draco shriveled into ashes. A wave of heat slapped my face, hard. The pile was now set alight, and so was the ground around it.

Draco smiled apologetically at me. "The Constellation of Draco represents a dragon," he explained.

"You don't say," I said flatly.

"Good," Corvus said as he edged around the flames. "Stay close to the fire. I don't want that woman popping out from the shadows."

"She can do that?" I asked.

Corvus nodded. "We believe she can live in any outdoor dark space." He looked out towards the forest. "Leo! Get back here!" Virgo gave him a questioning glance. "He was chasing a fox," Corvus explained with a shrug.

There was a loud roar from the forest. A few seconds later, he appeared from behind the trees thirty yards in front of me.

Leo was easily the biggest lion I had ever seen, and the most beautiful one too. His fur was golden, and his muscles so thick that he looked stronger than any human I had met. His mane was brown and red, covering his head and chest. He was taller than I, and had eyes that seemed to be made of molten gold. He was watching me, a bright intelligence in its eyes. It scared me to see such a human stare in those eyes—shrewd, calculating, keen. The lion approached us slowly then stood a few feet away, still staring at me. I noticed he had a pink scar next to his right eye.

"This is Andromeda," Virgo said. "She'll be fighting with us."

Leo gave a small snarl in acknowledgement.

"Hello," I said.

The lion looked away, focusing on Virgo, who caressed his mane affectionately.

"We have a problem, Leo," Corvus said. Leo looked up and met his gaze, his face serious, if any lion's face can suddenly become serious. "Darkness is here. She's working with Perseus."

Leo's face didn't move, but I heard a growl escaping from his snout. Virgo didn't step away. She kept caressing his mane gently.

"We can fight Perseus, and the other Star Children with him, but how are we supposed to fight *her*?" Draco asked.

"She might not even be powerful enough to hurt us, yet," Virgo said, pensively. "It will take some time before she becomes fully corporeal. I'm more scared of Perseus."

"What is she even doing here?" Corvus said in distress, as if he hadn't heard a word of what Virgo said. "She hasn't visited this planet, at least not in the form of Arianna, in thousands of years."

"*The sky he shall conquer*," Virgo said as she looked at the flames. We all turned to look at her. She looked at each of us. "That's why she's with Perseus. He's going to conquer the sky, and if he does that . . ."

"In Devil's name!" Corvus shouted, loud enough that I was sure our Star ancestors had heard him, and very possibly the Devil too. He slapped a hand on his face, so strong that it made Virgo flinch. "Why didn't we see that before?"

Leo growled, baring his teeth, which I noticed were sharp and big enough to cut a hole straight through me.

"He's right," Draco said as he pointed at Leo, apparently able to understand lion. "Prophecies are always weird, as if confusing the reader is their sole purpose. We couldn't have known, Corvus. There are many different ways to interpret each Prophecy."

"We should have!" Corvus said, walking in circles around the fire while the rest of us just looked at him. "Now it makes sense."

"What makes sense?" I asked.

Virgo looked at me with a sigh, as if tired of having to explain everything. "It's the oldest war in the cosmos," she said. "Light against Darkness. It's always been there, since the Universe was created."

"Light won the first battle that was fought," Corvus said as he kept walking in circles around us. Leo watched him as if he were a scurrying mouse. "Taking control of Destiny. But Darkness was still there, always present, and now that Perseus is prophesized to conquer the sky . . ."

"Darkness will help him so they can defeat Light and take control of Destiny?" I guessed.

"Exactly!" Corvus exclaimed, his hands buried in his hair as if he wanted to pull it all out.

"This is bad," Virgo whispered, quite unhelpfully. "We knew Perseus was planning to overthrow the Stars, but not with Arianna's help."

"This is a disaster!" Corvus said, although I was pretty sure this had been a disaster all along. "If Darkness takes over Fate and Destiny, or destroys them, then we're all as good as dead, in the best of cases."

"Darkness is not powerful enough yet or we would be dead already," Virgo said. She was leaning against Leo.

"But what happens when she grows stronger?" Draco asked. "It won't take her long—weeks, maybe a few months."

"I'm not saying we shouldn't worry about her," Virgo said calmly. "I'm just saying that we better focus on Perseus, who's *a lot* stronger at the moment."

"What can we do to stop him?" I asked, feeling invisible as the others argued among themselves.

"I don't know!" Corvus shouted. "He's got Alathea's book, so he probably knows how to kill all of us."

"Do we know for sure that he has the second part of the book?" I asked.

"Yes," Corvus said in a deeper tone, almost growling. "We've always known that the first part is somewhere in Rome, and the second one in Greece, and the third . . . Oh who cares about the third."

The entirety of our situation didn't seem to fit inside my brain. I couldn't imagine all the Stars in the sky controlling Destiny and Darkness taking over. What would a fight between Light and Darkness even look like?

"Hey," I said, making Corvus stop walking. "Let's focus on what we *can* do. We find Perseus and I kill him."

In theory, that sounded easy, something I could handle. But I knew that it would be much harder than that.

"At least we know where he'll be during the blood moon," Virgo said.

"Where?" I asked.

She walked back to her backpack and pulled out a large notebook. She leafed through the pages, and I noticed that she had drawn circles and mathematical equations and strange symbols I didn't understand.

"Well, asides from the blood moon, Uranus and Saturn will be conjunct, passing over Algol at twenty-six degrees in Taurus, quadrant to Mars in—"

"No," Corvus interrupted. "Please stop. Just make the explanation easier so we can all understand."

Virgo's cheeks flushed. "I'm trying to do that!"

"We don't understand all that," Draco said, motioning at her notebook. "Remember the rest of us are only half as smart as you."

Virgo glared at her notebook and then looked up at me, as if not wanting to explain to the stupid boys. Although, just like them, I really didn't understand what Mars had to do with this.

"I charted Algol's movements across the sky," she started. "And it will be in the same place as the blood moon will be, in a specific location where the star will be in full power thanks to other astronomical concepts too complicated to explain." She looked around our group. "Did everyone understand that?"

Draco and Corvus nodded. I understood too, or at least I thought I did.

"He'll be in Rome," Virgo said slowly. "At Palatine Hill, to be more exact."

"Where's that?" I asked. I had never heard of that place.

"Palatine Hill is Rome's oldest ruins. They're right next to the Colosseum," said Virgo, looking at her notebook. "Ara is there." She met my gaze and quickly looked away. "Ara is another Constellation. It represents a sacrificing altar. That's where Perseus wants to sacrifice you."

"Well, that sounds great," I muttered, not wanting to think too much about that. "So we know where he'll be."

Orion would be there too, alive, unless I didn't show up. Then they would kill him instead of me. No, they wouldn't kill him. Perseus knew that I wouldn't let Orion die. He knew that I would go save Orion, whatever price I had to pay. Even if it meant dying for him . . .

I looked around our small group. "So this is all we've got to fight Perseus?" I asked, my hopes dwindling.

"We have Aquila and Sirius too," Corvus said, and I really hoped they were as badass as they sounded. "Aquila is keeping guard nearby, and Sirius is in a village close by, working."

"Working in what?" I asked.

Corvus scratched his beard. "Sirius is the only one of us who works. He makes all the money so we can all live comfortably."

"So you guys aren't homeless?" I asked.

"Of course not," Virgo said. "We usually live in one of Sirius's houses, but we made an exception today because of you."

That statement made me feel uncomfortable, and I wondered how they had found me, but I was too tired to ask.

"You should sleep," Draco said as he looked at me. "You look like you haven't slept in a week."

"I haven't," I said.

ANDROMEDA

I walked closer to the fire and lay with my back to it, not wanting to scorch my face. The others didn't talk, but I could hear them shuffling around our small camp.

I closed my eyes, wishing that sleep could erase all my worries.

Chapter XI, Verse II

Into the bottom of the three Wise Wells it falls,
The water that cleanses every creature's soul.
Inside the Wells they shall be waiting,
The three women who know their dwellings.
The Weavers of destiny that choose your fate.
Fed by the element of their own souls.
Rooted by the judgment of the kings of Heaven.

CHAPTER 20

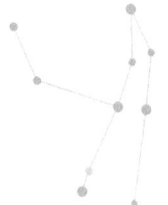

I MUST have slept for at least a couple of hours, because when I opened my eyes again everyone seemed to have moved. Virgo was sleeping next to Leo, her head resting on one of his front legs. Even though Leo could have ripped her apart with one scratch, Virgo's sleeping face seemed calm and peaceful. I noticed faint light coming from her hands, and realized that she had scars on them. I wondered how she had gotten those. Leo's scar next to his right eye also shone. It pulsed very slowly, and was bright—but not as bright as Perseus's scars.

The sky was fully dark above me, the moon hidden behind the canopy of trees.

Corvus was also asleep, sitting against the log Virgo and I had sat on earlier. He had pulled up the hood from his jacket, so most of his face was covered.

I noticed that Draco was still awake, looking at me from across the flames. He sat on the ground, his gaze intent.

I stood up, wiping leaves from my hair, and went to sit next to Draco. He didn't say anything, just stared at me silently while I watched the flames. They seemed to be moving with an invisible wind, dancing to a mute song, creating shapes that made my imagination ignite—the head of a horse, a man with three eyes, a river of fire.

"Can I ask you something?" I said after a few minutes.

"Sure," Draco whispered.

"If your Constellation is a dragon, then why aren't you a dragon? Or can you turn into one?" I asked.

Draco chuckled, and I assumed someone else had also asked him that. Maybe Corvus. "I don't know," he admitted. "I'm half-dragon, I guess. I can breathe fire, and sometimes I can make my nails turn into claws."

Since I had seen no dragons roaming Earth, I assumed there must be more to Draco's Constellation. I wondered what his Stars did—what Destiny they controlled.

"They protect treasures," Draco said, guessing my question.

"Treasures?" I asked.

The dark slit in Draco's eyes narrowed into a very thin line. "In the myth, the dragon Ladon protected a secret garden with golden apples. So the Stars in my Constellation control hidden treasures, and decide who gets to find them."

Out of all the Destinies, I would have never thought that hidden treasures would be one of them. But now I knew who to take on a secret quest. I wondered if Draco would have been able to find Alathea's book. It seemed like it was a treasure to many. Had his Constellation enabled Perseus and me to find the book? But Stars couldn't control our Destinies, so maybe they hadn't.

"What can Leo and Corvus do?" I asked.

Draco turned to look at the sleeping bulk of Leo. "His Constellation controls the ascension of kings and queens, or their deaths," he shrugged. "Anything that has to do with the royals, really. Although I have never seen him materialize any-thing except . . ." A dark shadow crossed his eyes, and I didn't ask.

Draco's gaze then traveled to Corvus and he smiled. His teeth were normal, I noticed. "He's the liar." He looked at Corvus's hunched shape. "A liar and a cheater."

I puffed my cheeks out. "I'll bet the Stars in his Constellation are having a blast blowing up marriages."

Draco laughed, but tried to choke it away by covering his mouth with his hand. The others didn't stir, not even the lion, who had started snoring. I wondered how poor Virgo was still asleep.

"I'm sure they are," Draco said. "Corvus can lie to anyone, and they'll believe him. A very useful skill along the years."

"How long have you guys known each other?" I asked.

Draco looked into the flames, and I noticed how his mouth twitched. Maybe I had touched a sore spot.

"I found Aquila first, around four years ago," he finally said. "Then we found Sirius and Leo a few months later. Then Virgo. Corvus joined us nearly a year ago." I looked at the three of them, wondering what they had been doing before Draco found them. "They've had tough lives," Draco whispered, motioning at Virgo and Corvus.

"So you've been trying to find more Star Children for the last few years?" I asked.

Draco brushed a fallen leaf from his hair. "Something like that. It's always been obvious that I'm not normal, but I never knew what I was." His eyes settled on Leo, whose mane shone red with the fire. "But it wasn't until I started finding the others that we began to wonder where we came from." Then his eyes went to Virgo. "She's the one that explained everything. She knew about Alathea's book."

"Hmmm," I said, wondering how she had known if they hadn't found the book yet. "And how did you find them?"

Draco smiled. "That was easy. I know a Star Child on sight."

"How?" I asked.

"I have a different sight," he said pointing at his reptile eyes. "I can see more wavelengths—infrared, X-rays, ultraviolet."

"So you can see my bones?" I asked, excited.

He nodded. "You have a very nice skull," he said. "The point is that Star Children emit a different light than everyone else."

"People emit light?" I asked.

"Infrared," Draco said. "Every human emits a little, because this planet as a whole emits infrared light. But Star Children don't. We emit a sort of light that I have never seen before. I don't even know how to explain how it looks." He scratched his head. "I've seen others, however, who I know come from other planets based on the light they emit."

I was beginning to put the pieces together. "So if humans emit infrared light because they were born on this planet, then inhuman people emit light from the planet they come from."

Draco smiled. "Yep, that's pretty much how it works. Or at least that's how I think it does."

"Are there many inhuman creatures on this planet, asides from the Star Children?" I asked, disturbed at that idea.

Draco's pupils dilated. "You'd be surprised how many of them there are. Most of them look human, but have supernatural abilities or can shift into other beings."

My heart thumped faster inside my chest. "Have you met them?"

He shrugged. "I've been unfortunate enough to cross paths with a few of them," he said, then shook his head. "They have their own battles to fight, as much as we do. And I'd rather they not get involved in ours and we in theirs."

We were silent for almost a minute, the fire crackling as it consumed the logs.

My eyes went curiously to Virgo. "What can she materialize?" I asked.

Draco's pupils expanded considerably. "We honestly don't know," he said in a more hushed tone, as if afraid she would hear us. "She was almost dead when I found her."

"Why?" I asked.

Draco shifted his weight, looking worriedly at Virgo. "You may have noticed that she's very thin," he whispered.

"I did notice," I said.

He nodded absently. "Our power comes from within us, so when we materialize something, we literally consume a part of ourselves. So we lose a little weight every time we materialize. And if we use too much of our power at once without letting it regenerate, then . . ." His gaze traveled again to Virgo.

"She used too much of her power," I whispered.

Draco nodded. "To have left her as it did . . . I can only wonder what she might have materialized," He arched his back for a second, then sat back normally. "She never talks about what she can do, not even after all this time. Like she's afraid of reviving a monster. She looks a lot better than she was before, but still . . . I'm not sure she's strong enough to materialize anything yet."

"Can't you guys guess what she can materialize based on the myth of her Constellation?" I asked.

Draco nibbled on his lower lip. "Virgo's Constellation is associated with too many myths for us to be able to guess. Since there are only three female Constellations in the sky—Virgo, Andromeda and Cassiopeia—Virgo became associated with most ancient goddesses. So her myths include those of Ishtar, Demeter,

Persephone, Dike, Athena and Artemis. She's powerful, there's no doubt in that, but we can't know for sure what she can do."

I stared at Virgo for a couple of seconds. She was still sleeping peacefully, her chest rising and lowering slowly. The flames played across her face, making her sunken cheeks look even thinner.

"You should go back to sleep," Draco said. "We still have some hours before sunrise."

I stared at Draco, but he didn't turn to look at me again, his gaze fixed on the flames that were the same color as his eyes.

I sighed. Now that I knew more answers, I felt more incomplete than when I hadn't known them. There were so many things that I had to worry about, so many emotions swirling through me, that my body seemed to have shutdown. I didn't want to know how it would feel when the shock fell away into pain.

I lay down a few feet away from Draco, my back to the fire. The dark forest before me seemed hostile compared to the warmth that radiated behind me. I wondered if Arianna was there, lurking in the shadows.

Corvus said she hadn't appeared in that form on this planet for thousands of years. So was Arianna just a face that Darkness showed? A physical representation of something so powerful that we couldn't begin to understand? I lay on my back, looking up at the sky. There were Stars there, hundreds of them. Did they look like us? Or were they literally just balls of fire? If Stars were just balls of light, then how could they control Destiny? I didn't know, and didn't want to know.

●———●———●

The sun had just begun to rise when I awoke. The sky was light blue, but there still wasn't much light. The light wind blew into the trees gently, and colorful leaves swirled lazily down every few seconds. I let myself lie on the ground for a while, then sat up with a groan, feeling sore.

I looked around. The fire was out now, logs and branches no more than skeletal ashes. Corvus and Draco were gone. Leo was still sleeping, lying on his side as he loudly snored like a strangled horse.

Virgo was awake too, sitting on the other side of the burnt logs. I stood and walked over to her. I noticed she was knitting what looked like a sweater.

"You knit?" I asked.

She gave a startled jump, nearly dropping the needles. Virgo looked up at me. She looked like she had rested well, her eyes alert. She breathed deeply.

"I do," she said.

I sat down next to her, watching how she threaded the marine-blue yarn into stitches. She would have made a very good grandmother, knitting sweaters for all the family.

"Why?" I asked.

She didn't look at me, and instead kept knitting, her hands moving gracefully. "It makes me feel . . . fuller."

"Who taught you to knit?" I asked.

She didn't meet my gaze. "The Weavers did."

"The Weavers knit?" I asked. I hadn't really thought that entities as powerful as the Weavers would knit. And how had she met the Weavers?

"That's why they're called Weavers," Virgo said. "They knit our Fates together, weaving them with our Destinies."

I didn't really understand what that meant, or how Fates could be weaved and knit. Before I could ask, the boys appeared. They were talking as they walked over to us.

Corvus's hair was still a wild mess, and his eyes red-rimmed. He had probably never slept in a forest before, or at least not in a very long time. He eyed Virgo's knitting with approval.

"Another sweater," he said.

Virgo nodded. "Winter's coming. Don't want any of us to be cold."

"Or die," Draco said, sitting in front of her as he watched her knit. He looked at my confused frown. "Virgo's sweaters are special. They're always warm to whomever wears them, and they're bullet-proof."

"Magical sweaters?" I asked. Even after all the things I had heard yesterday, magical sweaters seemed a bit ridiculous.

"Oh yeah," Corvus said, unzipping his jacket to proudly display his sweater. "Who cares about bullet-proof vests? These sweaters are immune to everything."

I wondered if the Weavers had taught Virgo that too. I assumed they must have, because I was sure there was no Magical Sweaters 101 class I could take.

"Did you get in contact with him?" Virgo asked.

"Yeah," Corvus said. He grinned at me. "It's time for you to meet the rich guy."

CHAPTER 21

"WHY KILL Perseus in a public park?" I asked. The sun was bright above our heads, and I had started to sweat already, despite the fresh wind blowing on our backs.

"It seemed like our best option," Corvus said.

We had been walking through the forest for two hours, the red, orange and yellow leaves from the trees floating in the wind. We walked at the edge of a large river to our left. The river was bright blue and green, making a beautiful contrast with the trees. The water looked inviting as it shimmered with the sun, but I knew it would be very cold.

Virgo and Draco walked a few feet behind us, and I couldn't hear what they were talking about. Every now and then one of them would chuckle or laugh. As usual, Draco was wearing dark sunglasses. Leo was behind them, walking silently, his head held high.

"Why not wait until he was alone in an alley or something?" I asked.

"We considered that," Corvus said. "But he would have been more alert, and he would have sensed us coming long before we managed to reach him." He turned to look at me, shielding his dark-brown eyes from the sun. "You haven't seen Perseus fight in a hand-to-hand combat, have you?"

"No," I answered. But I did remember how he had deflected Orion's punch in the hotel.

"He's an extremely good fighter, literally trained for that since he came into existence," Corvus said. "In the park, we knew he'd have his guard down. It would have taken a second for one of us to pretend to buy an ice cream while another stabbed him in the back."

"The cameras would have filmed you, and the police could have caught you."

Corvus shrugged. "If the police caught us, I would have lied saying that it wasn't us, and they would have believed me. We would've had enough time to escape the country. We've never liked the United States anyways."

Tiny rocks crunched under our feet.

"How do you know Perseus is such a good fighter?" I asked. "If he knew you, wouldn't it have been a bad idea for him to see you in the park?"

"He doesn't know me, or he didn't, anyways. He hasn't fought me but he has fought others I know."

Before I could ask whom, there was a shriek above us that made me look up, shielding my eyes from the sun. There was a golden eagle flying above us. Its feathers were dark brown with streaks of white in the wings. Even from afar, I noticed that the eagle was big. It seemed five feet long with a wingspan of at least nine feet.

"That's Aquila," Corvus said as he pointed at the sky.

Of course, that had to be Aquila. "What can he do?" I asked.

"In Greek mythology Aquila carried the thunderbolts of the god Zeus," Corvus explained.

"So he controls the weather," I said.

Corvus shook his head. "Only thunder and lightning."

"That's good as long as he knows how to aim," I said.

Corvus laughed. "He can do that just fine, trust me."

Aquila continued to fly overhead, spinning in circles above us as we continued. For some reason it made me feel less anxious to have the eagle there, watching out for any threats.

"So have you guys met any other Star Children?" I asked after a few minutes.

Corvus nodded. "Only a few more."

"Who?" I asked, curious.

"There's Gemini, the twins, but I personally hate them, so let's not talk about them," he paused. "We know Centaurus, but have only seen him twice. We also met Hercules a few months ago. But he didn't really care about us, not even when we told him that Perseus could try to kill him," Corvus said with a shrug.

"Why wouldn't he care?" I asked. "I mean, if Perseus is going to try to kill all of us then wouldn't he be interested in surviving?"

Corvus rolled his eyes. "He's a little bit like you. He doesn't believe in this sort of things. All he cares about is modeling underwear and getting another Olympic gold medal."

"I *do* believe," I snapped. "At least I do now."

"I know," Corvus muttered. He scratched his beard. "In mythology, Hercules killed Draco, Aquila and Leo, so neither of them wanted him to join us anyways."

"But those are just myths, right?" I asked.

Corvus seemed uneasy at this question. "As far as I know, there are no Greek gods roaming Earth, but still, those myths hold truth behind them, although we're not sure how much." His bitter gaze looked back at me. "If we had the book then maybe we would know."

"I'm sorry about the book," I said with a shrug.

Corvus muttered something incomprehensible, then let out a deep breath.

"Maybe we could steal the book from Perseus," I said.

"We could try," Corvus said.

He looked up at the sky. It was still early morning, the air fresh around us, but I could feel the tension, knowing that tomorrow night I would see Perseus again.

"How will we stop him?" I asked. The stark reality of the situation was starting to sink into my mind. Perseus had the power of the most dangerous Star, and all of the Star Children working with him were very powerful. *And* he was working with Darkness, one of the most powerful and dangerous forces in the Universe. *Too much power*, I thought.

Corvus shrugged. "I honestly don't know. But we have to try. Algol will have three risings, each time growing more powerful."

"Three risings?" I asked.

Corvus huffed and turned to look back, probably glaring at Virgo and Draco for not having told me. Then he turned back to me.

"We stole two Prophecies from Cassiopeia, I mean . . . Zia," he explained. "One about Algol conquering the sky, and the other about his three risings." Corvus mentioning Zia made my legs go wobbly, but I pushed her away from my head. It felt like trying to stop the current of a river, knowing sooner or later the water would burst through.

"But how will he rise three times?" I asked Corvus.

"It means that Algol will be at its maximum power three times. The Prophecy said that the first rising would be in a blood moon, which is tomorrow night," he started. "Then the next one will be when *the sun hides inside the night*. That most certainly means a solar eclipse. Virgo believes that it will happen in a total solar eclipse coming a bit before Christmas, when Algol will be in a certain position that gives it more power. But the last rising . . ."

"What about it?"

Corvus cleared his throat, as if the words were stuck there. "The Prophecy says Perseus will be victorious *when the sky goes full dark*, but we don't know what that means. It sounds similar to a solar eclipse, but we think it may mean something else entirely."

"So Perseus will eventually win," I said.

"No," Corvus said. "That's only one Prophecy," he turned to me. "You can kill him."

I felt that weight settling on my shoulders as if I were carrying a backpack full of rocks.

"Can't anyone else kill Perseus? You or Draco or Leo? Or maybe the police?" I asked. "He's causing terrorist attacks, after all."

Corvus chuckled. "The police wouldn't be able to kill him. He's too powerful. And even if they tried, they would need *a lot* of bullets. Only special weapons can truly kill a Star Child, anything else wouldn't be so effective. Mundane weapons could kill us, but most times they just make us bleed and leave scars—they're not always fatal to us." I absently traced the scars on my wrist. "And we can also die by drowning or asphyxiation, like a normal human would." Corvus paused. "In any case, it's in the Prophecies that *you* will kill him."

Our feet took us along the pebbled ground. In the distance, I could see a few buildings at the edge of the river. One was a three-story house, with white-washed walls and cracks everywhere. The other building was a small concrete shed, with a black door hanging on its hinges. At the sight of it, we both walked a bit faster.

I thought of the white knife Zia had given me to kill Perseus. He'd had the same knife, and so had Virgo, Corvus and Draco.

Could those knives be the special weapons Corvus had just described?

"What's Perseus's endgame?" I asked. "I get it, he wants to conquer the sky, but what does that actually mean?"

Corvus looked at the rippling water for a few long moments. "He wants to eradicate Destiny and Fate, give the Universe free will."

I considered that. Destiny felt like another prison, even if I didn't have it. With Prophecies, I had a bit more freedom to choose, even if my options were limited, but normal people didn't. They deserved that choice, right?

"That doesn't sound so bad," I said.

Corvus's head snapped back to me. "Didn't Virgo and Draco tell you last night? If there is no Fate and Destiny, then everything would erupt back into Darkness and Chaos, as it was before the existence of Light."

"And that's bad, right?" I did remember Virgo and Draco saying that it was bad, but couldn't recall the specifics.

"Life can't exist in Chaos, only Death."

"Then why would Perseus want to kill everyone?"

Corvus scratched his beard again until his skin turned red. "He believes that he can find a way to maintain a sense of order without Fate and Destiny. But there is none. It's as stupid as wanting a building to stay upright even though you want to remove the pillars that sustain it." He looked back at the swirling water. "Arianna must have convinced him that it was possible. But he'll end up destroying all life."

He shook his head, as if in disbelief that Perseus could believe in such nonsense. But could it be possible? Could there be free will without destroying the Universe?

I thought about the conversation that I'd overheard between Arianna and Perseus. "Arianna told Perseus that the only way to be free from his Prophecy was to fulfill it." I said. "I'm pretty sure Perseus wants to escape his own Prophecies."

Corvus raised a brow. "That's interesting," he turned to me. "It could be true," he conceded. "That by fulfilling our Prophecies we can escape them. Although I'm not sure how that would work, or why Arianna would tell that to Perseus." He shook his head sadly. "She's probably brainwashed him. Perseus will believe anything she tells him."

"Even if it's not true, Perseus believes that," I said.

Corvus nodded. "And he'll kill anyone who steps on his path to destroying Destiny and Fate, and maybe even Prophecy too." Corvus said. "He doesn't care who dies in his attacks."

I gulped, feeling the knot in my throat burning through my skin. "How did you even know Perseus was Perseus?" I paused, realizing that what I said had made very little sense. "I mean, how did you know Perseus was the Star Child Perseus?"

Corvus scratched his beard again, eyeing the old town warily as we approached it. "The first time Perseus used Algol's power was around a year ago, causing a suicide bombing. I was there." He gulped. "I saw the symbol drawn in blood and suspected a Star Child must have caused the attack." His eyes narrowed as he stared at the ground. "My suspicion was confirmed when Virgo and Draco found me in the hospital a few weeks later. Together, we began searching. When Virgo tracked the important Stars in the sky, she found that Algol was related to all the attacks that were happening, and we knew Algol was in Perseus's Constellation. So we went after him, tracking where Algol would cause the next attack."

Corvus kicked a large pebble into the river. It splashed silently, sinking out of sight. "Perseus must have realized we were searching for him, because the wolf tried to kill us a few times. If it hadn't been for Leo we would surely be dead." He cleared his throat, and I thought of the scar next to Leo's eye. "Then the attack in Paris happened, and the only person to walk unharmed from it was a red-haired boy. Draco saw him and knew he was a Star Child."

"So you followed him to New York," I continued, guessing where the story was going. "To that day he was selling ice cream at the park."

Corvus nodded. "At first we thought you were working with him, but we weren't sure."

I huffed. "Now you know I'm not."

Corvus looked up as we approached the village. It seemed very worn down, I realized, and very poor too. The rest of the buildings were small, all of them single-story structures. I wondered what Sirius was working on.

When I looked back, I noticed that Virgo and Draco were walking closer to us. Leo sat at the edge of the river, looking into the water. I assumed he would wait for us there.

I realized the buildings were houses, with laundry hanging from some of the windows to dry with the sun. Some windows had shutters, but I realized others didn't have anything but rags, making a sort of improvised curtain. Some houses were made of wood, and others of concrete, but they all seemed about to fall down on themselves. The doors were all closed so I couldn't see inside, not even through the windows, which were so dirty that they couldn't even be described as windows. I also noticed that most houses had a plastic chair outside. But there was no one sitting on the chairs. Where was everyone?

"Why now?" I asked as the question crossed my head.

"What?" Corvus asked.

"Why were we all of us born now and not before, or later?" I asked.

Corvus shrugged. "That's a question I ask myself every day."

One house had plastic buckets lined up against the wall, and another had fish hanging from cords at the front porch. I wiggled my nose in disgust, even though I was hungry. Breakfast hadn't been fulfilling, and I could feel my dear companion Hunger twisting in my stomach.

The ground around us was littered with plastic bottles and rotten fruits. Movement caught my eye, and when I turned to my right, I realized there was a gray rat next to a house, eating something I couldn't make out.

There were a few cars and a couple of scooters parked on the side of the muddy road as we walked further into the village. Most streets branched left and right into the forest that surrounded the village, and I wondered if there were more houses there. We passed by a couple of trashcans next to a house on my right. They were brimming with trash and smelled like radioactive decay. I wondered where they took the trash.

I stepped on fallen leaves that were scattered on the ground. We passed by a building on our left made of red bricks. It was the only one constructed from that material, so it stood out from the rest. It was two stories tall and with a bell on top. I assumed it must be a church, the only one here.

I didn't see any people around until we arrived at what I assumed was the main plaza. At the center were at least a hundred people crowded together. They all wore simple clothing—muddy shoes or sandals, plain T-shirts and blouses; the men wore trousers and most of the women skirts.

The plaza had an uneven pebbled ground, and there was a single large tree in the middle of it. There were benches surrounding the tree. At the edge of the plaza were stalls selling food and other goods, as if it were an open market.

Corvus fixed his eyes on the dense crowd gathered around the tree. I couldn't spot who he was looking for. I did notice, however, that right next to the crowd was a large camera set on a sliding platform, as if someone had been filming a movie. There was a man wearing a dark-blue shirt and sunglasses as he stared at a screen placed next to the camera, speaking excitedly with the man besides him.

"Where is he?" Virgo asked, standing next to us.

"I see him," Draco pointed to the middle of the crowd.

"I don't," I said.

Draco took me by the arm and we walked closer. Then he pointed again at the crowd, who parted on one side.

"You're kidding, right?" I asked.

Next to me, Corvus laughed and shook his head. "Sirius! Come here, boy!"

From the crowd, Sirius emerged and walked towards us. I noticed a small girl had a plush toy of him. She looked dismayed to see Sirius go. The rest of the crowd didn't notice, however. I realized they were too busy taking selfies and pictures with a handsome man dressed in what I assumed was a gladiator outfit. Although I didn't know what a gladiator would be doing in a Greek village. Didn't gladiators come from Rome?

My first thought at seeing Sirius as he came closer was that he did look very badass—just not in the way I expected.

"Sirius," Corvus said as Sirius stopped, standing in front of me. "This is Andromeda. She'll be helping us fight Perseus."

I looked down at him. Sirius was easily the biggest boxer I had seen in my life. His head reached my belly button, which he sniffed appreciatively. His mouth was black, just as the fur around his dark eyes. His broad chest was white, and so were his paws, as if he was wearing boots. The rest of his fur was dark brown, streaked with black stripes as if he were part tiger.

"He's a dog," I said.

"*Canis Major*," Draco said proudly. "But we call him Sirius because that's the name of the brightest Star in his Constellation."

"And it sounds better than *Canis Major*," Virgo said.

"Kids!" someone shouted.

I turned to see it was the man with sunglasses. He rushed over to us.

"It's nice to see you all again!" he said. His eyes settled on me and he frowned. "I hadn't seen you before, had I?"

"Nope," I assured him.

"She's a new friend of ours," Virgo said.

"Oh," the man responded.

"Steven!" another man shouted as he stood next to the camera.

Steven waved his hand dismissively at the man. "Well, kids, we've finished shooting our scenes here, just as promised. You already received the money, right?"

Corvus nodded.

"Great! I'll let you know when the first trailer drops."

"Cool," Draco said with a smile. "Thanks."

"No problem," said Steven. "I'll see you guys at the premiere. Take care of my star!" He patted Sirius on the head as the dog tried to lick Steven's hand.

"We will," Virgo said.

"I already called a ride for you kids. But are you sure you want that van instead of the car? It's a lot slower."

"That's alright," Draco said.

"If you say so . . ." Steven said. "I'll see you guys soon!"

He walked back to the camera at the same time as a large van pulled up next to us. The driver got out and said something I didn't understand—either he was speaking Greek or very terrible English.

Draco thanked the man and climbed into the driver's seat. I went inside, Sirius jumping in after me. Then Corvus and Virgo walked in, sliding the door close behind them. I realized that there were no seats in the van, only empty space—for Leo, I guessed. I hoped the tires of the van were resistant enough to hold his weight. I sat with my back against the wall opposite to the door, right below a small window. Corvus sat to my left, and Virgo and Sirius to my right.

"You know where the hangar is, right?" Virgo asked Draco as he began slowly backing up the van away from the plaza.

"Yup," he answered.

"So Sirius is a dog, and an actor," I said. "Why?"

"Why is he a dog or an actor?" Draco asked from the driver's seat. Corvus chuckled next to me.

"It's how we earn money," Virgo said.

"But why an actor?" I asked.

Corvus sighed. "Sirius is one of the most powerful Stars in the sky."

"Really?" I said.

Corvus nodded. "Sirius is the Star of fame, honor, wealth, and fortune." He motioned to the dog whose head was resting on Virgo's lap. "So he became rich and famous. Since he's a dog he needs someone to help him with more human matters. So we're Sirius's 'owners.' As long as we take care of him, he lets us keep all the money he earns."

"Haven't you been to the movies lately?" Draco asked without turning to look at me. "He's been in almost every superhero movie, and he was in a drama movie last year too."

I remembered the movie poster I had seen in Times Square while walking with Perseus. I turned to Sirius, who was in fact the dog featured on that poster.

"Wait," I said. "How could he be in a drama?"

"It was a movie about a police dog who gets shot protecting his owner," Virgo said.

"That *does* sound sad," I said.

Corvus nodded. "He's very good at acting like he's dying."

I actually laughed at that. Out of all the ridiculous things I had heard in the past few days, a famous, rich dog just seemed the most ridiculous of them all, even more ridiculous than magical sweaters.

I looked at Sirius again. His eyes were trained on me, with that sort of intelligence that I now recognized in the Star Animals.

I took a deep breath and let my head rest against the wall, closing my eyes.

"To Rome we go," Corvus whispered to my right.

I didn't open my eyes, letting the dread climb to my heart.

Chapter VIII, Verse I

The curse of black blood he shall be victim upon.
First he shall rise when the moon sits in high,
Dripping with blood of his wretched mortal pawns.
The second rising arrives when the sun hides inside the night,
With the madness of killing and the drunkenness of death.
Then at last he shall triumph when the sky goes full dark,
Taking the only light where hope was once found.

CHAPTER 22

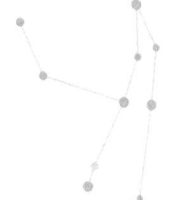

ROME hadn't changed since I had last visited it five years before. We rode silently through the paved streets. Sirius, Corvus and I sat in the back seats of the taxi. Aquila stood on the carpet at Corvus's feet. The driver had eyed the eagle warily, but hadn't said anything after Corvus lied to say it was just a plush toy. The driver seemed to believe it, even though Aquila screeched a couple of times. Virgo and Draco would ride a van with Leo. Virgo had suggested that we all ride the van, but it was a very small van and Leo had taken up all of the space. So they would meet up with us later.

I looked out the window, enjoying the view. On one side of the street cars were parked, wedged so tightly together that I wondered how the drivers would get them out. Tourists lined the sidewalks and plazas alike as if it were an invasion. It wasn't holiday season, but there still seemed to be a lot of people no matter where we drove.

The buildings around us were a combination of old and new, mostly old though. There seemed to be churches on every single corner. Some were wedged between two insignificant buildings, and others took up nearly half of a block. I noticed all of them were made out of stone, mostly white or brown. They had huge doors at the entrance, as if to let giants through. Columns and statues decorated the facades. Some churches were small; others were large, taller than the rest of the buildings, which were at most seven stories tall.

The churches were a stark comparison to other buildings, which were mostly colorful—painted in light orange, yellow, pink and red. Most windows had closed shutters, and I spotted a few with iron bars.

We passed by a church that was made of marble, with tourists pouring in and out of the large door.

Was there a god? I wondered. I had never been religious, but after what Corvus, Virgo, and Draco had explained I felt a surge of questions rising within me. There was no free will, as religion claimed. So did God actually exist?

I breathed out. Maybe it was better not to know the answer to that.

We drove by the river Tiber, which cut through the west side of the city. Its water was murky brown, and I remembered the stories Orion had told me about how, in ancient Rome, executed criminals would be thrown into the river. I wondered if there were still bones sitting at the bottom of the water.

The trees that lined the side of the street were almost bare. Even though the sky was completely clear, there was a tearing wind that made brown leaves and plastic garbage rustle past us.

In the distance I spotted the unmistakable curved dome of the St. Peter's cathedral inside Vatican City. It was light blue, lighter even than the color of the sky, but it was soon lost as we made a right turn onto another street.

The car had to slow down to avoid driving over the tourists who were walking on the middle of the street. I wouldn't have cared much if we did drive over them, but our driver seemed nicer than I.

I realized that there were stores at the bottom floor of most buildings. They had large windows displaying mannequins with clothes. The upper stories of the buildings had their shutters closed, and I assumed people lived there.

I noticed some pebbled streets, too narrow for cars to pass, so we had to go around them. People flocked through those streets in particular, where I spotted restaurants with terraces and stalls selling souvenirs.

We passed by a few plazas. There was usually a fountain at the center of each one. One was shaped like a sinking boat, and others had irregular shapes and marble statues of naked men. There were also obelisks everywhere—standing in the plazas, or next to buildings. Those were Egyptian, I knew, and I wondered why there would be so many of them in Rome.

Then at last, after an hour, we arrived at Sirius's apartment building, because, obviously, he had an apartment in Rome. As soon as the car stopped, I opened the door and climbed out of the car. The wind was blowing strong around me, ruffling my short hair, but I didn't mind it. The street was wide, with cars parked on each side, and didn't have many people on the sidewalk. I spotted an old lady walking with some grocery bags, and a couple of kids racing past her. There was also a group of people huddled close together down the street. Maybe some lost tourist group?

Corvus, Sirius and Aquila climbed out of the taxi after me. The group of tourists passing by us regarded Aquila with wonder as he perched on top of a fire hydrant, eyeing everyone with those creepy yellow eyes. They reminded me of Orion for a moment, and I had to bite back my frustration. Was he alright? Had Perseus or Lupus hurt him? I didn't want those questions roaming in my head, so I pushed them away again.

Sirius shook himself and sneezed. A small girl from the group of tourists narrowed her small eyes at him as she held to her mother's hand, as if she recognized Sirius from somewhere but wasn't really sure. I really hoped she didn't, because I didn't want the Sirius fan club gathering around us.

Corvus walked promptly to the entrance of the building and opened the door for us. For the first time, I looked at the building. It didn't look like much. It was five stories tall, the walls light orange with green shutters on the windows.

I walked through the glass door after Sirius. Aquila flew in, his wings brushing against my arm. The lobby was wide, with a red marble floor—it looked like raw flesh with thin and thick veins cutting through it. To the left was a reception counter with no one to attend to it. To the right were couches facing each other. At the end of the lobby was a spiral staircase. I noticed the stairs were wide enough for Leo. They were made out of white marble.

With dismay, I realized there wasn't an elevator. We all walked up the steps to the last floor, which had a wide double door. Corvus pushed it open and we all walked into the apartment. To my right was a kitchen. It had a large fridge, a sink, a stove, a washing machine, and a counter. Next to it was a round wooden table with five chairs. To the left was a small living room, with black velvet couches and a table in the middle. Against the left wall, behind the couches, was a large mirror. Next to it was a hallway with two doors on each side.

Corvus walked to the large windows at the other end of the room, and I heard the bark of a dog. I hadn't noticed him, or at least I assumed it was a he. His fur was exactly the same velvet black color as the couches. But I finally spotted him as he leaped from the couch and onto the floor, wagging his tail.

I had seen that dog before, at the park, when I had first met Corvus. It was a small black poodle. Sirius hurried to his side and the poodle stood on two paws trying to lick Sirius's face.

"Oh," Corvus said, as if suddenly remembering the existence of the small dog. He turned to me. "This is another Star Child." Corvus turned again to look out the window. "We found him a few weeks ago. He's *Canis Minor*, but we call him Maera because of his mythology."

"How did he get here?" I asked.

"Before going to find you in Greece we came here," Corvus explained with his back to me as he looked out into the city. I could see the river, and more buildings across from it. "We left Maera behind because we didn't want him to get hurt."

Aquila settled himself on the table with a shriek. I walked over to one of the couches and sat down, then heard a growl.

"That's Sirius's couch," Corvus explained. Sure enough, the dog was growling at me as he stood a few feet in front of me. I muttered an apology as I stood up, then walked over to stand next to the mirror. With his mouth, Sirius grabbed a fallen green quilt that had been left on the floor next to the couch, eyeing me reproachfully. Then he climbed atop the couch and arranged the quilt with his snout so he could use it as a pillow, settling his head comfortably in it. Maera climbed onto the other couch.

"Virgo and Draco are here," Corvus said. He walked to the entrance and opened both doors, looking down the stairs.

Outside, the golden rays of the setting sun were filtering through the window. In twenty-four hours, I would have to face Perseus. The blunt reality of it, of knowing that one of us could die tomorrow, was beginning to settle inside my head.

A low growl behind me made me turn. Leo stood a few feet away, watching me with interest. The room suddenly seemed very small. Virgo, Corvus and Draco walked into the apartment and closed the door behind them.

The lion lay down next to the windows. Virgo eyed him approvingly, then sat on the couch opposite from Sirius. Corvus remained standing next to the front door, looking at the setting sun.

Draco settled in one of the chairs. "Okay, so now—"

The front door opened, and a woman I assumed was a maid walked in with a mop and a bucket of water.

"*Ciao*," she announced. Then her eyes fixed on Leo, who was eyeing her as if she was a small mouse. Her clear eyes went wide with horror as her jaw dropped.

Corvus was immediately at her side. "*È solo un gattino,*" he said. *It's just a small kitten.* The maid closed her mouth, and her eyes returned to normal size. Her terror eased away, like when someone sees a monster through their window only to realize that it's branches from a tree playing tricks with the shadows. The lady stared at Leo as if he were indeed just a small kitten.

"*Ora non abbiamo bisogno dei tuoi servizi,*" Corvus said. *At the moment we don't need your services.* The lady eyed him, confused, but didn't argue. She walked out of the room, a frown on her face, then closed the door.

Corvus immediately went to lock it, letting out a sigh.

"So is that what you guys do every time someone sees Leo?" I asked. "You make them think that he's just a kitten?"

"It usually works very well," Virgo said with a smile.

Corvus leaned against the door, then slid to the floor as if he were exhausted. "Let's go over our game plan for tomorrow."

"We kill Perseus," I said.

"That's the idea," Draco said. "But we need something more specific."

"We stab Perseus in the heart with a knife," I suggested.

"Sounds good enough to me," Corvus said with a single nod.

"Virgo, Maera, Sirius and you will stay away from the fight," Draco said as he pointed a finger at Corvus.

Virgo seemed pleased at that, but Corvus shifted uncomfortably. Sirius gave a low growl of indignation, raising his head from his improvised pillow, as if he had already envisioned himself in the fight.

"Why can't *he* fight?" I asked as I pointed at Corvus. "He fought me in the park and in Times Square."

Before Corvus could argue, Draco turned to face him. "You're a good enough fighter, I know that. But you're not good enough for this. Lupus will be there, and so will Pegasus and Arianna." He shook his head. "You're not ready for this, Corvus, and I'd rather you stay with the others, keeping them safe."

Corvus set his jaw hard and looked away from Draco, staring at the floor. I didn't know the extent of their fighting skills, but Draco *did* seem physically stronger and faster. If he didn't think Corvus could deal with this fight then I was not going to argue against that, even though I would have preferred Corvus to be with us.

Virgo opened her mouth, then closed it for a few seconds, then opened it again. "We'll be in danger too, Draco, whether you want it or not. We just won't be fighting Perseus."

"I know," Draco said with a long sigh. "But you'll be in a safer place. Whatever Algol's first rising causes tomorrow, hopefully it won't reach you."

"If Algol is going to create some sort of attack, shouldn't we try to warn the police?" I asked. "Even if they can't harm Perseus, they can maybe evacuate the city."

Corvus huffed. "It's not our job to defend everyone in this city, only to fight Perseus and try to stop him."

"But she's right," Virgo said as she balled her bony fists. "We could try to warn—"

"No," Corvus said with a wave of his hand. "Whoever has been fated to die will die. We can't prevent that."

Draco sat back silently, his gaze switching between the two as they argued.

"Their lives *do* have value," Virgo said.

Corvus just shrugged. "I don't really care, Virgo. We can't save everyone. The best we can do is stop Perseus."

Virgo clenched her jaw hard, and her face went red with anger.

"Where will you guys go?" I asked. Both of them turned to look at me.

"If there is another attack, then we better get underground," Corvus said. He turned to Virgo, pensive. "We should probably go to the catacombs under the city."

"So that leaves Draco, Leo, Aquila and me to fight Perseus," I muttered, not liking my odds very well. But it was better than fighting alone.

Draco nodded. "We can do it." He let his elbows rest on his legs. "Perseus will expect you to go to Palatine Hill to save Orion."

"I know," I said, with dread.

"So you're going to go alone to Palatine Hill," Draco said. Before I could protest, he continued, "Leo, Aquila and I will hide close by. You let Perseus take you to Orion, so we know where he is, and, when Perseus least expects it, we'll attack."

I wanted to argue that it didn't sound like a very detailed plan of attack, but I had nothing better in mind.

"If something happens to me, find Orion and free him on the first chance you get," I told Draco. "He's the best fighter I've ever met."

His red eyes narrowed at Aquila, who gave a small shriek of acknowledgement.

"We'll deal with Lupus, Arianna and Pegasus. You get Perseus," Draco said.

I nodded.

"And stay away from Ara," Virgo said.

I had tried not to think too much about the altar. But it seemed like a sound idea to stay away from it, considering Perseus wanted to sacrifice me on it. "How does it look like?" I asked.

Virgo shrugged. "Like a rock altar, I guess."

That was a very unhelpful description, but I realized that none of them had ever seen the altar. So I didn't press on. I would just have to stay away from any rock with a flat surface that resembled an altar.

"And what will you do with Arianna?" Corvus asked.

Draco shrugged. "Like Virgo, I think she's not powerful enough to do us any harm now, or else she would have killed us at night in the forest." Corvus gave a small nod, but didn't seem too convinced. "I'd rather focus on Perseus and Lupus."

"Sounds like a terrible plan," I said. "But we'll have to make do with that."

Draco smiled.

"Alright then," Corvus said as he stood from the floor. "Guess we better get some sleep."

He walked out of the living room, and into the hallway. Then he banged one of the doors shut.

Draco sighed and shook his head.

"He's angry you're not letting him fight," Virgo said.

"He's not skilled enough for this fight, you know that. He'll get killed," Draco said. "I'm not going to let that happen."

"He'll be insufferable tomorrow," Virgo said.

"You can deal with that," Draco said.

He stood up and walked to the kitchen. He kneeled down to retrieve something from the drawers beneath it. I heard the clank of something hard and solid against the floor. Draco stood and placed four white carved knives on the table.

He looked up at me. "These are all the weapons we have to kill them. But it's all we're going to need."

I nodded, looking gravely at the knives that lay on the counter. One stab in the heart, that was all I needed to kill Perseus.

Draco walked to the window and stood for a few seconds looking outside, blocking my view of the buildings across the river. Then he closed the shutters, but not before I got a glimpse of the moon outside.

CHAPTER 23

I WOKE up sweating. There was no light coming through the cracks in the shutters, and outside the street was silent. The candle Virgo had left on the table in between the two individual beds was still flickering, burning low.

Virgo slept on her side, her back to me. I didn't feel tired anymore, not with the dread inside my stomach coiled like a snake. I swung my legs from the bed, and my bare feet touched the cold floor.

A tear fell from my eye. It felt hot as fire as it slid down my cheek. More tears began to burst from my eyes, blurring my vision, the dam of emotions inside me starting to break, slowly.

Virgo stirred and turned to look at me. I didn't even bother to wipe my tears. She sat up, resting her back against the wall. Her hair was a brunette mess around her, and with the light from the candle her cheekbones seemed sharper, almost cutting through her skin.

"I don't even know why I'm upset," I said as more tears slid down.

Virgo took a couple of seconds to answer, her eyes gently looking at me. "Yes you do."

The dam inside me burst apart, and all at once I was overtaken with a wave of emotions crashing painfully against my chest. I had never hated someone so much as I hated Perseus. Not even Zia. At the thought of her, my heart contracted like a black hole consuming me from the inside. Was I angry at Zia for all she had done to me? Or was I angry that Perseus had killed her? I wouldn't miss her; that was for sure. But still, knowing that it had been Perseus who killed her made me feel like a little part of myself had been ripped away. I had wanted her dead, but not like that. I had wanted her to suffer, but not at his mercy.

It was all just wrong. And Perseus—I wished I had never set eyes upon him.

But I blamed myself more than I blamed him. How could I have been such a fool to believe him? How could I have felt safe in his arms? His hands had touched my face, the same hands that had taken the lives of so many. I should have sensed something was wrong with him. I should have known he was a liar and a killer.

It made sense, I thought, that he cared about me. Who else but a monster would ever care for me? No one sane ever had. But for a moment I *had* wanted him. I should have known better—I would always be better alone.

My tears now ran freely, soaking my cheeks, and I didn't hold back the sobs that built in my throat. Rage flowed through my heart and into my veins—the pain so physical that I felt as if a hand were squeezing my heart until it burst.

I wiped the tears from my eyes. My vision was blurry, but clear enough to see Virgo still watching me.

"I hate him," I whispered in a hoarse voice.

"I know," she whispered back. "I know how you feel."

I looked into her brown eyes. I believed her.

"You thought you could trust," she said slowly.

"I can't really trust anyone," I said.

"No, you can't," she said. She looked at her bony hands. "I know exactly how you feel. I once trusted someone too, and paid a high price for it." Her eyes met my own. Her gaze seemed to deepen. "I was sold to . . . bad people." She was silent for a couple more seconds, tracing lines through her hands with her fingers. "I killed them all," she whispered. "But I nearly killed myself after I was done."

Her words were silent, but inside my ears I heard them as desperate screams. I looked her over once again. How she had more bones than skin in her body—a walking skeleton.

"I let my anger consume me and it nearly cost me my life." Her features hardened. "When you kill Perseus, don't let your emotions win. It sounds hard, but kill him without anger. Just kill him."

The candle flickered lower, nearly extinguishing. The room darkened. That was enough to let me see the dozens of scars on Virgo's hands. Then the light flickered back.

We were both silent for a while, and the only sound were my sniffs.

"Will you guys be alright hiding?" I asked.

Virgo hesitated for a moment. "I hope so."

She lay back down on her bed, covering herself with the blankets. "Try to get some rest before morning."

She turned her back to me again, but I knew that just like me she wasn't going back to sleep.

We all sat somberly around the table, eating French toast and bacon that Draco had prepared. I ate it without any appetite, but knew that I needed the energy.

Sirius and Maera ate scrambled eggs in their dog bowls, because apparently they didn't like dog food. Aquila had gone out very early in the morning to hunt, and ate the carcass of a squirrel next to the front door, leaving the floor bloodied. I wondered what the maid would think had happened in here. Would Corvus lie again and tell her it was ketchup? Draco had given Leo a couple kilograms of raw beef, which he dribbled on enthusiastically, making the apartment smell like a slaughterhouse, even with the windows open.

Virgo sat to my right, Draco to my left, and Corvus in front of me. In the middle of the table was a map of Rome. "We're right here," Draco said as he pointed at the map with his fork. The apartment was located in Northern Rome, east of the Tiber River and on the Second Municipality.

Draco looked at Corvus, who still glared at him resentfully. "You and the others will go here," he pointed again with his fork. A bit more to the north, around nine blocks away, were the catacombs.

"Palatine Hill is over here," said Draco. "Right next to the Colosseum."

That was a long way south, and I expected that it would take us half an hour to get there by car, without traffic. But we had no rush—the blood moon wasn't until night. That meant we had all day to get there.

"We'll meet back here after the fight," Draco said, looking at Corvus, then at Virgo. "If we can't do that then we'll see each other at the park in Villa Borghese, under the tree where we always eat our lunch."

Corvus and Virgo nodded.

Draco folded the map and handed it to Virgo, who put it away in a pocket inside her jacket. We finished eating without any further talk, listening to Leo gnawing on his meat. Once we were done, we all remained sitting in silence for some time.

"Well," said Corvus. "We don't want to be caught in the attacks so we better get going." He turned to look at Leo. "Let's get Leo inside the Roman aqueducts so he can follow you to Palatine Hill."

Draco nodded, looking at Leo as he finished swallowing a piece of meat. "He can follow my scent to find us," he said.

We took our plates to the sink, but didn't bother washing them. Draco put on his jacket and opened the front door. He walked out of the apartment and down the stairs. Corvus followed after him. Before I could walk to the front door, Virgo grabbed my arm. Her other arm was behind her back.

"Everything alright?" I asked her.

She nodded, then handed me what she had been hiding. It was a knitted sweater. I had to smile, even if sweaters had never been my favorite. Virgo smiled in return.

"I'm afraid I can't contribute much to the fight except for this," she said. "It's also knife proof, in case Perseus tries to—"

"This will be enough," I said as I pulled the sweater over my blouse, then zipped up my jacket.

From the stairs, Corvus shouted our names. We walked out of the apartment, closed the main door behind us, and rushed down the stairs. It was a bit after midday when we stepped outside. The sky was completely clear, and light blue. Even though the sun was bright, the air was chilly. Underneath my jacket, hanging from my belt, was the white carved knife Draco had given me. Having a knife again with me made me feel more alert, and every few seconds I patted my side to make sure that it was still there.

Aquila clung to Draco's outstretched arm. He seemed heavy, but Draco didn't seem to mind. Sirius and Maera were sitting on the ground next to us. Leo was waiting patiently in the lobby.

There were several pedestrians walking on the sidewalk, mostly adults, and cars speeding by on the paved streets. Corvus glanced at the street in front of us. I couldn't see it behind the white building, but I knew the Tiber river was there.

"We should get Leo around the building," Corvus said. "The entrance to the aqueducts is right underneath the—"

Sirius began barking as if he had been bitten by a radioactive snake, and Meara howled with such anguish it made my heart stop. Aquila shrieked, his wings flapping wildly, but he didn't fly away. Leo leaped through the glass door of the entrance, blasting it to pieces.

Around us, people turned, their jaws slacking and their eyes widening at the sight of the lion. There was a couple who screamed in terror and dashed away.

"Calm down," Corvus said as he tried to pat Sirius on the head. "What's wrong?"

My first thought was that the attack had started, and I expected bombs to drop from the sky at any moment, but the sky looked clear and tranquil as ever.

Leo roared.

"What the hell is—" Draco tensed, removing his dark sunglasses and looking down at our feet.

A rumble echoed around us, deep and loud like a moan coming from the center of the Earth. The ground began to tremble underneath me, making me dizzy. The windows from the buildings around us cracked and burst, making it rain glass. I dropped down to the street and covered my face with my arms. I heard the panicked screams and shouts of people around us.

A wail filled the air, like an air-strike siren. It sounded like a woman screaming.

"Earthquake!" Someone shouted from the other side of the street.

I looked up to see the man who had shouted, only to see him get buried by the building that had stood behind him.

Chapter XXIX, Verse I

There lies the altar in between the seven mountains.
Alive it is, the rock beating with its own heart.
Abandoned and forgotten in the olden city of the she-wolf.
A single sacrifice is enough to assure the victory of the Prince.
A life of Light taken and a new one of Darkness forged.
The Princess the only blood that can give the Prince his full force.
At the bleeding moon when Darkness is full upon.

CHAPTER 24

DUST from the fallen building enclosed around us in a greedy grip. I covered my face, coughing and feeling like I had swallowed glass. After a couple seconds it seemed to blow away with the wind, and I looked up again. The apartment building behind us was cracked, and seemed about to rip apart, with cracks snaking through the walls and the windows all shattered. The building across the street was now a heap of concrete, and I could see no movement among the rubble.

The ground was still shaking, and I wondered when it would stop. It was as if a giant's step was causing the ground to bounce up and down. Draco, Corvus and Virgo were kneeling around me. Leo stood protectively over us, his ears thrown back. Sirius was barking madly like a fire alarm, hurting my ears, and Maera was trembling in Virgo's arms. I hadn't noticed when Aquila had taken flight, but he was no longer with us.

The streetlamps on the sidewalk trembled like twigs cut from a tree branch. Twenty yards away, one of them fell over an empty car, shattering the hood, and the one right next to it fell towards a building, creating a dent on the wall from the impact. Further down the street I saw another building crumbling down like a Jenga tower, sending dust sprawling up. Screams of horror filled the air, and I clenched my fists in frustration. Cracks spread along the street, as if it were glass about to shatter.

Then the moaning around us stopped. Sirius whimpered. I could still feel the ground beneath me swaying and trembling. The alarm stopped abruptly. I remained kneeling on the ground, breathing fast.

A couple buildings had crumbled, and the ones that hadn't were about to. I could see a broken bathtub, a white door, some rags that had maybe been clothes, and water spurting out of a broken pipe, all of it mixed up with the rubble of bricks.

Thirty yards away from us, a large building had broken in half, as if a giant had stepped on it. All the streetlights, except one I spotted in the distance, were down. The street itself was filled with broken glass and rubble from the walls of the buildings.

Ambulances echoed somewhere far away.

"I should have known," Virgo whispered next to me. "I should have known it was going to be an earthquake."

"It's not your fault," Draco said silently, his hand on Virgo's back.

"So this was Algol," I said, my voice hoarse.

Virgo nodded. "I should have known," she sat down and buried her head in her palms. Leo snarled, his bright-golden eyes narrowed. Sirius began to walk around us, smelling the ground with his ears thrown back. "It never crossed my mind that Perseus could use Algol to cause earthquakes." She uncovered her face, and I could see the tears streaming down. "He always causes terrorist attacks by driving people's minds and desires, but a natural catastrophe . . ."

"Does it make a difference?" Corvus asked. His dark eyes were emotionless. "We knew people were going to die."

"But not . . ." Virgo's voice seemed broken. "Not like this. The earthquake probably damaged all of central Italy."

I took a deep breath, and my hand went to the knife at my hip, wanting to reassure myself that it was still there.

"Has Algol been the cause of many earthquakes before?" I asked, trying to contain my growing fear.

"A few big ones," said Virgo. "Not all. But there was one . . . Oh no . . ." Her face went suddenly very pale. "I didn't even remember."

"What?" Draco said, shaking her.

"It's . . . it was a long time ago," she said with wide eyes. "I investigated it a while ago, but didn't put much thought into it since I focused only on attacks of—"

"What?" Corvus asked, desperate.

"The explosion of Mount Vesuvius, the one that buried Pompeii, nearly two thousand years ago. That was Algol," she said.

There was silence among us for a couple of seconds.

"Are you sure?" Draco asked.

She nodded solemnly. "But that was because of a solar eclipse. Its shadow passed over Vesuvius when Algol was present." Corvus cursed, kicking away a piece of rubble. "Since this is not a solar eclipse, I can't know what's going to happen."

"But a blood moon is still a lunar eclipse, so we can guess it's really bad," Corvus said. "And the blood moon hasn't even started!"

There was a shriek above us. Aquila flew in circles, finally landing on the street at my feet. Aquila flapped its wings and squawked a couple of times. I didn't know how to speak eagle, but I guessed he said that the city was torn to bits and pieces.

"We have to move," Draco said, standing up and surveying the street.

People had begun to rush to the rubble to help the people who were trapped, climbing over the tiny hills of broken concrete. I noticed that a few more people were also emerging from the buildings that still stood. There was an elderly woman with blood running down her temple, carrying a small cat in her arms.

"I'm not sure we'll be able to hide in the catacombs anymore," Corvus said. "They won't be safe."

Draco considered this, biting his lower lip. "Then you have to get far away from here. Go north, as far as you can," he said as he helped Virgo stand. "Algol will be at full power at night so we should expect something else to happen—maybe another terrorist attack or another earthquake. Stay away from big crowds and stay alert." Virgo and Corvus both nodded solemnly. "When the fight is over, I'll go find you."

Virgo lunged at Draco and hugged him fiercely. "Please be careful," she said as she pulled back.

"You too," Draco said. He pulled away from Virgo and shook hands with Corvus, then leaned down to pat Sirius in the head as the dog licked his hand. He scratched Maera's fuzzy head too.

Virgo met my gaze. "We'll see each other again." She made it sound more like a promise than a hope. I swallowed the knot in my throat and nodded, wishing it were true.

Draco and I trotted side by side, with Leo behind us. I wondered what people thought of Leo. Maybe they assumed he had escaped from the zoo. Was there a zoo in Rome? But the lion was the least of their problems, and people were quickly distracted when more people emerged from the rubble, or when a new dead body was found.

Draco's sunglasses had broken in the commotion of the earthquake, so he tried not to make eye contact and kept his gaze down. Aquila flew over us, guiding the way. I realized that if we wanted a surprise attack on Perseus, the lion and eagle might give us away, but I didn't care if he knew we were coming.

The city of Rome was in ruins around us. I kept wondering how Perseus had become much more powerful than the rest of us and caused such mass destruction and death. If there was anyone who could answer that, it was me. I had been with him for days, and knew him more intimately than the rest of the Star Children. But I couldn't figure it out.

At the same time, I felt a chill snaking through my bones at the thought that if Perseus shed my blood, this level of destruction would become instantly available to him. He wouldn't have to wait for another eclipse—he could destroy entire cities as he wished. I couldn't let him kill me—for the good of the world, and my own good too, of course.

Draco and I jumped over a fallen streetlight that blocked the entire street. The street we were in was wide, thankfully, but the sidewalks were buried under the debris of all the fallen buildings. Among the rubble was a large TV, a broken dinner table, and a ragged blue couch. There were two ambulances parked in the middle of the street, and men with green and yellow vests tried to find people buried underneath, shouting things in Italian and English then waiting for a response. They also had a couple of dogs with them that sniffed around the rubble.

Most of the people had their clothes and faces covered in dust, a few of them bleeding or limping around the street, trying to find others or making their way to the nearest ambulance.

The air smelled disgusting around me—like vomit, fresh cement and feces. Maybe the plumbing system in the city had broken? There were certainly many pipes that had ruptured. I had passed by several streets with large puddles of water.

Aquila shrieked and turned right, so we did too. I noticed that the narrow street to our lefts would have been impossible to walk through. The buildings had collapsed on each other. I tried not to think how many people were dead inside of them, but knew from the ruin we had seen that there were probably thousands.

Some streets were blocked by the police, and many more too dangerous to walk through. What should have been an hour and a half walking to the Colosseum would extend to at least three hours, two of them already past.

We turned left onto a new street were most of the buildings had crumbled except for the stone church halfway down the block. Despite churches being some of the oldest buildings in the city I realized that many had survived. One of the statues decorating the church's facade had fallen in front of the entrance and broken, but the rest was still intact. The decapitated angel head from the statue stared blankly up at me as I passed by.

We turned right onto a new street. The large store windows on the bottom floors of the buildings were shattered. There was one building that had toppled down, and I could see a white plastic mannequin arm sticking out of the rubble.

Draco turned left at the end of the street and I followed after him.

Plazas were especially crowded, being the only debris-free place where people could gather. We passed by one where people were handing out free food and water to people sitting or standing around the central fountain, which I noticed had stopped spouting water from the top. The ground was fractured around the fountain, as if it would crumble at any moment and sink, leaving a gaping hole in the middle of the plaza.

"Have you seen this woman?" An anguished man said as he clutched my arm. His face was so pale that he looked about to faint, and he smelled strongly of vomit. I looked at the picture on his phone, which was hard since the screen was cracked. It showed a young woman with short blonde hair.

"No, sorry," I said as I pulled away and joined Draco as we edged around the plaza to get to the other side.

Most people were crying, alone or with others. A few were silent, their faces slack with shock. I could see their haunted eyes as I passed.

Draco and I didn't talk at all while we walked. The sound of ambulances hadn't died down, and the high-pitched howl was staring to deafen me.

We took a left turn at Aquila's directions and came onto a street next to the river. Thirty yards ahead of us I noticed that a bridge had collapsed into the river. Boats in the water carried people shrouded in blankets. There was also a large crane pulling a black car out of the water. I could see that the crane had already brought out two cars that were now in the middle of the street across of the river. One of them was crumpled as if it had driven straight into a titanium wall, and the other one was squashed like a pancake.

We continued through the streets until finally, nearly an hour later, we arrived at the Colosseum. The Colosseum seemed intact, and I wondered how many earthquakes it had withstood. It had fared better than most buildings, and looked less ruined than the rest of the city. The structure was taller than I remembered it, at least as big as a modern stadium, making me feel tiny as it towered above me. It was made of brown stone and had arcs with small columns in between them. I noticed many chunks missing, as if the structure had been part of a mass shooting and still bore bullet marks of the damage. Those seemed old, though. The dying sun emitted an eerie orange-red glow that shone through the arcs and made it seem as if the Colosseum was bleeding light. Its wide shadows spread across the ground.

Draco and I stopped on the street in front of the Colosseum, sitting on the sidewalk with our backs against the wall to catch our breaths. The street was empty of cars, and people walked freely on it. I spotted many police officers, firefighters, and nurses with bright vests. There was an army of ambulances parked in the plaza, in between the Colosseum and the small marble arch to its right. Wounded people crowded around the ambulances, and others helped by bringing buckets of water, medical supplies, coats, blankets and food.

I would have expected Perseus to choose the Colosseum for his sacrifice—it seemed more appropriate considering how many people had died there—but Ara was in Palatine Hill, the ruins right next to it. They weren't visible from where we were sitting, but Draco pointed at a path on our right, lined with trees, that presumably led to the site. At the end of the path was a marble arch, but I couldn't see beyond it.

Leo had disappeared, probably not wanting to be so visible, and I didn't worry much about where he may be. Aquila flew above us and silently settled at the very top of the Colosseum. He was nearly the same color as the walls, so he was hard to spot.

Draco and I remained sitting for a while, the sounds of commotion loud around us, but I ignored them. My mind was strangely empty, not able to focus on anything except the green patch of grass that sprouted from the sidewalk next to me.

After some time, I felt Draco's head jerking up, and he squinted at the ruins on our rights. I couldn't discern what he was looking at, but his muscles tensed.

"He's already there," he said in a low voice.

CHAPTER 25

THE ANCIENT ruins didn't seem like much to me—they were just more rocks. Going along with Draco's plan, I had entered the ruins alone, and walked aimlessly for a while, trying to find Perseus or Orion, but there was no sign of them. I also tried to spot any flat-surfaced rocks that could resemble an altar, but there were none. All the rocks were coarse and ragged, tall as pillars or round like boulders.

After a while, I went back towards the entrance and decided to sit down. I was sure Perseus would come to find me. I sat on some old stairs; they were cold and made of cement. On both sides were crumbling red-brick buildings, but now most of them looked white. The place was so worn down, the structures no more than two stories tall and with walls missing, that the earthquake probably hadn't affected much. I imagined the buildings would have been taller once, but there were no remains of the upper floors. I realized that the ruins were similar to the city after the earthquake—minus the rubble and dead people.

The buildings at my sides looked like they had once been small brick houses. The open arch to walk inside the structures was blocked by iron bars, and when I had tried to peek inside, I couldn't see anything through the dark. The only modern addition to the site was a couple of trashcans placed alongside the buildings, and a few signs I had seen at the entrance pointing to the bathrooms.

Directly in front of me, right across the narrow and pebbled street, were the remains of other buildings, no more than brick walls and a few heaps of earth and stone. There was an iron fence a few feet away from me that surrounded them, preventing me from walking closer.

Across from that, in the distance, and half-hidden behind tall trees, was a six-story tall structure. The only things that remained of what must have been a very impressive palace or temple were three arches that had caved in to create a large room inside them. It had openings on its other side like small windows, which were cut out like more arches.

I couldn't see the city from the ruins, nor hear the wails of the ambulances and police cars. It seemed like the ruins were part of another world, abandoned and forgotten, surrounded by large trees that had claimed back their territory from humans. I hadn't seen anyone in the site, not a single soul, and that had made me feel more dreadful. The sun had sunk lower, right below the buildings behind me. No wind blew, but I still felt cold inside my jacket, even with Virgo's magical sweater.

There was movement from the corner of my eye. I turned sharply to my right, and my stomach shrank. Perseus was walking straight towards me, striding casually over the pebbled path. He wasn't wearing a jacket, only a long-sleeved shirt and jeans. His red hair was disheveled, and, as he came closer, I noticed the dark patches under his eyes. My heart began to beat faster with every step he took. He stopped right in front of me.

He eyed me from head to toe, then took a step back and leaned against the iron fence. We were no more than five feet apart, but it felt like inches.

"Where's the wolf?" I asked.

"I came alone," he said, his voice hoarser than normal. "I needed to talk to you."

"Where's Orion?" I asked.

He shrugged. "He's nearby. I didn't hurt him."

I clenched my fists, not sure whether to believe him or not. "Where is he?"

Perseus's gaze traveled back to where he had come from. "He's here in the ruins. I'll take you to him."

Every muscle in my body knotted. It was a trap, but if I wanted to see Orion alive again, I had to follow Perseus and hope the others were nearby, waiting to attack.

Even though the sky was still light blue I could feel the darkness closing in. The moon had started to rise in front of me—a white orb that would soon turn red.

"But before I take you to him, we need to talk," he said, his hands gripping the iron fence tightly.

"About what?" I hissed.

His black eyes stared intently at me, and I could almost see the sadness inside them. "I'm sorry," he said. I opened my mouth to respond, but didn't know what to say. I hadn't expected him to apologize. "I should have told you the truth from the beginning. About . . . me," he said, motioning at himself. His eyes stared at the ground for a moment, then back up again, the sorrow inside them deep as a bottomless pit. "I can't control it."

"You mean Algol?" I asked.

He gulped, his Adam's apple bobbing. "I really can't, Andromeda." Perseus's mouth twitched, and he held tighter to the railing. "I thought that I could control Algol if it ever awoke inside me, but it controls me." His eyes pleaded with mine to understand. "It's as if it's a different *me,* taking control over my thoughts and actions."

"Why did you need to tell me this?" I asked.

He shrugged. "The hospital, New York," he looked towards the entrance of the ruins. "This . . . I-I just wanted you to know that it wasn't on purpose."

I had no answer to that. Was he sorry that he had to kill me too?

"I really wish we could have worked together," he said, not meeting my eyes.

"Worked together to destroy the Universe?" I asked.

He turned back to me sharply, his expression dumbfounded. "What? Who said anything about destroying the Universe? Why would I destroy the Universe if I live in it?"

I swallowed hard. "Then what *do* you want?"

He hesitated, his hands tightening on the iron fence again. He shook his head, and chuckled, as if this were so funny. "I just want freedom," he whispered. Those words hit me like a bullet in the chest. "Destiny, Fate, Prophecy—they're a prison." He met my eyes. There was a weariness inside them that I hadn't seen before, as if he were an old man who had fought wars all of his life and was tired of it. "We all deserve the freedom to choose."

I set my jaw hard, fighting back the tears that had unexpectedly gathered behind my eyes. Those words resonated inside me like the ring of a bell. Didn't I want that freedom too? No, I didn't. Corvus, Virgo, and Draco had said that the Universe would collapse without Fate and Destiny. And besides, Perseus wanted to kill me, so there was no way we could ever fight for the same thing. He talked about freedom after he had murdered thousands in the attacks he had caused. He would achieve *freedom* even if it meant killing every single person on the planet.

Perseus didn't want freedom—he only craved destruction.

I was aware of the sun below the horizon, and of all the shadows gaining ground around me. Night was fast approaching and the moon would turn red soon. I needed to find Orion, *now.*

Perseus pushed away from the railing and motioned me to follow him. I walked a few feet besides him, every muscle in my body alert. The weight of the knife was like an itch I couldn't scratch. I needed to kill him. Every cell in my body commanded me to do it, yet I had to hold back, just for a little longer.

We passed by more ruined buildings. Perseus studied them with interest, seemingly taking detail of everything. Once we were out of that path we turned right into another one. This path sloped slightly upwards, and had strange patterns on the ground, as if the street had been reconstructed a couple of times, creating a mosaic of different stones. To the right were more lonely walls that gave way to some ancient-looking stairs which led to a cluster of trees. To the left was a small hill. Perseus continued straight.

I wondered how he could be so calm, knowing that he was about to sacrifice me. But I was strangely calm too.

We continued forward, passing by more skeletal remains of ruins and olive trees on both sides. The very light green of the leaves looked almost white. They were perfectly still, as if the trees were holding their breaths to see what Perseus and I would do.

"This is where Rome was founded," Perseus said abruptly after about ten minutes of walking.

"What?" I asked.

Perseus didn't turn to look at me. "Palatine Hill. This is supposedly where the demigod twins Romulus and Remus were suckled by the she-wolf Lupa after they were abandoned. The brothers founded Rome." He looked at the ruins around us. "And the first emperors built their homes here."

Then he was silent again. I eyed him warily, but he didn't say anything else.

These ruins, compared to Delphi, seemed darker, surrounded by large trees that cast wide shadows over most of the site, as if the forest that had once been here wanted to reclaim its land. There was a tense silence around us, and not even birds chirped, as if they had fled the site knowing what was about to happen. The air around me smelled like rotten wood.

I ignored the ruins and instead became more aware of Perseus. His arms dangled at his sides, but his muscles were tense, telling me that he, too, was ready for a fight.

Darkness had started to settle around us, the sky above becoming a darker shade of blue with every passing second.

We finally arrived at an open space, and I quickly took in my new surroundings. To the left were more ruins, protected by a fence. There was a tall, ragged pillar that had probably been part of a wall once, but the rest of the ruins were just slabs of brown-red stones, none of them taller than me. They were the remainders of where walls and pillars had once been placed. I couldn't make out much more except jagged pieces of rocks. To the right were tall shrubs, covering some ruins behind them that seemed like they had been buried under the earth, as if they had sunk through time.

There were sparse trees here and there, a few of them growing in the distance behind all the ruins. I realized that the ground underneath me was muddy, and that there was no grass.

As I continued walking forward, I heard a muffled cry to my right and turned. My heart nearly beat to my throat. It was Orion. I hadn't seen him before, but at once I spotted his large shape sitting with his back against the remains of a stone pillar and hurried to his side.

He had been tied, his legs bound together and his hands behind his back. Behind him were stairs that went up into nothingness, as if leading to heaven.

I kneeled at Orion's side and took the gag from his mouth. "I didn't think you would be stupid enough to come for me," he growled in a raspy voice.

I nearly laughed out loud, but contended myself with biting my lip. The sky had turned completely dark above us, and the only light came from the full moon, which I realized was as good as any streetlamp. Orion had looked better. He had a bruise on one cheek, a split lip, and his hair was a wild mess. The white in his eyes was red, and I assumed he hadn't slept much in the last couple days, if at all. I took his cheek in my hand, feeling the fuzz from the stubble he hadn't shaved, feeling the warm relief that he was alive.

"Why did you come back for me?" He hissed. "Now we're both dead."

"It doesn't have to be that way," Perseus said behind me.

I turned and gave a startled jump, noticing the wolf behind Perseus. My eyes averted, looking away from the wolf's eyes, and looked instead at Perseus's shadowed figure. His face was pale as the moon.

"I'll let him go if you do as I say," Perseus said to me.

"No!" Orion roared. "Come on, Andromeda. Just go."

I didn't turn and focused solely on Perseus. "Let him go now."

Perseus shook his head, the muscles in his jaw twitching. "I give you my word that I'll free him after."

"He'll kill me," Orion growled in frustration. "You seriously don't believe what he says, do you?"

I had hoped that Draco and the other two would have already shown up to help me, but there was no sign of them. Draco had said that they would attack Perseus when he least expected it, and this would have been a great moment to do so.

"Fine," I said. "I'll trust your word."

Orion grumbled some curses at me, which I ignored. The moon above us seemed to have become just a bit bigger, and I knew that in a while longer it would turn red. Where the hell was Draco? I couldn't kill Perseus with the wolf there.

Perseus smiled. There was a current around me, making the leaves from the trees stir, but it wasn't wind. My scars erupted in sudden pain, and I heard Orion grunt. I knew he felt it too. My insides were churning, as if attracted to a magnet and repelled by it at the same time. Hunger arose inside of me, stronger than before. I needed to eat. No, I needed to consume.

The ruins seemed to dissolve away as Arianna's form took shape. Her face appeared out of nothing, like it had been there all along. Her clear blue eyes were more brilliant than ever, as if the moon shone within them. Her hair coiled around her head in curls, and I noticed she still wore a black dress.

Arianna stood next to Perseus, but her feet seemed not to touch the ground—if she even had feet. "Let's get along with it, we don't have much time left," she said, her voice lulling. "I see you did manage to bring her back." Perseus looked like he was about to throw up.

"I didn't want to have to do this," he said to me, trying to swallow. "I'm sorry. It's the only way I can be free."

I looked around, but didn't notice any particular rock that resembled an altar. But I knew that Ara was close by.

"I'm sure you are," Orion grumbled behind me. I turned. He stared intently into my eyes, his own dark amber. "What the hell were you thinking? You surely must have known that this was a trap."

"I did know," I assured Orion, who frowned. Then I turned back to Perseus and Arianna.

I smiled.

Chapter IX, Verse III

Alone she walks amidst the uproar.
In chains that bond all except for her soul.
Prisoner of blood, free of her damnation.
The Prince she will slay for her own survival.
Or die by his hand in a rage of delusion.
The demon shall rise to meet his own rival.
Or lose his own heart in the raptness of sorrow.

CHAPTER 26

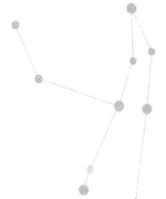

A DEAFENING roar boomed from my left. Before Lupus could react, Leo leaped from the edge of the open space, jaws open to reveal a row of sharp teeth. Leo crashed with the wolf, who had been standing behind Perseus and Arianna, and both animals tumbled to the ground, rolling and snapping their teeth. They were the same size, and seemed equal in strength.

Perseus jumped forward, away from the animals. Shock rippled through his face, but Arianna didn't seem surprised, her expression still as stone.

There was a rustle behind me, and Draco jumped out of the shrubs. He stood right next to me and I took a few steps back. Before Perseus and Arianna could turn to look, Draco had already inhaled. He blew, and fire erupted from his mouth like a flame-thrower, bringing bright-red light to our surroundings. Perseus jumped out of the way, stumbled, and fell safely away from the fire. With a shriek Arianna was gone, the leaves from the trees rustling without any wind. Perseus hastily scrambled back to his feet, eyes fixed on me.

"Go!" Draco yelled.

I gripped the knife and slid it from my belt. Its weight felt familiar. The carvings on the handle squirmed at my touch, as if they were fighting each other to death. Perseus's eyes widened in surprise, then narrowed in concentration. Somewhere deeper in the ruins, Leo and Lupus were still fighting, their growls filling the air. I lunged at Perseus, but he didn't move.

Orion shouted a warning behind me, but it was too late. With a dull pain on my right side, I was knocked flat down, my vision swirling. The knife flew from my hand, and all I could hear were shouts and growls around me. I had never been kicked by a horse before, and could feel the hoof print marked on my side.

I struggled to my knees, and immediately felt a strong arm seize my waist, pulling me up. My ribs felt like a truck was crushing them. Still dizzy, I took in what was happening in a detached sort of way, as if I were watching from a distance. Perseus had managed to get on top of the horse, and had hoisted me up with his arms around me, leaving my legs dangling off the horse and my torso sprawled across it, right on his lap. Pegasus whinnied, then began racing away by hoof. I bounced up and down, trying to free myself from Perseus's grip.

The horse flapped its giant wings and jumped into the air, flying towards the night. I let out a surprised scream. I clung to Perseus's arm for dear life, and he held me even tighter, crushing my lungs, which made it hard to breathe. If he had wanted to kill me by dropping me to the ground, he could have done it, but didn't.

"What are you doing?" I demanded furiously.

I wasn't even sure he had heard me with the roar of the wind around us. I used my other hand to grip Perseus's leg. If I fell, I would be sure to take him down with me. I tried to pull myself up so I could sit on the horse, but he was still flying upwards, and the best I could do was hold on as my legs thrashed wildly against the air. Pegasus's wings flapped rhythmically, like a slow helicopter, while the cold wind slapped at my face. The horse's body was warm under me, and his coat soft. His mane fluttered with the wind, brushing my back like silky strands of hair.

I looked down at the ground below us. Draco's fire had set a tree in flames, casting light around the open space. But we were so high up that Draco and Orion were two minuscule shapes, running towards the ruins. Leo and Lupus were in the open space. Leo was on his side, trying to get up, but Lupus lunged at him and sunk his claws into Leo's chest. I heard the roar from the sky.

Pegasus flew away from them, turning into a new direction. I realized he was still flying atop the ruins, not towards the city. I looked up at the moon, and my heart skipped a beat. It was starting, a coppery-red light touching the edge of the moon.

There was a screech next to me. There were no clouds in the sky, but I was suddenly blinded by a white light that sizzled past me. Lightning struck the ground, and the sound of thunder made my ears ring as if a hammer had crashed down on them.

Pegasus whinnied and swerved madly in the sky like a faulty helicopter. Perseus held on tighter to me, cursing loudly. Aquila screeched again. I closed my eyes, and felt the heat of the lightning sizzling past me. The smell of burning flesh reached my nose, and I noticed that Aquila had hit Pegasus on his wing. The horse whinnied again in pain, swerving lower.

"Come on!" Perseus shouted encouragingly to the horse.

I could hear Aquila screeching in the distance, and lightning struck the earth again, this time further away. The horse swerved down like a roller coaster and I felt my insides swirling as if they were in a blender. One of my ribs crunched against the back of the horse as we landed. Breath was knocked from my lungs and pain erupted from my side as if I had been stabbed. Perseus let go and I fell off Pegasus, flat on my face. My nose burst with pain, but when I touched it, I found that I wasn't bleeding. I took in a few strangled breaths then stood up, feeling as if my legs had turned to spaghetti.

I looked around and realized I knew where I was. We were right next to the three six-story tall arches I had seen earlier. They curved inward, like an elongated dome cut in half, and were spacious—each big enough to host the stage of an outdoor concert. But now they held nothing except jumbled pieces of rock. The curved ceiling had round holes as decoration.

There was something in front of it that from a distance I hadn't been able to see. My stomach churned as I looked at it. It was a large rock, half as tall as me, and its surface was mostly flat, if a little uneven. It was enclosed by another iron fence, as if it were important. I didn't need Corvus, Draco or Virgo here to tell me that the rock was Ara, the sacrificial altar. The simple sight of it seemed to turn my organs inside out.

A few feet away were columns of stone, but those were at least four times as tall as me, and wide enough that I could have lived inside them. They seemed to have been in recent renovation, the one furthest away with a scaffold still around it. In the distance were the skeletal walls of the ruins I had been in when I had waited for Perseus, the ones that resembled a little brick village. With the darkness around me they looked more solemn, like a town abandoned to let death sweep through its streets.

Pegasus whinnied loudly, bringing my attention back to him. I looked at the horse, who was standing right next to the huge middle arch, one of its wings singed at the edge. It was bleeding, too, but that didn't look fatal. Perseus was trying to calm down the horse, caressing his mane, his back to me.

I didn't have the knife, but didn't care. I lunged at Perseus and knocked him flat on the ground. He struggled underneath me, but before he could flip me around I punched him in the nose. He roughly pushed me backwards, and I fell hard on my back. Pegasus tried to crush me with its hooves as if I were an ugly spider he wanted to kill. I rolled away from him, closer to the arches.

I was about to stand again when my scars began to burn. The pain felt as if my naked back was pressed against a sheet of ice. My tongue shriveled inside my mouth, and suddenly I couldn't find enough air around me. My throat contracted.

Above me, most of the moon had turned orange—blood red on one edge and white on the other. Perseus kneeled next to me and hoisted me to my feet.

"Come on," he said, as if expecting me to cooperate.

I didn't know what Arianna had done, but I felt weaker. With a shaky fist, I feebly punched Perseus in the gut. His abdomen was solid as a stone wall, and my hand throbbed in pain. Instead of punching back he simply held both of my wrists and dragged me towards the altar.

Every single instinct told me to stay away from it. It looked just like any other ordinary gray rock in the ruins, but there was something that set it apart from all others. Maybe it was that I recognized it as another Star Child, and wondered vaguely if the rock had a sort of consciousness.

Perseus dragged me to the iron fence, and I could do nothing except grip the fence with both hands as my last barrier against the rock. Aquila screeched above me, and lightning crashed down a few feet away, making my ears thunder with pain. Pegasus whinnied loudly, but I barely heard him with my ringing ears. For a second, I was glad Aquila had come back to help me. But that feeling vanished as soon as the horse flew again into the air, presumably chasing after Aquila.

Now I was completely alone with Perseus.

He crouched down next to me, trying to pry my fingers free from the fence. "Please, Andromeda," he pleaded. "I don't have any other option."

"Yes you do," I growled. "Don't let a stupid book tell you what to do and just let me go."

My hand burst in fiery pain, and I screamed. Perseus had hit my fingers with a rock. I knew that probably a few of the fingers in my left hand were broken, but I didn't care. I yelled in outrage, letting go of the fence, and turned to punch Perseus on the nose with my right hand. His nose had already been bleeding, but now more blood spurted out of it.

"Andromeda!" Draco shouted in the distance.

Perseus turned towards where the shout had come from, opposite from the big arcs, then back to me. He held the rock tighter in his hand, and hit me in the head. My brain seemed to burst like a balloon. Dark spots danced in my eyes and didn't seem to go away. Vertigo took over me and I felt my stomach suddenly heavy, as if I had swallowed petroleum.

There was thunder in the distance, but it seemed far away, maybe on the other side of Palatine Hill, or near the Colosseum. Had Pegasus lured Aquila away so he wouldn't be able to help me?

"I'm sorry," Perseus whispered in my ear. "I'm sorry, Andromeda. I did care about you."

I couldn't even answer him. My jaw seemed to have gone slack and my tongue numb.

"Andromeda!" Orion roared.

He was close by. I opened my eyes, but saw everything blurry. Orion stood right in front of the tall stone column next to the altar, at most thirty feet away. Draco was beside him, both of them still like statues. A blur of gray passed next to me, staring intently at the two boys. Lupus was limping, his front paw curled onto his chest, and he had four straight lines running through his side. The blood oozing out of them made his fur look black. I couldn't spot Leo anywhere.

I willed Orion and Draco to move, but they didn't. They simply stared dumbly at the wolf, who was licking his teeth as if ready to eat them both. Then Arianna was standing next to them, her pale figure hovering beside Orion. I realized she was nearly as tall as him. She began tying something around his neck. Was that a rope? It was, I realized as my vision cleared a little, and she was fastening it around his neck. Then she went to Draco and did the same, faster. I didn't even know where she had pulled those ropes from, then looked up and realized that the ropes had already been there, at the top of the column behind Orion and Draco. There were at least a dozen ropes tied together in a small loop on top of a large concrete box. Some ropes were long and dropped all the way to the ground, while others were only a couple feet long. Someone had left them there during the renovation, which still seemed to be in progress, and I cursed whatever stupid worker was responsible for it. Arianna whispered something into Orion's ear, then vanished from the ground. I blinked, then noticed that she was standing at the top of the column, staring down at the boys. If she managed to knock that concrete box to the other side of the column, the ropes would hang Orion and Draco.

I knew I could free them. The rope wasn't a lock, or any sort of door or safe, but it was still something closed that I could open.

My attention was pulled away from them as two arms grabbed my waist. Perseus hoisted me up towards the rock. It was uneven. But I realized, with an electric chill down my spine, that it seemed to perfectly fit the curves of my body.

There was a vibration coming out of the rock too, I could feel it on my back. They were small thumps, like the beat of a heart, in unison with my own heartbeat.

I commanded my body to fight Perseus, but couldn't muster enough strength to even slap him across the cheek. Perseus climbed onto the rock, kneeling next to me. My sight cleared a bit more, and I noticed he held a white knife in his hand. Had he had it all along, hidden inside his shirt? I wondered if it was the knife Zia had given me. Perseus sat on top of me, his weight crushing my abdomen, and I squirmed away, trying to escape. Blood ran from his nose and down his lips and chin, but he didn't seem to care.

I looked up at the moon. I had never seen a blood moon before. It was a dark shade of red, truly looking like it was bleeding. I looked back at Perseus, whose eyes were narrowed at me.

The ground began to sway underneath me—up and down and side to side. Another earthquake? Perseus winced, as if someone had punched his face, and he let the knife drop next to him on the rock, scraping my leg, which immediately felt like it had been dipped in acid. There was a loud wailing in the distance, and a boom like an explosion. The beating of the rock accelerated, the vibration sharp on my back.

Perseus screamed, as if he were being ripped apart. What was happening to him? Was he using Algol's power? He seemed to get heavier on top of me, my abdomen feeling like it was being crushed by a whale. Arianna's voice seemed to come from everywhere around me, as if she whispered through the wind.

"Kill her now," she said.

Perseus shut his eyes, and the ground stopped trembling abruptly. Or at least I thought it did because I couldn't hear the alarm anymore, but I still felt like everything was lurching back and forth beneath me.

Perseus picked the knife and gripped it tighter, still without opening his eyes. Then he did open them, seconds later, and I noticed how dark they were—blacker than the sky.

He held the knife high.

CHAPTER 27

IN THAT moment, knowing the certainty of my death, I had a single second of clarity. But that single second was all that I needed for the truth to hit me.

I took too much from her, Perseus had told me when I had asked about his eyes. Now I understood.

I knew what made Perseus so powerful.

That simple knowledge gave my body a shot of adrenaline. I kicked Perseus in the crotch, and he fell from the rock, too surprised to defend himself. I sat bolt upright, ignoring the sparks blinding my vision.

I scrambled away from the altar, falling to my knees on the ground, and turned my attention to Arianna. She still stood at the top of the stone column, pushing the concrete box towards the edge. Orion and Draco were being dragged backwards by the ropes tied around their necks, towards the column, but they made no noise, their eyes still fixed on Lupus.

The wolf growled, but didn't move. Maybe if it lost eye contact then Orion and Draco would be able to free themselves.

"Arianna!" I shouted at the top of my lungs, feeling my head spinning again. I stood on trembling legs. She turned to look at me with a frown, probably puzzled that I was still alive.

I closed my eyes. The hunger was still there, lurking inside me. It had been there since I had first met Arianna at the psychiatric hospital, I just hadn't known what it meant. Now I knew what the hunger asked for, the same thing it had asked of Perseus.

The hunger inside me grew as I felt Arianna move closer to me. "Are you sure you want to take that path?" she whispered. "Everything has a price."

I opened my eyes again. Arianna was standing right in front of me. I glanced at Orion and Draco, their bodies still paralyzed, and the rope around their necks tight. Arianna had almost managed to push the box over the edge. I didn't know what the price to pay would be, but I was willing to pay it to save Orion. I wouldn't let Arianna and Perseus take him away from me. He was the only person I had left—the only one I had ever cared for.

The hunger was there, gnawing at my bones. I looked into Arianna's unnaturally brilliant-blue eyes. She didn't look surprised, as if she had expected everything to turn out the way it had. She suddenly vanished and appeared again on top of the column. She kept pushing the slab, faster. I cursed under my breath.

I was tackled from behind and fell to the ground, the air knocked from my lungs. I gasped for breath. Perseus scrambled to his feet. He gripped my ankle and began dragging me backwards—towards the altar. I clawed my nails on the muddy ground beneath me, my fingers bleeding.

I closed my eyes, feeling that hunger, that emptiness inside my chest, that figureless beast that had followed me for days. Instead of pushing away the hunger, I let it take shape inside me, guiding me towards what it wanted to consume. The hunger became sharper, a pang that made my tongue shrivel and my stomach contract. But it also made me aware of the darkness around me. I had never felt it before, but I could now. It was a current, like water in a river, except it didn't need containing. It flowed all around the Universe—shapeless and strong. Invisible to the eye, but present once the hunger guided me to it. I could feel it like a silk veil around me, grazing my skin, tingling my scars.

I was vaguely aware of Perseus pulling me atop the rock again. My back scraped the rough surface, and I could feel the beat of the rock like the pulsing of my own heart. I opened my eyes. Perseus held the knife high above my head, gripping it so tightly that his knuckles were as white as the blade. The moon above us was bright red, just as his hair, and the sky around it black as his eyes. I couldn't see the darkness anymore, but felt its current like a suffocating wind.

"Kill her," Arianna's whisper came from all around us.

Perseus hesitated, gripping the knife hard. That was all I needed. I screamed, feeling all my scars burst in pain at once. I could have counted them if I had wanted to, traced them blindly through my back, shoulders and arms, knowing exactly where each one of them was.

I was blinded by a sudden light, and it took me a second to realize it was coming from me. Instead of subsiding, the hunger inside me seemed to crave for more, leaving me feeling hungrier than before. So I took in more, my soul drinking from that invisible current that flowed all around me—that power that fed all life and death.

I began to lose my grip on reality, not caring about anything else except the growing hunger, which was making me feel more and more hollow. I was so thirsty, so hungry, and with every passing second it seemed to become worse, as if I were drinking salt water that only made me more dehydrated. The darkness came into my body through my scars. I could feel all of them burning, but at the same time they felt as if made of ice.

The pure-white light was blinding around me, but for a split second, it brought me back to my senses. His face materialized inside my thoughts. Orion. He was still trapped and about to be hanged.

Open, I commanded inside my head, trying to focus all of my thoughts to the rope that was tied around his neck. *Open!*

I couldn't tell if the ropes had snapped or loosened, but instantly felt that something inside me had ruptured. It was as if my power had been contained inside my body in a little box, and the box was now broken. I could feel my power running loose inside me.

I screamed again, not in pain but in frustration.

"Andromeda!" It was Orion's voice, but so far away.

The hunger inside me, that beast, seemed to be taking away everything from me—my breaths, my heartbeat, my sight, my hearing.

Stop, a voice inside me said. But I couldn't. I needed to keep consuming, the hunger demanded it of me.

So I kept devouring, my soul absorbing all the darkness around me. I couldn't stop, didn't want to. It was addicting, increasing my hunger, like a hole growing bigger and bigger inside me.

Then it was gone. Someone had taken it away from me. *Perseus*. I opened my eyes, not remembering I had closed them. The light was still around me, poking through my clothes like laser beams.

From somewhere around me, I heard Arianna yell in outrage. Then she was above me. She pinned me down to the rock, which I realized I was still lying on. Her weight felt too real on top of me, too physical, knowing it had not been so before. She held the white knife in her pale hand.

The light from my scars became fainter, but I could still feel it pulsing with my own heartbeat.

She smiled, her eyes shimmering. With a wave of horror, I realized what I had done. Arianna had given me darkness, power, which now resided inside me, but in exchange I had given her a piece of me. For darkness to live inside my body I had needed to take something else out—my own flesh. It had been an exchange.

I couldn't see Perseus, or anyone else, my eyes fixed like nails on Arianna. But I did hear the shouts and roars of commotion somewhere around me.

Arianna held the knife above me. "Alathea must have been wrong," she whispered, her face expressionless.

Arianna drove the knife down towards my chest. My only thought was that being stabbed didn't hurt as much as I had expected it to.

"What?!" Arianna demanded, her face a mask of anger. It seemed to deform her features, making her face inhuman—her eyes seemed to sink into her skull, her nose looked bigger, her ears so small they were almost inexistent, her cheekbones too sharp, her chin so pointed it was almost triangular.

She was pulled back abruptly by Orion, who tackled her down to the ground. I rolled away from the rock and landed hard on my back, my breath knocked away from me. My hands went immediately to my chest, my jacket was torn, but there was no blood. I opened the jacket to find my sweater intact.

Bless Virgo and her magical sweaters! I immediately regretted having thought her sweaters ridiculous. I would wear that sweater for the rest of my life.

I stood up, and surveyed the scene before me. Leo had appeared again, fighting the wolf. They were inside one of the arches, and their roars echoed as if magnified by a speaker. Leo had a bleeding gash across one cheek, and I could see blood dripping from his chest too. Lupus looked worse, though, limping with a broken leg and with wounds on his side. Both animals stood a few feet apart, growling deeply as if challenging the other to attack first.

Orion was still battling Arianna right next to the column where he had nearly been hanged. Arianna punched him in the gut, making Orion double, and her eyes fixed on me. Draco came out limping from behind the column, then kneeled a few feet in front of it. Arianna didn't seem to notice him as she glared at me. She took a single step in my direction. Draco inhaled.

My instincts propelled me to jump behind the altar. I fell to the ground painfully and curled into a ball, my heart beating out of my chest. Arianna's shriek pierced my ears like needles. I didn't see the fire, but felt the scorching heat around me as if I were inside a giant oven. It was suffocating, my skin feeling as if I were being roasted alive.

Just when I felt that I couldn't take any more heat, it was gone. The rock was still hot behind me, but I breathed in cool air. I stood up a few seconds later, once I was sure Draco had stopped breathing fire. Arianna was gone, but I knew that she was far from dead. Orion breathed hard, sitting on the ground, and so did Draco as he kneeled. The roars to my right distracted my attention.

Lupus lunged at Leo and bit the side of his neck. Leo roared in pain, and Lupus took that distraction to race away, running deeper into the ruins. I didn't think that would do much good to his broken leg.

"Where's Perseus?" I asked as I turned back to Orion and Draco.

Orion raised his head, and I noticed the purple bruise encircling his neck. Draco's neck was swollen too. I looked at the column and realized that Arianna had managed to push the concrete slab over the edge. It was cracked in half, the ropes entangled around it like dead snakes. But both Orion and Draco were alive. I sighed in relief.

"I don't know," Draco said in a wheezing voice. Orion shook his head.

Then I heard the whinnying of the horse, and looked up. The moon was still blood red, although less now. The white horse was easy to spot in the dark sky, flying away to the other side of the ruins. I muttered a curse at Perseus inside my head. That coward had escaped.

Lightning hit the side of the horse. A figure fell from the horse close to the little brick town. After flying in awkward circles, Aquila landed next to me on the ground. He didn't look good either. One of his wings was bleeding badly, as if the horse had bitten it. I didn't have time to focus much on him, though. My gaze was fixed on where Perseus had fallen. I looked around wildly, but the white knife was nowhere to be found. It didn't matter. My feet were running before my mind knew it.

"Wait, Andromeda!" Orion shouted raggedly. His voice sounded as if his throat had been crushed, which I guess it had been, a little.

I knew I should have stayed with Orion; he was safe now. But I couldn't. There was a rage inside me that poisoned my heart. Perseus had betrayed me. I had cared for him. I had trusted him. I had *liked* him.

He didn't deserve to escape—he only deserved death.

Chapter IX, Verse I

A war of centuries be fought, after so long they have waited.
To the Stars no lies be told, but believed they must be.
The Prince shall awake when she comes to his aid.
By each other's hand one of them shall be dead.
The Princess and Prince to death they shall battle.
After three wars one will have triumphed.
To ashes and blood one will be slaughtered.

CHAPTER 28

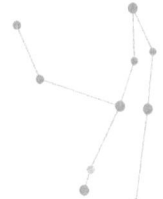

PERSEUS had landed close to the stairs I had sat on while I waited for him to find me. I could see a very small puddle of blood right next to the concrete stairs. I climbed up the steps, two at a time. The eerie red glow of the moon bathed my surroundings in a strange orange reflection. I arrived at a wide landing with a brick ramp leading up. I raced forward; it was the only way to go. I could see splatters of blood, dark and wet against the stone ground. Then I arrived at an ancient brick building. It was so dark inside that I couldn't even see the walls of the room. I hesitated for a second, then stepped in. I was able to make out the shadowed form of the stairs at the end of the small room. I ran for them, my footsteps silent.

The stone stairs curled upward, they smelled of acid sweat. The walls were cold as my bleeding palm slid along them, trying to support myself as I ascended.

Then I was outside again, standing on a wide terrace. I turned to look at the building behind me. Its facade was in renovation, with scaffolds around it, so I couldn't make much of it. Ahead of me, the terrace stretched at least thirty feet. It had a marble railing decorated with ceramic flowerpots, the flowers all dead.

In the distance I could see the giant three-arch structure I had just been in. I couldn't see the altar from here, it was hidden behind some trees, but I could see the arches illuminated by light. Maybe Draco had made a fire?

I was tackled from behind, and stopped myself from falling on my face with my hands. The fingers in my left hand, which I knew were broken, felt as if I had just ripped them off. I struggled to get away from Perseus and kicked wildly, not seeing clearly what I was hitting. I must have hurt him, because Perseus groaned and fell away from me.

I scrambled to the edge of the terrace, my back against the railing, holding my left hand in pain. Perseus stood before me. His nose was badly broken and had swelled like a giant, deformed grape. Dry blood caked his mouth and chin. He held the white knife in his right hand, and I realized that blood slid down his other arm. The skin of his upper arm had been singed, and I could suddenly smell roasted flesh.

"I should have killed you in the park," I growled.

Perseus smiled, that goofy grin he always gave me, his teeth still intact but stained with blood. "But you didn't."

Perseus lunged forward, and I lurched to the left, crashing with some ceramic pots that smashed to the ground below the terrace. I fell on my side with a grunt of pain. Before I could scramble to my feet, Perseus had pinned me down. Sizzled arm or no, he was still stronger than I.

He held my throat with one hand, and with the other the knife. I gagged on the smell of his burned flesh. His hand trembled slightly as he held the knife. His other hand tightened around my neck, and dark spots began to swirl in my vision. I tried to breathe, but could only get a couple of ragged breaths into my lungs.

Perseus looked into my eyes and hesitated, as if they reflected something that he feared. I wondered if they looked black, like his. But I hadn't consumed that much darkness, had I?

"Come on, you bastard," I hissed, trying to force the last of my breath out. "Kill me then."

His black eyes met mine. They were big as ever, as if wanting to get a last look at me. The knife was trained on my left eye—the sweater wouldn't save me this time.

Perseus screamed and plunged the knife down.

My back hit the grass hard. Black spots blinded my vision. The sun was bright above me, which only hurt my eyes more, so I looked away from the light.

"Andromeda," Zia said. She hauled me to my feet and quickly inspected me. "Are you alright?" Her blue eyes were wide with concern.

"Yes," I answered. The spots had left my vision, and nothing hurt.

Zia eyed me cynically, then turned to Orion. He was standing a few feet to my right. Her gaze pierced through him like sharpened knives.

"Sorry," Orion said even before Zia asked him to apologize.

"You better be," Zia said.

Orion walked closer to me, his eyes yellow as the sun above. We were almost the same height, but he looked smaller with his hands behind his back and his head hanging low with embarrassment.

Zia looked at both of us. "You should never harm her, Orion. Remember, she's the only person you'll ever be able to trust."

"I know," he said sheepishly. "I was just trying to get the soccer ball." He motioned at the white and black ball lying a few yards away from us, at the edge of the large backyard.

"By pushing me away from it?" I demanded.

His eyes narrowed. "I said I was sorry."

Zia sighed. "Alright, enough of games." She looked up at the sky. The sun was still high up, indicating it was probably an hour past midday. The black and gray clouds in the distance hung heavily in the air, covering the horizon. "There's still enough time to go for an ice cream, and walk around the park to see the ducks."

"Ducks!" Orion exclaimed excitedly.

At the same time, I said, "Ice cream!"

"We can do both," Zia said with a smile.

"Can we watch a movie after?" I asked.

"And build another pillow fort?" said Orion.

"And eat brownies and popcorn?" I asked with a wide smile.

Zia looked at both of us with a serious expression before it broke into a grin. "We can do anything you want." She looked at the dark clouds again, which seemed to have moved closer to us. "Just go get your jackets before we leave."

Orion and I raced back inside the house.

I opened my eyes. Perseus was still on top of me, his face contorted in rage and sorrow. He had plunged the knife right next to my face, cracking the concrete floor as the knife stuck there. He breathed hard, once, twice, thrice. Then he stood up on trembling legs, taking a step away from me.

I stood up too, not even feeling my legs anymore, taking support from the railing. The solid touch of it gave me a sense of strength. Perseus held his arm where the lightning had struck him. There was a loud whine in the sky, and Pegasus landed behind Perseus, making the floor tremble underneath me. The horse regarded me fiercely, his mouth snapping as if he wanted to bite my head off. I noticed that his wing was still bleeding, and he had a gash on his side that was blackened red.

Perseus turned around and took a step towards the horse.

"I understand now," I said in a hoarse voice, still feeling his hand tight around my neck. The answer had always been there—the only thing I would have had to do was look up at a night sky.

Perseus stopped midstride but didn't turn, making me look at his red hair.

"I understand that Stars can't shine without Darkness, but Darkness can survive without Light. The more Darkness there is, the brighter a Star can shine," I said, feeling my bones tremble. "That's why your eyes are black, that's why you're more powerful than the rest of us—because you took Darkness. I understand now."

Now I knew too, that he couldn't completely control Algol. His body craved more Darkness, and every time he fed it Algol would attack.

Perseus straightened his back, but didn't turn to look at me. "I knew you would understand."

He walked forward, towards his horse and climbed onto Pegasus's back. Pegasus flapped his wings, ready to fly off.

Perseus looked at me. Our eyes met one last time. No words passed between us, but we both knew what was left unsaid. The Prophecy hadn't been fulfilled tonight, but someday it would be. I couldn't ignore the truth anymore.

The horse flapped his wings and jumped off the terrace, knocking down another ceramic pot. The horse snorted once again and flew into the night—towards the slightly orange moon.

Footsteps thundered behind me, and I turned to see Orion barreling into the terrace. He had a knife raised high in his hand, probably borrowed from Draco. He let his arm dangle back down once he realized that Perseus and the horse were gone.

He walked closer to me. Orion's neck was bleeding where the rope had been tied, and it was starting to swell. But despite his injuries his yellow eyes were still bright, nearly the same color as the moon. He looked me up and down, as if assessing the damage.

He looked back at the sky where the horse was now a white dot in the distance, then kneeled down to pick up the knife Perseus had left. He gripped it tight. "He could have killed you," he said. His voice sounded raspy, as if he had swallowed a handful of sand.

"I know," I said, still feeling Perseus's hand around my neck.

"Why didn't he?"

I shrugged. I had seen it in his eyes. He had hesitated at the altar. He hadn't wanted to do it. But Orion was right; Perseus would have gained more by killing me than by not doing it.

Why? I wondered too.

Orion limped to my side and placed a hand gently on my shoulder. "Let's go, come on."

He pulled me away from the edge of the terrace, back towards the stairs. We didn't talk at all as we made our way back to Draco. I could feel Orion sagging next to me, ready to collapse at any moment.

We finally came to the three large arches again, and I noticed that Ara, the altar, was burning. Draco had his ears covered, and it was until I walked closer to the rock that I realized why; it was moaning, and wheezing, as if a man were trapped inside.

Draco pulled his gaze away from the altar and entered one of the domed arches, where Leo lay on his side. My gaze was intently fixed on the altar. It moaned louder, weeping. The flames made the rock sizzle, and it was already black, and dripping to the ground as if it were melting. I was transfixed until Orion pulled me away, towards Draco.

With effort, I pulled my gaze away from the altar, but could still hear its cries of pain behind me. Leo's eyes focused on me, and he purred. His side was bleeding. He had claw marks on his broad chest and side, and a bite on his neck. Draco sat crossed legged next to the lion, trembling.

"I think there are still some ambulances in front of the Colosseum," he said, his voice barely audible as he held his strangled throat. "You guys should go."

"What about you?" I asked. "And Leo and Aquila?" I said motioning at the other two. Aquila was perched on a large rock a few feet away from Leo. His chest was heaving slowly and his wing dripped blood where Pegasus had bitten him. It seemed like a nasty injury, and I wondered how the horse hadn't bitten him in half.

"Just bring some water, bandages, and alcohol," he said. "We'll wait here," he looked over at Leo and Aquila.

"But—"

Orion nodded to Draco and pulled me away, past the altar. It was still burning, and the moans had turned to strangled cries of agony. Orion kept pulling me, and we left the altar behind.

My head was spinning, and I leaned on Orion for support. My feet dragged my body along. The next thing I remember, blue and red lights were flashing before me, stinging my eyes, trying to pierce through my skull. There were people talking to me, alternating between Italian and English, but I couldn't understand them.

A woman talked to me soothingly, but I could only see her lips moving. Then I noticed that Orion wasn't next to me anymore, and I couldn't spot him. The Colosseum stood in front of me, the moon rising just above it. It was yellow now, with small traces of orange. I noticed some odd figures next to the

Colosseum, and it took my eyes a couple seconds to adjust—they were dead bodies, piled up together. There were dozens of them, left uncovered. The sight of it burned into my brain.

I couldn't stop him, I thought. I had failed to kill Perseus. Algol would rise again, and the deaths of those people would be on me.

The woman dragged me inside one of the flashing ambulances. Then I closed my eyes and slept, thinking in my sleep that I had to wake up and go back to Draco. I tried to open my eyes, but they were heavy as iron gates. I didn't dream, only heard the moaning cries of the altar, calling me back so I could burn with it.

Then I was awake again, very suddenly. I lay on a small bed inside one of the ambulances. My body felt like I had been dragged across Rome. I sat upright, and a bolt of pain seized my head as if thunder had struck it.

"Lay back down," a woman told me. I couldn't make out her features very well. "You have a concussion," she was saying. "A fracture in your skull . . . three broken fingers . . . your ribs . . ."

Then she was gone. My brain wasn't working properly, but it seemed like my body knew what to do. I was grabbing stuff from the ambulance, putting it inside a backpack I had found. I would need all the bandages I could find to help Leo.

Then I was out of the ambulance, lights flashing before my eyes as I walked among more ambulances and people sitting on the ground. Someone gripped my arm. I turned, trying to pry my arm free, then realized it was Orion. He was lying on a stretcher, right next to an ambulance. With the light now illuminating him, I could see that his neck was swollen purple, his breaths ragged. His eyes looked at mine, as if pleading at me to stay with him. But he nodded, knowing I had to get to the others. Then he closed his eyes, and his hand went a little limp.

My heart gave a start, but then I realized that he was still breathing, his broad chest rising and falling slowly.

"He'll be alright," a man dressed in white said next to me. He walked to Orion, examining his neck slowly. Orion only moaned in his sleep, but didn't wake. "It's nothing fatal," the doctor assured me, but his frown told me that he wondered how Orion had gotten that injury on his neck. "He'll be up and about in a few days."

I nodded, turning to see Orion's sleeping face before I walked away.

CHAPTER 29

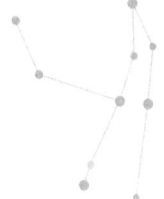

THE FOREST was dense around me, and I had no notion of where I was going. A large backpack was slung across my shoulders, carrying enough food and water to last a few more days. I also had some matches so I could light fires at night, and some toilet paper.

It had been two days since the blood moon.

I had a bandage around my head, and whenever a cold breeze swept by it hurt more, as if the wind was leaking through the crack of my skull and freezing my brain. Three of the fingers on my left hand were tied to small sticks, which I knew would be enough to set them straight again. Two of my ribs were broken, and I knew I should have taken a few days to rest, but I just couldn't. My torso was an ugly patchwork of bruises I had accumulated along the fight; the gash on my leg was painful and my feet were sore, but I kept walking.

The forest was beautiful around me. The leaves were all yellow, and the ground dark-red with fallen leaves. They crunched under my feet as I walked. The sun shone directly above me, making the colors seem more vibrant. Birds chirped around me, their happy tunes filling the air. I could hear the flapping of their small wings above me. Sometimes it made me look up, wary that it would be something else.

I was passing by a large tree when I stopped. I don't know what had suddenly made me realize I was being followed. I simply felt it.

I turned around. Orion stood in between two smaller trees, his eyes the same color as the leaves. He walked closer once I turned, then stopped two feet in front of me.

"You didn't come back for me," he said. His voice was still a little choked and hoarse.

"I knew you'd be alright," I said.

The birds had flown away, their chirping echoing in the distance.

Orion was wearing a heavy black jacket, but it was open at the top, and I could see his neck. He had a black and yellow line where the rope had been. It was a bit purple at the edges. His cheek was also bruised, making one of his cheekbones seem bigger.

"I helped Draco find his other friends," he said as he absently traced a finger through his bruised neck. "I thought you would want to know they're all alright."

I released a breath I had been holding. I was relieved that Corvus, Virgo, Maera and Sirius hadn't been hurt.

Orion took a deep breath and leaned against one of the trees, crossing his arms. When he spoke, faint mist came out of his mouth from the cold. "The Italian government has declared a state of emergency in the country. This is the worst earthquake they've had in decades. It was a magnitude 8.5, and spread throughout all of central Italy. They've counted at least two million people dead." He said, sounding like a news reporter. His yellow eyes were trained on me, as if wanting to see how I would react. I wasn't at all surprised, having seen the destruction in Rome myself. In a way, I felt sorry, and a bit guilty too, for the deaths of those people. But I had buried those feelings in the same place where I buried the memories of the patients at the hospital and the victims at Times Square. "The first earthquake killed about half. Then the second one came, and whatever hadn't been destroyed in the first crumbled down."

I knew there had been another earthquake, right before Perseus had tried to kill me at the altar, but I hadn't realized the extent of the damage. That's mainly why I had tried to stay in the forest and not go to any cities or villages. I didn't want to see any more crumbled buildings or dead bodies.

Orion took a deep breath, bringing me out of my thoughts. "So we're Star Children, and our power is to materialize thoughts," he said. I nodded. Orion had probably spent enough time with Draco to know everything. "And since my Constellation represents the hunter, I'm good at hunting down people and things," his eyes narrowed at me. "And you're the chained princess, good at opening locks. Or on a bigger scale, freeing prisoners or putting them behind bars."

"That's what my Constellation does," I said, carefully.

Orion nodded thoughtfully. "Right, because we can only manifest a fraction of our Constellations' power."

"Yes," I said.

He nodded again. "Except Perseus, who found a way to become more powerful than the rest of us."

"Where are you going with this?" I asked.

Orion's face hardened. "Right on the blood moon, while we were busy fighting, there was a breach in every single prison in central Italy." I was about to say that it could have been because of the earthquake, but Orion spoke first, as if guessing what I would say. "The earthquake caused damage to the prisons, and a few deaths too. But the breach happened *after* the second earthquake, at the same time, in every single prison, even in the ones that hadn't been much damaged." His eyes traced my face, which I felt had gone a bit pale. "Did you know about that?"

"No," I answered, a little too quickly.

Orion noticed too, regarding me with those fierce eyes. I hadn't known about that, but knew well enough that I had caused it. I had been too focused on consuming Darkness that I hadn't noticed anything else around me. I didn't want to think of the consequences of having freed so many criminals and the harm they could cause in destroyed cities and villages, which were in their most vulnerable states.

Orion remained silent, looking intently at my face. He knew I wouldn't talk further about the matter.

"So what are you going to do now?" I asked.

"What are *you* going to do?" he asked, looking suspiciously at my backpack.

I clung to the straps of my backpack. "I'm going to walk."

Orion's eyebrows drew together. "That doesn't sound like a good life plan."

"It does to me," I said. "Where will you go?" He didn't answer right away. "Back to New York, to be with Rose? No wait, you can't go back to Rose." Orion raised a brow. "She's Perseus's adopted sister."

Shock rippled across Orion's face. "His sister?"

"Yes," I answered.

Orion considered that, his features tensing. "Hmmm," he said after a couple of seconds. "I'll look into that."

The tension grew denser around us, to the point where I felt it would drown us both. After a few seconds, I spoke.

"She's dead, Orion," I said, in such a hushed voice that I wasn't sure he had heard. He hung his head low, not looking at me. "She's dead."

There were a couple more seconds of silence. "She did care about us." He looked up to meet my gaze, then his own set hard. I felt my muscles stiffening. "She did."

"Yeah, she cared so much about you that she kissed you," I spat out. Orion's face went blank. He didn't respond, but that was as good an answer as any. "She abused you, Orion. Can't you see that? Zia was sick, a monster. She hurt you in many more ways than she hurt me." Orion's jaw was clenched, but strangely his gaze was cool, as if this wasn't such a big deal.

He looked away from me, his jaw set so hard I worried he might crush his teeth. I didn't ask how many times Zia had kissed him, or if she had gone further than that. I knew he wouldn't answer me.

I gave a frustrated growl. How could Orion still care about Zia? How could he protect her secrets even after she was dead? How could he not realize the wrongness of what she had done, the emotional abuse that he would have to carry because of her actions?

"She cared about you too, Andromeda," he said, his voice tight as if he were being hanged again.

"Don't tell me that!" I said.

Orion faced me. "She was harsh because she knew that we would live in a harsh world all of our lives. She was training us for this!"

"Then why didn't she tell us the truth in the first place?" I shouted.

Orion was about to answer but shut his mouth, then opened it again. "I don't know why she decided to keep the truth a secret. But everything she made us do was because she knew we would need it for later on." I didn't answer. "Have you forgotten the good times we spent with her?" Orion asked. "Or did you just decide to forget them?"

I pressed my lips tight, and my head began to throb. I could feel my brain beating inside my skull as if it were my heart.

"Do you remember when we were little and lived in France? She used to take us to the park every weekend to eat ice cream and see the ducks," he started. "The road trip we took to the theme park when I turned ten. When she taught us how to ski, how to swim, how to fix a motorcycle. That one time she took us to the beach to watch the seals. And when—"

"Stop!" I said as I clutched his jacket tight with my right hand. My own throat felt as if a rope was tightening around it.

His eyes bore into my own.

"Have you forgotten?" he demanded. "She's dead. The least you could do is try to remember all of that."

I tried to swallow the knot in my throat, but couldn't. I pushed all of my feelings and memories away to the back of my head, trying to forget about their existence. I let go of Orion's jacket and began walking away.

"Where the hell will you go?" Orion asked.

"Wherever my feet take me," I answered.

Orion grabbed my shoulder and turned me around, forcing me to face him. "You still have your Prophecy with Perseus to worry about."

"So you believe in the Prophecies too?" I asked.

"After everything that's happened . . . I have to." He held my cheek with his warm hand, and I realized that my face had been cold. "Algol will rise again and you're the only one who can stop Perseus. Corvus, Draco and Virgo are looking for you because they need your help." He paused. "You can't escape what's coming."

I pulled away from him, instantly feeling the cold slapping my cheek again. I had helped Virgo, Corvus and Draco with Perseus at Palatine Hill—and had failed to kill him. I didn't want them to bring me into that mess again. I would only cause more trouble. "I can try." I walked away, and he followed after me. He strode ahead of me, blocking my path. Orion took hold of both of my arms, and I tried to pull from his grasp.

"You don't need to run away anymore, Andromeda," Orion said. His gaze softened. "You're free now, as you've always wanted."

"I just need some time alone," I said. "After everything that's happened."

Orion wasn't convinced at that. I could read it plainly in his face. But I couldn't tell him the truth. Better let him think that I was running away from Perseus and my Prophecy.

"Promise you won't come after me this time." I said. He opened his mouth to reply. "Promise me!"

My shout resonated across the forest, and my head throbbed with a new wave of sharp pain. Orion looked at my face, his eyes burning into my flesh. Then he slowly leaned forward, and gently pressed his forehead against mine. I could feel his breath on my cheeks and mouth—it was warm. I pressed my hand to his cheek. It was soft, he had shaved recently; he had never liked having a beard.

"Promise," I whispered.

He held on tighter to my arms, as if afraid I would run away at any moment. He closed his eyes for a few seconds, then opened them again. I had always loved that shade of yellow, like all the autumn trees around us. He pursed his lips, as if he was about to say something he would very soon regret.

"I promise," he whispered back. "Just promise me we'll see each other again."

I nodded. "I promise."

He pulled his head away, slowly, looking into my eyes as if trying to commit them to memory. He didn't let go of my arms until a few seconds later.

"Try not to flirt with any other strange guys, alright?" he asked. I had to smile, and he did too, a little awkwardly. He gently placed his hand on my cheek again, brushing his thumb against the bridge of my nose, making my skin tingle with warmth. "And for the love of all that's holy—let your hair grow again."

"I'll think about that," I assured him.

His smile widened a little, but then vanished a second later, and he pulled his hand away. He took a few steps back. I became suddenly aware of the hunger inside my chest—of the beast that lived in me. He nodded at me, and I nodded back.

I turned and began walking away. I could feel his eyes on my back, but despite every single muscle in my body wanting to, I didn't turn around. I put one foot in front of the other, trying to get away as fast as I could. I knew that if I turned around he would still be standing there, looking at me.

I didn't trust myself to look back, and I knew that I had to stay away from him, and from people in general. I had tasted the sweet power of Darkness, and it had left a hole inside me, one I would never be able to fill again.

If I kept fighting Perseus, and if I got involved again with the Star Children, I knew that the temptation would be too great—to consume more Darkness. The hunger felt like an ache inside my soul. It was as if I had been deprived completely of food and survived only on liquids. It made me almost always feel distracted, thinking about consuming again so I could feel satiated, but I knew that consuming would only make the hunger worse. I repeated that over and over inside my mind, trying to convince myself. I felt like a prisoner in my own body—but I could live with that kind of prison.

I wondered how Perseus managed to live with so much Darkness inside him. It had gone so far as to take away his eyes.

What else had it taken from him? And how long could he keep consuming until he had no more flesh left? He was exhausting his own power—or was he feeding it so it would grow? I didn't want to find out.

I walked faster, feeling my ribs aching in protest.

I could never tell anyone what I had done, what I had discovered. Yes, it had made me more powerful, but if I had known the price of it, felt it before, I probably wouldn't have done it. My steps faltered, and I nearly fell down. But if I hadn't, Orion would have been dead. I raked my short hair with my broken nails. For him, I would have consumed all the Darkness in the Universe.

But every time one of us consumed Darkness, Arianna would become more powerful, her form more physical, and I didn't want to know what she would be capable of then.

I simply *couldn't* go back. Corvus, Virgo, and Draco were wrong thinking they needed my help. It would be better for everyone if I just disappeared—the temptation of Darkness far away.

The sun hid behind clouds, and shadows seemed to invade the forest. I walked, shivering with sudden cold. Even that small shiver sent a sharp pain through my head and ribs. I took a deep breath, and mist came out of my mouth as I exhaled. I couldn't feel Orion's gaze on my back anymore. Maybe he had decided to walk away too.

I clutched the straps of my backpack so tight that my hands hurt, and my broken fingers felt as if I were drilling holes into them.

I *had* to leave, even if Orion never understood why. I had no other choice. I couldn't help the others fight Perseus—not anymore. Not without compromising myself and hurting others.

But I've always wanted to escape, I reminded myself. I had always wanted to be alone, and now, for the first time in my life, it was possible. I breathed out, releasing my death grip on the straps, letting my arms dangle at my sides.

This has always been my dream, I told myself. To disappear from everyone I knew; to sit down and enjoy the sun's warmth on my back without worrying anyone would beat me. I smiled. I finally had what I most dearly wanted—to just walk and let my feet guide me to an unknown destiny.

I was free.

ACKNOWLEDGEMENTS

THERE ARE so many people who have helped me get this book into your hands.

To Harrison Demchick, who more than an editor has become my creative writing professor and mentor. It's been almost eight years since we started working together and you've read all of my worst and best drafts. Thank you for helping me make my stories as good as they can be and following me along in this journey. I wouldn't be where I am without you.

To Ally Machate, for always being so kind and supportive of all of my books, and for helping me navigate the path to publish this book.

To everyone else at The Writer's Ally, including Julie Haase, who helped me get this book into its final shape

To Emily Hitchcock, Clair Fink, Doug Davis and the rest of the team at Storehouse for their guidance and hard work to make this book get to its final form.

To Tyler Wagner, who after two meetings convinced me to take a bold step forward to publish this book.

To Sam Lydon, my first official beta reader. Thank you for your friendship, support, and our fun talks in lab. To Abby Dowse, for being my second official beta reader and for all of our fun adventures in the Bay Area.

ANDROMEDA

To Alba Medina and Gina Diez Barroso for being great mentors.

To Hesam Panahi, Patrick Ray and everyone else at Lilie who have helped me move this project forward and take it out from my computer and into the world.

To everyone in the AgFunder team for being so supportive of my writing, especially Manuel Gonzalez and Andrew Finkelstein.

I'm fortunate enough to have amazing friends who throughout the years have supported me on this journey and cheered me along. Alejo Isaza, thank you for being with me both in the best and worst moments of my life, for always being at my side when I need someone to lean on, and for understanding me so well. Ana Sofi Guerrero for always having my back, for supporting me with all of my books, and for always listening to my voice notes which are long enough to be podcasts. Melissa Ruiz, who has the kindest heart, thank you for the great adventures we've had, and for always motivating me and supporting me throughout our friendship. Val D. Ibarra, for our long talks about our futures, our shared jokes, and for our friendship. Daniel Koh, I couldn't have asked for a better O-Week father, and I am so thankful to have met you and to have your friendship. To Kenzie Pickett for always being there to listen to my rants and ideas, and for being a great roommate and friend. Gargi Samarth, you know me so well that you were able to write the most epic bio anyone has ever made of me for O-Week, and I am grateful for our friendship and our random talks in the quad.

I also want to thank my O-Week group: Jerry, Everett, Ben, Claire, Hamza, Jack, Julia, Mark, Priyanka, Yoshwa, and Mauricio. Thank you for being amazing friends and for all of your support.

To D'signLab and Augusto Aguilera, who created the most beautiful book cover I have seen. Thank you for taking the concept

I had and turning it into a work of art that went beyond any of my expectations. And I can't thank you enough for all the support you have given me.

To Caro, not only my sister but also my best friend. Thank you for reading all the crappy first drafts for most of my novels and always giving feedback and ideas. I wouldn't have made it this far in life without you at my side.

To my mom, who has supported my writing from the first book I wrote, and who has always fought for my voice to be heard. Thank you for dedicating so many years to us, for always being present, for supporting and helping me to follow my dreams, and always motivating me to be myself and do my best.

To my dad, for his unconditional support and always motivating me to chase my dreams, no matter what they may be, and for always helping me find new opportunities. Thank you for helping me become who I am today.

To Abu, who has a heart made out of gold and who has always cheered me on in every project I've taken and been there to support me even in the hardest moments of my life.

Lastly, I want to thank you, dear reader, for taking the time to explore the world of the Star Children. I hope you enjoyed meeting them, and I promise there's a lot more coming . . .

ABOUT THE AUTHOR

A T 17, Sofi became the youngest published author in Mexico. She is the author of "The Lost Origin", and "Star Blood" series. She won the award "Writers of Tomorrow" and was named one of the most influential women in Mexico by *Quien* magazine at 19. Sofi wants to keep one foot in the future and get involved with technologies that are making fiction turn into reality through science. She holds a B.S in Bioengineering from Rice University and has worked at Hilton lab doing research in epigenetic engineering and synthetic biology.